HONORABLE PROFESSION

A NOVEL OF AMERICAN POLITICS

ANDY KUTLER

Black Rose Writing | Texas

ISBN: 978-1-68433-847-4 (Paperback); 978-1-68433-889-4 (Hardcover)
PUBLISHED BY BLACK ROSE WRITING
www.blackrosewriting.com

Printed in the United States of America
Suggested Retail Price (SRP) $19.95 (Paperback); $24.95 (Hardcover)

Honorable Profession is printed in Garamond

*As a planet-friendly publisher, Black Rose Writing does its best to eliminate unnecessary waste to reduce paper usage and energy costs, while never compromising the reading experience. As a result, the final word count vs. page count may not meet common expectations.

PRAISE FOR
HONORABLE PROFESSION

"Andy Kutler knows Washington and politics from the inside out, and his novel spans the great divides of our politics: gender and generation; ideology and principle, in a way that will speak to you regardless of which side you're on."

—Paul Begala, campaign strategist and former White House official

"A brilliant, lengthy, and engaging political thriller of 2021, author Andy Kutler's *HONORABLE PROFESSION* is a must-read drama...a one-of-a-kind novel fans of the political drama genre will not want to miss."

—Hollywood Book Reviews

"Gripping and creative...The characters in this book are unique, multi-dimensional, and believable, with each one coming to life on the page following layers of personality and history...Their strengths make them powerful. Their flaws make them relatable."

—IndieReader

"A fresh, engrossing take on the political novel with a striking hero....the book as a whole is such an enjoyable and satisfying one..."

—Kirkus Reviews

"*HONORABLE PROFESSION* is an important, compelling book with great relevance to American politics today. Andy Kutler has crafted a winning story for people who believe in the virtue of public service, and believe government can be an instrument of good."

—Bob Kerrey, Former Governor and United States Senator

For Maddie and Ben

HONORABLE PROFESSION

PROLOGUE

It started as a quiet Tuesday in the United States Senate. No bombshells from former aides claiming sexual misconduct. No pitchfork-wielding protesters testing the bounds of the First Amendment. Not even a single corruption charge filed by the local United States Attorney.

It was still morning, though. The day was young.

Inside the Dirksen Senate Office Building, a hearing plodded along, as stale as the traces of cigar smoke that still lingered, years after the last match had been struck in the room. Rows of chairs sat half-empty, reflecting the lack of interest among Washington elites for a handful of obscure government officials discussing airspace security in the 21st century.

Thirty-year-old Dan Cahill sat at the witness table; his microphone muted. He was attentive, but the grandeur of the hearing room was having little effect on him. To those on the dais, he appeared like most agents of the United States Secret Service, wooden and stoic. They had no inkling of his simmering contempt for the Democratic subcommittee chairman, lording over the room like the King of England.

Dan had once envisioned a possible career in these stately surroundings, serving at the right hand of his home state senator, John Warner, or even a legend like John McCain. He had such great reverence for the storied institution then – a fact he was reminded of when he entered the hearing room earlier that morning, absorbing the splendor of it all, from the regal carpeting to the framed oil portraits of past chairmen lining the walls.

He had chosen a far different path after college instead, one that required him to tamp down his pastime of partisan politics. It wasn't difficult; the demands of the Secret Service were beyond relentless, leaving little time for his wife and daughter, let alone the suffocating quagmire of modern-day campaigning.

"On a related matter, Ms. Patterson," drawled out Wendell Blackwell, the ancient Senator from Tennessee, "we'd like for you to share with the subcommittee your thoughts on the Administration's budget request for the next fiscal year and whether you will be able to increase staffing to adequate levels for the Secret Service's protective activities. Or will this be another year of treading water in the deep end?"

Dan gave a sideways glance to Barb Patterson, the raven-haired Assistant Director for Protective Operations seated on his left, wondering if she would respond as she wished, or as she had been conditioned by her years of government service.

"Chairman Blackwell," Patterson began evenly, striking a tone of deference and patience Dan both admired and abhorred. "As our CFO told this subcommittee in the Spring, we believe the four percent increase over current year levels will enable the Secret Service to maintain sufficient staffing in future years for both our protective and investigative functions."

Dan smiled to himself, his question answered. Patterson was an icon in the Service, and would never stray from the company line, despite the enormous strain the current presidential campaign was placing on a gravely overstretched workforce. After twenty-two years on the job, her loyalty to the Service and the Director was absolute.

Their paths first crossed six years ago, when he was a rookie agent working the Winter Olympics in Salt Lake City, and Patterson was in command of the sprawling security operation. A native of Midland, Texas, she had been away from the Lone Star State for more than two decades, but those who worked for Patterson knew that underneath her polished exterior there still lurked a brassy, plainspoken soul. Maybe that's why Dan was disappointed she declined to take a swing at the Tennessean. Or at least point out any deficits in the agency's funding were hardly the blame of a president who had used much of his two terms in the White House to redouble the focus of the federal law enforcement and national security communities on the counterterrorism mission. It was Blackwell and his Democratic colleagues who historically short-shrifted agencies like the Secret

Service, prioritizing social welfare, foreign aid, and other spending programs instead.

"But Ms. Patterson," Blackwell persisted, "according to media reports, your number of protectees has more than doubled since 9/11. National Special Security Events have gone up. Your Director told us last month about his plans to triple the number of cybercrime task forces you currently have in the field, both domestically and abroad. Now, I'm no mathematics wiz, but if y'all are going to sit here and tell us that a four percent increase is going to cover all that, when your attrition rate hasn't budged, well that dog just won't hunt."

Patterson remained still, waiting for the Chairman of the Senate Appropriations Subcommittee on Homeland Security to ask an actual question. The awkward silence was finally broken by Blackwell and an exaggerated sigh of frustration.

"With that, the distinguished ranking member, Senator Mobley, is recognized."

The senior senator from Oklahoma, a bolo-tied, fourth-generation cattle rancher, opened a binder and began reading from the talking points assembled by his staff and printed in 48-point font, the man's vanity keeping his reading glasses tucked away in his suit coat pocket. As he rambled on, the question morphed into a sermon denouncing the invasive, Constitution-hating vendetta against the traveling public by the oft-criticized Transportation Security Administration. Dan tuned the man out, his own eyes wandering to Patterson's graceful fingers gently drumming the table.

Dan had thought of her, more unprofessionally, on more than one occasion. At forty-four, the Assistant Director was ancient compared to his wife Michelle, but Patterson was in the Service's gym every single morning, the rowing machine and free weights keeping her lean and firm. Aside from the shapeless black pantsuit, her elegance was uncompromised by her trade, evidenced by her painted nails, subtle makeup, and the touch of Chanel perfume that seemed to be drifting in Dan's direction. While he had imagined his superior between the sheets, he couldn't quite imagine her enjoying the experience. The woman was permanently stern, as if auditioning for an American Gothic sitting. He tried to shake the boorish thoughts occupying his mind. He owed this woman mightily, starting with Salt Lake City. She deserved far better from him.

Senator Mobley concluded his scripted rant without asking a single question of the witness panel, bolting from his high-back chair like the land-seeking settlers from his home state more than a century ago.

It was all such a spectacle to Dan, and he longed to be back at the White House among his select few. He may have lacked experience as a congressional witness, but he had no shortage of confidence in his abilities as a federal agent. He assumed it was that aura of self-assurance drawing the attention of the femme fatale with porcelain skin and ginger hair seated just behind Chairman Blackwell. Betraying his young family was unthinkable, but four years of marriage hadn't blindfolded him. He enjoyed the game, and knew he cut a decent figure with his athletic frame and square jawline. A few inches over six feet, he wasn't packed with muscle, but his body was taut, a product of regular five-mile runs and a demanding home workout routine. His chestnut-colored hair was close-cropped and parted to one side, and neatly accented by thick, arched eyebrows.

As the chairman called on the junior Senator from Maryland, Dan peered once more at Blackwell, glimpsing again the man's alluring aide in the background. She flashed him a brief, coquettish smile, but with the C-SPAN cameras rolling, Dan remained expressionless, making just enough eye contact with his fair-skinned friend to keep things interesting.

"Thank you, Mr. Chairman," began Senator Dvorak, a retired technology executive. She was only in her first term but already a grating thorn in the Service's side, and both Patterson and Dan braced themselves for what they knew was coming.

"Ms. Patterson, you said in your prepared remarks that, quote, widening the zone of restricted airspace over the Washington Metropolitan Area is integral to protecting the White House Complex, unquote. I have shared with your office the scores of petitions and correspondence I have received from my constituents on this matter. As you know, we have quite a few private airfields in Maryland that will be greatly inconvenienced, if not put out of business, by what you are proposing. Exactly how certain are you your proposal will prevent another 9/11 from happening in Washington? What assurances can you give this subcommittee?"

Patterson bent to the microphone, her voice still calm and level.

"Senator Dvorak, we Texans are brought up with two rules. One, don't make promises you know you can't keep. And two, only drink the water upstream from the herd."

There was light laughter in the audience, and even the Senator from Maryland offered a faint smile.

"As you know," Patterson continued, "there are no absolutes in our line of work. But everything we do – our procedures, our training, our methodologies – is aimed at minimizing risk. That is the foundation of the proposed expansion. But we are sympathetic to the concerns that have been raised. Special Agent Cahill is currently the acting chief of our Air Security Program, and I'd like for him to share with you some of our ideas to minimize the impact of the new restrictions on smaller airports and the private flying community."

On cue, Dan began regurgitating the same points he had made to the House and Senate authorizing committees the day before. It had been his maiden appearance as a congressional witness and his nerves were frayed at first, overcome by the pageantry of it all. Now the back and forth already was getting tiresome. He had rotated into the air security program two months ago and was informed just last week he would be covering on the Hill for a branch chief away on paternity leave.

As he walked the subcommittee through the various mitigations the agency had developed, the faces of his interrogators became almost lifeless. It was, Dan had learned, the practiced stare of those whose positions were already cast in stone. As he completed his final point, heads began turning toward a commotion behind the dais. Paul Sheffield, the tanned, barrel-chested Chairman of the Committee on Appropriations, emerged without warning, the door to the anteroom quickly closing behind him. He was followed by a train of aides as those in the audience sat up in their chairs, his appearance a surprise to all. Sheffield leaned into the ear of his subcommittee chairman and whispered a few words before settling into one of the vacant leather chairs, eyeing the prey before him.

Just forty-two years old, Sheffield was the youngest full committee chairman in the history of the Senate. The fact he had ascended to helm the single most influential committee in all of Congress at his age was a testament to his policy mastery and political skills. In just his second term, he had managed to curry favor with just about every legislator and lobbyist operating under the Capitol dome.

Dan hadn't been briefed on this, he simply understood politics better than most among his agency brethren, having once led a chapter of College Republicans. It was a challenging outpost in the People's Republic of Massachusetts, so Dan spent most of his junior year traveling the country, railing for Bill Clinton's removal from office and fighting for Republicans to hold their majorities in the House and Senate. They prevailed, but it was the first time the President's party actually gained seats in a midterm election in half a century. Dan nearly erupted when he heard the Democrats spinning that into vindication for Clinton, just months after the man admitted to perjury and his dalliance in the Oval Office.

And now, after making it through the Service's screening process, vigorous training, a five-year stint in the Boston Field Office, and selection to the prestigious Presidential Protective Division, here he was. Forced to bend a knee before a committee of majority Democrats, a few of whom were the same bozos who rallied to Clinton's side a decade ago.

Dan leaned into Patterson's ear, keeping his voice low as he watched Sheffield pull a Blackberry from his suit coat and start thumbing buttons.

"Why the hell is he here?"

Patterson turned to meet his eyes and signaled a look of caution. "Steady, Dan. I'll handle this."

Blackwell banged the gavel again. "We're now going to move into closed session so we can discuss the more sensitive facets of the Secret Service's airspace security proposal. We will need all members of the press and the public to depart the room. Exceptions are for cleared staff and remaining witnesses only."

Those seated at the press table and in the rows of chairs behind the witness table gathered up their laptops and personal belongings and began filing toward the exit, grumbling about the unscheduled closed session. As the C-SPAN engineers powered down their equipment, Dan knew something was amiss. Components of the draft plan were certainly classified, but there had been no arrangement with the subcommittee to discuss those elements today, nor were they even in a properly secured space to allow it. A Capitol Police officer pulled the heavy oak doors closed, completing the public exodus. With a nod from his subcommittee chairman, Sheffield toggled the button on his microphone.

"Assistant Director Patterson, as you know, I have long been one of the Service's most faithful supporters. And I have made every effort to ensure the agency's budget requests are fully funded year after year, even as other agencies have faced substantial cuts or rescissions. With that said, I wanted to personally stop by and discuss with you a matter I consider of utmost importance. My apologies for the dramatics in closing this hearing, but it is also an issue of some sensitivity. That is, the decision of the Secret Service to continue the prohibition of general aviation aircraft flying in and out of Reagan National."

Dan could feel the rising heat in the room, though the issue wasn't unfamiliar. After the 9/11 terrorists had commandeered a 757 and piloted it into the Pentagon, the Federal Aviation Administration, backed by the Secret Service, the Pentagon and anyone with an ounce of sanity, immediately barred private aircraft from operating out of Reagan National Airport. The proximity to the White House, the United States Capitol, and a metropolitan area of six million people was simply too close. The restrictions sailed through without dissent, part of a battery of emergency measures hastily implemented to safeguard Washington and New York from future attacks.

Behind closed doors, the decision was assailed from every corner of the Capitol. High-powered industrialists and lobbyists coveted their private air service into an airport so close to the corridors of power, as did Members of Congress who were permitted to travel as guests in such aircraft. Politically impossible to voice such complaints in public, the restrictions still remained in place years later.

"Mr. Chairman," Patterson began, "if I could just point out the Secret Service has no jurisdictional authority to make such decisions. Our role is merely advisory, and to provide a security recommendation to the FAA and Department of Home—"

"Ms. Patterson," Sheffield interrupted, glimpsing a large wall clock. "I have appreciated your frankness in the past, so let's dispense with the kick-the-can routine. We will hear from DHS and the FAA next, but you and I both know neither of those bureaucracies has the political muscle, let alone the *cojones*, to defy a finding from your agency."

"No disrespect intended, Mr. Chairman. I was just pointing out the Service makes its recommendations based on security risks and threat assessments. It is up to others, namely the FAA, DHS, and the White House, to evaluate those risks against other considerations, and determine the appropriate course forward."

"Let's talk about those other considerations. As my high school economics teacher used to tell us, there is no free lunch, and your oftentimes draconian measures do have consequences. Does the Service have any idea how many jobs have been lost, and how many families have been harmed, by grounding these aircraft at National? How about the lost revenue to the Airport Authority, requiring my Commonwealth of Virginia to slash the budgets of other programs to make up the difference?"

"No, sir, that is not our—"

"I might add, it's been seven years since September 11. Do we not have sufficient defenses and countermeasures in place now to prevent another such tragedy in the metro DC area that would allow us to ease up on these job-killing regulations? What in God's name have we spent all those millions of dollars on?"

"*Hundreds* of millions."

Dan's microphone wasn't on, but his voice seemed to echo across the cavernous hearing room.

"I beg your pardon?"

Dan felt the wrathful eyes of his superior but pulled the microphone in close. "I said, hundreds of millions, Mr. Chairman. And not a nickel of that money has been spent fixing the problem at hand."

The Assistant Director remained motionless even as Dan could feel her fingers wrapping around his throat. But Dan could not stop himself. Sheffield's eyes were cold as he motioned for the witness to continue, but not before sharing a look with Patterson that Dan failed to register.

"Sir, our agency has taken the position that general aviation flights could resume the minute these operators agree to submit to the same screening procedures and security measures as commercial operators. Background checks on pilots, hardened cockpit doors, electronic screening of passengers and baggage —"

"Son, we all greatly appreciate the dedication of the Secret Service to its mission. But we are also tiring of the agency overreacting and cooking up half-baked, feel-good security measures without any regard to the public and the taxpayer. Do you know how many of these operators would go belly up if they had to comply with such onerous, hare-brained regulations dreamed up by bureaucrats who don't understand how the real world works? How many of these folks are you willing to put out of business?"

Dan felt his temperature spike, the word *bureaucrat* nearly launching him out of his seat. Before he could respond, Patterson leaned forward and spoke into her microphone. "Mr. Chairman, your concerns are certainly valid, and I assure you, we will give every consideration—"

Sheffield held up a palm, silencing the Assistant Director, his eyes drilling holes into those of Dan.

"What's an acceptable number, son? How many of my constituents in Northern Virginia will have to lose their jobs because of such callous, naive overregulation?"

Dan glared right back at the chairman. "Would you rather they lose their lives, Senator? Because if they do, their blood will be on your hands."

The room became deathly still. Dan could sense Patterson frantically searching for a way out. There would certainly be a reckoning back at headquarters.

Fuck it. He'd had enough of the sanctimony.

Sheffield's face was contorted in smoldering rage, the powerful chairman unaccustomed to anyone addressing him in such a manner.

"What did you say?"

"All it takes, Senator, is one individual to load a cannister with a biological contaminant onto a Cessna, and crop dust hundreds of thousands of people in this area to their deaths. Could the Pentagon intercept it, shoot it down? Maybe. And even if they could, do you really want that downed aircraft tail spinning into Georgetown, or Alexandria? So, if you're asking which I value more, the jobs of a few hundred airport workers, or the lives of a few million people in the metropolitan area, the choice is easy. For me, at least. I wish it was for you."

· · ·

The trio of Secret Service agents marched wordlessly down the long corridor on the ground floor of the Dirksen Building, whisking past hearing rooms and committee offices as their heels clicked out a cadence on the marble floor. A well-honed veneer masked whatever thoughts they were harboring as they fled what now felt like a crime scene. Patterson was fourteen years his senior, but Dan struggled to match her strides, her Ferragamos pounding an angry tattoo. Brett Hodges, the Service's chief liaison to Capitol Hill, was a few steps behind Dan, and as the lobby doors came into view, the veteran, bullet-headed agent closed the distance.

"You stupid piece of shit," Hodges hissed in Dan's ear, with the same menacing air he once used as a beat cop in Philly. "You realize how many ways you have fucked us?"

Dan didn't turn. "Sheffield won't —"

Hodges was short, muscular, and built like a fireplug. He grabbed Dan by the bicep and braced him against the wall. "You don't know a goddamned thing about Sheffield! Or his staff director, Diana Cribbs. That witch wrote the book on grudges and settling scores. They'll come after us now with the long knives, gouge every nickel they can out of our budget and probably zero out my shop. We are fucked, just because you couldn't keep your mouth shut, dickhead."

Dan was taken aback by Hodges' venom as he felt the man's hot breath on his face. But he wasn't cowering either, and his body went rigid as he leaned closer to the smaller man. Dan knew he had flouted a sacred, unwritten rule, and reprimands were coming, but the tantrum from Hodges was out of bounds. He waited for Patterson to step in. A United States Senator, even a Democrat, wouldn't even some score against the Service, or compromise the agency's mission, because a single agent spoke a little truth to power.

Patterson's eyes flickered up and down the hallway, spotting only a few staffers milling about, each immersed in their own affairs. No one had noticed the two younger agents standing nose to nose with fists clenched.

"Damn it, Brett, let him go," she ordered. "We'll take this outside."

Hodges released his grip, the two men still glowering at each other. The agents continued into the main lobby and past the turnstiles and magnetometers, pushing through the heavy glass and steel doors. They were outside now but still within the Capital Police security perimeter, where a bunker mentality continued to prevail years after 9/11. Armed officers in tactical gear patrolled the sidewalks, while concrete ballasts and other barriers prevented any public access to the neighboring streets.

The agents mechanically slipped on their sunglasses, the sun beating down a surprising warmth on a late autumn afternoon. An agency van idled against a nearby curb, a perk of traveling with a member of the Senior Executive Service.

Patterson turned to the liaison. "Brett, you mind taking a cab back to H Street? I'd like a private word with Dan."

"Gladly," grumbled Hodges, who headed for the taxi queue. He turned one last time. "Your father's name won't bail you out of this one."

Dan took a step toward him. "What did you—"

"Dan," barked Patterson, opening the side door. "Get in the fucking van!"

Seething from the jab, Dan climbed into the backseat next to Patterson, cursing under his breath. The driver pulled away from the curb and past the security checkpoint, gunning the engine toward Massachusetts Avenue.

"What the fuck, Dan?"

"I screwed up. I know that. But—"

"You're damned right you screwed up. Hodges dills my pickle and he's hardly my idea of a refined liaison officer, but he's spot on. His office will be cleaning up this mess for months. There'll be a shit storm at headquarters, and the political hacks at DHS will be having coronaries. The Director is going to have to call Sheffield and kiss the man's ring."

Her voice softened. Barely. "Look, I know you don't have much experience with these circuses, but you walked right into it. Sheffield is slicker than a boiled onion, and he was putting on a show. All we had to do was play our part."

"A show?"

"A show. The cameras were off, and the press had left the room. The lobbyists had left the room. Who didn't leave the room? The staff. Those kids sitting behind their bosses, including that pretty little cowgirl you were eyeballing, had one job. To memorize everything they heard and leak it to all those industry people and union representatives who have been hounding Sheffield for months over this issue. The same people he kicked out of the hearing room so they wouldn't see him back off once he got his questions on the record. He wanted to rake us over the coals, but only in private, so he could check a box with his political patrons while sparing us any kind of public black eye. His staff would have spread the word he tore into us and did everything he could to convince the Service to reverse course, but to no avail. The pressure would have eased off, the campaign dollars would have flowed again."

"And the airspace proposal?"

"It would have gone through quietly, without any trumpet blasts, or interference from the chairman. He'd quietly tell his K Street compadres he went bare knuckled, but we wouldn't budge."

Fuck. For the first time, Dan understood what he just stepped in. He rubbed the back of his neck.

"And now?"

Patterson clicked her fingernails on the butt of the Sig Sauer .357 holstered on her hip. "I'm not sure. Politically, nothing has changed, he still can't come out publicly against the proposal. But personally, he lost a lot of face today. The staff will talk, and word will get out. He'll be looking for his pound of flesh."

"My flesh."

"Yes, if we're lucky."

"Why didn't you warn me?"

"Frankly, I wish I would have," Patterson said irritably. "But I wasn't expecting a junior agent to get his cows runnin' and into a pissing match with the chairman of the Senate Appropriations Committee."

The van turned off Pennsylvania Avenue and barreled up 7th Street.

"What do I do?"

Patterson offered a grim smile. The only kind she knew.

"We got a saying. I'd rather be a fencepost in Texas than the King of Tennessee."

"Meaning?"

"Meaning, pack your bags for Tennessee."

Dan wanted to laugh, until he remembered how foreign the concept of humor was to Barb Patterson. She was working her Blackberry now, already moving on to manage the next crisis in the world of protective ops, while a knot started to form deep within Dan. He quietly stewed, absorbing the magnitude of his blunder while silently cursing every conniving politician in America.

CHAPTER 1

December 2023
Las Vegas, Nevada

Two years to go.

Like most civil servants within striking distance of retirement, and a long-awaited pension winking from the horizon, Dan had drawn a mental circle around the date some time ago. More recently, a daily countdown had slipped into his subconscious, a recurring reminder that 721 days from now, he would have given twenty-five years of his life to Uncle Sam. From that date forward, he would experience life from an entirely alien perspective. A nice consulting gig perhaps. Nine to five workdays supplemented with long lunches and occasional overseas junkets. All bookended by that which he hadn't known since the days before he was sworn in: tranquil nights of deep slumber, uninterrupted by anyone or anything.

Such as the trilling cell phone beckoning from his nightstand.

Dan groaned, longing for the day he would be emancipated from the anxieties that pulled on the sleeve of those in his profession. The haunting sensation that monumental disaster was just an eye blink away. In just under two years, he would be liberated from it all, reveling in a new existence where his weightiest decision might be whether to play the back nine or the full eighteen. Free from an around-the-clock obligation to uphold the law and safeguard the public. Free to sleep the sleep of the carefree, liberated from any worry or dread the country might be on the brink of plunging into the unthinkable.

But not tonight, Dan bellyached to himself in a bedroom as black as the night outside, where only the dim glow of his cursed phone was visible. He plucked it off the nightstand and freed the device from its charge cord.

"Yeah?"

"Boss, Pablo here. We got an issue here at the Platinum."

"Hold on," Dan mumbled, sitting up and swinging his legs over the side of the bed. His groggy state was no match for the calm and measured tenor of his on-site agent. Pablo Maldonado was more than dependable, and from his voice, Dan knew intuitively whatever warranted the urgent call was momentarily in check. It gave him the few precious seconds he needed to orient himself. Rocketing from dreamland to an operational environment was never optimal, and one of his first lessons learned as a supervisor. Better to lose a few seconds shaking off cobwebs than make a cognitive mistake while mired in the fog of sleep. He squinted to read the clock on his phone – 1:10 in the morning – and raised the device to his ear again.

"Go."

"Principal retired two hours ago, with his, uh, secretary. A few of his guys decided to stay up and party. And now they might have an underage girl in one of the suites."

Shit. "Might?"

"Hotel management can't confirm. It's possible they're not getting a good angle on the facial recognition. Also, possible they're covering their asses, throwing the shit in our lap. You want us to call Metro PD?"

"No, I'll call them. Try and keep this quiet. We don't need a bunch of uniforms in there. I'll call their special services guys and meet you there. What floor you on?"

"44th. North wing. Elise will meet you downstairs."

Dan ended the call, muttering something coarse under his breath as he rubbed the sleep from his eyes.

"That couldn't have been good."

He leaned back on the pillows, appreciating the silhouette of her shapely form against the moonlit window. She was laying on her side, her head propped up with one hand while the other reached out to caress his forearm. He bent toward her, kissing her lightly on the cheek as he brushed her lips with his thumb.

"Sorry I woke you."

"You have to leave?"

"Just have to parachute in for a few hours, so we don't have to nuke one of our European allies. I'll be back before dawn. Buy you breakfast?"

"Love to," Nicole yawned, "but I picked up a shift from Marisa. I'm on at nine, and I need to go home and shower."

Dan smiled wryly. "I thought you did just shower."

She was a cocktail server at a posh resort in Summerlin, the tony suburb ten miles from the center of Las Vegas and ten blocks from Dan's condo. The clientele was mostly a mix of higher-end gamblers who shunned the bustle of the Strip and retired locals who patronized the trendy restaurants or hot spots within. The money was good for a single mom of two middle-schoolers, with the expected drawbacks. High on the list was the drunken pawing and finishing every midnight shift smelling like an ashtray. Last night the cloud around her was particularly noxious – enough secondhand smoke to choke a camel – and Dan had led her to the shower the second she walked through the door. She complied, gliding by him in the bathroom as she grazed her fingernails across his chest and began unbuttoning her blouse. She was in her work attire, and though it wasn't as provocative as some of the trashier costumes passing for uniforms in the downtown properties, the black mini-skirt and heeled boots were enticing enough. Dan quickly peeled off his clothes and followed her right into the shower.

Barely an hour later now, her hair still damp, she smiled back at him.

"Well, as you recall, I still needed a shower after our shower, but you wouldn't let me out of this bed." She yawned again and wedged her head back on the pillow. "Rain check? I'm off on Saturday."

"Deal," Dan said, giving her a kiss before rolling out of bed. He rummaged through his dresser for a fresh undershirt and boxers. Even in total darkness, Dan could slip on a suit mechanically, a pre-dawn ritual he perfected over more than two decades.

He finished knotting his tie, catching his reflection in the dresser mirror. He had certainly aged over the span of his career, beginning with the extra twenty pounds now layering his midsection. Living on his own hadn't encouraged the healthiest of diets. Two back surgeries to repair herniated discs had wrecked his running regimen, and with his executive protection days long past, maintaining peak conditioning hadn't topped his priority list for some time. It nosedived once he hit forty. He had more than two decades of training and experience in the field though, so handling himself if push ever came to shove was never a question. And he never missed his monthly, rust-shaking visits to the shooting range.

Still, he couldn't hide the advances of middle age. His face was fleshier now, with more lines, but his hair remained thick and neatly cropped, other than a few encroaching gray strands.

His dressing complete, Dan headed downstairs, grabbing an energy bar and a stale croissant as he passed through the galley kitchen. Outside, the familiar outlines of the other starter homes in his small, gated community were barely visible, a thick haze settling into the valley and dimming the street lamps lining the checkerboard roads. With the streets devoid of any traffic, he made the Strip in twenty minutes flat, winding his car toward a soaring high-rise dwarfing the properties on either side.

The Platinum Tower Resort and Casino was the latest power player in the panoply of mega-resorts flanking the southern end of Las Vegas Boulevard. The construction phase had eclipsed two years and more than $2 billion, with an innovative design encasing the entire 54-floor structure in silver-tinted glass. The Platinum boasted nearly 6,000 rooms, making it the eighth largest hotel in the world. As with most of its contemporaries, the property also sported a pulsating pool scene, entertainment and musical venues, and of course, a 130,000 square-foot casino. Like the Wynn and Bellagio, it catered to the chosen few, those who complemented their high-stakes gaming with luxury spa treatments and high-end shopping at all hours of the night.

Of the thousands of gamblers and partygoers under the resort's roof at the moment, only one mattered to Dan. He was one of the Platinum's most eccentric and renowned players, though few of the hotel's other visitors had any clue the man was even in-house. He visited roughly twice a year, tethering himself for hours at a time to private baccarat and pai gow poker tables in a room cordoned-off from the rest of the casino. The few gamblers allowed entry presided over financial empires and multi-million-dollar operations. Just one placed his bets under the watchful eye of the United States Secret Service.

Dan pulled his government-issued Dodge Charger to a stop just outside the main entrance, waving his credentials at a nearby attendant who wore a deep frown. A decade-old relic that screamed police cruiser was hardly what any self-respecting valet would consider curb appeal. The precious real estate out front was normally reserved for the gentry and their glitzy Lamborghinis and Hummers.

He barely had one foot out of his car before he was met by Elise Shusterman. Though the young agent could have passed for a college student, an academy instructor had once vowed to Dan that pound for pound, she was the toughest trainee in her class. The Brooklyn native and triathlete was in just her second year, a recent graduate of City College of New York whose family had worn NYPD blue for three generations.

"Elise," he nodded, straightening the holster on his belt. "I see I'm not the only one who got a wake-up call."

"Yes, sir. We've got the end of the wing sealed off, and Metro arrived ten minutes ago."

"Omirou? Still on-site?"

A quick headshake. "Galanos wanted him out of here. He's on his way to the Waldorf with the DL."

After dispatching Shusterman to report to the Detail Leader at the most elegant hotel on the Strip, Dan headed for the main entrance, shouldering his way past the other arrivals, most of whom sported young faces, bare skin, and a tapestry of tattoos. The assault on his senses began as he neared the entrance, led by an earsplitting blare of electronic slot machine chimes and an invisible cloud of tobacco fumes. The doors were held open by pair of buxom sirens in silver body suits, welcoming revelers and directing the better clad of them to STEEL, an exclusive nightspot open only to those whose name appeared on a magical list. Dan glimpsed his watch with a yawn. 1:50. While America slept, Vegas was hitting its stride.

It was his fifteenth year in the city, a remarkable number given the unending reassignments and transfers marking most Secret Service career paths. Dan's track had wandered from the norm since the day of his high-speed derailment in the Dirksen Senate Office Building so many years ago. As Barb Patterson had predicted, his impudence incited a firestorm at headquarters. Chairman Sheffield graciously accepted the Director's personal apology and spared the agency from reprisal, but Dan received no such quarter and remained very much in the man's crosshairs. It was left to Patterson to find a place for Dan somewhere in Secret Service oblivion.

It wouldn't be Tennessee, and Dan had at least managed to elude South Texas, where a small, forgotten troop of agents once kept watch over the feeble Lady Bird Johnson, her statutorily-mandated protection continuing three decades after former President Johnson's death. She passed away just months before Dan's misstep with Sheffield.

Instead, Dan caught what seemed like a break. The investigative side of the house desperately needed another body in Las Vegas, where the Service was urgently expanding its outreach and casework. Financial crimes had been spiking for years regionally, particularly among the casinos and the nascent tech companies sprouting up in the metro area. The Director approved the transfer, satisfied Dan's removal from the Presidential Detail alone would quench Sheffield's bloodthirst, no matter the final destination.

Dan's relief soon gave way to a festering resentment, disgusted by the willingness of his superiors to make his career a sacrificial offering. Until that fateful moment at the Senate hearing table, he had a promising future ahead, unassisted by his father's influence. His abilities and potential were respected by both peers and supervisors. Now, whispers would follow wherever he went.

The transfer was welcomed even less at home. Vegas would mark the third relocation for the young couple in just four years of marriage. As a political campaign consultant, Michelle was dubious about her career prospects in the West, a solar system away from the epicenter of her trade in Washington. But with their daughter, Megan, just turning four and Dan still relatively early in his career, he had little choice but to accept the assignment without complaint.

They made every effort to connect with their new community, joining a neighborhood pool, and later filling Megan's weekends with Girl Scouts and youth soccer games. Dan was rarely around to enjoy any of it. He plodded away as a criminal investigator, striving to impress his new supervisor. The perennially sullen man, lacking both intellect and imagination, wasn't much of a leader, and with the office in the middle of a review by agency inspectors, morale was ebbing.

Dan did his part, closing a number of headline-worthy cases over the years, and when Washington finally decided to clear out the upper ranks of the office, he was elevated to Assistant Special Agent in Charge. That made him second in-command, managing eighteen special agents and half a dozen investigative and administrative support personnel.

A year later, facing another likely forced move, Dan made a watershed career decision, opting to remove himself from consideration for future promotion. It was a trade-off the Service offered to veteran agents. Dan would remain a senior GS-14 for the duration of his career, with no further advancement in the civil service system. That entitled him to remain in Vegas, exempt from future transfers to a protective detail or other field offices. Megan, just entering her freshman year in high school, would have the stability Dan lacked in his own childhood, and equally important, Dan now controlled his own fate. No re-assignment to headquarters, and no random transfers to Tennessee, Timbuktu, or any of the other 140 field offices and protective details operated by the Secret Service.

He hadn't imagined the possibility when first sentenced to the desert, but he considered Vegas now a choice assignment. The caseload was consequential, and an infusion of exceptional leadership had transformed the entire character of the office, improving operational efficiencies and lifting morale to new heights. A highly prized network of partnerships was developed with sister agencies and local industry leaders, further elevating their stature in the community.

A bell chimed, announcing the elevator's arrival on the 44th floor. Dan stepped off, one hand reflexively adjusting the 9mm Glock strapped to his hip while the other checked his tie knot. He knifed past the trio of black-sport coated security men standing awkwardly in the elevator lobby, offering only a professional nod and brief flourish of his badge. They parted quickly, resuming the onlooker status they had been relegated to by the federal agents. There had been little protest, the men content to keep their distance from the powder keg Dan was headed toward.

His outward composure reflected the confidence he had in his team. In addition to Shusterman and the shift agents, all relatively junior, there were two protective intelligence agents and two supervisors on-site. Pablo Maldonado was Dan's subordinate in the Las Vegas office, and responsible for the protective footprint at the hotel. Just under six feet, he was a broad-shouldered gym rat with a strapping build and quick mind. He had eleven years in and arrived in Las Vegas last year from the Vice Presidential Protective Division with a file full of commendations. Alec Heath was the Detail Leader, a senior agent shuttled in on occasion from the Los Angeles Field Office for short-term gigs like this. Though lacking much of a personality, he had proven to be a quietly efficient, reliable DL. Like Maldonado, Heath was a clear-eyed professional, and Dan trusted them both implicitly.

He immediately spotted Maldonado, squared off with another individual roughly halfway down a gilded corridor that seemed to stretch to Utah. Their raised voices carried the entire length, the tension and friction palpable. As Dan drew closer, he recognized the bulk of Demetrius Galanos, the security chief to the President of Cyprus. They had met often over the years, and though Dan lacked any affection for the man, he was sensitive to Galanos' credentials, including his special forces background. That was also two decades and a fractured vertebra ago, adding plenty of excess pounds to what was already a stout frame.

Galanos was waving his arms in agitation, the aggression and wrath unmistakable. He loomed over Maldonado, outweighing the American agent by at least fifty pounds, as he jabbed a meaty finger in the air and spittle flew from his mouth. Maldonado leaned in, undaunted and prepared to snap the man's finger in two. An older man, diminutive and paling by the second, stood nearby. The translator, Dan surmised. Likely discomfited from standing just feet away from two armed killers. They all turned at the sound of Dan's heavy footsteps, with Maldonado's face registering no small measure of relief.

"My men," Galanos rasped, now stabbing his finger in Dan's direction. "Free. Now."

Dan held up his palms. "Hold on, Demetrius, I just got here. Give me a minute alone with Agent Maldonado."

The foreigner gave his watch an overdramatic glance as Dan led his colleague back toward the elevator.

Dan kept his voice low. "Where are they?"

Maldonado's eyes burned with intensity, and beads of perspiration dotted his forehead.

"CJ has them. They're in their suite, cuffed and on the sofa. Metro is in there, too. They were amped up on something, maybe Molly. Cannerella had to baton the bigger guy. Fucker's going to need some stitches on his scalp."

Dan grunted in approval. The agency-issued, collapsible baton had a one-inch steel ball on the end, packing a wallop of non-lethal stopping power.

"They're calming down now," Maldonado continued. "I think they know they're in a shitload of trouble."

"Weapons?"

"We took a knife off one of them, and brass knuckles, if you can believe it, off the other. No guns, they were off-duty."

"The girl?"

"Metro has her in another room, one floor up." Maldonado paused. "She's fourteen years old, sir. A runaway from California. They want to take her to the hospital and get a formal statement."

"Fourteen? Jesus. Is she hurt?"

Maldonado set his jaw. "They got rough."

"Rape?"

"Not sure. If they didn't, they sure as hell were going to."

"Is she willing to talk?"

"Sounds like it."

"Omirou is at the Waldorf?"

"Still en route. Heath has Drew and the PI crew with him, plus the rest of Galanos' guys. Day shift is inbound."

"Did you call Jimmy?"

Jimmy Wu was a former captain with the Metro Police Department, now head of security for the Platinum.

Maldonado nodded. "On his way. Told his people to give us whatever we needed."

"What we need is a lid on this, and whatever tape they have on the girl."

"Working on both."

Dan stomped back down the hall, Maldonado following on his heels.

"Here's what's going to happen, Demetrius. Your two guys will likely be taken into custody by the local police. I don't want to hear any bullshit about diplomatic immunity, because your men committed a crime in plain view of Federal officers. I'll make sure they're taken out of here quietly. Likely through the service elevator and whatever back door we can find."

Galanos listened to the translation, his lips curling in consternation as he considered a response. Perhaps attempting to sniff out a possible bluff. Dan knew immunity wasn't an impossibility under such circumstances. It was a murky area with little precedent, but instinct told him to err on the side of detention and let the lawyers sort it out later. He was relieved to see Galanos dropping the bombastic routine, likely uncertain of what standing, if any, his men had.

"Thank you for your professional courtesy." The remark came through both gritted teeth and the translator. The sarcasm needed no translation.

"Fuck you, Demetrius," Dan fumed. "That's the same service elevator those gorillas brought a child up here to rape and assault."

The translator worked quickly through Dan's scolding, chafing at the coarse words as he replicated them in his native language. Galanos became beet red again, the vein on his temple nearly bursting from the skin.

"You and I will go to the Waldorf together and speak to your President. Is that acceptable?"

Galanos waited for the completed translation, never taking his eyes off Dan, before barking a few surly words and storming down the hallway toward the delegation's main suite.

"What did he say?" Dan asked the translator, rivulets of perspiration streaming from the man's forehead.

The man's smile was pained. "Nothing I can repeat out loud to our gracious host or believe is anatomically possible. But I suggest, sir, you arrange your own transportation to the Waldorf."

CHAPTER 2

Dan left *Terrible's*, the ubiquitous Vegas convenience store, and climbed back into the driver's seat, liquid treasure in hand. He thumbed the keyless ignition, wincing sharply as a string of painfully discordant musical notes filled the Charger. His finger shot to the mute button as he cursed the 90s Sirius channel and everything that decade stood for. A sleepless night followed by high-decibel Sheryl Crow was a toxic recipe, but his newly acquired coffee, one of his favorite brews, would at least sustain him through the marathon meeting awaiting.

Only a few hours had passed since Dan returned to his warm bed. Nicole barely stirred when his head hit the pillows. Sleep was elusive, with Dan still wired after his spat with the head of state at the Waldorf. Anxiety also nagged at him, knowing there would be repercussions once headquarters learned of his very undiplomatic exchange. After a fitful hour, he rolled out of bed once again, this time suiting up for a short run through his neighborhood. Desperation maybe, and certainly questionable judgment considering the years of neglect of his physical conditioning. He logged a punishing two miles before staggering home, winded and aching. Some warrior. An hour later, he was showered, shaved, and back in the Charger, stopping at *Terrible's* for a much-needed infusion of caffeine.

He eased the Charger out of the small parking lot and onto West Charleston Boulevard, weaving into rush hour traffic before hooking an illegal U-turn, known in Secret Service parlance as a Federal Left. He turned onto Las Vegas Boulevard and drove north, miles away from the Platinum and her gaudy, sister resorts bracketing the eight-lane width of the Strip. Here, closer to the old downtown, the boulevard tapered to just four lanes, lined with dated structures blighted with decay. It was the seedier Las Vegas few out-of-towners were familiar with, and though it had shown some signs of improvement in recent years, it was still dotted with the dated motels, sketchy pawn shops, and flashy signage that catered to the downtrodden and dispossessed.

Just beyond this bleak landscape was a drab assortment of government office buildings. It wasn't a choice location, but the real estate was priced to entice tight-fisted government procurement officers. Most agencies here served local constituencies, assisting veterans, Social Security recipients, low-income housing tenants, and so many others with sorting through mind-numbing regulations and mountains of paperwork giving bureaucracy a bad name. The area was also home to the law enforcement community, including field offices for the FBI, DEA, and Secret Service.

His cell phone buzzed, and Dan tapped the button on the car's navigation screen, recognizing the number as he waited for the Bluetooth to kick in.

"No, you can't have any money."

"Wow," rang a young woman's voice. "I haven't heard that one in days. Let me guess. You're here all week, folks."

"I'm here all week, folks," Dan said at the same time. They both laughed.

"Hey, Dad."

"Hey, Megs. How's school?"

Dan cursed himself the second the words left his mouth, having forgotten the sensitivity of the subject.

"Okay," Megan answered. "Other than the guy teaching my Comparative Politics class. He's a little to the right of Sean Hannity, and mom's freaking out about it."

He could hear the cereal being shoveled into her mouth. The girl was as lean as a rail but could put away every morsel of food in a one-mile radius.

"That's your mother. How're your mid-terms going?"

"Eh."

Dan swung the car onto Clark, the contours of the county building emerging ahead, just blocks away. "Hate to cut you off, but I've got a meeting I need to run to. What's up?"

"Wanted to see if we could move dinner to Sunday. We have a protest on Saturday night at the admin building."

They had just recently agreed to get together every few weekends, but scheduling remained a challenge given Dan's unpredictable calendar and Megan's recent spate of student activism.

"No problem. We still going to that dog restaurant?"

More laughter. Music to a single father's ears.

"Yep. *State Street Dogs*. You're going to die."

"From what you told me about their menu, I probably will."

"You can bring Nancy," his daughter teased.

"Nicole. And I've told you, she's just a friend."

"Right. I know guys who would love to meet more of your *friends*."

One block to go. "How's your mom?"

A pause. "Okay, I guess. She's pissed about the grades, said you guys might cut me off."

There was hesitancy in Megan's voice, and Dan sensed she was holding something back. Megan and her mother agreed on politics but little more, and the unease between the two had been ratcheting up for months. It started with Megan's decision to stray from the path of law or medicine her mother had been hoping for since the academic awards began piling up in high school. So much had changed with Megan in a few short years. She had begun to open up during their recent dinners, and Dan was struck by how the shy, withdrawn little girl he once doted on had transformed into such a worldly, headstrong young woman. One clearly growing weary of the constant barrage of doomsday admonishments from her mother. How Dan had ever been so close to his former wife was a mystery for the ages.

"Kind of hard to make such threats when I'm writing the checks. Look, we'll talk on Sunday night. Gotta run."

They ended the call just as an armed guard finished checking Dan's license plate and badge. An iron gate encircling the parking structure slowly retracted to admit the Charger.

Ten minutes later, a dozen others were seated with Dan around a long, mahogany conference table. He looked mournfully at his now-empty paper cup as he waited for the private conversations to wind down.

The mix of cops and prosecutors at the table was familiar. For more than a decade, Dan had served as his office's primary liaison to local law enforcement and invested considerable time in building trusted partnerships with his Clark County peers. They were capable and cooperative, willing to share information whenever needed, and Dan made sure that was a two-way street.

He felt the eyes of Phil Engel from across the table, and he gave the man a curt nod. Gangly and thick-bearded, Engel was a senior agent in the local FBI office, and like Dan, a regular attendee at these meetings. The Bureau man offered a disbelieving head shake, conveying sympathy for the fix his Secret Service colleague was in.

Disingenuous ass, Dan thought, forcing a smile.

"Dan, you're holding that gas station muck like it's the last coffee on Earth."

The room quickly quieted, and Dan proudly tipped his cup to the woman seated at the head of the table.

"Late night. And I'll take my gas station muck over your Starburnt every day of the week."

Jennifer Pham scoffed. "First case I worked here was a whack job who threw his coffee on an attendant at a Shell station on Sahara. Gave the girl third degree burns on her face and hands. The perp said it tasted like the instant crap the Army once gave to him and countersued for his eighty-nine cents back."

"I know that Shell station," Dan grinned. "Best Colombian blend north of Bogota."

Pham smiled back, shaking her head. Dan liked the rotund, no-nonsense District Attorney for Clark County. Born and raised in the city, she was the oldest daughter of refugees who fled Saigon in the chaotic days leading up to the final withdrawal of U.S. personnel from Vietnam. After four years at the University of Nevada, Las Vegas – known locally as UNLV – she put herself through UCLA Law School, then landed a plum position as an Assistant U.S. Attorney in Manhattan, putting drug lords and crooked hedge fund managers behind bars, before returning to Las Vegas to run for District Attorney. She was tireless and conscientious, and singularly focused on the crushing casework managed by a bustling office of more than one hundred prosecutors.

A paunchy, harried figure came through the door, pushing his horn-rimmed glasses up as he offered Pham an apologetic look.

Dan didn't know the younger man, but Pham nodded in greeting, clearly expecting the newcomer. She directed one of her staff to the chairs lining the back wall, freeing up a space at the table.

"Everyone, this is Elliot Partain, one of Jeff's people."

Partain found a seat and opened a leather-bound notebook. "Sorry I'm late. The boss apologizes for his absence. He's in Denver but asked me to convey his strong interest in this case and his wish to be kept fully informed."

Dan eyed Pham carefully. Jeffrey Kendrick was the United States Attorney for the District of Nevada. Appointed by President Vance, the federal prosecutor was a prominent figure in the state, and Dan knew he and Pham had a close partnership minimizing the overlap between their two offices. His surrogate's presence was a red flag, as Kendrick reported to masters in Washington who could trump Pham's authority on nearly any matter.

"Of course," Pham smiled. "He can join the club." She nodded to an aide who activated the telephone console in the middle of the table.

"Ms. Rainey," Pham called out, "you with us?"

"I am," responded a clear voice, one Dan suspected was some 2,500 miles away.

Pham addressed the table again. "We have with us this morning Elizabeth Rainey with the State Department in Washington. She'll be listening in."

Those last four words, Dan knew, were chosen with precision, the DA marking her territory. Pham turned toward the uniformed officer at her right.

"Doug, why don't you start us off?"

"Doug Cunningham here," the man intoned for the benefit of their listener. "Chief of Investigative Services, Metro Police Department."

Dan knew the veteran officer well. They were roughly the same age, but the hulking Cunningham had graying hair and a red, bulbous nose. He was quick-tempered and prone to speaking without thought, but he was also an earnest cop, and led what Dan considered an exceptional team of officers and detectives. And while no one would accuse Cunningham of being the most soft-spoken man in the department, he always shunned personal credit, directing every accolade or commendation to those under him. It was a trait Dan wished he saw more of from the managerial ranks of his own agency.

The veteran officer slipped on a pair of reading glasses and began reciting his notes.

"Victim is Tonya DeLong, a white, female, 14-year-old with no known local address. Parents are William and Deanna DeLong of Stockton, California. Reported their daughter missing nine months ago. We have more on Tonya from Social Services, which we can dig into later. It's not exactly Afterschool Special material. According to the victim, she was approached by one of her assailants, we'll call him Thug One, on Quincy Street, just before midnight. He came by private car. Local outfit, and we're still tracking down the driver. Thug One makes the pitch, she gets in, and they're driven to the Platinum. Hotel security somehow passes them through to the loading dock. From there, we believe, but haven't been able to confirm, they took a service elevator to the 44th floor—"

"Hold right there, Doug," Pham injected. "I want your people all over Platinum management for this. Let them know I'm considering charges for criminal negligence, and abetting, and God knows what else we can come up with. And their security team better start giving us 120 percent."

"Yes ma'am," Cunningham responded dutifully, though they all heard the skepticism in his voice. The overseers of the Platinum would not be easily bullied, its corporate principals brandishing political connections from Carson City to Capitol Hill.

"From the service elevator, her escort brought the girl to a suite, where Thug Two was already waiting. The two men negotiated her price and gave her half the money up front. They popped a few pills – Ecstasy laced with something, we're waiting for the lab reports – and things got out of hand. No intercourse with either of the suspects, sounds like they were working their way up to that. She tried to leave, said the men were losing control and getting more...physical. That's when they roughed her up pretty bad. She's got deep contusions on her face, back and buttocks, a skull fracture, and lacerations to her lower lip and right eyebrow. She was taken to University Medical Hospital and they'll keep her there indefinitely for observation. Parents are on their way in from California. We've taken into custody the two suspects, both members of President Omrow's—"

"Omirou," Dan corrected, rhyming it with zoo.

"Omirou," Cunningham mimicked. "Thug 1 and 2 are on the President's security detail, and we got positive ID by the victim from their passport photos. Nicos Demetriou, age thirty-one, and Christakis Nouris, age twenty-seven. They're being held in county detention at the moment."

"Fourteen years old," uttered one of the newer assistant district attorneys, horror-struck. The others at the table were less moved, too familiar with the darker underbelly of the city.

"Ms. Pham, can I jump in?" The voice over the speaker phone sounded crisp and alert.

"Go ahead, Ms. Rainey."

"Liz, please. Good morning, everyone. I'm the Assistant Secretary of State, Bureau of Diplomatic Security."

Shit. Not the GS-13 flunky Dan expected. The lady was a heavyweight. As head of the Diplomatic Security Service, the respected arm of the State Department protecting both American diplomats overseas and foreign officials visiting the United States, Rainey was one of the highest-ranking officials in Foggy

Bottom. By statute, the Secret Service protected visiting heads of state, namely foreign presidents and prime ministers, and an occasional Pope. DSS was responsible for the next tier, including cabinet ministers, ambassadors, and other diplomats. With side trips to Vegas common among foreign visitors, Dan had intersected often with DSS. They were pros.

Alarm bells began sounding for Dan. Barely three hours had passed since he stood in front of President Omirou. Rainey's personal involvement signaled how rapidly the matter had already escalated.

"I'm with our General Counsel and Director of Domestic Operations. For everyone's situational awareness, Cyprus' embassy here in Washington has already filed a formal protest with the State Department over the arrests. They are demanding the men be immediately remanded in their custody and deported so they can be investigated and tried in their own country."

The men and woman gathered around the conference table reacted as one, all frowns and scowls. Except Partain, the aloof Assistant U.S. Attorney.

"That's a joke, right?" asked a disbelieving Pham, even with her years in the trenches.

The Assistant Secretary's voice remained calm and even. "As a career security professional, yes, I consider that a joke. Like each of you, I'm under no illusion these men would ever serve a day behind bars in their country. But as a diplomat, this standoff is a serious dilemma for the Department."

"Let me make it easy on you, Ms. Rainey." The DA's eyes swept across the room, full of assurance. "This is no standoff; this is a slam dunk. I can already think of half a dozen charges we'll be filing here, including multiple violations of Nevada state law."

Pham spoke as if Partain wasn't in the room. A tug-of-war with the U.S. Attorney was surely coming, but that far exceeded his junior lieutenant's pay grade. She did glance at Engel, the FBI man. In high-profile cases, the Bureau typically asserted jurisdiction as fast as they could slip on their blue windbreakers. But in what was surely heralding danger for Pham, Engel was locked into a neutral expression, declining to show any display of support. While the Bureau may have regarded the matter as entirely local, it was more likely they wanted nothing to do with what was shaping into a political minefield.

Big cases, Dan's father often warned, *big problems*.

"Ms. Pham, let's stand down on the turf war. It's unnecessary and counterproductive. I would like to collaborate with you and your team on this, but there are issues at stake here beyond the rap sheets of these two men. This country is a vital strategic ally, making this situation exceptionally delicate."

"Cyprus?" exclaimed Cunningham. "A vital strategic ally? They even got an army?"

Dan wanted to bury his face in his hands. He liked Cunningham but riffing like a small-town yokel only weakened Pham's hand. There were a few moments of awkward silence until Rainey's voice came back on the line, cooler now.

"Rest assured, Mr. Cunningham, they have a number of assets and facilities tying into our counterterrorism operations in the Med and beyond."

Cunningham folded his arms defiantly. "Which has exactly what to do with two would-be rapists in Southern Nevada?"

"Nothing," Pham responded for Rainey. "But I expect we're about to hear a national security claim here."

"Fuck that," mouthed Cunningham, his eyes urging the DA to dig in, but Pham kept him quiet with a raised palm.

There was another pause on the line from Washington before Rainey responded, her voice softer now. "Look people, I have two young daughters of my own. I'm revolted by what happened there, and I want those two bastards to serve some real time in an American prison cell. But we can't ignore the atmospherics."

"Atmospherics?" asked Pham.

"Fucking politics," Dan grumbled.

"I beg your pardon, who was that?"

He cleared his throat. "Dan Cahill, Secret Service ASAIC, Las Vegas Field Office. My guys—"

"Yes, I know what your people did, Agent Cahill, and I have no objection to their conduct. We will defend it vociferously to the Cypriots."

"Before you let the assholes go."

Pham looked at him pointedly and Dan averted his gaze, already regretting the words. Rainey hadn't exactly been swinging an iron fist. She seemed to be playing it straight, coping with a four-alarm fire in Washington while building bridges with the duty-bound public servants on the ground. But his stomach was on full churn mode. While he hoped Washington would support Pham and her prosecutors, he had worked foreign dignitaries long enough to know diplomatic niceties were soon going to eclipse every other consideration.

"Ms. Rainey," Pham said, looking for calmer waters, "perhaps when the forensic investigation is complete, we can review—"

"Let me it put this as plainly as I can," Rainey interrupted, revealing her first sign of strain. "The Secretary of State has already put a call in to the Attorney

General. I expect within an hour, you'll have an order from the appropriate authority to release those men."

There was a chorus of objections in the room, plus an assortment of colorful and disparaging remarks about the Nation's capital.

Rainey waited until the room was quiet again. "This is a White House decision, not subject to further debate. That said, it's up to us – me and your team – how we manage it from here. No one is telling you to return their passports yet. We want to see justice served. The Department is just looking for some time to sort through this."

"How much time?" asked Pham.

"It's just past noon here. Release the men but hold their passports for the day. We'll re-connect later this afternoon. Can you keep a lid on this with the local press?"

"No promises," sighed the DA, and Dan could hear the defeat in her voice. "We can control our people. The hospital staff will respect the victim's confidentiality given her age. But the hotel folks aren't under any obligation and will likely talk. We can clam them up for hours, maybe, but not days."

They discussed a few other administrative matters before the call ended. The meeting broke and Pham asked Dan to follow her back to her office. She collapsed in her chair, gesturing for the federal agent to close the door.

"When is the delegation scheduled to leave?"

"Tomorrow. They're on a noon British Airways direct to Heathrow." He waited a beat. "For what it's worth, Rainey seems square. Maybe if—"

"Rainey won't be calling the shots, the White House will, and you know better than I do those men will have their passports by the end of the day. If State is coming down hard on us, and there truly is a counterterrorism nexus here, then DoD and the intel community are coming down ten times harder on them."

"Any chance the Bureau jumps in?"

Pham gave a scornful look, answering his question. "Have you ever been in a meeting where Phil hasn't said a word? His SAC will see nothing but headaches here, whatever the Hoover Building tells him to do. And if they had no role in the arrest and can't score any points with the press, the risk-gain arrow is pointing the wrong way."

"What about the girl?"

"My guess is the parents will want to extricate her from this and try and help their daughter move on and return to some kind of a normal life. My husband was an AUSA in Northern Virginia years ago. He handled more than a few cases back then of foreign diplomats running amok in DC."

"And?"

"And, from what I remember him telling me, there are people in Washington who can arrange for the girl to get a decent settlement out of this."

Dan shook his head, appalled. As if the girl would ever return to any kind of normalcy. Just go back to high school, try on some prom dresses, and forget what those animals tried to do to her. What they *did* do to her.

"A payoff. One check and these—"

"A very nice check, Dan. It would likely set her up for years, get her into rehab, counseling or whatever else she needs. Maybe save her life. I don't like the idea of a payoff any more than you do, but if it's a *fait accompli* these men will walk, she should at least get something out of this."

"You mean, besides the cuts, the skull fracture, and the psychological trauma? What's that worth nowadays, five grand? Ten?"

Pham leaned back in her chair, a deep scowl on her face. "Do you have a better solution? Since I know you don't, then get the fuck out of my office."

. . .

Three hours later, Dan was in his own downtown office, pounding away on his keyboard as he fielded yet another request from the manpower shop in Washington, this one ordering three bodies for a jump team. The Las Vegas agents tagged by Dan would join with others from the field to support an upcoming POTUS trip to Toronto. His desk phone buzzed, and he picked it up, recognizing the number on the digital screen. He cursed, knowing there was only one reason for the call.

"Cahill."

"Dan, it's Jen Pham."

"Are you fucking kidding me?"

"I wish I was, but they're out. Twenty minutes ago, with their passports."

"What the fuck? Their passports?!?"

"Nothing I can do, Dan. DOJ made the claim, said the interest of America's security superseded the victim's interest here."

"Jesus Christ. They'll be on that London flight by lunchtime tomorrow. And never set foot on American soil again. Guaranteed."

"DOJ promised to carry the fight through their channels."

Dan dismissed that. "Any possibility of extradition?"

"Slim. We have a reciprocal agreement with Cyprus in place. But there are waivers, and given the sensitivity in this case—"

"So, we're done." It was a statement, not a question.

"I'm sorry, Dan. I know you were personally invested in this."

"No, a 14-year-old girl was personally invested in this," burned Dan, slamming the phone down.

Ten minutes later, he was still leaning back in his chair, staring at the ceiling. A thousand thoughts raced through his mind as he deliberated his next move, weighing the implications of just one short phone call. He inhaled deeply, finding the name in his Contacts and placing the iPhone to his ear. His personal phone. There would be fingerprints, but he was past caring. A gruff voice picked up.

"Stuart Valentine."

"Stu, Dan Cahill here."

"Agent Cahill, good to hear your voice. How's Megan doing?"

"Doing alright. A year and a half to go at UNLV. How's Ingrid?"

"All good. Not sure if you heard, but she left UC-Davis a few semesters ago. Working with a private coach to make one of the pro teams."

"That's fantastic, Stu. Please send her my best wishes. Megan owed half her career saves to all those workouts with her."

"Sure thing. That was a hell of a team. Hey, don't mean to cut you short, but I'm on deadline for a story on the school board election."

"Still covering local politics?"

"Pays the bills," Valentine lamented, a man drowning in tedium.

"Well, I might have something for you. A little sexier than a school board election."

"That could be paint drying. What d'ya got, Dan?"

CHAPTER 3

The rich aroma intoxicated Dan the moment he passed through the glass doors. The demure smile from the olive-skinned barista completed the seduction. Either the young woman had a fetish for middle-aged men with soft bellies, or their mutual familiarity was a sign of his dependency issues with caffeine.

A two-level structure that once housed the city's premiere pawn shop, *Sacred Grounds* was owned by a family of Conservative Jews who imported many of their decadent blends from the Middle East. Just blocks from the field office, the cafe had become a safe house for Dan and his superior, where they could discuss more sensitive matters away from the prying eyes and ears of their subordinates.

He spotted Anthony Jarrett at the window bar. A long-limbed figure with the frame of a middleweight boxer, the Special Agent in Charge of the Las Vegas field office gestured toward Dan with the two ceramic mugs in his hands. Dan had received the man's urgent text – punctuated with a few choice adjectives – just as he was finishing an early morning meeting with the information security wonks at Zappos. His stomach lurched the instant he saw the hyperlink Jarrett had included. A single click later and the front page of the *Las Vegas Review-Journal* filled his phone screen, topped by headlines pronouncing attempted rape, a miscarriage of justice, and shadowy bureaucrats with political agendas.

Washington may have been three time zones to the east, but Dan could feel the storm winds swirling up and down Pennsylvania Avenue. Political appointees from the Pentagon to Foggy Bottom were surely on the warpath by now, incensed about the leak after the White House had ordered a lid on the story. An order someone had deliberately flouted.

Even Nancy Drew would have nailed Dan as the source. It was no small skill to leak information without attribution, so Washington would know it was an experienced operator. It would also have to be someone privy to the Platinum case details, and on familiar terms with the local scribes in Vegas. That was certainly in Dan's job jar. Jarrett relied on his ASAIC to engage with the press as necessary, offering quotes and background information to news outlets covering protective visits or breakthroughs in criminal cases. Though Dan had some latitude, every exchange with the press, on and off the record, was required to be coordinated with the agency's public affairs shop back in Washington. The Service's media flacks were fanatical about ensuring headquarters and field personnel were singing from the same sheet music.

By now, the agency's lead spokesman was surely apoplectic and warming up an electric chair. Far sooner than Dan had anticipated, as the R-J story had reached publication in breakneck speed. Barely twenty hours had passed since he spoke to Stu Valentine, offering just a loosely-worded tip and a few strategic bread crumbs, but this was the era of 24/7 digital news, where speed, legwork, and occasional ethical lapses separated those who published from those who perished. And so, while Dan was tossing and turning in bed, the R-J was already fully vetting and sourcing a sensational exposé, one fitting a political narrative the newspaper's conservative owner favored as it rippled across the Valley and drew nationwide attention.

Dan climbed onto a stool, palming the steaming mug shoved toward him, hoping it wasn't spiked with some deadly poison.

"Is this your version of a last cigarette?"

Anthony Jarrett laughed, his deep baritone sounding like a cross of Mufasa the Lion King and Dr. Evil.

"Gallows humor. I love it. Actually, I thought you might be hung over."

"This time of day?"

"I figured it had to be booze," Jarrett said, his smile evaporating. "Why else would you make that phone call."

"What phone call?"

"Come on, Dan."

There was no edge to Jarrett's voice, but the man had always been a superb investigator, and this wasn't exactly the Lindbergh baby kidnapping. Dan could not meet his superior's eyes. The decision to call Valentine hadn't been a difficult one, but he never intended to deceive his boss and friend, a man he had so much regard for.

Jarrett was recruiting poster material. As a criminal investigator in the Detroit field office, he amassed countless awards and an exemplary service record. When it came time for his first protective posting, he was selected for the Presidential Detail and the Service's tactical assault squad, considered the elite of the elite. Five years later, he was handpicked to command the Las Vegas office, and the dreadful reign of the previous SAIC soon became an afterthought. Jarrett was diligent and decisive, with a magnetic personality, and in their three years together, had formed an unlikely and unshakeable personal bond with his deputy.

His stint in Vegas wouldn't last much longer, the man destined for a much loftier post in the agency. Yet for all his professional success, Jarrett remained as grounded a person as Dan knew. A loyal friend, a doting father to his twin daughters, and a conscientious leader.

"How's my girl?"

Dan sipped his scalding brew, thankful for the redirect. "Good. Having dinner on Sunday."

"Maybe someday you can see her more than once every blue moon."

"I doubt she could take that much of me."

"Tell me about it," Jarrett said with a crooked smile. He set down his coffee. "Have you read the article?"

Dan nodded as Jarrett pulled a phone from his suit coat.

"Funny thing," Jarrett continued. "You know how I found out about it? An email from Ed Schumann, just as my plane touched down at McCarran."

Schumann was Jarrett's FBI equal. He had six times the manpower as Jarrett, and though they had a relatively friendly co-existence, the competitive spirit between the two rival agencies ran deep. Jarrett thumbed open the article, scrolled for a moment, then handed his phone to Dan.

"My favorite part."

Dan skimmed the words quickly, anxiety surging through his bloodstream. Halfway through, he read the incriminating passage for the second time that morning.

According to a senior law enforcement source, U.S. officials in Washington ordered the diplomatic passports returned to the suspects, paving the way for the two men to flee the country. Once overseas, the source confirmed, extraditing the men to the United States to face a trial becomes almost an impossible task.

"Well, since your face just got three shades paler, I see you spotted the magic words."

Dan remained quiet as Jarrett snatched the phone from his hands.

"You had to mention the passports? Did you expect Pham to fall on her sword for you and say she was the leak?"

Dan sipped from his mug again.

"The shit storm is already rolling in. And not just at HQ. From what I'm hearing, heads are exploding from Pennsylvania Avenue to the State Department. The Director is catching buckets of hell."

"What do you want me to say, Tony? The victim's a kid, for Christ's sake. And it's the White House and State that gave those two a Get Out of Jail Free card. I didn't sign up for that kind of political BS."

"Actually, Dan, you did. We all did. Because we don't make decisions, we execute them, even if we have to scrape the political BS off our shoes every day."

"I thought we enforce the law."

Jarrett gave him a hard stare. "Hey, it's me. Drop the holier-than-thou attitude. This ain't no classroom exercise at Beltsville. Did you ever consider the possibility it isn't just politics? That there might be real CT implications to giving this country the middle finger? And stop with the look."

"What look?"

"The one you're giving me now, that says you'd rather be banging that casino gal with the legs than listening to my lectures about procedure. But this time you better listen to what I tell you. I might be the only friend you have right now."

"This won't stick to you, Tony, if that's what you're concerned about."

Jarrett glared at him. The worst kept secret in the office was his name was up for a Deputy SAIC slot on the Presidential Detail. He was a lock for the bid, a move that would one day lead to a senior leadership post in the agency.

And though Jarrett was almost always unflappable – his even temperament a perfect counterbalance to Dan's constant grousing and sarcastic jabs – the man was on the cusp of explosion now. Dan chewed his lip, knowing his rash comment could not have been more insulting. Even worse, Dan was in the man's debt. Unlike his predecessor, who considered Dan radioactive after his expulsion from Washington, Jarrett had always treated him as a confidante rather than his lesser.

"First of all, fuck you. This isn't about me, and you know that. My only concern is the jeopardy you've put this office in. And if it sounds like I'm taking all this personally, you're motherfucking right I am. Apparently, you trust me so little I had to hear about this from the Bureau."

"Come on, Tony—"

"Second of all," Jarrett continued, "you're right. It won't affect my bid. Because you're going to take the brunt of the blowback. Headquarters will give that article one read, and no matter what kind of interference I run, they'll know where the leak came from."

"I don't want you to run interference. I'm sorry. I wanted to tell you, but think about the position that would have put you in. You green light me to talk to the press, then it's your ass, and goodbye PPD. You don't allow it, well, no disrespect, but no way was I going to let it pass. I had to do it, Tony. I had to. You can't understand that?"

Jarrett stiffened. "You don't think I put myself in the shoes of that girl's father? What I would want if that was one of my daughters?"

"Then you know why I did it. And I'd do it again."

Both men were quiet for a full minute, nursing their coffee as the strain eased.

"What's going to happen, Tony?"

Jarrett mulled the question over. "Well, I don't think they'll send you packing. Even Dunton knows it'd be like trying to run Jurassic Park here after the fat guy locked up the computers and bailed. You're the fat guy, by the way."

Dan smiled, appreciating Jarrett's version of an olive branch. "Have you heard from HQ?"

Jarrett waved a hand. "They're probably sheltering in place, waiting for the fallout. My guess is Dunton will call you up and tear you a new one."

"Dunton is a jackass."

It was one of the more charitable words Dan could have used. Bill Dunton was the Assistant Director of Investigations, with the authority to stick his nose into any criminal case in the field, anywhere and anytime, which he often did. The man obsessed over arrest and conviction statistics, and every open case was a personal affront to him, as if tainting his own spotless record. His disdain for the agency's foray into electronic crimes was also well-known, his analog mind unable to adapt to digitalization and the emerging technologies so impactful to the financial sector. The man was a relic, like the snub-nosed revolver strapped to his ankle.

"He's more than a jackass, he's a dinosaur who thinks the Pinkertons are still cutting edge. He's also stonewalled me every time I've tried to get more bodies out here. But he's our boss, and after the Director receives a cursing from White House, he'll beat the hell out of Dunton, and Dunton will beat the hell out of you. So, you may want to think about stowing that attitude and playing nice."

Dan sighed in surrender. Jarrett was a savvy operator, and the one colleague Dan could speak to openly.

"This isn't like what happened with me and Sheffield, Tony. I knew the second Barb Patterson hauled me over the coals back then I'd fucked up. I didn't fuck up here, Washington did."

Jarrett shook his head. "That thought should go over well at headquarters." He downed the last of his coffee, his cheerless expression unsettling Dan. The man was normally a pillar of optimism, constantly preaching to his younger agents the key to adversity was converting every problem into an opportunity.

"Look, brother, everyone, including the Director, is in unchartered waters. My advice – take your lumps when Washington calls, and keep your mouth shut. How many years you have left before you put in your papers?"

Dan held up two fingers.

"You're that close, old man. Don't screw your retirement up over this. I don't like what happened any more than you do, but there is a damn good reason why field agents don't talk to the press about these things. Whatever your personal feelings about this case, or the paper pushers in DC letting those meatheads walk, you broke the rules. So, take your medicine, and here's a crazy thought – apologize."

Dan's face went blank, and Jarrett had to laugh. The SAIC knew him well.

The senior agent consulted the clock on his phone and rose from his stool.

"I need you, Dan. You're a model manager. Efficient, practical, and the younger agents think you're way funnier than me. You may not have noticed, but those kids look up to you. And though you try your damnedest to make us all think otherwise, I know you care about this job. About the mission."

"Nice speech."

"They taught it to us at SAIC school. And every word of it is true. Keep that temper in check, and don't fuck this up any further."

"You know, even the fat guy in Jurassic Park got more love than that from his boss."

"Maybe. But he also got torn apart by the raptors."

They both heard the cell phone vibrating in Jarrett's pocket. He removed it and read his screen.

"Shit," he grunted, picking up the call. "Jarrett." He was quiet for a full minute before he spoke again. "Yes, sir. I'm with him now. Yes, sir, I will pass the message."

Jarrett ended the call, looking pensive.

"Well, I was wrong. It won't be Dunton beating the hell out of you. It'll be the Director himself."

"I have to call him?"

"No such luck," Jarrett said with a tight smile. "You fly out tonight."

CHAPTER 4

Washington, D.C.

Beams of light poured through the windows of the spacious corner suite perched eight stories above H Street. Erected a quarter century ago, the structure was a sleek design of brick and glass, a significant upgrade from the pedestrian spaces the Secret Service once squeezed into on the upper floors of a commercial office building in downtown Washington. Though just a block from the White House complex back then, and thus a prime location operationally, it was the sort of shoehorning one might expect for an agency tacked onto the Treasury Department from birth, in the twilight of the Civil War.

The founding mission of the Secret Service was to safeguard the integrity of the U.S. monetary system. Abraham Lincoln signed the order creating the small Treasury bureau in April of 1865 – hours before he went to Ford's Theater – hoping to stem the flow of counterfeit currency flooding the war-ravaged country. That mission would evolve, most notably in 1901, when the Service received its first protective authorities following the assassination of President William McKinley.

Most considered the agency ill-suited for Treasury. The economists and Wall Street barons managing the department had a long tradition of paying little mind to the organization, preoccupied with expanding markets and diffusing trade wars instead. The authority and resource needs of a law enforcement bureau like the Secret Service were second fiddle to virtually all else.

It was that indifference that fueled the Service's unabashed enthusiasm for joining the Department of Homeland Security in 2003. In the years that followed, many would quietly regret the move, loathing the sprawling, inept new bureaucracy brimming with political appointees and micro-managers flaunting thin resumes.

The H Street headquarters building at least provided some standoff distance from the new overlords at DHS. Equidistant from the White House and U.S. Capitol, the compact facility housed just a fraction of the agency's personnel. The vast majority of the 7,000-strong workforce, including an entire division of uniformed officers, was in the field, assigned either to protective details or field offices scattered across the globe, from Tampa to Tokyo. While Dan recalled attending occasional briefings during his time on the Presidential Detail years ago, today marked his inaugural visit to the vaunted eighth floor. There was a time when he pictured a place for himself here, rubbing shoulders with the privileged few who commanded the organization and carried its celebrated legacy on their backs. He almost laughed now at that absurdity, just one more lofty aspiration added to the trash bin.

"Are we keeping you awake, Agent?"

Dan lifted his shoulders, suppressing a yawn as he focused his eyes again on the Assistant Director for Investigations. The man was impeccably groomed, from his perfectly coiffed mane and thin mustache to the pocket square peeking out from the breast pocket of his custom-made suit. It was all undoubtedly stitched together by the same legendary Bangkok tailor patronized by every agent ever posted in the Far East.

Bill Dunton was mostly a stranger to Dan, their career paths never intersecting. He had heard much about the man, none of it positive. Tony Jarrett was certainly no fan, convinced Bill Dunton was singularly devoted to Bill Dunton, with one eye always affixed to the Director's chair he hoped to occupy someday. His service record was both unblemished and unremarkable, with enough checked boxes to impress the politicos on both ends of Pennsylvania Avenue. He was flanked at the table by the agency's public affairs czar, and – most unnerving to Dan – the thirty-year agent who ran the Office of Professional Responsibility, more commonly referred to in municipal police departments as Internal Affairs.

"Sorry, sir. Red eye from LAX. Landed an hour ago."

Dunton either didn't hear him or didn't care.

"Just so you are aware, in addition to half of Washington breathing down our necks, the Director got a call from Jock Wainwright at Langley, informing us exactly what kind of support his people and the Pentagon rely on Cyprus for. I can't tell you what that is because the shit is classified so high the Director is the only one in the building cleared to hear it. That should give you an idea of exactly how deep of a cow pie you just stepped in."

Dan gripped the armrests of his chair. He could see the Director frowning, the man clearly ill at ease listening to a veteran agent dressed down like an academy trainee. With the calming voice of Jarrett in his head, Dan resisted the baiting from Dunton and waited for the Director to speak. In his rolled shirt sleeves and loosened tie, the former college wrestler appeared haggard, a telling sign of the unfathomable pressure he faced day and night in arguably the most taxing job in the world.

Dan had once felt some of that pressure. They all had. Knowing any moment, one operational miscue could trigger the worst imaginable tragedy for a family, a government, and a nation. An error or oversight that would blacken the records and consciences of every serving agent and officer. The kind that haunted Jack Kennedy's detail, and drove those men to alcohol and lifelong despair. And the Director was unable to ever escape the eye of the hurricane.

The older man opened his palms. "Look, Dan, Bill isn't exaggerating. Our asses are in a sling over this. You did everything by the book, right up until your unauthorized contact with the press. There are material consequences to that level of stupidity, and your fuckup here is your flagrant disregard for a critically important internal policy."

"Talking to a reporter out of school."

The Director glanced at the OPR head. The two men shared a look Dan was unable to decipher.

"You admit it."

"Yes, sir," Dan replied, struggling to recall the words he had rehearsed repeatedly during his six-hour flight. "I know I should have given a heads up to Public Affairs, but no offense Ed, your guys don't exactly move fast, and these shitheels were getting their passports back. I know Stu Valentine. Our girls were high school teammates, and we've known each—"

Dan's words trailed off and he swallowed hard. The Director was already shaking his head, and Ed Trudeau, lead spokesman for the agency, was noticeably cringing.

"Jesus Christ," carped Dunton, "high school teammates."

The Director leaned forward, his eyes flaring. "I don't care if Stu Valentine was the best man in your wedding. Or he donated an organ to save your first born. There is no gray area in that policy, Dan. No room for individual discretion or interpretation in the field. No room for personal relationships with friendly media people. You cannot have such conversations with the press, period, unless specifically authorized by Ed and his shop. The agency has been burned too many times on that front."

Dan remained quiet as the Director exhaled deeply and sat back in his chair.

"How many years you got in, Dan?"

"Twenty-three," Dan answered, his voice terse, unsure where this was going.

"If you were some kid on his first rotation, and this was just a local brushfire, I'd tell Tony Jarrett to smack you around a bit. Have Bill send you a nasty note for your service jacket. And it all would have been soon forgotten. But you're no kid, and this brushfire has already turned into a towering inferno at the White House and State. You had a problem with those men getting their passports back, you should have raised it through channels. We could have worked this through State or —"

"With respect sir, by the time we were on our second, or third, or twentieth phone call, those two would have been on a plane home."

"Which they are anyways," the Director retorted, unaccustomed to interruptions from the lower ranks. "And now we've got one royally pissed off head of state who's managed to have two cabinet secretaries and the White House Chief of Staff call over here to bark at me like junkyard dogs."

"Sir," injected Trudeau, "may I say something?"

The Director, red-faced now, fought back his next words and motioned Trudeau to proceed. The spokesman was a slight, balding man, with enough polish and articulation to suit him as the public face of a notoriously buttoned-up agency. Few would have believed the man was once a glass-chewing, All-American goaltender for the Harvard hockey team.

He turned to Dan. "You and I go back a ways. Wet-nosed kids on the Detail once. I've asked around about you since this all broke. People speak highly of you. Took a body blow all those years ago and bounced all the way back. A squared away agent and respected supervisor. But I hope the Director throws the book at you, because if he doesn't, that policy won't be worth the paper it's printed on. I'm going to have agents and officers all over the country with a personal agenda, or an ax to grind, having whispered conversations with reporters and bloggers every time they get passed over, disagree with an operational call by a supervisor, or take issue with something POTUS said or did."

Dan's fists were clenched. He knew Trudeau had a point and the rebuke was deserved. Yet it was what they hadn't discussed that continued to gnaw at him.

"Permission to speak freely, sir."

The Director nodded warily.

"Careful, Agent," snarled Dunton.

"I know what the rules are and why they're there. If I was in Ed's shoes, I'd be leveling the heavy artillery too. But we're all sworn law enforcement officers. And I know you have different considerations in this building, but sometimes in the field we have to—"

"You self-righteous son of a bitch," bristled Dunton. "You think none of us has ever spent time in the field? You have any idea how much we've tried to save your ass? How much trouble you have caused this agency?"

Dan ignored the AD and faced the Director again. "I'm sorry for all the hell you've caught over this, sir. But try pitching that bullshit about an internal agency SOP to the parents of a 14-year-old attempted rape victim."

Trudeau's face turned as crimson as Dunton's pocket square. Before he could utter a word, the Director raised a hand, silencing them all.

"Give us a minute," he commanded his headquarters staff.

The senior agents all stood. The Professional Responsibility chief had still not spoken a single word, but he joined the other two in shooting a withering, contemptuous scowl at Dan before exiting the room. Dan braced himself, fearing what the lack of witnesses portended.

The Director leaned forward, planting his elbows on the table as he laced his fingers together. His face, lined with the ancestry of his Cheyenne heritage, was taut with anger and exasperation.

"The review board met yesterday. They want you on the beach for two months pending a formal review."

The words hit Dan like a sledgehammer. The beach was an agency euphemism for paid administrative leave. A form of purgatory for those under investigation for misconduct. He expected nothing more than an admonishment, and at worst, a formal letter of reprimand. There couldn't be a soul among his brethren, even Bill Dunton, who believed the two men should have been allowed to skate.

Yet here he was, facing a suspension. And it was clear the Director wasn't finished.

"Off the record, Dan, there'll be a transfer when the investigation is complete. Anne is talking about sending you to Liza Walker's detail."

Dan remained motionless, stunned into silence. Anne Van Sloan was the agency's Deputy Director, responsible for personnel decisions, particularly among the higher grades. Reassignment to the Secretary of Homeland Security would not only put him back on a detail for the first time in years, it was the bottom rung on the protection ladder. He hadn't contemplated for a moment his career and time in Vegas might be in jeopardy. He slumped in his seat as he continued to absorb the blow.

Then he thought of the girl again. The photographs he had seen. The bruises. Her eyes. The torn underwear. He straightened, pushing back any pangs of regret.

"They have an ASAIC opening," the Director continued, "so you get to remain a supervisor. They've got a solid group there. Oscar Ruiz is the SAIC, not sure you know him. It's a good set-up, but we can frame it as a demotion, and publicly, we will. That will satisfy the West Wing and Foggy Bottom."

"I'll resign."

The Director folded his arms and fixed his eyes at the ceiling. Dan knew he was fraying the man's patience, a good man by all accounts, but he no longer cared. It was over.

"You're not resigning."

"I've been in Vegas for fifteen years now —"

"By your choice."

"My daughter is there. My—"

The Director twisted his face into a scowl. "You think you're the first agent who had to make a difficult move to an assignment he didn't want? Who had to eat a shit sandwich just to get a higher grade and an extra five hundred bucks a month?"

Dan shifted nervously in his seat, unable to argue the point. Agents had been making such sacrifices for decades. It was particularly wrenching on families, no matter how prepared they were for unexpected or undesirable moves.

"Sir, I've got twenty-three years in. Doesn't that count for something?"

"In my book, it counts for everything, which is why we're giving you an ASAIC slot on a detail. Maybe you don't appreciate some of the other suggestions I've heard. One of the ADs wants to send you to the Uniformed Division to supervise magnetometers for a year."

"But DC—"

"I can't leave you in Vegas. That ship has sailed. And Dunton doesn't want you anywhere in the field."

"The suspension—"

"Will stand. Two months minimum, son. Nothing I can do about that. The ADs were all in agreement, in a room where we have spilled blood over where to order sandwiches from. I can't ignore that."

Dan slumped in his seat. He had given his entire professional life to the Service and had already endured one public flogging that had stained his career for more than a decade.

"I can't do it, sir. I have to resign. I'm sorry, sir, I'm not trying to make this sound like an ultimatum, but—"

"Son, did you hear who I said is calling me about this? Who wants your head on a platter? The Pentagon. CIA. State. DIA. They all want you shit-canned. Hell, I'm surprised I haven't heard from the Secretary of Education yet."

"I get it, sir, but that doesn't—"

"Dan, do the damn time. You sit on the sidelines for a couple of months, work on your tan or golf game, then help run a quiet little detail until you put in your retirement papers. Finish your two years, get your pension, then go back to Vegas and cash in running private security for some casino exec. But you leave now, under this cloud, who's going to hire you?"

Dan nearly gasped. "A cloud? For blowing the whistle on two men who sexually assaulted a fourteen-year-old girl. And I'm under a cloud, because I wouldn't let it get swept under the rug?"

The Director's eye twitched. "Son, you take that sanctimonious tone with me one more time and I will throw you out of that window. No one is sweeping anything under the rug. And I'm trying to salvage your career." He paused, leaning back in his chair. "What the hell is going on here, Agent?"

Dan cocked his head. "Sir?"

"I knew your father. He was my first shift leader, and then I ran his counterfeiting squad at WFO. The man bled Secret Service blue. Would have shipped out to Madagascar if he was asked. Something is different here. Almost like you're wanting to resign, and you were just looking for a reason. Maybe something has been eating up your insides all these years, after getting cashiered out of PPD, and now finally you've lit the fuse. So, talk to me. Do you *want* out? Is that it?"

Dan quietly brooded. "Permission to speak freely again, sir?"

"Knock that shit off. Say your piece, son."

"I know I fucked up with Sheffield on the Hill, and this is coming off as my second strike. I broke the rules in speaking to that reporter, I get it. But I did it because we have people in this town who were perfectly willing to let those two apes walk after sexually assaulting a child. I couldn't just let that go, and it doesn't have a thing to do with my loyalty to this agency, my future career, or my father. For the record, sir, I'd do it again. In a heartbeat."

The Director shook his head in resignation. "You're just never going to accept any responsibility for your actions, are you?"

"I already—"

"I've heard enough," the Director interrupted, standing and moving behind his desk. "I've got thousands of men and women under my charge, and just about every single one of them understands their role in this organization, our chain of command, and how we comport ourselves in this job. Contrary to your belief, we do look out for our own. But it's your choice here, son. Just like it was fifteen years ago. Just like it was two days ago."

"Is there any way I can stay in my current—"

Seated at his desk, the Director stopped flipping through a stack of phone messages and squinted at Dan with vacant eyes.

"This meeting is over, Agent Cahill. Resign or move to Liza Walker's detail, I no longer care. But I want your decision by the end of the week."

CHAPTER 5

January 13, 2024
Las Vegas, Nevada

Tucked away in a colorless strip mall, *State Street Dogs* was an affront to every cardiologist west of the Mississippi. Caregivers in the Chicagoland area, birthplace to the small restaurant chain, would likely be more forgiving, understanding an occasional Polish with the works was necessary to sustain those subjected to oppressive Lake Michigan winters.

The outpost in Green Valley, operated by a gregarious family of transplants from Schaumburg, catered to the most gluttonous in a city priding itself on excess. Displaced Midwesterners flocked to the small establishment when it opened more than a decade ago, salivating over Chicago-style Vienna dogs slathered in relish and mustard, and Italian beef cooking in its own juices.

It had been nearly a month since Dan – no longer tethered to a volatile schedule and feeling little urgency to create something called a resume – began meeting Megan weekly for dinner. He balked when she first suggested a hot dog joint, but it didn't take him long to join the legions of *Dogs* aficionados. Nor was it helping his waistline, as he found himself envying his daughter's metabolism. Despite a two-year absence from competitive play, her frame remained pencil-thin and stood out among the scale-tipping patrons filling the booths and tables, even as she matched their consumption, calorie for calorie.

"I thought you were going to be really pissed," Megan breathed in relief, dunking her kielbasa in a cup of some concoction called beer cheese.

Dan waved dismissively with one hand, still chewing the last bite of his Italian beef sandwich. He took a swallow of Diet Coke and wiped his hands on a napkin.

"That's your mom's job," he said. "It was a bad semester. You'll bounce back."

Dan believed it. He hadn't been much of a presence during Megan's high school years, but knew she had been an academic wonder, graduating third in a class of more than four hundred. She embraced every challenge then, excelling most in math and the sciences, and bringing home enough scholastic awards to wallpaper her bedroom. The girl was full of self-initiative, requiring little nudging from either parent, each convinced their daughter's future was limitless.

Megan had her own ideas. Spurning academic scholarship offers from San Diego State and USC, she chose to stay close to home, enrolling at UNLV. Midway through her freshman year, her mother nearly melted down after Megan detoured away from biological sciences to pursue a liberal arts degree.

Dan was irked as well, having felt the pain of writing both alimony and tuition checks, now so their daughter could answer trivia questions someday about 18th century French poetry. Unlike Michelle, he muzzled any criticism, recalling his long-held resentment toward his own father for pushing him into a criminal justice program at Boston College for the sake of a family legacy.

By the middle of her sophomore year, Megan's grades had begun to seriously slip, leaving her mother wringing her hands and even Dan a bit troubled. He had little regard for grade point averages and test scores though, his own marks in school middling at best. In the end, Dan elected to give her space. He wasn't nearly as close to Megan as his ex-wife was – the absences were too many – but there was one quality of his daughter he knew all too well, beginning with her first tryout for travel soccer at the age of nine. She finished everything she started.

Megan put her sandwich down and shifted uncomfortably on her stool, twirling a French fry in a pool of ketchup. Her father took notice, knowing her propensity for devouring anything deep fried at the speed of light. He could only imagine the restaurant tabs for the on-again, off-again boyfriend that Megan seemed to regard as mostly a distraction.

She certainly had her suitors. Blessed with her mother's Mediterranean features, she had bronzed skin, thick eyelashes, and a warm, inviting face. Her sable ponytail had been a constant since childhood, accentuating the dark, oval eyes that had such fierceness to them. Eyes that were avoiding his at the moment.

Megan braced herself. "I'm thinking about taking a break from school."

"You want to go to Tahoe with your friends again?"

"No, Dad. A real break. Like a year."

So much for finishing everything.

"A year? You've only got a year and a half left. Why?"

Megan leaned forward, and despite his frequent absences over the years, the look of intense eagerness he saw was not unfamiliar. It was how intrepid climbers gazed upon a beckoning peak, steeling themselves for some great challenge. Dan liked to think her dauntless spirit came from his DNA. She certainly hadn't inherited it from her mother, a case study in risk-aversion.

"The election," Megan said, her eyes alight. "It's less than ten months away. So much is happening here, Dad, and I want to be a part of it. I don't want to be sitting in a classroom."

It was as if the warmth coursing through him had been doused with ice water. He hoped she might want to don her goalkeeping gloves again, maybe take a crack at a walk-on slot on the school team. Or embark on the sort of adventure every college-age kid fantasized about, like backpacking across Europe or exploring remote Indonesian beaches. But joining a political campaign? It was the one substitute Michelle would accept for the sin of their daughter shelving school for a year. She had dragged Megan to a Hillary rally before she was a teenager.

Politics. Dan recoiled at the thought, and he tried to mask his irritation as the word gnawed at him. Since his banishment from Washington all those years ago, he had stopped following the inter-party insanity, staying informed just enough to know if the country was on the verge of war.

Election years were an unwelcome exception. There was no refuge from the political ads engulfing Nevada every campaign cycle, and with the state a perennial, blood-soaked battleground, it had all become increasingly vicious. Skirmishing was already underway over the coming presidential contest, and the nuclear tactics once reserved for the closing weeks of an election were visible even now in January. The salvos from candidates, party committees, and Super PACs plastered every media outlet day and night. Each ad seemed to employ the same sinister voice-over, warning of chaos and carnage, and an opposing candidate who was a threat to all humanity.

For better or worse, Nevada mattered. A small state with few Electoral College votes, its early primaries and hotly competitive districts made the state a priority for both political parties. And with the margins so close in Congress, even a handful of House seats could sway power to either side. Once reliably Republican but tilting blue in recent election cycles, the national spotlight had become a fixture here every campaign season.

Megan's political affiliation was no mystery, the result of Michelle's endless diatribes about income equality, social justice, and the other usual suspects of liberal causes. She had led her high school Young Democrats club, and since arriving at UNLV, volunteered her Saturdays at the State Democratic Party. Just last month, she became a lead organizer of a campus-wide protest against a steep tuition increase proposed by the State Legislature. The combined faculty and student strike drew nationwide interest, and Dan admittedly felt a twinge of pride when he saw Megan quoted in the *Los Angeles Times*.

"Which campaign? Sheffield?"

"Fuck, no," Megan blurted. The reaction surprised Dan, considering he had never shared with her his past with the man. The now-Vice President was the current frontrunner for the Democratic presidential nomination.

"Sorry," she continued. "I mean, I'll vote for the guy, if he's the nominee. But he's got millions in the bank and all kinds of staff. I've been working at the State Party on the coordinated campaign. Mostly House races, plus all the local seats. The guy I'm interning for, Marc Powell, has me on the State Assembly, which is great because that's where Eleanor Jeschke sits."

"I thought they hired you to put names in a database?"

Her smile was rueful. "They did, but I just go to all their senior-level meetings instead."

"Jeschke," Dan repeated. "Isn't she the one who proposed the tuition increase?"

"Yep. You wouldn't believe some of these Republican clowns in Carson City."

"Oh yes I would. And that clown car has plenty of Democrats squeezed into it too." He paused. "And you want to do this full time now?"

Megan nodded enthusiastically.

"Are they paying you for this?"

"No."

"Have you asked? The worst—"

"—they can say is no," Megan finished her father's familiar refrain, which was also his father's familiar refrain. "I'll ask, but they only have a few paid staff. I figure I could move back in with mom and keep working weekends at the Cosmo."

Dan finished his soda and came to a quick decision, even as he dreaded the blistering phone call he would surely be fielding soon from his ex-wife. "I'll tell you what. The job at the Cosmopolitan will keep you in pocket change, whatever it is you do there."

"I'm the special assistant to the Spa Concierge."

"Right. Remind me, why does a spa need a concierge?"

"All the big resorts have them. They sort of manage the guest experience. Ours are a little high-end. Like, suppose you need an exfoliation treatment, do you go with the shea butter bamboo or the lemon blossom stone scrub?"

Cahill shook his head in wonder. "And they need an assistant for that?"

"Dad—"

"Anyway, keep the job. I'll keep paying your rent for that fleabag campus apartment you share so you don't have to move back in with your mom. If you finish school after the election."

"Are you serious?"

"Unless I come to my senses and change my mind, yes."

"And that's it? I expected you to blow a gasket over this."

"Leaving school?"

"Yeah. And being a Democrat."

She laughed, a sound he treasured these days. Megan had some tough years to be sure. She was in middle school when her parents' once-idyllic union crumbled to pieces. Then a gruesome compound fracture early in high school, leading to two surgeries, nine months of rehab, and a permanent move from midfielder to goalkeeper. A year after, her maternal grandmother, with whom she was so close, succumbed to the COVID-19 pandemic.

The divorce may have been the greatest jolt. He and Michelle had managed to keep their widening differences mostly concealed from Megan during her early years, but the move to Vegas deepened the rift. Dan hadn't expected the caseload of a smaller field office to be so substantial, and with a constant flow of protectees parachuting into the city, he saw far less of his home and family than they had all anticipated when he left the Presidential Detail. It was the last straw for Michelle.

Dan shrugged. "I can live with it. At least the school part. A Democrat, that's a tougher pill. Maybe we can find you a therapist or something."

"Mom says you were brainwashed when you were working for Bush."

Dan gave a tired sigh, having heard those exact words before from his ex-wife. "As I've told your mom a thousand times, I didn't work for Bush. I served on his detail. And just his last two years."

"Dad, you wouldn't ever vote for Pierce, would you? She's a total Nazi. Makes Trump look like a moderate."

Dan smiled, refusing to take the bait. He was forty-six now, not twenty-six. And despite his aversion to Rebecca Pierce, the favorite to win the GOP nomination, politics had become little more than a communicable disease to him.

He had despised both parties for years, though his equal opportunity revulsion had made little difference to Michelle. To her partisan ears, his neutrality was the moral equivalency of sleeping with the enemy.

The Nazi remark struck a nerve though, just as it had when Michelle used it against Bush long ago. Dan considered the forty-third president a class act, undeserving of the endless smears and mockery from the left. More infuriating was Michelle's constant implication that serving on the man's protective detail meant subscribing to his every policy and social whim. Dan had political convictions in his younger days, but like every man and woman in the Secret Service, partisan leanings would never exert even a speck of influence on his professional conduct.

And whatever leanings he once had were a distant memory. Since that fateful exchange in the Dirksen Senate Office Building, he felt nothing but contempt for Democrats and Republicans alike. He still voted though, a right he would let no one take from him. The lone exception had been the 2020 election. He voted for Trump in 2016 – the prospect of a second President Clinton unthinkable – then watched in horror the man's four-year wrecking ball of a presidency. If only Paul Sheffield's name had not been on the same ballot the next time around, even just as a running mate.

As Megan awaited a response about Rebecca Pierce, Dan knew it was time to downshift. Their dinners were a rebuilding project and subjecting his daughter to his excessively bleak worldview of American politics was an unnecessary risk.

"Back to your schooling, I'm fine with you taking a year off. I'm just concerned once you're out, you might not go back."

"Oh, I'll go back. I know I need a degree. I'll finish, just not now."

Dan was reluctant to push things any further. He picked up the check and reached for his wallet.

"How're you fixed for cash? You good?"

"Yep. They're giving me another shift at the spa. How about you, Dad? You doing okay?"

"I'm getting by. Huge demand at the Red Cross for plasma these days."

The grin he wore was forced. There had been a hefty price tag to resigning from government service just short of the 25-year mark. Had he stayed, his reward would have been a sizeable monthly pension check, one he would have started collecting at the age of forty-eight. It would have continued indefinitely, even if he kicked off a second career. By walking away early, he wouldn't see those checks until he hit retirement age, with the added insult of a significantly reduced payout. By walking away from the carrot, they were now clobbering him with the stick.

"So, what are you going to do now? Where are you going to work?" Megan grinned. "I can put in a good word for you at the spa. What do you know about Turkish bathing rituals?"

Dan signaled the waitress again, mostly to buy himself a few seconds. Speaking to his child about his unemployment was beyond humbling. The past month had lasted an eternity, the inertia testing his sanity as he struggled to fill his days. It was a challenge adjusting from a schedule where free time came in unexpected bursts to one where it had no end. Nicole wasn't the answer. He enjoyed her company, but conversation wasn't her strong suit, and after her own War of the Roses-style divorce a year ago, she had little interest in anything resembling a relationship.

He met Jarrett every Friday for lunch. The SAIC caught him up on agency scuttlebutt, after reminding Dan how the office was falling apart without him. The other day he put the question to Dan of whether he had any regrets. He batted it away, though the same question had been circling his own thoughts for some time.

Jarrett also harangued him about joining the private security game. It was tempting. Even without the retirement windfall, Dan was comfortable with his savings, but he desperately needed something useful to do. Something purposeful. Now that he was on the outside watching from the stands, it was easy to see what a fulfilling career he once had.

Private security and executive protection were certainly among the most lucrative options. The demand for former Secret Service agents in the consulting field proliferated every day. Once his resignation became known, Dan fielded a number of calls from old colleagues. Many were embedded with CEOs and corporate boards, retained to quell jittery shareholders and investors fretting about threats from hackers and hacktivists. A Secret Service badge could be gold in those boardrooms, where executives readily cut whatever checks were needed to have the most credentialed security operators in the world protecting their lives and livelihoods. Half a dozen serious offers were dangled in front of Dan, from Seattle to Tel Aviv. Generous pay supplemented with expense accounts, private secretaries, and the promise of a civilized lifestyle. And yet he couldn't pull the trigger, or even think about leaving Vegas right now. Partly because it would all pale against the memory of serving in the most exclusive law enforcement organization in the world. Partly because of the young woman seated on the pleather stool across from him.

"You almost ready to head out? You said you have to be on campus by seven, right?"

"Actually, Dad..." she answered, trying to suppress a smile.

"Uh, oh."

"I was wondering if you might want to come with me."

"You said it was a student meeting."

"It is, but we're supposed to bring a guest. My academic advisor is leading it, and I really want you to meet him."

"Meet the legendary Walter Becker?"

Megan's eyes widened in surprise. "You remember his name?"

How could he not? The man received more favorable press than a conquering war hero.

"Please, Dad? I really want you to hear him."

"I don't know, Megs, I have a very busy schedule."

She beamed, knowing his sarcasm better than anyone. "Is that a yes?"

"It's a yes."

"Awesome. But I have a favor to ask."

"Another one?"

Megan slurped her Coke again. "I'm serious."

"Okay, shoot."

"Whatever you hear tonight, I want you to have an open mind."

"With Becker? Why? What am I going to hear?"

"He's special, Dad. I've told you he's the best prof I've ever had, hands down. But he's so much more than that. There's something about him."

Dan wasn't sure where this was heading, but he gave Megan an assuring nod. "Open mind. I promise."

"Really listen to him, Dad, he's amazing. You might hear some talk of the election."

Dan's face must have fallen.

"He's not like that, Dad. He's like you, fed up with politicians from both parties. You said it yourself. All they do is lie, and all they care about is winning elections and making the other party look bad. And what pisses me off about that the most, is that I want to go into public service. To represent people, and fight for those who don't have money, or a voice. But public service is such a joke. If you say you want to run for office, it's like you automatically have this black mark next to your name. Like you're in it for the money or power."

Dan was moved by the depth of her sudden emotion. There was also something in her words, jogging a memory from long ago.

"An honorable profession," he murmured.

"Huh?"

"Robert Kennedy. We learned it in junior high, back in the Prehistoric Age. He once called politics an honorable profession."

"Yeah, exactly. That's what it should be, Dad. Honorable. Something decent, and something people admire. But it isn't. Not anymore."

"What does that have to do with Walter Becker?"

Megan smiled. "What do you think?"

"I don't know. He's going to make a big speech about how we need to make politics an honorable profession again. Something like that?"

Megan rose from her seat, pushing the check toward her father.

"Something like that," she said, a coy smile playing at her lips.

CHAPTER 6

If there was ever a political candidate to appeal to disaffected voters like Dan Cahill, it was Rebecca Pierce. Billing herself as a no-nonsense, take-no-prisoners champion of small government and traditional ideals, the retired Army general's populist rhetoric and demands for sweeping change to American governing institutions had seized the imagination of Republican voters, all in a matter of weeks. She wasn't the first candidate to bond with the aggrieved, and others had proven equally adept at channeling such widespread animus. But the intellect and polish she brought to the table were unmatched by any of her predecessors, widening her appeal across the electorate.

Long ago, Dan would have touted Pierce's prescriptions for change as just the tonic a fundamentally broken government so desperately needed. But his eye was far more practiced these days, seeing her posturing and meaningless slogans as window dressing for the naked ambition at her core.

It had been two weeks since Pierce saturated the airwaves on New Year's Day with a long-anticipated announcement of her candidacy, having been purposely cagey about her plans for months. Her long-simmering feud with the current Administration was well-known, and as a confederation of conservative activists and media figures began openly hyping her as presidential material, she had waited in the wings, allowing the public cries of support to reach a crescendo.

Her New Year's Day ad marked the beginning of the end of the GOP presidential primary. It caught fire the moment it aired, as her media team targeted self-described Republicans, conservatives, and independents across the digital sphere. The short clip sparked heated discussions at kitchen tables, water coolers, and across social media. Within days, there were few remaining of any ideology who hadn't seen or heard of it.

Soon after the New Year's Day release, half a dozen other Republican candidates laying groundwork in Iowa and New Hampshire ended their exploratory bids. They united behind the retired general, wisely hitching their political wagons to the heavily favored horse, and the Pierce campaign became an unstoppable force.

The ninety-second introduction to voters was brilliant in its execution and simplicity. Wearing a sleeveless blue dress baring her toned arms, the 55-year-old candidate was seated at a large oak desk at home, flanked by American flags. Behind her, framed photographs filled the wall, some with her husband and three children, others capturing the uniformed general posing with knots of officers and soldiers.

As Pierce spoke to the camera, her eyes were steady, and her manner poised and pleasant. The words, with just a trace of a Georgia drawl, were meticulously crafted to appeal to listeners whose political and social views had been previously collected and tagged by an underworld of data mining outfits. For those drawn in by her narration, every word rang true, as if hearing from a long, lost soulmate.

> *Hello America.*
>
> *My name is Rebecca Pierce, and I am running to be your next President and Commander in Chief. Happy New Year, in what promises to be one of the most pivotal and consequential years in our nation's history.*
>
> *I want to introduce myself to each of you, tell you something about my background and experience, and share with you my ideas for how we can bring strength, prosperity, and virtue back to our country.*
>
> *From the training grounds of West Point to the battlefields of Afghanistan, I've had the privilege of serving this nation for more than thirty years. I am proud and humbled to have been just the second woman in the United States Army selected to serve as a four-star general. That was no easy climb. And now, I'm here to announce my next battle – my candidacy for President of the United States.*
>
> *If elected, I promise to lead this great country with conviction and strength. And restore our core national values – faith, family, and integrity – to our framework of governance and to our everyday lives. As many of you know, when the President asked for my resignation, he said it was because there was never any give or take with me. He's right. Because I will*

never support this Administration's practice of taking from you and me, and giving to others, on every single domestic and foreign policy. It is a practice that is fiscally and morally bankrupt, and I will put an end to it.

But wait, there's more.

As a former infantry and air wing commander, my highest priority from the very first day I'm in office will be to provide a safer and stronger America. I never lost a single fight on the battlefield, and I will never lose one on the global stage. But the capitulation and appeasement policies of President Vance and Vice President Sheffield have weakened America abroad. Like all of you, I'm shocked and incensed by how our great country has been pushed around by the Russians, the Chinese, the Iranians, and so many others. They take advantage of the Administration's weakness because they know we lack the political courage to strike back.

Come November, those days will be over. So will the days of shortchanging our brave men and women in uniform. I will give them the weapons, the technology, and the pay raises they deserve. We will no longer cower from our enemies, and every elbow they throw will be met by a fist to the mouth.

But I need your support. If this sounds like the kind of leadership you want in the White House, I'm asking you to make a donation this month of just $20. That $20 is all I need to begin our epic fight to take on the Washington insiders, and break the stranglehold the corrupt and incompetent have on our great nation.

I've been a fighter all my life. And now I want to fight for you.

Join me.
Join the fight.

CHAPTER 7

The heart of Las Vegas Boulevard stretches from the Mandalay Bay Resort to just past the Wynn properties, a distance of some three miles. In between, an expanse of billion-dollar behemoths lights up the nighttime sky. The four properties at the intersection of Las Vegas Boulevard and Tropicana Avenue alone offer more than 14,000 hotel rooms. And yet not a single square inch of all that real estate, famously known as the Strip, actually lies within the Las Vegas city limits.

The origins of that odd distinction trace back to midway through the last century, in the midst of the first real growth spurt to hit the burgeoning desert community. A handful of casino managers pulled off the unthinkable then. They called a truce in their bare-knuckle rivalry, locking arms against a mayoral gambit concerning a patch of land just outside the city boundaries. The parcel was roughly a mile wide and a few miles long, and bracketed the portion of Las Vegas Boulevard then housing the most prosperous casinos. The mayor sought to annex it all, a brazen ploy to expand his tax base and raise much-needed revenue.

The casino operators pushed back, galled by the proposed land grab that would leave their establishments underwriting the city's growing debt. Led by the Flamingo, they flexed their political muscle, cajoling Clark County officials into declaring the land an unincorporated town outside the city limits. The tract was given the name Paradise, to be governed by the only municipal board in American history comprised entirely of casino men.

By the late 1950s, as the Rat Pack and their pals were packing showrooms from the Dunes to the Sands, another newcomer was beginning to plant roots in Paradise — the University of Nevada, Southern Regional Division. The college adopted the Rebel name and mascot to signify its independence from the main University of Nevada campus in Reno and graduated its first class of twenty-nine students in 1964. Known today as UNLV, the school had grown to an enrollment of nearly 30,000 undergraduate and graduate students, with 150 different academic programs and a faculty of more than a thousand instructors.

It was here on the UNLV campus in Paradise that Dan sat in misery, surrounded by several hundred turbo-charged, doe-eyed collegians, mutually dedicated to saving all humankind. In comfort, at least. Greenspun Hall, the glittering home to the College of Urban Affairs, was a far cry from the creaking facilities Dan recalled from his Boston College days. The five-story, environmentally friendly structure offered an abundance of technology-infused classroom and faculty office space. It housed media facilities for the campus radio and television stations and featured the largest auditorium on campus with 432 seats, every single one currently occupied.

Amid the ocean of youth was a scattering of older faces closer to Dan's demographic. He and Megan found two seats in the back while other late arrivals stood along the walls to the side and rear. The turnout was impressive, the clamor from the private conversations and small discussion groups pulsating across the auditorium.

Dan was vaguely familiar with the man at center stage. Walter Becker was a campus legend long before his recent news-making, when he led the UNLV community in open revolt against the State Legislature. A popular instructor, he had few detractors. Most were members of the State Board of Regents who had sided with Carson City's efforts to scale back the university's deficit spending. Since the Legislature backed away from the proposal last month, the man had been the toast of the town, his name spoken with near reverence in so many corners. Whatever the merits of their cause, Dan sure couldn't recall any of his college profs drawing such veneration from their pupils.

While Megan chatted away with fellow revolutionaries nearby, Dan studied Becker, holding court on the main floor. He was near the lectern with a small gathering, his hands chopping through the air like a symphony conductor. He was a dominant figure despite his diminutive size, and even from a distance, Dan could discern the glint in his eyes. He had a surprising spring in his step for a man with such a lithe build and well north of seventy. His bushy, tousled hair was battleship gray, and though his oval face was lined with wrinkles, his darkened skin suggested the man found time for the outdoors. His attire was vintage Fred Rogers; khaki slacks, with a cable-knit navy cardigan over a powder blue, button-down Oxford.

A quick search on his phone and Dan found a *New York Times* profile, published a month ago during the height of the tuition skirmish. He quickly scrolled through the column, learning Becker had lived most of his life in Las Vegas, his father a commercial delivery driver for one of the oldest businesses in the city. An undergrad during UNLV's early years, Becker was part of the school's first four-man cross country team, and later a regular in the Las Vegas Marathon before a degenerative hip condition limited him to neighborhood walks. He lived alone, having lost his wife of more than four decades to an aneurysm.

Dan's attention was drawn back to the floor, where Becker's students were retreating to their seats. The professor stepped to the lectern, the room quickly quieting.

"People, let's try and keep the noise down," Becker began, a microphone amplifying his voice. "The longer the Board of Regents hibernates, the lower your tuition bills will be."

That brought appreciative laughs and the audience clapped in approval.

"It's so nice to have so many of you here this evening. I see many old friends, and quite a few new ones. For those who are new to this gathering, it started somewhat smaller. It was near the end of the fall semester when Evan Worley and I met for lunch at the Student Union. As his faculty adviser, it was Mr. Worley who opened my eyes to just how adverse the State Assembly's proposed tuition increase would have been to not only his family, but our student population at large. I love this university and could not have asked for a more supportive administration these last many decades. Nonetheless, I felt compelled to speak out.

"The next day, Mr. Worley brought two of his classmates, Miss Cahill and Miss Jacobs, to the same corner table at the Union. Within a few weeks, there were more than a hundred of us, packed into Wright Hall, assembling protest signs and talking points for the first public hearing on the proposed increase. Someone, I can't recall who, scratched out three simple words on a sign that became a clarion call during that hearing. End This Now. Three little words that turned into a rallying cry, a front-page headline in the *Review-Journal,* and eventually carried our side to victory."

The students cheered triumphantly, and Dan joined in, on behalf of his checkbook.

"Tonight, we have filled an entire auditorium with those who also wish to end things now. But 'things' have changed, haven't they? When the Legislature yielded on the tuition fight, we said this wasn't the end, but the beginning. This had to be about making your voices heard, for years to come, far beyond the boundaries of UNLV, so this state, and this country, reflect your values, and your vision for the future. There is so much, so many values, we in this room share. Compassion. Equality. Justice. And above all else, a common conviction we as a people can do better.

"We also share an impatience for those in elected office who purport to represent us yet embrace the polarizing causes and bumper sticker catchphrases dividing the American people, eroding our values, and diminishing the institutions they serve. Some of you are disillusioned by a political system seemingly rigged in favor of the most prosperous and connected amongst us, particularly those already in Washington. I hope not. While some see the system as flawed, I see it as a work of art, designed more than two centuries ago by some of the most perceptive and inventive minds this world has ever known. They managed to devise a structure and framework of governance both ingenious and revolutionary. And the pinnacle of that brilliance was its allowance for change. Not changing the Constitution, as some on the campaign trail are foolishly prattling on about. But change in our representatives and leaders, and change in our policies, provided there is a will and movement to do so."

Dan gave Megan a quick gander, his daughter pitched forward in her seat, enraptured by Becker's words. Dan couldn't deny the man's eloquence. And all of it independent of notes or prepared text, the words simply pouring from the man's head and heart. He was good.

"Once, it took armed conflict to bring about change. But we have graduated from rebellion and civil war to the power of words and ideas to right our political wrongs and reset our moral compass. So, starting tonight, let us see if we can follow a similar path. Let us see what we, as a small group of common citizens, can do to build our own will, and our own movement, and bring desperately needed change to our political system. Just as our Founders envisioned so long ago."

A wave of cheers cascaded across the large room as a number of students and their invitees, Megan included, leapt to their feet in approval. Becker waved the ovation down and leaned again into the microphone.

"Mr. Worley, Miss Cahill, Mr. Newsome, and Miss Jacobs, will you join me down here? I think our audience has heard enough from the senior citizen bloc."

Dan pivoted his knees so Megan could squeeze past. Three others rose from the masses and descended to the main level, joining the professor on the small stage.

"I jokingly refer to this quartet as the Four Horsemen of the Apocalypse. Hopefully there are others in the room old enough to understand that reference. We're going to break into smaller groups now, each led by one of these fine young people, so we can discuss—"

Megan stepped forward, clearing her throat, intentionally loud, catching Becker's attention. One of the others, a bookish-looking young man with a mop of unruly hair, joined her at the podium. Becker stepped back, a question mark on his face.

The young man spoke first. "Sorry about the interruption, Professor, but we have a small presentation to make." His head swiveled to the audience. "Thanks everyone for coming tonight, especially our guests. It's like Parents Weekend here. I'm Evan Worley."

"And I'm Megan Cahill. We wanted to take a moment to recognize Professor Becker for everything he did for us students before the holidays."

"When we had our first organizing meeting," Evan continued, "Professor Becker said a movement would have to have a leader, just like a winning football team has to have a quarterback. I remember he asked each one of us, who was going to be the one who wanted the ball? With that in mind, Professor, we wanted to give you a small gift."

Evan stepped back as Megan threw her hands in the air. From somewhere in the audience, a football materialized, a wobbly spiral landing softly in Megan's goalkeeper hands. She handed the football to Becker, who turned it over, reading the words neatly hand-painted onto the leather.

"To Professor Becker," he read aloud, an embarrassed smile on his face. "Our star quarterback. Signed, Team Walter."

There was another round of sustained applause and Dan joined in again as Becker held the ball aloft. The man eyes were glistening as he responded to his admirers.

"Thank you, everyone, this means a great deal to me. More than you know. But now we must return—"

Megan cleared her throat again.

"Does anyone have some water for Miss Cahill?" asked Becker with mock annoyance, the crowd laughing along.

"One more minute, Professor. Evan?"

"As you know, Professor, we have a pretty big election coming up in November. The Nevada Primary, where the two political parties select their presidential nominees for the fall ballot, is less than six weeks away."

"Which is why I no longer turn on the television."

"The Vice President, of course, is currently the heavy favorite for the Democratic nomination, with no real opposition."

"So it seems. And he doesn't seem to be faring well."

Evan shared a smile with Megan before he continued.

"No, he doesn't. And it's the opinion of those gathered in this room there should be another name of that ballot, one standing for equality, justice, and progressive values. That name is Walter Becker."

The audience erupted again, and this time Dan felt his seat shaking as many of the students stomped their feet on the floor. The professor, dazed by the turn of events, tried to reassert control of the room but to no avail. It was Megan who finally came to his rescue, quieting the room again so Becker could speak.

The professor's eyes fell to the floor.

"A kind, albeit misguided expression," he said softly, his eyes crossing the room, connecting with his young supporters. "And I thank each and every one of you for it. It's apparent all of you have taken advantage of the recreational narcotics currently permitted in our state."

Becker awaited the expected retort from Evan or Megan, but they remained mute, the smiles broadening on their faces.

"Why are you looking at me like that?"

Megan gave an exaggerated shrug. "Like what?"

"Like how Tom used to look at Jerry as he was holding a fork and knife."

Evan's voice was buoyant. "No idea who that is, but you suggested we gather here tonight to build a consensus. To turn our frustration and our will, you said, into a movement for change."

"I did."

"We agree," Megan said.

"Kids, I appreciate—"

"We want to build that movement, Professor," Megan finished, "and we want to make a statement here in Nevada. With you."

"With me? Running for President? We want to be taken seriously, no? Kids, look, such an exercise would only be a distraction from the issues we're seeking to draw attention to. Again, I appreciate the sentiment, but this is supposed to be about you. Your future. And we're going to discuss tonight what you can do to change things. You can organize, you can demonstrate, you can—"

"We're going to organize and demonstrate. For you."

Becker grimaced and Dan detected the first sign of weariness with Megan's cheerful persistence.

Welcome to my life.

"Kids, I might have once been more than intrigued by the opportunity, but I'm just too old for the game now. And not exactly qualified to be on a presidential ballot. I haven't any experience in government, or even—"

"Isn't that the sort of candidate you've said we need more of?"

Becker chuckled. "Turning my own words against me, Mr. Worley? Look, everyone, I'm so flattered by this. More than flattered, I am truly honored. But practically speaking, it's impossible. There are procedures to follow. The primary is next month, and you just can't add a name to the ballot."

"Actually, you sorta can," Evan smirked. "You just need to file the necessary paperwork with the State Party by January 15 and pay a $2,500 fee."

Becker seemed to breathe easier, having found his escape hatch. "Which leaves you two days to collect $2,500. I cannot allow you—"

Megan removed a folded envelope from her pocket and handed it to Becker.

"What's this?" Becker asked, opening it.

"$426."

Evan handed a similar envelope to Becker. "$210."

The two other students standing near the front produced their own envelopes. The young woman handed them to Becker.

"$88 from me, $176 from Marques."

Another student rose from the third row and made his way to the front, handing his envelope to the dismayed instructor.

"$28."

From the back of the auditorium, Dan watched the procession of students as they stood, one by one, and delivered envelopes to Becker. The professor stood still, his feet cemented to the linoleum floor as a mix of emotions crossed his face. As the last student returned to their seat, Evan looked up from a small notebook he had been tabulating numbers in.

"That's more than $2,700. The State Party office opens at eight tomorrow."

"I – I don't know what to say. I can't—"

"Hell yes, you can," Megan cut in. "Do you know how many students we had to hit up to raise that kind of cash? We had to promise everyone you would outlaw blue book exams."

The audience laughed, but Dan felt the anticipation seizing the room. Almost every attendee was leaning forward in their seats.

Becker took a deep breath, scanning hundreds of hopeful faces as he gathered his thoughts. The words came out slowly, his audience straining to hear the professor's voice, brittle now with feeling.

"There are no words to adequately convey my gratitude for this incredible gesture. You have my profound appreciation and affection. Every one of you. You deserve a response, a well-considered one, and one I'm just not prepared to offer at the moment. But I know the clock is ticking, so I will propose a bargain. Let's continue with our plans for this evening, where we hoped to discuss those ideas and principles we wish to coalesce our movement around. As we're discussing these, I will give your request due consideration and share with you my thoughts before we break for the evening. Deal?"

"Deal," Megan and Evan responded in unison, and there were smiles all around.

"And let's keep that $2,700 quiet," Becker said heavily. "I just spent a month telling the world you kids were broke."

CHAPTER 8

With the room still abuzz over the prospect of a presidential campaign, Becker reclaimed the microphone, separating the attendees into smaller groups. Each was tasked with identifying economic and social inequalities, and then exploring potential legislative and legal remedies that could underpin their movement.

For Dan, it was like stepping into a Young Communists meeting from the 1930s. He politely declined the overture from his seat neighbors to participate, just as he would've politely declined an invitation to be waterboarded. He surveyed the room instead, the decibel level ramping up quickly, and reflected on what he witnessed earlier. Setting aside the farce of putting their professor on a presidential ballot, even Dan, with his hard-boiled cynicism, was moved by the students' affection. The man was clearly more than just a classroom figure.

Dan found Becker across the room, standing near the fringe of one of the more robust discussion groups, quietly observing. Dan thought it probably a façade, the man more likely mentally conjuring some sort of exit strategy, allowing him to graciously spurn his hero worshippers without bruising any feelings.

He felt sympathy for Becker. The students, his daughter included, shouldn't have put the old man in such an awkward position. Had they not contemplated the ridicule he would be subjected to? Or the folly of taking on a sitting vice president? Paul Sheffield may have flatlined in national polls, but he still had ample power and prestige, plus the endorsement of every party loyalist in the state. Even if the students made a serious effort to cobble together a legitimate campaign, the political atmosphere was utterly vicious. Why throw a 76-year-old to the wolves, including a sure trouncing at the polls?

While beyond futile, such a potential contest did hold one appeal for Dan. The sharp-witted professor would likely have a field day if he ever had the opportunity to meet Sheffield on the debate stage. Not that the Vice President wasn't a formidable campaigner. A seasoned pro on the stump, he had prevailed handily in four Senate elections in Virginia. He was also a tenacious fundraiser, with a record-topping war chest that long ago warded off others from contesting the nomination. Yet for all his qualifications and attributes, warning bells were sounding day and night within the Democratic Party, and it was no secret why.

It seemed like ages had passed since Dan had faced off with Sheffield during the airspace security hearing. Still a young lawmaker then, Sheffield was considered a rising star, with a resume that couldn't have been scripted better by Hollywood. After earning a degree from William & Mary, he became an osteopathic doctor in the Army Reserves, with the government covering his medical education bills. He completed a tour in the first Gulf War, and when his military obligation ended, electoral politics awaited, with Virginia Democrats gleefully recruiting him into their ranks. He became a United States Senator on his very first try for public office, skating to an easy victory against an aging incumbent in failing health.

Re-elected three times, Sheffield had become a master at bridging the partisan divide within the Commonwealth, and his popularity spanned from the Piedmont to the Northern Virginia suburbs. He consistently drew support from independents and even Republicans, and could have held his seat for life if he hadn't been aiming higher. But he was, of course, and when then-Michigan Governor Chet Vance asked him to join the Democratic ticket four years ago, his ascent continued.

Sheffield's presidential campaign, however, had been clouded with uncertainty from the day it began. It was largely an era of peace and prosperity, yet the approval numbers for the Vance Administration languished. Able pollsters understood why. While the public appreciated a steady hand on the tiller, especially after the ineptitude of the previous regime, they found the Administration wholly uninspiring. Most attributed that to the 82-year-old Vance. Following his not-so-surprising announcement in the fall to step down after a single term, Sheffield's camp all but measured the Oval Office for curtains.

The Vice President formed a juggernaut of a campaign, stocked with Democratic party veterans and mountains of cash from a well-tapped donor base. It stalled almost immediately. Support among the party faithful was tepid at best, and by the end of the year, his poll numbers had plateaued. The data analysts drilled down, finding much of the cautious issue-straddling that fueled his political rise at home in Virginia was an albatross nationwide. The progressive wing of the party resented Sheffield for falling in with Senate Republicans on taxes and immigration. Party moderates were derisive as well, branding Sheffield's recent embrace of clean energy and gun control policies as a ploy to curry favor with politically essential Democratic constituencies during the primary process.

Most disquieting for party operatives in Washington was a perception of Sheffield locked into the minds of most voters. While the man had carefully manufactured an image of someone who shunned the partisan fray, much of the country instead saw a crafty politician lacking passion and conviction. A placater of both allies and adversaries who considered incremental progress a triumph, and bold leaps perilous risks.

Compounding the angst of national Democrats, the likely Republican candidate continued to ride the crest of a populist wave. A newcomer to politics, Rebecca Pierce was one of the two highest-ranking women in the history of the Army. She had traded her uniform for business suits and blue jeans, barnstorming through Iowa and New Hampshire with unabashed zeal. Her digital media footprint was fresh and imaginative, and she was breathing new life into whistle-stop campaigning. She drove from town to town, her caravan passing crowds of cheering supporters waving handmade signs with battle cries such as "Pierce Another Glass Ceiling" and "Fights Like a Girl." She was embraced by women voters of all political stripes, pulling back suburbanites who had drifted left in recent years, and convincingly promising an end to all things Washington stood for.

Her appeal was little surprise. Pierce was a graduate of West Point and the Army War College, and a decorated helicopter pilot in between. She held command positions in the Iraq campaign and at U.S. Central Command before taking the helm of U.S. Army Forces Command. After earning her fourth star and appointment as Army Chief of Staff, she was widely expected to succeed the retiring Chairman of the Joint Chiefs. But President Vance passed her over, citing an inflammatory address to her alma mater, where she slammed the fecklessness of international institutions and spoke glowingly about a radical congressional proposal to remove civilian leadership from the Department of Defense. The right upbraided Vance for what they framed as a political move against a highly decorated soldier, and chided him for the missed opportunity to make history at the Pentagon.

Pierce, emboldened by the national attention, escalated her feud with the Commander in Chief on the public airwaves, ridiculing Vance's once lackluster support for the post-9/11 wars abroad. Enraged by the break in protocol, the White

House demanded Pierce's resignation. She complied, but not before eviscerating more of Vance's policies on her way out the door. His vice president wasn't spared.

Establishing herself as a darling of conservative media, her support snowballed. A flush outfit calling itself the First Patriot Committee financed a national ad campaign promoting Pierce as the future of American leadership. She called for militarizing the homeland security mission to safeguard the porous southern border, inner city streets, and even schools and churches. All while dismissing her critics, and branding them with words like treachery, betrayal, and corruption.

Dan socially distanced himself from politics, and generally viewed Washington as a cesspool, but even he was troubled by the undertones of her messaging. With choices like Sheffield and Pierce, it was little wonder a group of college kids were so galvanized and desperately searching for an alternative.

"Dad!"

The call came from the main floor, where Megan was now standing with Becker by the podium, motioning for her father to join them. He stood reluctantly, easing his way down the long aisle and feeling the academic's appraising eyes with each step. The professor greeted him warmly, grasping Dan's hand with both of his as Megan made the introductions. She then excused herself to referee a spat in the back corner of the auditorium, leaving Dan shifting his feet while silently cursing his daughter.

The older man couldn't hide his amusement.

"Your daughter is an insightful thinker with sound judgment. But I suspect you're questioning that at the moment and considering multiple forms of corporal punishment."

Dan nodded. "Not just corporal, Professor."

Becker laughed. "Please call me Walter. Come walk with me, Mr. Cahill. I need to stretch my legs, and you have the look of a man who'd prefer not to explore voter registration strategies for convicted felons."

Dan followed him to a nearby exit, where they passed through a set of glass doors and into an outer corridor. Dan welcomed the reprieve, the cacophony of voices fading the further down the darkened hall the two men strolled. They continued past a series of deserted classrooms until all that could be heard were their own soft footsteps.

"You must be very proud of Megan, though I do wish she'd reconsider leaving her studies."

"If you're trying to win my vote for president, that angle will definitely work."

"No subterfuge here, Mr. Cahill. I'm quite a fan of your daughter. I've been teaching political science for four decades, and I've never met a young person so committed to the notion of engaging in public life."

"You've inspired her."

"Possibly, but I suspect politics may be in her blood."

Dan laughed. "Blame her mother. She was talking to Megan about John Kerry and other hopeless causes while she was still in the womb."

"What about you?"

"What about me?"

"Any hopeless causes you might have some soft spot for?"

"I'm a Patriots fan in the post-Brady era, if that counts."

"You're talking to a UNLV basketball fan, so yes, that counts." He paused. "That sounded like a note of disdain for John Kerry. Does that make you a Republican?"

"We must have a bad connection. You're breaking up."

Walter's smile widened. "Not comfortable talking politics?"

"Not used to it, I guess. Tried to avoid it for years, and at work, well —"

"They don't exactly encourage it in the Secret Service?"

Dan flinched, unaccustomed to strangers knowing his past vocation. He gave a long sigh, no longer caring, the divorce final now.

"It's drilled into you from the first day to keep a lid on personal views. The Service doesn't want public perceptions that it's political in any way. The agency protects the office, regardless of who occupies it."

"I thought that was obvious."

"That's because you're a logical thinker. Something of an endangered species in Washington these days."

"Even if you can't speak of personal views, surely that doesn't mean you can't hold them. Do you vote, Mr. Cahill?"

"It's Dan. Yes, mostly."

"Mostly?"

"I skipped the last one."

"Tsk, tsk. I'll spare you the lecture I give my non-voting undergrads. Though it is an inspiring speech if I may say so."

"I'll bet. What about your voting undergrads back there? What are you going to tell them?"

"This nomination business? I'm open to any advice. It would be quite the undertaking, no?"

Dan did a double take. "You're considering it?"

"I think I owe them that. Consideration, at least. Don't you?"

"Sure, I guess."

"Speak, Mr. Cahill. I could use an opinion from someone old enough to remember the twentieth century."

"I'm also someone who'd rather join a leper colony than talk politics." He paused, giving the question some thought. "If you do go through with it, you may want to manage some expectations. Megan, for starters. She probably thinks you can win."

"You don't think she's that naive, do you?"

"I think we all were at her age. She's also wired differently than the rest of us. I'll tell you a soccer story. When she got to high school, she made the varsity team as a freshman midfielder. They won two games that year, but she vowed to the other two freshmen they'd be State champs by their senior year."

"Were they?"

"Their *junior* year. With her as captain, playing a new position after breaking her leg in three places."

"Well then, with her in my corner, how can I lose?"

The professor pointed to a bench, and the two sat side by side. Dan noticed the man was breathing a bit heavily.

"Megan says you walk five miles every day."

"Used to," he said, massaging a sore spot on his lower back. "I'm down to two now, just to campus and back. Old age, I guess. And by these evening hours, I'm pretty spent. Don't get old, my friend."

They sat in silence for several moments.

"Can I share a small secret with you, Mr. Cahill?"

"It's still Dan. You're a Marxist?"

Becker chuckled. "Worse. An optimist. And what I'm about to tell you, you may think I'm in need of psychiatric care."

He began absently rubbing his hands together, something Dan had seen his own father do time and time again. Arthritis.

"You're going to say yes?"

Walter nodded. "I told the kids I would share with them my decision in the morning. But once those young people started pressing envelopes into my hands, there was really no other answer I could give."

"So, the bribery worked," Dan grinned. "You'll fit right in when you get to Washington."

Walter smiled back. He stood, resuming his walk as he clasped his hands behind his back. Dan fell in next to him.

"Do you know how I came to Las Vegas, Mr. Cahill?

He searched his memory. "I think I read your parents were immigrants. You came with them?

"Nope. I was born in Chicago, on the very day Harry Truman defeated Tom Dewey."

"I thought it was the other way around."

Walter clapped him on the back. "Very good, Mr. Cahill. My parents were political refugees. My father, like his father and grandfather before him, served in the German Army, even though he considered the Nazis utterly despicable. He survived the war, then attended Leipzig University, where he met my mother. They saw what was happening with the Soviets and fled East Germany for the United States. Couldn't speak a word of English between them. They came through New York, then on to Chicago where my mother had a cousin. My father was one of those bootstrap immigrants Rebecca Pierce doesn't talk about much. He thought Chicago was no place to raise a family, so he brought us out West in 1954. Found work driving a truck and stuck with it for the rest of his life. And after everything he experienced, do you know who he considered the saintliest figure in America? President Eisenhower. The man who vanquished his birth country. My father was convinced Ike was not only an intelligent, exceptional leader, but also at his core, a kindly, good-hearted man."

The professor stopped, turning to Dan. "I know I'm not exactly presidential material. But I also know Rebecca Pierce is no Dwight Eisenhower. And no one is standing up to her."

Dan shuffled his feet again.

"Your daughter freely shares every thought that crosses her mind. And yet with you it's like conversing with a mime."

"You realize you'll be laughed at?"

Walter nodded. "Thirty minutes ago, I would have considered the thought laughable myself. But I'm a 76-year-old widower with no children. That's nothing to pity. I've had a good run, and I'm grateful for every minute I've spent on this Earth. My clock, however, is winding down, and given the chance, I do have some things I'd like to say."

They resumed their walk, the auditorium drawing nearer. Dan heard a sigh from the professor.

"I care, Mr. Cahill. Maybe too much, but I do care."

"I can see that. I guess I cared once, too."

Walter snickered.

"You doubt that?" Dan was surprised by the indignation in his own voice.

The professor touched his arm. "No, Mr. Cahill. I doubt you ever stopped."

They reached the main foyer again, hundreds of muffled voices reverberating through the walls.

"I understand from your daughter you might have some extra time on your hands now, I sure could use a companion in all this."

It was Dan's turn to laugh. "Running mate? Campaign manager? Oh, I'm in."

Walter opened one of the doors, peered in, then eyed Dan again. "Fortunately for you, it's probably somewhat early to be settling on a running mate. And I believe the position of campaign manager, or managers, will soon be filled by some of those young people. But I would enjoy having someone closer to my age at our side."

"I don't want to get involved," Dan said before gesturing toward the clusters of students inside. "And I don't think an old grouch like me would fit with this group."

"You don't have to get involved, but your forthrightness and insight would be most welcome. Just come listen. What do you say? I would enjoy your company. As would Megan."

The last three words sealed things. Just as Walter knew they would.

"I'm free tomorrow," he conceded.

"Is that a yes?"

"For tomorrow."

CHAPTER 9

January 15
Thirty-Eight Days to Primary Day

The windows rattled again in their frames, buffeted by the fierce gusts ripping across the treeless subdivision. If this had been Oklahoma or Kansas, accustomed to yearly onslaughts of deadly tornadoes, a stampede to the nearest storm cellars and emergency shelters would have already been underway. But this was Las Vegas, where valley windstorms were common, and a tradeoff locals were more than willing to abide. Less a threat to public safety, and mostly a nuisance to anyone with a tee time, contact lenses, or having to walk a dog with an impatient bladder.

Adjusting to the desert climate hadn't been as challenging as Dan first anticipated. Summers were oppressive, as he learned that initial August when his rubber-soled running shoes clung to the sun-softened blacktop on the streets and sidewalks. But aside from replacing a wardrobe of woolen business suits with more breathable fibers, Dan gradually became fond of the arid conditions. There was much he would not miss about Washington, but its soul-withering humidity topped the list.

Winters were more of a surprise. The Spanish translation of "Nevada" was snow-capped, a reference to the Sierra mountain range 400 miles to the north. In Southern Nevada, Januarys were generally mild but occasionally frigid, with snow sometimes visible atop the highest peaks in the Spring Mountains, just thirty minutes outside of Las Vegas. A brisk cold front had swept into the valley earlier that afternoon, and with the mercury hovering in the forties, jackets were piled on a bench near the front door.

Nestled in the Royal Crest neighborhood barely a mile from campus, the Becker home was a modest, split-level structure. Purchased by Walter and Hannah decades ago, it resembled most Vegas dwellings, with a clay tile roof, vaulted ceilings, and ceramic flooring. All prescribed features for the sun-soaked environment.

The scent of hot cocoa hung in the air, and a gas fireplace radiated enough warmth in the living room to keep the small group more than cozy. The house was impeccably furnished, reflecting Hannah Becker's affinity for all things Pottery Barn.

Familiar faces from the previous evening were seated around a large coffee table, each seemingly convinced the louder they spoke, the more likely they would be heard. Tuning out the crosstalk, Dan found himself lamenting his momentary lapse in sanity when he accepted Becker's invitation. He had at least arrived with a credible excuse for departing early, an option he summarily abandoned the moment he was greeted by an elated Megan. Most parents were as welcome in a collegian's life as a bout of mono, and if that wasn't the case here, he wasn't going to squander the opportunity.

He took a long pull from his Heineken, his second now, listening to Megan tangle with Evan, her accomplice from the previous evening. Walter was slouched in an easy chair as he too monitored the pair quarreling over the scope of the governor's latest infrastructure investments. Dan ignored the competing voices in the room, watching his daughter with rapt attention. Her stubborn resolve was familiar, but it was the complexity and coherence of her arguments absorbing him.

As she skillfully articulated her rebuttal points, Dan knew he was glimpsing a side of her he hadn't seen before. The young woman before him was nearly a stranger, with a growth and maturity that surely began long ago in her adolescence. Years he missed, simply too consumed by work responsibilities that left little room for home and family. At least, that's what he once convinced himself of. Now, he was left haunted by the errant choices that had marked his life, including the one that now had him lounging on the professor's vintage upholstered sofa instead of coordinating a protective detail for the Prime Minister of Whateverstan.

Megan finished with Evan and wheeled over a large white board, apparently a familiar feature of Walter's classroom. *Issues* had already been scrawled across the top, with *Us* and *Them* underneath. She hushed the other conversations, waving a dry erase marker.

"Okay, we've agreed we have to define our platform for the campaign. So, let's focus on what we want up here."

Walter sat up straighter.

"May I make a suggestion? From what I'm hearing, we have no shortage of ideas and issues to frame the campaign around. I'm certain we could pull together a long and very worthy list. Our challenge, however, is our shortage of time. We cannot engage the electorate on so many issues, nor do we want our potential supporters to have any ambiguity about what we stand for. Let me suggest we narrow this platform to just a few core, impactful ideas, the ones we believe are central to the campaign. This will focus our message and allow us to articulate positions that potential supporters can relate to."

"That makes sense," Evan said, perched on one arm of the sofa. "Maybe we emphasize issues setting you apart from Sheffield, so we're giving voters a clear choice."

A senior, Evan was the elder statesman among the students. Dan learned he came from a family of limestone miners and was the first Worley to attend college. Politics had been his singular focus since the age of fourteen, when corporate negligence led to an elevator accident that killed six miners, including his uncle and cousin, in their small Churchill County community. Beneath the rumpled clothing and windswept hair, Dan saw a pleasant-looking boy, one who seemed to both charm and rankle his daughter.

"I have an idea," volunteered another student.

Dan remembered her as Krista SomethingorOther, one of the four who had stood behind Walter the previous evening. He had to resist staring at the girl, reminding himself she was his daughter's age. But she was a knockout, fair-skinned with honey blond hair and indigo eyes.

"What about a middle-class tax cut? We know Sheffield votes like a closet Republican, especially on tax cuts for the wealthy. So, we come out with something just for the middle class, and contrast that with his voting record. It would have mass appeal with working people and show who Sheffield really stands with."

Walter turned to Evan. "Mr. Worley?"

Evan had been shaking his head while jotting down notes in a tattered, spiral-bound notebook.

"Too easy for Sheffield. He'll just say he agrees working people should get a tax cut. What about foreign policy instead? He keeps trying to one-up Pierce by trashing the UN and calling for troop pullouts everywhere, but he's undercutting his own President. We could double down on what Vance started, talk about the U.S. leading the world again."

The professor offered no reaction as he turned to his other, newly minted co-manager.

"Miss Cahill?"

Megan capped her marker and sat down next to Walter.

"I know this is going to sound lame, but maybe we should just take politics out of the conversation, and just talk about the most important issues facing this country."

"I thought I just did."

"No, Evan, you suggested we pick an issue Sheffield and Pierce agree on, just so we can sound different."

"It's not so lame," Walter soothed, "and I'm with you wholeheartedly. So, start us off. Suppose we could eliminate all political considerations. What issues would you have up there?"

Megan tapped the marker against her chin. "Jobs? Wages? That's what everyone cares about, Democrat or Republican. Maybe we can come up with some job creation package."

"Well, that sounds like an economic stimulus, which is somewhat of an old saw." He faced the group again. "Expand your reach, everyone. And let's get outside the box. Maybe the issue most Americans care about, is an issue no politician is talking about."

"Climate change?" offered Evan.

Walter smiled. "We're in a Democratic primary, Mr. Worley. Climate change doesn't get more *inside* the box." He hesitated. "Sorry, I'm asking you to read my mind, and that's not fair." He paused a few moments, gathering his thoughts. "What about cancer?"

"On a happier note," Krista deadpanned.

They all laughed, including Dan. But Walter remained serious.

"I want this country to cure cancer."

Dan fought to keep his face composed. Sure, why not? Wave the magic wand, save millions of lives. He wasn't expecting much tonight, but hearing Becker repeat such a tired mantra was still a disappointment. And it instantly reminded Dan why he reviled the political arena, where candidates shamelessly pandered for every vote and made outlandish promises they never intended to keep. Even Becker's faithful student leaders appeared doubtful.

Evan spoke first. "That's outside the box? Who doesn't want to cure cancer?"

"Wasn't that an Obama thing?" added Megan.

Walter leaned forward. "Yes and no, Miss Cahill. He did propose an initiative to eradicate the disease. But from what I've read, their progress was modest at best. I want something far different, and far more enterprising. But I don't want just a clever slogan, or anything merely aspirational. It should be grand and far-reaching, but also implementable."

The students were quiet, and Dan could see their doubts fading, the young people latching onto the concept now, as if the old coot had solved the riddle of the universe.

He didn't notice the old coot eyeing him intently.

"Mr. Cahill, you look like a man with something to say."

"Nope." He pointed at the students with his bottle. "This is their show. I'm here for the free beer."

"Come now, Mr. Cahill. The perspective of someone who eschews politics would be welcome. Give us the everyman viewpoint."

"This everyman tends to rain on parades."

"My mom calls him Chief Dark Cloud," confirmed Megan.

More silence, and Walter's smile faded. "Please, Mr. Cahill. I want to hear your thoughts on this."

Dan took a deep breath. "Look, I'm not faulting you for swinging for the fences, especially when Sheffield has decided on a bunting strategy. And I'm sympathetic. I lost my father to cancer, and the issue will certainly resonate with the public. But whatever the differences, Sheffield will say you're copying Obama's idea, and you'll come off sounding starry-eyed to most voters. Like Bernie Sanders with free college. You can't have it both ways. You can't say you want to be taken seriously, then offer some far-fetched pipedream as your central platform."

Dan stopped himself, realizing he may have overstepped. Evan and Krista looked shellshocked, unused to hearing their living legend second-guessed. Megan eyed him intently, more difficult to read.

"Sorry, I'm not trying to sound—"

Walter held up a hand. "No apologies necessary, Mr. Cahill. I asked for it, and you're raising some very germane points. I'll strike you a deal. Give me some time to refine the idea, then let you take another pass, see if you're still convinced it's a far-fetched pipedream."

Dan laughed, sitting back on the sofa. "Oh, no. I'm about ten seconds away from getting tarred and feathered by these kids, so that little mic drop is all you're getting out of me."

"That sounds like a challenge," Walter said with a smile, as Dan pantomimed locking his mouth with a key and throwing it away.

Megan tapped the white board with the marker. "Okay, so cancer, anything else?"

Krista raised a hand. "What about calling Sheffield out on choice. He voted to de-fund Planned Parenthood twice, and also voted for the Hyde Amendment."

The befuddled Evan mouthed the words across the table. *The Hyde Amendment?*

Megan answered him. "Prohibits federal funding for abortion services. Krista, I'm not excusing the guy, but most Senate Democrats from the South voted for the Hyde Amendment."

"Virginia isn't the South. Not anymore. The state voted for Obama, Hillary, even Vance."

"But Sheffield is pro-choice," Evan argued. "He supports *Roe v. Wade* and—"

"He voted for the Hyde Amendment and to ban late-term abortions. We need to win women, and if we don't stand up to people in our own party who—"

"I'm not running on abortion."

The words stopped Krista in mid-sentence. They were delivered gently, but the finality in the professor's tenor was unmistakable.

"I didn't mean you should, Professor, I just meant Sheffield has voted with the pro-lifers on—"

"I know you feel strongly about this issue. I know others feel similarly. Including me. I was marching on choice issues with Hannah when Jimmy Carter was in office, for heaven's sake. But I don't see how it can be characterized as one of the more significant issues this country is facing today. It's highly divisive, and I don't think we want one of the pillars of this campaign to rest on the nuances of a medical procedure."

"If we don't win women—"

"I want to win everyone, Miss Jacobs. And I want us to identify problems shared by all Americans, not just those who vote with us. We have limited time to talk about truly existential issues, and we can't fritter away any of it on something as obscure as the Hyde Amendment."

Krista was stricken. "How can we not talk about choice issues? Sheffield is trying to have it both ways. And Pierce is promising to only appoint judges who agree to some pro-life pledge."

"I'll talk about the issue if asked, but do we elevate it to that white board? I want others to chime in, but I'm sorry Miss Jacobs, my vote would be no."

The young woman looked at her two peers, her eyes pleading. "Do you agree with that?"

Evan's face was apologetic as Krista fixed her eyes on her roommate and closest friend on campus. Megan swallowed hard, sympathy in her voice.

"We've only got a month, Kris. Maybe—"

"Wow, I can't believe this." Krista stood, gathering her belongings while glaring again at Walter. "I thought you were going to be so different. I thought you were going to be the leader Sheffield isn't. And you won't even stand up for women."

Walter frowned. "Oh, Miss Jacobs. I hope someday you reconsider that thought. I know how disappointed you must be, and I truly admire your commitment to an issue you care so deeply about. Please stay with us. We need you."

He found nothing but defiance in her eyes. She turned her back on the others as she collected her coat and left the house without another word. The living room was quiet, and Dan could see the anguish in Megan's eyes. Walter spoke first, his voice gentle.

"I'm truly sorry we lost such a bright, capable ally. But please understand, everything I say and do as we move forward may not please all of you. I'm quite new to this, and I haven't given much consideration to the long list of issues out there. If either of you feels as Miss Jacobs does, by all means let's talk privately, so you can determine if you're comfortable with the platform we run on."

Evan thrust a hand up. "Not trying to change the subject, but when we do figure out this platform, how do we tell people about it?"

"Spend millions on television ads," Megan remarked.

Evan nodded. "That's my point. We don't have millions, or even hundreds. Which brings us to fundraising."

"That's an easy one," Walter said. "There won't be any."

Evan shot a questioning glance to Megan before turning back to the professor.

"We're not fundraising?"

"No, we're not. We're going to give new meaning to the phrase shoestring budget."

"I understand your concern with big money," Megan said, "but what about just small donations, maybe nothing over $100? We can still say it's a grassroots campaign, and we—"

"Nope. Not one dollar."

Dan recognized the tone. The professor held as much interest in collecting campaign contributions as he did in adding abortion to their platform.

Megan chewed her lip. "That's really going to limit what we can do."

"We don't have time to raise money, let alone spend it. And what do campaigns spend money on? Advertising, staff, offices, the list goes on. We don't need any of that. We'll have a web site and use it to publicize our platform. We'll use social media, which I trust you kids know something of. And we'll knock on every door we can find. I can think of a few modest expenditures that make sense, like yard signs for busy medians, but I can contribute my own funds for that, which I believe is allowed by federal election law. We'll have no cash flow, and that will work in our favor. No reporting requirements, no filings, and no pack of volunteers to manage and process it all. Trust me, this won't limit our campaign. It will free it."

Evan exhaled. "I guess we'll need to get creative in how we get the word out."

"Oh, I'm counting on it. You are the most creative young people I've ever been around. Use that."

"We'll have to go completely digital," Megan noted. "So, maybe we figure out where we stand on all the major issues, post your positions on our web site, and then share them on social media. We could build events around each one, like a health care rally at a medical clinic, or an education speech at a school."

Walter smiled. "I like where you're headed, Miss Cahill, but given our limited time and resources, I come back to my earlier point. We must focus on a smaller, simpler platform. One far easier to communicate."

"Web site has to be the priority then," Evan said. "Building one isn't rocket science. Some of these outfits will host a site for cheap, and their servers are solid. I can have something up tonight if you want."

Walter looked at Evan in surprise. "Tonight?"

"Or whenever we have the content ready. I've been working on the design for a week. We were going to show it to you the other night as a surprise, but we were having connectivity issues at Greenspun. I'll DM you the prototype, and then we can decide if we need any U/X testing."

Walter wrinkled his nose. "You'll what me the what?"

"I'll email it to you," laughed Evan along with the others.

"I can ask someone from the State Party to come talk to us. Give us advice."

"That would be very helpful, Miss Cahill, but I'm skeptical they would willingly assist anyone not named Sheffield."

Megan shrugged. "I work with a guy. The worst he can say is no."

Her father gave a satisfied smile.

Evan cleared his throat. The young man's forehead seemed permanently creased in worry.

"What about your announcement and kickoff event? We'll need a huge turnout, large enough to get everyone's attention. Maybe a rally on campus?"

Walter gave a forceful nod. "Yes, indeed. But I think we want to demonstrate we have broader appeal beyond UNLV. I have an idea, a place owned by one of my dearest friends. Let me phone him tomorrow and discuss it with him, see if he's amenable."

"I feel like we're just scratching the surface here," Evan grumbled. "Like there are a thousand things we're not thinking of."

"There are, Evan, and that's okay. We're navigating unchartered waters here. We'll take this one day at a time, lest the currents drag us too far downstream. Why don't we all sleep on this, give some more thought to our platform, and we'll see where we all stand tomorrow."

"One small item," Dan said, surprising them all.

"The floor is yours, Mr. Cahill."

"Any skeletons in your closet?"

"Dad!"

Evan gave the professor a look of apology. "He's right. Not that you have anything, Professor, but once your name is out there, people are going to dig."

Megan rolled her eyes before pointing an accusatory finger. "Have you ever murdered anyone? Are you part of a drug cartel?"

Walter smiled at first, then turned more solemn. "I didn't want to have to share this with you. But I also don't wish to see it splashed on the front page of the newspaper."

He took a deep breath, and the room became still.

"We have a homeowners association here, with a fiendish president who spends every waking moment dreaming up new bylaws and regulations. I purposely send in my monthly checks a week late, just to irritate the man."

Evan and Megan laughed, and even Dan smiled in appreciation.

"Professor, I'm starting to learn you're my kind of guy."

CHAPTER 10

January 16
Thirty-Seven Days to Primary Day

The rumble from Dan's stomach could have been mistaken for distant thunder. He peered behind the counter again, watching a high schooler jab a wooden peel into the coal-fired oven and spin an assortment of pizzas baking inside. Megan stood nearby, scrolling through her phone while nibbling on some sort of powdered-sugar fried dough she had collected from a sample basket near the register.

"How do you live without coffee?"

Megan looked up from her screen. "Huh?"

"You said you were up until three in the morning. You had classes starting at eight-thirty. Then work. And now you're headed to another evening meeting with Matlock."

"Who's Matlock?"

"Never mind. How did I get roped into this again?"

She licked the sugar from her fingers. "You offered me a ride from work to Becker's house. Then suggested we pick up dinner for everyone. So, I guess you roped yourself in."

Dan grunted in acknowledgment. Was he that desperate to get out of the condo?

"Did you come up with any ideas for the platform?"

Before Dan could answer, his stomach sounded off again, irritable about the tasteless greens still digesting from his lunch. He eyed the basket of fried dough hungrily until a small boy reached in, oblivious to his smudged fingertips tainting every piece.

"It was a toss-up between single-payer health care and outlawing all fossil fuels."

"Which did you choose?"

"Neither. I was busy on something called LinkedIn."

"Ugh, it's such a snoozer. You should try Facebook. It's like Instagram, but for old people."

"I'm already on it. All I see are photos of my friends' kids holding up participation trophies."

Megan laughed. "Well, we know *you* don't have any of those photos."

Dan winced.

"Dad, I'm kidding."

He nodded, absently.

Megan punched his arm. "Really, Dad, it was a joke."

He met her eyes. "I'm sorry, Megs."

"About what?"

"I should have a phone full of photos like that. Every decent father would."

"Every decent father wasn't in the Secret Service. Besides, I don't want a decent father. I want you."

She managed to keep a neutral expression for a good three seconds before her face widened into a grin. "I'm here all week folks!"

He couldn't help but share in her laughter, a sound that always pulled Dan back to her younger years. She was so carefree and lighthearted then, a stark contrast to her parents who attacked their careers with an almost joyless vigor. Other than the sparkling eyes that first melted him in a delivery room twenty years ago, it seemed everything about Megan had changed. His once-precocious little girl in pigtails and princess dresses had grown into an intensely focused, upright young woman. She had come so far, and though Dan's life was pockmarked with missteps and wasted opportunities, she was easily the best part of it. It shamed him to consider how much he had missed, and while joining a couple of campaign meetings and splurging for some pizza wouldn't make up for so much lost time, he hoped it was a start.

"Seriously, Megs, if I could go back and do it all over, I'd—"

"Dad, you don't—"

"No, I mean it. I drove by Cashman Field the other day, and it made me think about the State finals – what was it – four years ago? Coming back from that busted leg, it was the first time I saw you play goalie. First time I saw you play that entire season. And I barely recognized you out there. This confident, strong girl, leading that team, owning that net. And all I could think at the time was, when did this happen? How did I miss it all? And when I was listening to you the other night, standing at that white board, I had the exact same thought. When did this happen?"

He rested a hand on her shoulder. "If I haven't said this to you before, I'm saying it now. I'm so proud of you. And I'm sorry I wasn't there more for you."

Megan blinked away the tears. "I – I'm glad you came with me the other night. I'm glad you're here now."

Another teenager set three boxes on the counter, wisps of steam escaping from the edges. Dan swiped his credit card before turning back to his daughter, handing her a napkin from a nearby dispenser.

"You know you're breaking the cardinal rule of college by hanging with your old man."

She dabbed her eyelids, her smile back in place. "An old man who keeps paying for dinner."

Twenty minutes later, they were back in Walter's living room, picking up from the previous evening. Dan intended to drop Megan off with the pizza and return to Summerlin, but after ten minutes of roasted garlic wafting through his Explorer, he opted to resume his place on the sofa, at least for a slice. They were seated around Walter's coffee table again, greasy paper plates and empty boxes littering the floor.

Walter wiped his hands on a paper towel, noting Evan's forehead creases already in overdrive.

"So, Mr. Worley, how long do we have?"

The young man made the mental calculation. "Five weeks."

"Well, my friends, I've given some additional thought to the idea I put forward last night. With our limited time and resources, I suggest we focus on a single issue. An idea grander and more ambitious than anything currently out there in the public sphere. And one I'm certain will resonate with voters of all political persuasions."

"You're going to cure cancer?"

"No, Miss Cahill, *we* are. This country. I want to propose the greatest marshalling of American resources since the Manhattan Project. It's a simple proposition. If this country can harness the sciences to manufacture a weapon to take so many lives, surely we can harness the sciences to preserve them."

Evan gave a sardonic smile. "If we had any money, that'd be a great campaign ad."

"I've come up with a three-pronged strategy, and–"

"Three prongs? What is it, the Marshall Plan?"

Walter turned to Dan. "That's actually a fitting analogy, Mr. Cahill. Let's start with the government. We make the Director of the National Institutes of Health a cabinet-level official, reporting directly to the President. He or she will chair an advisory board comprised of the Secretaries of Health and Human Services and Treasury, the bipartisan congressional leadership, and the medical research community. The board must be government-wide, nonpartisan, and informed by the best experts."

"You've given this some thought," noted Megan.

"Second, the people. That is where the resources, every penny, must come from. We will ask every American to take a pledge. A promise to donate some amount of money – we set a modest threshold – to a trust fund by a certain date. Not a tax to be collected by the government. A donation, from volunteers, tax deductible of course. The goal will be for some number, let's say fifty million Americans, to take this pledge, and collectively raise billions of dollars every single year."

"That doesn't sound like much."

"No, Mr. Cahill? The entire annual budget for the National Institute of Cancer is $6.5 billion."

"Is that where the money would go?" Evan asked, chewing on a piece of crust.

"Ah, part three, the money. Certainly, adding to the Institute's budget would be a priority. I think we could also drastically increase funding for research and experimentation going on in the medical and academic communities. And establish grants and scholarships to double the number of researchers and doctors on the front lines."

Megan saw her father's raised hand and gave an exaggerated sigh. "Here comes the rain."

"You want to center your entire campaign around a proposal relying on people to voluntarily give their money to the government?"

Walter gave a thin smile. "That's exactly what I want to do, Mr. Cahill. Paul Sheffield and Rebecca Pierce are both talking about what they want to take *from* the federal government. And look at it this way, we'll certainly stand out."

"You certainly will."

"I've been working on a more detailed one-page summary we could post on our website. I'll send that around shortly and I welcome all input and suggested changes."

"You don't even need us," Megan said, only half-jokingly. "You're doing all the work."

"That's clearly not the case, Miss Cahill. Speaking of which, I understand you and Mr. Worley have given some thought to the road ahead?"

Evan nodded, flipping through his notebook. "We need a slogan. I thought about just "Walt" but that would sound a little Hillary-ish."

Dan chortled, drawing a few cross looks, and one bemused smile from the candidate.

"A little? But you're quite right, Mr. Worley. We need a slogan. Something idea-oriented."

"And something about change," Megan added. "You're different, we need to get that across."

"Okay, we can brainstorm independently on that one. Next?"

Evan surfed again through the spiraled pages. Dan was beginning to see the disparate styles between the two co-managers. Evan, the meticulous record keeper, wore every emotion on his sleeve. Anxiety was his constant companion and he fussed over every detail. He didn't just cross every t and dot every i, he anguished over them. Megan was equally expressive, but otherwise a sharp contrast, perennially bright-eyed and upbeat, even when Dan suspected she was beset with her own worries and frustrations. There was great divergence, too, in their approaches to every task and challenge. Evan, cautious and methodical, while Megan was like her father, prone to shooting from the hip.

The young man looked up. "We really need someone to be the press secretary. Word is getting out, and I've already gotten one call from the *Scarlet & Gray*, and another from some AM radio channel. It can't be me – I don't know how to talk to those people."

Walter turned to his left. "How about you, Mr. Cahill? Have you any experience dealing with the media?"

Dan glanced at his daughter, who purposely avoided his eyes. A conspiracy, it seemed, was afoot.

"Contrary to whatever you may have heard, I'm not sure I'm the person you want speaking on your behalf. Especially to the media. And remember our deal. I—"

"Yes, yes, you don't want to be involved. Perhaps you could simply screen the calls for us? Find out who they are with and what they want. Sort through it, bring it back to this group, and we'll discuss as a team how to handle. How does that sound?"

Dan flashed a half-hearted scowl at Megan. "It sounds like I'll be involved."

"Good!" Walter exclaimed, gently slapping the table. "It's settled. Everyone formally welcome Mr. Cahill to the team."

"I'm not on the team! I'm returning phone calls. That's it."

They all smiled, amused by his annoyance as Walter spoke again.

"What else is on your list, Mr. Worley?"

The young man shuttered his eyes for several seconds before fluttering them open again.

"We haven't really talked about our strategy on the ground. Are we just campaigning in Vegas, or other places as well?"

"Like Washoe County," Megan added, referring to the home of Reno and half a million people, some 400 miles to the north. "The rest of the state will be impossible. I know you want to compete for every vote, Professor, but no way can we campaign in all those rural counties."

Dan eyed his daughter, impressed again. It was an astute calculation. Outside of the two population centers in the north and the south, Nevada's remaining fifteen counties were sprawling expanses of open land with sparse populations. And not exactly crammed with progressive voters.

"No, Miss Cahill, you're right. We'll focus solely on Clark and Washoe Counties."

"Do you know anyone in Reno?"

"A few colleagues at UNR. Perhaps some of your peers have likeminded friends up there."

"I'll check," Evan said, glancing down again at his notebook. "Okay, I have one last idea, but it's kind of a longshot."

"This is Las Vegas, lad. As Hannah used to say, sometimes you have to bet against the house. Let's hear it."

"Hope Sullivan."

"Who?"

"Yes," Megan declared emphatically, her face lighting up. "Brilliant!"

Walter and Dan were stupefied.

Evan tried to help. "RebelGirlProductions?"

Walter shook his head. "A student drama club?"

"No," Megan laughed. "Hope is a student here at UNLV. She's got a huge Instagram following all over the country. Like, a million followers."

"Because of her pictures?" asked Dan, incredulous.

Megan groaned. "Posts, Dad." She turned to Evan, apologetic. "He uses Facebook."

"It's really her vlogs," Evan explained.

"What the hell is a vlog? Is that Russian?"

Evan laughed and turned to the still-mortified Megan. "Your dad is amazing." He smiled at Dan. "A video blog. She posts one every week on her YouTube channel. They're hilarious, and they get shared big time. Only thing is, I don't know if she's political."

The professor fought back a yawn. "You want her to make videos for us for her Instagram followers?"

"Well, that would be an added benefit," said Evan. "But at the least, she can tell us how to use social media to promote the cancer idea, or whatever our platform is."

"I appreciate your enthusiasm, all of you, and I know I have to embrace these more modern forms of communication. But I'm not sure older voters would understand—"

"It's kind of a no-brainer, Professor," Megan injected. "We need Hope, or someone like her. One of us could run your social media. We could create our own Instagram account, or build a Facebook page. We'd get plenty of likes and shares, but it wouldn't translate into votes. My boss at the State party talks about this all the time, calls it the action gap between expressing support and actually going out and pulling a lever. Hope is just on another level. She knows how to use her platform to reach people and change the way they think, and how they act."

"You make it sound like a science," Walter said.

Evan nodded. "That's exactly what it is."

"Then I suppose we should meet her. Can you set it up?"

Megan looked at Evan. "Do you know how to reach her?"

Walter yawned again, settling deeper into the sofa cushions.

"Uh, kids, maybe we should call it—"

The professor straightened. "Oh no, you don't, Mr. Cahill. I'm just gathering my second wind. *Miss* Cahill."

"Yes?"

"I have a special assignment for you. We are going to find a print shop to produce two large banners with our campaign slogan on it, whatever that is. Your job will be to make sure for the next five weeks, that banner is held up by two of our volunteers, every day, at a busy intersection during rush hour. One in Vegas, one in Reno."

"Got it," Megan said, as her father wondered where she would possibly find time in her frenetic life to manage this. "Assuming we can find someone at UNR who can dig up some volunteers for me."

"Mr. Worley, your turn. The Golden Knights have a home game on Thursday night, and another one on Sunday afternoon."

"I get to go to hockey games?"

"No. You and some of our cohorts get to stand outside of them. We're going to make small programs for the games and print our slogan and platform on the back. I'll cover the tab. We'll hand those out for free outside the stadium, however many we can afford."

Evan shook his head. "Man, where are you coming up with this stuff?"

"Hannah was attached to quite a few local political campaigns. They were all cash poor and needed to employ alternative means of reaching voters other than the airwaves."

Megan turned to her co-manager. "Evan, if you could design something in Adobe, we could print the programs ourselves. Save a ton of money."

"Done."

"The banners and programs will help," Walter continued, "but that's only a start. Meeting voters face to face is a must. We need to think of places where large crowds gather, and away from the tourists. Anywhere we can drum up support."

There was agreement around the table, and Evan volunteered to begin organizing field events.

"One last piece of good news. I spoke to my friend, Charlie Drummond, and we have a venue to make our grand announcement."

"Where have I heard that name before?" Megan asked.

Dan knew, recalling the name from the *New York Times* profile on Becker, but remained quiet.

"It's large, free, and a perfect backdrop from which to introduce our platform. Evan, I'll need you and Megan to work with my friend in setting things up at his place."

"No problem. How much time do we have to prep for it?"

Walter eyed a nearby grandfather clock and gave a tired smile. "Fourteen hours."

CHAPTER 11

January 17
Thirty-Six Days to Primary Day

Dan turned over in his bed, the soft vibration from the nightstand prodding him from a deep slumber. Even half asleep, the déjà vu washed over him, stirring memories from a month ago. Another ringing phone at another ridiculous hour, and a call that became the catalyst for his downward spiral, bringing a two-decade career to an abrupt and unceremonious end.

He wanted to throw the warbling phone through the window but could only curse his own idiocy for parking the device within easy reach. He didn't have to. A civilian now, he was permanently off the clock, his 24/7 obligation kaput. And if not a duty officer calling, he could also safely assume it wasn't Publishers Clearing House or Gal Gadot on the other end. But old shackles were difficult to cast off, and Dan angrily snatched the phone from the nightstand. He thumbed it on, springing to a sitting position as he saw an image of the incoming caller flash on the screen.

"Megs."

"Hey, Dad, you sleeping?"

"No, I'm knitting you a scarf for your birthday. You okay? What are you doing up this late?"

"I'm twenty. That's what 20-year-olds do."

Dan wiped the sleep from his eyes. "Okay, so why are you waking *me* up this late?"

"I was just thinking about Professor Becker."

"That's...disturbing."

"Seriously, about the event in the morning. Evan and I are going down super early to set things up. Would you mind giving Becker a lift?"

"What am I, an Uber? Doesn't he have a car?"

"He does, but someone running for President shouldn't be driving himself around in a Toyota Prius."

Dan stifled a yawn. "Lyndon LaRouche used to run for President from a prison cell. He did all right."

"Who's Lyndon LaRouche?"

"Are you serious about this, Megs?"

"It's not presidential, Dad."

"A Prius? You're all Democrats, it's totally presidential. What do you want, Megan, a motorcade? Maybe a counter-sniper team?"

There was silence on the other end, and Dan feared he stepped too far. She had to be distressed about an event they were still scrambling to organize, one likely to either springboard or sink their fledgling hopes. Evan had been tasked with drumming up media interest, but logistics for the rollout were Megan's responsibility. One that would be suffocating and stress-inducing for the most experienced operator, let alone a college sophomore and part-time assistant to a spa concierge.

"I just don't think he should be driving himself."

Dan sighed, laying back down. "It's *Becker*, Megan. Not exactly Bruce Springsteen rolling into Madison Square Garden. If he can drive himself to the grocery store, he can drive himself to North Las Vegas. And I wasn't kidding about the Prius. It's probably a good story for him, shows he's down-to-earth and planet friendly. Man of the people."

More stubborn silence, a personality quirk Dan knew could be traced to his ex-wife.

"Come on, Dad, he's not going to be treated like a real candidate unless he looks like a real candidate."

"He's *not* a real candidate," Dan snapped. He ran a hand through his hair, cursing under his breath. So much progress the last few days, and now he was kicking sand in her face.

"Sorry, Megs, that's not what I meant."

"Whatever."

A word that riled every parent in America. Suggesting concession, it was anything but. His daughter would throw herself into a pit of scorpions before backing down.

He sighed, knowing full well where *that* personality quirk came from.

"I just don't want him to get lost, Dad, and show up late to his own event. And once he's there, that place is huge. I checked it out on Google Maps. What if he goes to the wrong entrance?"

Dan shook his head. The man was the savior of the free world but couldn't be trusted to find his own campaign rally.

"Please, Dad."

He had once stood his ground against a United States Senator, a foreign head of state, and the leader of the most exclusive law enforcement organization in the world. But he was no match for his willful daughter. The imploring was too much.

"Text me his address. Start time is at ten, right? Tell him I'll be there at 9:15, on the nose."

"Thanks Dad. You're aces."

"On the nose, Megan. I'm leaving at 9:16 with or without him. Punctuality counts."

"Wow, it's like you're back in the Service."

Oh yeah, Dan grunted to himself. *It's just like that.*

.   .   .

"I'm sorry they shanghaied you into this," Walter said, lifting his paper cup and tipping it in Dan's direction. "But I do appreciate the tea."

Dan returned the air toast from his own brew. His other hand was on the steering wheel as he weaved the Explorer through Walter's neighborhood.

"Well, if I'm going to drive Miss Daisy around town, I better make sure we're both awake. Megan says that's all you drink."

"Yes, doctor's orders. Horrible, cruel doctors."

Dan had pulled up to Walter's home at precisely 9:15, surprised to find the professor seated on a bench swing on his front porch. He was dressed in his standard apparel; pressed khakis and button-down Oxford. Given the momentous occasion, he had added some flair to the ensemble. A tweed blazer with elbow patches, of course. All that was missing was a smoking pipe clamped between his teeth.

He eased the car to a halt at a red light and gazed out the windshield. In the distance, the upper floors of the Platinum were visible, the morning sun bouncing off the plated glass, pulling Dan back to that tumultuous episode like a riptide and instantly reminding him of all he had lost.

Twenty-three long years of service – literally half his life – vanished into thin air. The dues he had paid; standing post in monsoon-like conditions in the Philippines; in bone-chilling temperatures in the mountains of Utah, and in the scorching heat of Crawford, Texas. The relationships he had sacrificed with family and friends to devote himself entirely to his craft. Now, before his savings were depleted, he'd have to prostitute himself before some corporate headhunter and jockey among other retirees for a cushy position somewhere in Corporate America. His ambition no longer to protect U.S. presidents or foreign heads of state, but silver-spooned, white-collar executives instead. The sort who were consumed with hollow status symbols, like having a rough-hewn former Fed riding shotgun to a liveried chauffeur, while they sat in the back, sipping their martinis from behind tinted glass.

The light turned, and Dan motored the Explorer toward I-15. Glancing at his passenger, Dan was surprised by the man's composure considering what loomed a few miles away. He recalled past drives with other principals as they huddled with their aides, pouring over prepared speeches and scribbling in last minute edits. Walter, however, seemed impervious to what awaited ahead, his demeanor unchanged from what Dan had seen all week.

"A question?"

Walter turned to him. "I'm expecting a few of those today."

"You don't look nervous," Dan said, accelerating up the freeway ramp.

"Should I be?"

"Well, it's not like you'll be performing Shakespeare out there, but there's an expression on the campaign trail. This ain't beanbag. Are you ready for it?"

"I'm too old for word games, Mr. Cahill. Can you elaborate on beanbag?"

Walter sounded genuinely curious. Dan was beginning to understand the man was chronically sincere in every conversation.

"It means, it might get rough. Standing in front of a classroom full of students who stare at you with gaga eyes is one thing. But what you're stepping into can be pretty cutthroat. I saw it up close. Opponents digging into your past, your personal life, even your family. The media picking apart everything you've ever said and done. Wackos blasting you on Twitter and Facebook."

Walter sipped his tea. "Dante's Inferno, no?"

"That's exactly what it is. Rings of hell. And you're not nervous about it?"

"Well, now I am."

Dan laughed.

"I confess, Mr. Cahill, I am feeling somewhat...anxious."

"I'd sure as hell be."

"But maybe I'm more prepared for it than you know. Let me tell you something about being a teacher, and what it's actually like to stand before students, not all of whom are so...gaga-eyed. My very first year as an educator was at a high school in rural Mississippi in 1970. I was quite the idealist back then. A wishful, world-class do-gooder, and I wanted to go where I could be a part of a changing world. The Supreme Court had struck down school segregation sixteen years earlier, but, well, let's just say the South was still very much a work in progress. And that's where I wanted to be.

"It was my first teaching position, and I was assigned 11th grade social studies at Jefferson Davis High School. Yes, *that* Jefferson Davis. You want to talk about daunting? Try being a 22-year-old, Nixon-hating, Vietnam-protesting liberal, responsible for teaching Civil War history to Mississippi schoolchildren. In a building named after the President of the Confederacy."

"Hostile audience?"

"You have no idea. My first day, I shared with my students – mostly white faces, mind you – what we would be covering in the coming weeks. That provoked considerable dissent, to say the least. My offense? I intended to explore some of the root causes of the war, including perspectives not quite welcome then south of the Mason-Dixon Line. I wanted to open their minds a bit, but I may as well have thrown sticks of dynamite. The fury in that room, Mr. Cahill, fueled by generations of blind and rampant hatred, was palpable.

"I stood there, listening to the most vicious invective I had heard in my life. The hateful voices of direct descendants of slaveholders and Klansmen. That moment was an eye opener. The first time I truly understood the divide in our country. I stood there as student after student rose from their seats and marched out of my classroom in protest. Eighteen of them left that morning."

"Yeesh," Dan muttered as he changed lanes. "Was that the end of your stay in Mississippi?"

"Not quite. Thirteen students remained. Eight black faces, but five white ones as well. Five sons and daughters of the Confederacy, whose great-grandfathers had surely fought and likely died in that war, had stayed to listen, and to learn. They all pulled their desks into a small circle, and we spoke. Honestly, respectfully, and sometimes painfully. Not all of the remaining white students were angels. A couple were as like-minded as their departed classmates, but wanted to state their case, and were at least willing to listen to mine. And for an hour, that Mississippi classroom seemed like an island of civility in a vast, hate-filled sea. The experience stayed with me for the rest of my life."

Dan exited the freeway near the old downtown district, turning left onto Las Vegas Boulevard near the world's most famous drive-thru wedding chapel. His passenger was slouched in his seat now, still lost in the poignant memories from his youth.

"How long were you down there?"

"Less than two years. My mother fell ill, and I came home to help with things and pursue my graduate studies. Stayed in Las Vegas ever since."

A few more turns and they arrived at their destination. As Megan had suggested, it was a sprawling facility. Dan followed the signage to a large surface lot fronting a long, low-rise structure reminding Dan of the old General Motors assembly plant in Framingham, just outside Boston. There were only a few empty spots, quite a distance from the main entrance, and he made a mental note to chat with Megan about the finer points of advance work.

Walter was sitting up straighter now, his earlier calm beginning to fade.

"Any regrets?" Dan asked.

"About coming here?"

"About going to Mississippi," Dan answered, handing the professor a bottle of water.

Walter gratefully unscrewed the cap and took a long drink.

"It wasn't easy. I suppose I should have been content some were willing to hear me out. But I can recall at the end of the first day, sitting alone in my sweltering room at a local boarding house, dwelling on one question. How do I get through to those other eighteen kids? How do I open their minds to something they consider utterly unthinkable?"

Dan glanced at the venue in the distance. "We're still talking about Mississippi, right?"

"Right," Walter winked.

"Did you get through to any of them? Open any minds?"

"No fairy tale ending, Mr. Cahill. By Thanksgiving, the school wanted to fire me. But another teacher there, a local native, stood by me, and convinced the school to keep me on in another capacity. I began teaching mathematics, which I had no training for. But it was a living, and at least I had far fewer angry parents screaming at me."

"Your new friend down there probably saved your life."

"Not just a new friend," Walter said, a light returning to his eyes. "My future wife."

Dan's jaw fell. "You're kidding."

"Hannah was born and raised there. And somewhat of an outcast. She was Jewish, and a member of a congregation pre-dating the Civil War. Can you imagine, a quarter century after the end of World War II, the son of a German soldier and the daughter of Holocaust survivors, falling in love in the cradle of the Confederacy?"

"Now that does sound like a fairy tale." Dan paused. "I know you've lost her. I'm sorry."

"Nearly five years now. I admit, Mr. Cahill, it hasn't been easy. One of the reasons why I'm still teaching. I can't imagine spending all day in that house without her. You're divorced, I understand?"

"Celebrating eight years of freedom next month."

"So, you're unmarried and unemployed. Ever consider working on a political campaign?"

"Only if there weren't any openings at the city morgue."

"I'm starting to think you don't see a victory within our reach."

"Do you?" Dan asked cautiously.

Another wink. "I guess that depends on how you define victory."

They exited the car, and Walter studied the building in the distance with a blank, unreadable expression Dan had not yet seen from the man. It was the look he once had, Dan imagined, a generation ago. Walking into a Mississippi classroom, all alone in a new world, careening between infinite hope, and abject fear.

CHAPTER 12

"Ain't that something?"

The pride could be heard in the older gentleman's voice, but his question barely registered, his guests distracted by the true showpiece of the historical display. It was a mural-sized, black and white aerial of World War II-era Las Vegas, mounted on a 16-foot wall, and Walter and Dan were exploring every inch of it. For a photograph of that vintage, the resolution was spectacular, and the two became quickly engrossed in the details. A handful of hotels and other establishments were visible in the foreground, bunched across the original downtown, with Packards and Buicks dotting the paved highway that spanned the length of the image.

"How many people lived here then?"

"Oh, maybe 18,000 or so," the older man drawled, answering Dan while chomping on an unlit cigar. He used it to point to an intersection near the center of town. "There's our old plant right there, on the corner of 2nd Street and Wyoming Avenue, before we moved it to this location in '58. That's the old Jackpot Motel, and see those? It was wartime, so those were horse-drawn trucks lined up to take on their morning loads and deliver our goods to the markets and stores in town. We literally tore out the engines and hitched each truck to a team of horses. Engines were useless with the government rationing gasoline and rubber tires."

They stood on a polished floor of Brazilian cherry, the contemporary, well-appointed interior resembling nothing close to what Dan had imagined for an industrial plant. According to their host, the million-dollar refurbishment of the main atrium was intended to be a monument to his family's history, impressing and educating visitors and touring schoolchildren. The collection of artifacts and images provided a guided expedition through the company's rich, century-long heritage.

Walter grazed the glass frame with his fingertips, his eyes drawn to ant-like figures idling near each truck. "He wouldn't be in here, would he?"

Charlie Drummond smiled. "Not yet. 'Bout another decade 'till the Becker clan rolled into town."

Walter stepped back from the picture, returning his focus to the present and their host.

"So, Charlie, what should I expect?"

Drummond folded his thick arms, still gripping the cigar. The father of four and grandfather of nine was a hulking figure. He matched Dan's height, with wide shoulders and a barrel chest making him as fearsome as his gridiron days at the University of Wyoming. His dark, leathery skin was a testament to long hours mending fences and herding cattle at a family ranch in western Colorado. He and Walter were roughly the same age, but there the similarities ended, as the buckle on Charlie's belt and his worn Stetson spoke to a different, more rugged upbringing. All that was missing was a set of Colt Peacemakers strapped to his waist.

Dan peered down the empty corridor. Megan and Evan had been on-site for hours already and should have met Walter on arrival. That was ten minutes ago, the same time Drummond pulled up in his Ford F-250. There were more cars than Dan expected on a Saturday morning, but he now knew the plant was no minor operation. The Drummond Milk Company was a dairy processor, providing milk and other commodities to virtually the entire metropolitan population, including most of the larger resorts on the Strip. The care and feeding of hundreds of thousands of residents and tourists every day kept the plant churning, so to speak, around the clock.

It was a setting for the campaign rollout that surprised them all when Walter first revealed it. For the fifteen years he had lived in the valley, Dan had been oblivious to the existence of a working dairy in the heart of such a vibrant, cosmopolitan city.

The owner shrugged at Becker's question. "Honest, Walt, I'm not sure. After you called, I sent an email to our workers, all eight hundred of them, telling them we were going to make a little Vegas history today. But I also made it clear no one was taking attendance. Won't likely be too much of a crowd, with only two days' notice, and this being a Saturday. We got just one shift working, since weekends are off-days for most. Family time for a lot of my people. I'm sorry it had to be today, Walt, but weekends are the only days we'd have enough room to—"

Walter waved a dismissive hand. "I promise you our expectations are modest, Charlie. A small gathering will suit our purposes just fine."

Charlie pocketed the cigar and hooked his thumbs in his belt. "Earl called me a short while ago. He and Les have been working with your people, setting things up on the dock. It's the only wide-open space we got where you won't be standing in a puddle of milk. Good news is, even if only a few dozen show, we can still make it look crowded on the platform."

"You really don't know how many people are out there?"

Charlie smiled at Dan through tobacco-stained teeth. "I just got here too, friend. But my secretary claims we'll have a respectable showing. Two television cameras already set up, she said."

Dan stared at him. *Television cameras?*

They followed their host down a length of corridor that seemed to have no end. What was once a small block building had been transformed into a modern engineering wonder occupying nearly eight acres on Dakota Avenue, right on the boundary of North Las Vegas and its quarter million inhabitants. Drummond shared the story of the family business with Dan as they walked, taking him through the century of changes the dairy had endured growing alongside such a booming community.

There wasn't much to Las Vegas when the original facility first opened. Before the first cornerstones were laid on downtown landmarks like the El Cortez and Golden Nugget, Charlie's grandfather began trucking in raw milk from a handful of family dairies in California, bottling it or converting it to other products. A small fleet of trucks driven by men like Karl Becker would then fan out across Southern Nevada, delivering the refrigerated goods to hundreds of homes and retailers. By the turn of the new century, the dairy had evolved into a thriving, multimillion-dollar operation, serving a market of more than two million people and continuing to expand year after year while swatting away out-of-state competition.

The trio neared a set of swinging doors where Megan and Evan awaited, their faces reflecting both high spirits and deep trepidation. Walter suddenly halted, his wan face filling with unease.

"You okay, Professor?"

Walter gave Dan a feeble, unconvincing smile. "I think so. This is somewhat different than my university lectures."

"Can't be any rougher than that Mississippi classroom, right?"

Walter eyed the double doors, drawing in one last deep breath as he motioned his two students over.

Dan tapped his daughter on the shoulder. "Site lead meets the principal at the arrival point."

"Yeah, I know. What do you think I'm doing?"

"This isn't – never mind."

Walter turned to Evan. "How's it look in there, Mr. Worley?"

The young man tried to smile. "It's not empty."

"Ah, see? Progress." Walter stood in front of his two students, placing a hand on each of their shoulders. "I want to thank the two of you, no matter how many or how few people are out there. A month from now, when this is all said and done, I'll either be the winner of the primary, or the laughingstock of Nevada. But we will finish what we started. Agreed?"

"Agreed," they answered as one.

Walter held their eyes. "Let's have fun with this. Let's make our mark out there. And let's give voters in this state something to think about."

He gave a nod to Dan, who together with Charlie pushed through the doors, leading the entourage on to the loading dock. For a fleeting moment, the sequence took Dan back to another campaign trail, what seemed like a lifetime ago. They passed through the entryway, and his eyes became saucers, overwhelmed by the sight before him. The loading dock swelled with a massive, cheering crowd.

The students he expected. It was the others – plant workers and their families he surmised, numbering perhaps in the hundreds – that staggered him. The gathered crowd came to life the moment the professor stepped into view, feting him with a rousing welcome that thundered across the platform. The slow-moving bulk of Charlie and Dan cleared a path for Walter like a pair of Notre Dame linemen, but it was no easy task. The capacity crowd was densely packed in, shoulder to shoulder, on floor space half the size of a high school gym.

They pushed through waves of adoring faces, young and old, with a sprinkling of small children waving hand-drawn signs. They were all gathered in front of a lectern placed at one end of the loading dock, while cameras from the local ABC and FOX affiliates sat perched atop makeshift staging Charlie's crew had erected to one side.

With a broad grin, the owner stepped to the podium, adorned with one of the campaign's gold and blue signs, the ink barely dry on the words A NEW VOICE. He lifted his outstretched arms, attempting to quiet the onlookers, but the din only became louder.

"What a crowd!" Charlie boomed into the microphone, and another wave of applause was unleashed, carrying on for a full minute. He patted the air again, the boisterous response finally subsiding.

"I sure hope no one is clocked in, or we won't be making payroll this month. I want to welcome all of you, our staff, your families, and everyone else joining us here this morning. I stand before you today, not as your employer, but as your fellow Nevadan. I am so proud and humbled by each of you. You've all heard me say this before; we have the best employees here at Drummond Milk. The best workers, but even better people. You have come here today, most of you, on your day off, grabbing your loved ones, your neighbors, and anyone who cares about the future of our state and our country. You came to listen to what this man beside me might have to say.

"Most of you are familiar with the history of our great company. We have always prided ourselves on our ties to the local community, and the contributions we have made to our schools, veterans' clinics, homeless shelters, and so many other charitable organizations. I'm not going to recount those and pat ourselves on the back. I mention it because it was a creed handed down from my Grandpa Aiden, to my father Robert, to my sisters and me. Community before prosperity.

"What I'm announcing today is a mighty switch for us. The Drummonds have never been shy about our political views, but only under our own roof. We have enough horse sense to separate our business from our politics. Especially when our company has much of its fate in the hands of politicians and regulators, whether they're in Clark County, Carson City, or Washington, DC. Over time, we've played the game like everyone else, supporting candidates and officeholders of all political stripes, in the interest of our business."

He inclined his head toward Walter.

"Today, that comes to an end. Because today I stand next to someone who we here at Drummond Milk consider family. Someone who has served this community for decades. For those who have not yet met Walter Becker, he can be a chatterbox at times. But he's also whip-smart, tells-it-like-it-is, and has more kindness in his heart than anyone I've ever known.

"We were tykes when we first met. Just a couple of five-year-olds, dumb as rocks. His daddy worked for my daddy at our old plant on Wyoming Avenue. I had an attitude about that, and made sure Walt heard about it nearly every day in grammar school. He was teased quite a bit back then. I remember the day Walt got into it with one of his tormentors. A classmate nearly twice his size, who was making the observation that the squirts couldn't hit as hard as the big boys. Walt decided to test that theory and socked the much larger boy right in the stomach, dropping him like a sack of potatoes."

Charlie paused.

"Let me tell you," he continued, patting his stomach and knotting his face in mock pain. "That pee-wee packed quite a punch."

The crowd burst into laughter, hooting and hollering in delight. Charlie exchanged grins with Walter before addressing the crowd again.

"And Walt Becker is going to drop Paul Sheffield like a sack of potatoes next month!"

The folksy defiance in Charlie's words had its desired effect. It took some time before the crowd quieted enough for the man to continue. When he did, he was no longer smiling, his expression far more serious.

"So, can this pint-sized slugger become President of the United States? That I don't know. But you know our motto here, Walt. It's been on every container of milk since my grandfather came up with it. *For Goodness Sake.* Now, you can't use that. It's been trademarked and I'll sue you into oblivion. But that is why we are all standing with you today. For the sake of goodness in our political system. So, with that said, I want to introduce you to a great Nevadan, an extraordinary teacher, member of the community, and my oldest and dearest friend, Walter Becker."

The crowd erupted with another roaring ovation as Walter joined Drummond at the lectern, waving and offering a short bow of gratitude. The applause and shouts of support continued, and when he was finally able to be heard, there were pools in Walter's eyes and a catch in his voice.

"Charlie, you old son of a bitch. I told you not to do that."

The audience laughed along as Walter drew a deep breath. "Thank you so much, my old friend. We do indeed go back a few years. I cannot put into words how much I treasure our friendship. Like everyone else here this morning, I am so grateful for everything your extraordinary family has done for this city and our state."

Walter momentarily closed his eyes, summoning his next words. "You may be asking yourselves, why would a 76-year-old teacher, with no political experience and no interest in living anywhere near that morass known as Washington, DC, run for President of the United States? The answer, my friends, is not that I'm lonely, or bored, or a kook. Like so many of you, I'm simply worn out by political candidates who care more for an orthodoxy or self-righteous political dogma than they do our country and our communities."

Walter paused, waiting for another wave of hand clapping to subside.

"I sure wish my father was here today. He wanted to move his family out of the Chicago tenements and to a better life, so he brought us out West, and found work as a delivery driver at a ramshackle milk bottler in a dusty, desert town. He earned a modest living, but when he retired, he stubbornly refused to accept his Social Security, stuffing every uncashed check in a drawer at home. An immigrant, he never thought his adopted country owed him. All he desired was an opportunity to give back, and it was a life lesson I've always tried to follow.

"I have been a teacher my entire life, contributing to our community in my own small way. I'm sure I will be mocked for my political inexperience, my age, or some of my unfiltered ramblings. But I hope the platform we put forward is given serious consideration by all. We believe it is something our entire country can unite behind, and from which we can achieve great things for our nation."

His eyes searched the audience. "I want you to meet Hector and Daniela Alvarado. Where are you two?"

Dan saw their hands go up, the middle-aged couple standing off to the side. There was a scattering of applause, the pair clearly unknown to most others.

"These two have been married for more than a quarter century. Hector owns a prosperous landscaping company he started from nothing, and Daniela manages the day-to-day operation. They came here as a young couple from El Salvador, became great American entrepreneurs, and are now my next-door neighbors. They have two grown sons, both now second-generation Americans and United States Marines. The Alvarados are expecting their first grandchild in August. For all their good fortune in life, Hector and Daniela are now facing the sort of life challenge each of us fears. A month ago, a tumor was discovered lodged inside Hector's brain. It is inoperable."

Walter stopped, watching Daniela wipe a tear from her cheek as the crowd remained hushed. The professor let out a long breath before continuing.

"Hector is a strong man, with access to the very best health care and oncology services in Southern Nevada. But Hector doesn't know how many of his grandchild's birthdays he will be around to celebrate. This isn't an insurance issue, and Hector doesn't want to become a talking point for the bitter debate we've had for years about health care reform. He's a realist, who understands how deadly his illness is, despite the quality of his care.

"What he and I and so many others cannot understand is how such a horrifying disease has continued to curse the human race for generations, with no effective cure or treatment in sight. For all our wondrous advances in science, medicine, and technology, how can this remain so elusive?"

Walter slapped the lectern with each word. "That. Must. Change."

"Nothing should take higher precedence in Washington than protecting American families from death and disease. Forty percent of us will be diagnosed with cancer at some point in our lives. The numbers for this year alone are astounding. 300,000 Americans will be diagnosed with breast cancer. Another half-million with lung cancer. 190,000 Americans will learn they have prostate cancer, and 25,000, like Hector, will learn they have brain cancer. Worst of all, thousands and thousands of young children will be diagnosed with some form of cancer. 23,000 of them with leukemia alone."

Walter paused, inhaling deeply. His words were softer now, but the forcefulness remained.

"We lose a dozen people in a mass shooting and it incites a national debate. Marches, fundraising efforts, calls to action. We lose thousands to cancer and nothing changes. *Nothing.* The heartbreak in these families is unimaginable, and yet our leaders pass their time in Washington as if this can't be helped, as if there is nothing more we can do beyond the usual research and treatments. As if this is all so...acceptable. Well, my friends, on my watch, none of this will ever be acceptable.

"The centerpiece of our campaign is a bold new National Cure Initiative. Our objective is to mobilize America, in a way we haven't seen since World War Two, uniting Americans of every race, religion, political affiliation, and income level. Together, we will eviscerate these deadly diseases and create a truly watershed moment in our nation's history.

"Am I dreaming? Paul Sheffield would surely tell you that. As would Rebecca Pierce. But not Jonas Salk. Salk was an American physician, who waged a personal war against polio – another horribly crippling disease. He and his team of crack researchers spent seven years developing a vaccine. Sixty-five years later, Jonas Salk is hardly a household name, yet consider the impact his discovery has had on our national health. The extraordinary efforts of one team of physicians and researchers have literally spared millions of lives.

"I say to Paul Sheffield, Rebecca Pierce, and every voter in Nevada, dreamers might be just what we need at the moment."

More cheers of approval, and Walter pushed on.

"What separates the National Cure Initiative from past efforts to combat cancer, is that this Initiative will not be led by the government, but by all of us. It will depend *not* on the charity of politicians on both ends of Pennsylvania Avenue, but by contributions directly from the American people. At its heart, this initiative is about personal sacrifice. Asking ourselves, what am I prepared to do for my countrymen and the greater good? It starts with a goal of fifty million Americans volunteering to join us in this cause. Volunteers who will pledge to contribute $200 every year, or about $17 a month, to a special trust fund administered by the National Institutes of Health. That alone would raise some $10 billion, an amount equal to nearly twice the entire annual budget for the National Cancer Institute.

"Beyond strengthening and accelerating existing programs, this trust fund will educate a new generation of researchers and specialists, and provide grants to the universities and research centers on the cutting edge of discovery and potential breakthroughs."

Walter's determined eyes swept across the masses before him.

"It can be done, my friends. Each of us can squirrel away $17 a month. We can give up a few restaurant meals each year. We can go door to door in our neighborhoods, collecting more for this great cause. We can sacrifice, my friends. As a country, for our country.

"So, there you have it, my fellow Nevadans. A simple platform. I know there are many more issues and challenges facing our country, but the Cure Initiative alone could make us all infinitely healthier and stronger. It requires nothing more than selflessness, dedication, and yes, patriotism. I hope you will consider supporting me, and more importantly, this great Cure Initiative we are proposing. Our campaign represents a new voice for everyone here, and a new future for our nation, one putting the health of our families, friends, and communities above all else. Thank you, and I will see all of you on February 22nd."

The raucous cheers rose up from every corner of the loading dock. As Walter began greeting the hordes swiftly enveloping him, Dan stood by, surprisingly moved by the vigorous address. It had been far more eloquent and compelling than he expected, hitting emotional chord after chord. Most impressive, the man spoke entirely from the heart, the speech once again delivered extemporaneously, electrifying everyone within earshot with each heartfelt word. And in that moment, watching so many of the spectators pressing toward the candidate just to shake his hand, Dan could not let go of a thought he would have considered utterly preposterous an hour ago.

People are going to vote for this man.

. . .

For nearly an hour, Dan found himself at Walter's side, gamely attempting to keep each admirer an arm's length away. Megan and Evan threw themselves into the frenzy as well, collecting names and phone numbers from eager new volunteers while capturing images of an exultant Walter mugging with supporters.

Once Walter was finally able to extract himself from it all, Charlie shepherded them to the main entrance. The students remained behind, and after expressing his gratitude and exchanging an emotional farewell with his oldest friend, Walter finally left the plant with Dan. As exhilarating as the event had been, both men welcomed the cooler air and open space, relieved to leave behind the concert-like atmosphere.

"Your impressions, Mr. Cahill?" Becker asked, as they slowly weaved through the other cars in the plant's expansive surface lot.

Dan considered a response as he tried to ignore the stir in his stomach. It was well past the lunch hour, and the dry toast and granola parfait he consumed hours ago had been as satisfying as a cupful of sawdust.

"Nice little kickoff. You knocked it out of the park."

"May I impose on you for one last favor today? I have a medical appointment in Henderson I'm already late for. If you could drop me there, I could take a taxi home."

Dan sighed to himself. He was famished, and his lunch date with Nicole on the other side of the valley would have to be cancelled, but he couldn't refuse the request. The professor looked entirely depleted.

"No problem, I'm headed in that direction anyway."

They had just reached the Explorer when a fashionably dressed young woman with a hurried stride caught up to them, her heels telegraphing her approach. Dan remembered her standing on the platform with the news cameras, typing into a phone rapid-fire throughout the speech.

"Professor Becker?"

"Yes?"

"Sophie Howell, FOX 5," she said, offering her hand. "We'd like you to come in for a live spot on the six o'clock broadcast this evening. Can you make it?"

Dan intervened before Walter could react. "We'll let you know."

The journalist regarded him as if he had just stepped off a spaceship.

"You'll let us know?" Her voice dripped with contempt. "Connie and Trey have been number one in this market for three years. Their last in-studio guest was Governor Tibbets."

Dan shot Walter a warning look. It was well known the local Fox station skewed as conservative as its parent organization, and Dan suspected Connie and Trey had little interest in Walter beyond using the man to splash mud on the Vice President. Walter gave him a playful wink, fully aware of the hazards ahead.

"I would be delighted, Ms. Howell."

The woman slipped a business card into Dan's hand. "I'll be back at the station in an hour. Call me. You're his press secretary?"

Dan scowled. "Do I look like a press secretary?"

The woman shrugged, already moving away. "Blue blazer, in way over his head? Oh, yeah."

CHAPTER 13

"Forget the Prius," Dan muttered to his daughter. "You're going to tell me *that* looks presidential?"

They were watching Walter from behind the glass separating the studio set from a connecting observation area. A floor producer led the professor to a sofa where the two news anchors were arranging themselves. Walter sat where directed, exchanging pleasantries with his hosts as a technician expertly threaded a small microphone under the source of Dan's derision, a fire engine red UNLV sweatshirt.

Megan whispered back. "Why didn't you say something when you picked him up?"

"I did. He called it his lucky sweatshirt and threatened to wear it until Election Day."

Megan twirled the end of her ponytail in her fingers. Between the earlier rollout and the live television cameras now wheeling into position, Dan was surprised the girl hadn't chewed off every fingernail.

"Well, he *is* going to the game right after this."

No, Dan thought to himself, *the two of us are going to the game right after this.*

He and the Explorer had been conscripted once again, this time out of fears the late scheduling addition could jeopardize the man's 35-year streak of attending every home basketball game. With the KVVU studios located in Henderson and Becker scheduled for a mid-show segment, it was going to be close. Megan pleaded with her father to skirt whatever traffic laws necessary to get the professor to the arena in time for the pre-game ceremonies. Evan managed to have him named an honorary co-captain.

On set, it wasn't just Dan questioning the professor's wardrobe. Subtle disapproval still marked Connie Bannerman's face as they waited to return from a commercial break. An ominous sign, as Dan knew the platinum-haired anchor – a fixture on the Nevada airwaves for two decades – wasn't likely to be welcoming of Walter's politics.

Megan looked at him curiously. "What was that?"

"My stomach. I haven't eaten since breakfast, and Sergeant Slaughter says no snacks for two weeks."

"Who's Sergeant Slaughter?"

Dan shared the story of his new boot camp coach at Lifetime Fitness, a former Army drill instructor whose philosophy on nutrition seemed rooted in sadistic deprivation. He started to describe the latest assault on his cardiovascular system – warriors are built from burpees, the man preached – when Megan shushed him, pointing at the floor producer twirling a finger in the air.

A red light affixed to one of the cameras illuminated, and the grim-faced Bannerman was instantly transformed, wielding a thousand-watt smile likely visible from deep space.

"Welcome back. We're joined now by a special guest, lifelong Valley resident and UNLV political science professor Walter Becker. Thank you for coming in tonight, Professor. I see you're ready for the big game."

"Thanks for inviting me, Connie."

"Earlier today you announced your candidacy for the Democratic nomination for President. Yet you've never run for office at any level before. Why the presidency, and why now?"

"I was asked, Connie, by a group of young people who care very deeply about their country and the direction we're headed. They are dissatisfied with the current choices before Nevada voters."

"And why you?"

Walter smiled. "I suppose they needed someone who met the minimum age requirement. I just made it."

It was a quality quip, and Dan hoped it would resonate more with the viewers at home than it had with the anchor, busy studying her blue note card for the next question.

"As we've seen in Iowa and New Hampshire, the Vice President has struggled to gain traction with Democrats here in Nevada. Why is that?"

"I think voters are looking for fresh ideas, Connie, and new voices. People who have spent their entire careers inside the Washington Beltway tend to be somewhat detached from reality."

"Is that why Rebecca Pierce is surging on the Republican side? Fresh ideas and a more realistic perspective?"

"No, Rebecca Pierce is surging because she espouses reckless ideas and empty slogans, all designed to rouse her supporters and inflame division among others. Like other vacuous figures from our past, she's an opportunist, purposely appealing to our worst instincts."

The blunt words momentarily froze the anchor. "The polls tell us differently," she countered, "that the general is a strong leader who will restore—"

"All we know from the polls is there are many who confuse volume and bluster with leadership and strength. Have we not learned that lesson before with the megalomaniacs of our past?"

Troy Alexander, the co-anchor, jumped in. "Professor, you issued today a national call to arms for fighting cancer. Talk to us about that. It seems we've heard this before."

"We haven't, Troy, because what I'm proposing would be truly unprecedented. It starts with the premise cancer is not political. Think about how many Americans and how many families are touched by this disease, killing millions every year and devastating millions more. A disease that doesn't care how much money you have, whether or not you have insurance, what political party you belong to, or which God you pray to. We have to fight this disease as a country, and yet Washington has barely even suited up for the challenge. We need a bold stroke, a game changer, beginning with significantly more resources for the National Institutes of Health and the National Cancer Institute."

"So, more money."

"Resources, Troy. Financial and human. Yes, more money for these organizations to expand their experimentation and testing. But we also need to invigorate our research efforts with a new generation of innovative, scientific minds. Think about what this country accomplished during World War II. Do you know how many people worked on the Manhattan Project then?"

The co-anchor, with his styled hair and whitened teeth, perked up, welcoming an interplay usually absent from their in-studio interviews.

"Thousands, I imagine."

"185,000, Troy. Physicists, scientists, engineers, and machinists, working at secret facilities around the country in pursuit of a single objective. And the war itself, sixteen million soldiers, hundreds of thousands of weapons, ships and airplanes. Do you know how we paid for it all?"

"War bonds," answered Connie, jumping in. The senior anchor minored in history at the University of Texas.

"Right, war bonds. The government asked Americans to underwrite the war, offering a modest return on their investment when it was over. Eight-five million Americans – half the country then – bought those war bonds. They raised $185 billion. That's 2.7 trillion in today's dollars. And do you know what else this country did when those sixteen million men went off to war?

The two anchors looked at each other blankly.

"We mobilized," Walter continued. "Converted our manufacturing from consumer goods to war material. Instead of cars and refrigerators, we built tanks and bombers. Much of it was done by women, most of whom had never seen, or been allowed, inside a factory before. And we sacrificed. We had mass rationing across the country, from gasoline to fresh meat, to keep our soldiers fed and equipped. Every American, young and old, contributed to the war effort then. Everyone contributed because everyone believed in what we were doing. It was our finest moment, and that's why I want another call to arms, as you put it. This is a national problem demanding a national solution. And I believe the people will respond."

Connie pursed her lips. "But another tax, in this downturn, isn't that—"

"Wait, Connie," her co-anchor said, placing his hand on her forearm as she blinked at the surprise interruption. "It's not a tax, is it, Professor?"

Walter waved a hand. "Of course not. We're talking about voluntary contributions from those who chose to participate."

"You mentioned enlisting more people in the fight. How exactly do we steer more young Americans into this field?

Dan studied Troy Alexander, pushing aside his aggravation for the man's tanned features and cool bravado. Like Connie, his partisan inclinations were well-known, his family name synonymous with GOP politics in Southern Nevada. But while Connie had attempted to bait Walter into sniping at the Vice President, her co-anchor seemed to be on an entirely different tack.

"An excellent question, with so much importance. We certainly have world-class doctors and researchers committed to this fight, but we need reinforcements, another generation, to join them. So, let's use this new funding to offer medical training and scholarships to those willing to serve their country in this capacity. Our military already does this, offering medical education in return for a few years of service. The Vice President himself was a beneficiary of such a program. I want to expand that concept and invest in our own people."

"Professor Becker," Connie jumped in, "a source with the Sheffield campaign has suggested you are deliberately using this terrible disease to garner sympathy, and pull at heartstrings, just for the sake of drawing more votes. What's your response?"

Walter raised an eyebrow. "What source is that?"

The twitch in Connie's smile was barely noticeable, the anchor plainly irked to have her question answered with another question. "An anonymous source with the campaign."

"I would say anyone who would make such a charge or repeat such a charge on live television without attribution, has clearly lost their way. The notion that I, and these bright young students running my campaign, would use the grief and suffering of others to score political points, is quite frankly, offensive. I'm sorry to hear you doing their bidding, Connie. I think in your younger days, you too once believed public servants were capable of decency, and nobility, and not simply out to relieve some insatiable thirst for electoral power."

A producer frantically signaled the anchors, the pair having lost all sense of time. The segment was already two minutes over.

"And we'll have to leave it at that," Connie said, facing the camera again, her forced smile long gone now. "Thank you again for joining us today, Professor, we hope—"

"One last question, if I may Connie," interrupted Troy, vexing both his producer and co-anchor. "How serious is your campaign, Professor? Are you simply trying to raise awareness about an important issue, or do you believe you can actually win the Nevada primary?"

"The two go hand in hand, Troy." Walter turned away from the two newscasters and smiled at the camera. "And sometimes, you have to bet against the house."

. . .

The car doors each closed with a thud, the noise echoing across the darkened parking garage. Dan sat behind the wheel, waiting for one of his passengers to break the silence. He watched his daughter in the rear-view mirror as she collapsed in the back seat, clasping her hands together on the top of her head.

"That was amazing," she murmured.

Walter tapped his watch. "Tip-off in twenty minutes. Think we can make it?"

Dan pushed the ignition, turning to Walter as the engine purred to life. "What was that?"

Walter feigned innocence. "What was what?"

"Going after Connie Bannerman. You'll be lucky to get another television interview anywhere again."

"Dad, she so deserved it."

"She was goading me to attack the Vice President."

"Gee, the guy you're losing to?"

Walter tipped his head back and closed his eyes. "She had an agenda, Mr. Cahill, and I wasn't going to be party to it. If I'm going to appear on those kinds of shows, I'm going to do it on my terms."

"Jesus," exclaimed Megan from the back seat, the light from her phone casting her face in a soft glow. "Hope posted you and Connie going at it all over social media. She's already got 4,000 likes on Instagram...1,200 shares on Facebook...they keep going up."

Dan glanced at Walter. His eyes were still closed, but a satisfied smile slowly crept across his face.

"Holy crap!"

Dan looked in the mirror again. "Now what?"

"Evan just texted. Two radio stations have called, and the local NBC affiliate."

Walter didn't miss a beat.

"Sounds like a job for our press secretary."

CHAPTER 14

January 21
Thirty-Two Days to Primary Day

Libraries were generally foreign soil to Dan, who had yet to crack open a book this century. He did recall fondly the scattering of study tables in the Marshall High School library, particularly one dimly lit corner, just out of sight of the head librarian's desk, where he and the captain of the gymnastics squad often made use of their free period together. An airy smile crossed Dan's lips as he thought of Kelly Redding and their extracurricular pursuits, somewhere between Physical Sciences and World Geography.

Some three decades later, here he was, sequestered among endless stacks of books, partially listening to a 21-year-old recite the procedural obscurities of state mail-in balloting laws, partially reminiscing about the virtues of dating a gymnast.

The popular Flamingo Road branch had serviced the south-central part of the city for half a century, and most who lived in the adjoining neighborhoods considered the facility a community treasure. Among the library staff, their most faithful patrons were like family, and for Walter Becker, who could navigate every stack and shelf blindfolded, the library was a second home. He and Hannah had been loyal patrons for decades, and thus, his quiet request to one of the senior librarians yielded unfettered access to the fully enclosed and soundproofed Archibald Francis Room. Normally used for community meetings and other small gatherings, it was now serving as an informal campaign headquarters.

Dan was tipped back on the legs of a plastic chair, the pleas of his daughter still ringing in his ears. Shuttling the professor around in the evenings, she reasoned, would preserve his energy for the daily rigors of the campaign trail. A better solution might have been to continue meeting at Becker's house, but Dan could certainly sympathize if the man wanted to declare his home a campaign-free zone.

He ultimately agreed to continue his driving duties for one reason; he lacked a plausible excuse not to. Other than his morning torture sessions with Sergeant Slaughter, there was little else on his daily calendar.

"So, the sum conclusion," Walter pronounced, "is we didn't quite make the splash we hoped this week."

"Not with the papers," conceded Megan. "The *Review-Journal* mentioned the launch, but it was buried in an article about Sheffield's struggles in Iowa. We got nothing in the *Reno Gazette*. On the plus side, FOX5 and KNBC ran stories at the top of their broadcasts the other night, with teasers on their web sites."

"And the clip from your interview with Connie and Troy is still on fire," Evan added. "You heard about Hope?"

"Ah yes, our Instaface hacker. The clip is still virtual?"

Megan laughed. "There's so much wrong there I don't know where to start. But yes, it's viral, and she gave it the hashtag ThisGuy. You'll be trending soon."

Walter turned to Dan. "Do you have any idea what she just said?"

"I don't speak Klingon."

"You're ThisGuy," Evan explained. "Trust us, it's a good thing."

Walter held up his hands in surrender. "Okay, back to that which I actually understand. What about our event on Monday at the VA center?"

Evan frowned. "We sent out the press release yesterday. No word yet from any local media. Hope managed to get some play on the digital side."

"You sound discouraged."

"I thought there'd be more interest. That the locals might actually cover a Nevadan running for president. We're getting next to nothing, and the few mentions we do get, they make us sound like little kids opening a neighborhood lemonade stand."

"The lemonade stand is just fine for now. There's an old baseball adage; take the singles and doubles, they'll add up."

Megan gestured toward the glass wall providing a full view of the main floor. A squat, muscular man was weaving his way through a maze of research tables, his gait slightly uneven.

"Hurricane Marc. Right on time. Brace yourselves."

The visitor pushed through the heavy doors and shuffled awkwardly into the room. Marc Powell was in his early forties, with a dark complexion and mocha-colored eyes. His salt and pepper hair was closely shorn, with a matching, stubbly beard. An oversized, scarlet sweatshirt with Marines emblazoned in gold across the front fit comfortably over his burly frame. What he wore under his loose-fitting cargo shorts explained the unusual stride; a pair of gleaming metallic prosthetic legs.

He looked like a man hounded with worry. There were dark pouches under his hooded eyes, and his mouth was turned down in what may have been a permanent sulk. The campaign team stood to welcome their caller, exchanging handshakes before the professor invited him to sit at the head of the table.

"That's the hot seat, Mr. Powell," Walter said lightly. "We saved it just for you."

Powell grunted in return. The man was clearly wary of his hosts, his posture remaining rigid as he lowered himself into the chair, like a hostile witness taking the stand. With his hands interlocked on the table, he struck a pose that somehow looked both indulgent and prickly.

"Marc is my boss down at party headquarters," Megan began. "He pretty much runs the Democratic Party in the state."

Powell screwed his face up in annoyance. "I don't run the Democratic Party in the state. I wear different hats and pitch in where needed. Candidate recruitment, data analytics, campaign messaging, communications, even a little fund raising."

"He also brings donuts every Saturday."

"I thought we had an agreement. I come, you don't talk."

Dan felt his teeth grinding and resisted the urge to put Powell in a choke hold. Megan, he noticed, was still beaming, impervious to the man's snark.

"Megan tells us your official title is Political Director," Walter said. "Which means you likely have exponentially more wisdom and experience than all of us put together. We're very grateful you're here."

"I'm here because this girl, who we assigned to data entry, but instead parks herself in my office every Saturday morning asking six-part questions more suited for, say, a political science professor, wouldn't clam up until I agreed to come. I'm happy to answer as many questions as I can but read my lips; I'm here as a courtesy. I'm a strong supporter of the Vice President, and though the State Party will remain neutral in a contested primary, no one in our shop will be shedding any tears if Sheffield runs away with it."

Dan looked at the man in quiet disgust. Hearing a senior party official offer a full-throated endorsement of the most lackluster, milquetoast candidate in presidential history was just another indictment of the state of political affairs in

America. The attitude was mystifying as well. While Dan hadn't expected much enthusiasm from the man, he also hadn't expected such open hostility toward two college students and a senior citizen.

"You honestly want him to be our nominee?"

Powell turned to Evan.

"We support candidates whose values and records reflect what our party stands for, and who stand a realistic chance of winning. Like him or not, Sheffield is a solid, lifetime Democrat. He votes right on the issues, and he's hands down our best hope for holding on to the White House. Our *only* hope."

"Um, hello?"

Irritation flickered across Powell's face the second Megan opened her mouth. Dan straightened in his chair.

"Why're you being such an ass?"

"Dad!"

"I'm being an ass, buddy, because I've seen this movie before. Hell, I was in it. I was a Bernie supporter in '16. A true believer then. I thought the party had strayed from our core values, like economic equality and social justice. I hated Hillary, both for her politics and the shit her people pulled on us during the caucuses. I'm sure you've heard about it. It took me months to get over that. Hell, I never got over that. I voted for her in the general – I had to – but I sure as hell wasn't going to do anything else. Didn't knock on a single door. Didn't make a single call. Didn't donate a single dollar. But truthfully, I never considered the upshot of her losing. Cabinet appointments. Judicial nominees. The Constitution. Well, you know what happened. The presidency went into the toilet, and it took forever until we could right the ship with Vance. The Vice President is no Gandhi, I get it. But we need a Democratic candidate who can win in November. It's that simple."

There was a long silence at the table. Megan was sagging in her seat now.

"So why are you even here? You said yes as soon as I asked."

"I'm here because my position requires it. We have ourselves a contested primary and the Party is neutral, obligating me to consult with any declared and certified candidate who asks. I'm also here out of respect."

Powell turned to Walter, his manner softening. "I'm an admirer, Professor. I loved what you did for the students, and your stand against the State Legislature. I also respect the democratic process. You followed the rules and have every right to be on the ballot next month. So, I'm happy to set aside whatever personal views

I have and be as helpful as I can. To a limit." He turned back to the group. "Fire away."

Their eyes darted across the room, each waiting for someone else to step in front of the bull. It was Megan who spoke first.

"How do we win?"

There was light laughter around the table, and even Powell cracked a small smile.

"Well, I don't know what your strategy is, and I don't want to know, but I assume it ends with getting the most votes on February 22nd. So maybe you have some questions that will help you win those votes."

Evan tugged at an ear lobe as he feverishly leafed through his notebook. The page flipping continued until Walter leaned forward, waiting for Evan to meet his eyes.

"Lad, I understand your reticence. To say you are in unchartered territory is a great understatement. We all are. No one here, including Mr. Powell, will think less of you for asking questions. I assure you, once upon a time, Mr. Powell was quite the novice at all this as well. Go on."

Megan also gave Evan a reassuring nod. He took a deep breath and turned to the strategist, who was still smarting over the novice jab.

"Who votes in the primary?"

Powell grunted with approval. "Bravo. The magical question."

"What's the magical answer?" posed Megan.

Powell's voice changed again, full of intensity. Another mood shift.

"Remember, you're not trying to win every single Democrat out there. You're trying to win the majority of those who show up to vote. So, target your campaign messaging. Our primary numbers are going up, but it's still a minority of registered Democrats statewide. Roughly 100,000 party members voted in the 2020 caucuses. Five times that number voted nine months later in the general election. The good news is, we're expecting better turnout now that we've moved to a primary. Those caucuses were a pain in the ass for a lot of people."

"Great," lamented Evan, sinking lower in his chair. "We just need to reach 100,000 people in a month, with no commercials, no direct mail budget, and no organization outside Vegas."

"My advice? Forget about Reno or anywhere else outside Vegas. You don't have time or money to make a difference there. We've got just over three million people in this state, and three-quarters of them are here in Clark County."

"So, we need to reach 75,000 Democrats with no money. How?"

"We find them and go door to door," Megan suggested, "and really up our game on social media."

Powell pointed at her. "And that's where you're going to piss us off."

Megan arched her eyebrows. "Huh?"

Powell turned again to Walter. "I'm sure you've seen the public polling out there. Sheffield's approval numbers are respectable, but his support is an inch deep, and he's getting clocked in matchups with Pierce. So, your instinct is probably to go negative, foot stomp all the reasons people are lukewarm about him. And what happens? The press eats up the David versus Goliath story, embarrasses the guy, and the attacks you hit him with get repeated and amplified for months by the other side. Only this time, the Rs say, see, even his fellow Democrats think he's weak and unprincipled. And they'll use you. What you saw from Connie Bannerman was just the opening act."

Walter tented his fingertips together. "Interesting words you chose, *weak* and *unprincipled*."

Powell's smile was wolfish. "Well, that was just a hypothetical attack." He turned serious again, the man an emotional chameleon. "Whatever slant you take, I promise you, it will be used against us in the general. And let me be brutally candid. You will be dividing this party at the worst possible time, when we're trying to build momentum nationally for the August convention. Right now, Sheffield would win here with seventy, maybe even eighty percent of the vote. You cut into that, take fifteen, even ten percent of his votes, you'll change the narrative of his win. The media will say this is more proof his candidacy is on life support. That a meaningful portion of our base is still looking for an alternative candidate."

"You mean they'd tell the truth," muttered Megan.

"I think I can allay your fears, Mr. Powell."

"Oh?"

"I have no intention of attacking the Vice President. I have no intention of even mentioning his name."

It was as if a pistol shot had gone off in the room.

"What?" Megan and Evan asked simultaneously, the duo nonplused.

Walter folded his arms, his eyes level and serious.

"I don't like coronations, Mr. Powell, and I don't like the notion that in our democratic system, we shouldn't voice any dissent because it may signify the existence of, heaven forbid, competing ideas. But I won't be attacking the Vice

President because, frankly, he isn't worth the time. Let *me* be brutally candid. The Vice President is lifeless, uninspiring, and, to quote a nameless but highly insightful man, weak and unprincipled. He lacks vision of any kind, and every Democrat knows this. But in the end, he is no threat to this country. He would be a guardian of the status quo and nothing more. Rebecca Pierce, with her perverted definition of nationalism, her assault on every civil liberty and Constitutional principle not associated with the right to bear arms, and her blind ignorance and willful antagonism towards the sciences, that is where the mortal danger lies."

Powell rubbed his stubbled jaw. "So, you're going to focus your campaign on Rebecca Pierce?"

"No," responded Walter. "We're going to focus our campaign on an extraordinary proposition that could save millions of lives. One that will resonate with voters across this state and across the political divide."

"I've read that proposition, Professor. Personally, I love it. Others will love it. But it won't change votes. It'll be dismissed as Fool's Gold, offered by a marginal candidate desperate for attention. Sheffield's people will tell anyone who will listen not to waste their vote in the primary chasing unicorns. And weakening the party's nominee in November."

It was another harsh dose of reality and it plunged the room into gloomy silence. The man had the bedside manner of an executioner, but as much as it pained Dan to see his daughter brought back to Earth, these were truths she and Evan needed to hear. They were welded to the virtue of their cause, creating a fairly large blind spot. He hoped after hearing Powell out, the two might chew a bit on the realities of the challenge they faced.

Unlike their candidate. The professor leaned forward, unfazed by Powell's premonitions.

"You read our one-pager on the National Cure Initiative?"

"I did."

"And?"

Powell shrugged. "Like I said, good stuff. You did your homework."

Walter pointed a thumb toward his two students. "No, they did their homework." He leaned back in his chair. "Tell me, Mr. Powell, as the Political Director of the State Party, would you like to see your nominee running on an issue like the Cure Initiative?"

"I would."

"And yet your anointed candidate's representatives here in Las Vegas are out there mocking it and calling it a tax increase in disguise. Just like Connie Bannerman. But here's a thought, Mr. Powell. Instead of those who ridicule and distort an idea you and I agree is not only good policy but good politics, perhaps we would be better served by candidates who embrace it. Candidates who haven't become so smitten with caution and compromise, they've forgotten about the limitless possibilities of what this nation can aspire to."

Powell was quiet for several moments before turning to Megan. "Is this what his classes are like?"

"Every single one."

"Professor, you said the real target here is Rebecca Pierce. I agree. So, why don't we find a way to work together to bury her in this state?"

"Great," Megan said. "But first we need to get Sheffield out of the race."

Powell shook his head, but Dan perceived a hint of amusement in the man. The operative checked the wall clock and rose from his chair.

"I'm out of time. Look, Sheffield has the entire Nevada Democratic establishment behind him. He's got the best strategists, vote counters, and fundraisers, not to mention a building full of hired help back in Richmond. He's got infrastructure here, and infinite resources. What do you have? An appealing personal story, and a lot of gung-ho young people."

Powell saw the reactions to his words and held up his palms. "I don't mean that in a negative sense. At all. On the contrary, I admire all of you. I have a job and responsibilities that go with it, but don't think for a minute there isn't a part of me wanting to sit at this table and plot the greatest upset in American political history."

"Why don't you?"

They all turned to Dan in surprise. Powell eyed him for a moment before turning to Walter again.

"Your only hope over the next month is to beat Sheffield on the ground. I started volunteering for my congressman in San Diego the day I came home from Walter Reed with these peg legs. The man held his seat for more than forty years. He told us all the time; winning elections is about pounding the pavement until you start making some footprints. Maybe ninety percent of the folks who plan on showing up at the primary have already decided to vote for Sheffield. That's a hell of a lot of minds to change in thirty days. Find a way to get your name and story out there, then send out all these kids to do what Megan said. Knock on doors, the right doors, one at a time."

Megan grinned. "Any chance you'll give us the right addresses?"

"You're entitled to them. Every qualified candidate is. Just ask Delia to give you the lists, that'll keep your hands clean. You'll get the address of every registered Democrat, but you'll also be able to see who voted in the 2020 caucuses."

Powell started to leave before turning again. "Who's in charge of your Hispanic outreach?"

His question was met with silence as Megan and Evan exchanged a look. He gave a weary sigh.

"Know your demographics, people. A third of registered Democrats in this state are Hispanic. A third. You better come up with an outreach strategy. Older voters, too. A quarter of Democrats here are over the age of 65. Plus the quarter-million military retirees in the state. And they all vote."

He ambled to the door before stopping one last time.

"Professor, there are lot of people back at the office, and maybe a few in Richmond, hoping I convinced you to back out. I told them, and I'm telling you, that's not my job. The State Party doesn't cheer for the home team or the visitors. We're just the umpire, calling balls and strikes until we have a winner."

Walter rose to shake the man's proffered hand. "I understand, and we're grateful for your time and guidance, Mr. Powell. It was very much appreciated."

They all said their farewells and the door closed behind their visitor.

"Well, that went well," Evan said, slumping again in his chair.

"Did anyone else hear it?"

"Hear what?" Evan asked Walter.

Dan nodded. "I did." He pushed back from the table and hurried from the room.

Evan turned to Megan, who shrugged her own puzzlement. Evan caught the professor's eye again and made a second attempt.

"What did you hear?"

Walter locked his hands behind his head and leaned back, his eyes fixed on the ceiling. "An opening."

· · ·

Powell was nearly to his truck when Dan caught up. The man's artificial appendages certainly didn't seem to slow him. He turned at the approaching footsteps in surprise, perhaps expecting the man's firecracker of a daughter.

"No, I'm not donating to your campaign."

"Good, because they're not taking donations."

"That figures." Powell hesitated. "Dan, right? Megan is a good kid. Got her head screwed on right."

"She says she's learning quite a bit from you."

"I can't get her out of my office. And I wish I had ten more just like her." Powell smiled unexpectedly. "You're a bit different than the usual cast of characters we see on these campaigns."

"Saner?"

"Older."

"They cut me a deal. I drive the future president around, I get to spend more time with my daughter."

"You could take her to a Knights game instead."

"I wish. This is how she wants to spend every spare minute of her life."

"She's got the fever."

"I think of it as a plague."

"What can I do for you, Dan?"

Dan folded his arms. "You came because you had to. Can't play favorites in a primary, but happy to explain rules and process. Like an umpire, you said."

"That's right. Just calling balls and strikes."

"But that's not what you just did."

Powell did not respond, his face impassive.

"Those weren't balls and strikes. You were telling them how to win the game."

"What makes you say that?"

"You told them how and where to mine for votes. You didn't send them to Reno or Pahrump. You told them to hit Democrats, Hispanics, older voters, all here in Vegas. Voters Sheffield needs. At the same time, you told them not to rough the man up. I don't get it."

Powell leaned against the side of the pickup, hooking one arm over the bed.

"Crap," Dan said. "Sorry. You need to sit down?"

"Nah, I'm good."

"Those things titanium?"

"Carbon fiber. The tread is heavy-duty rubber." Powell read the question on Dan's face. "Fallujah, 2004. IED turned our Humvee into scrap metal. I was in the back seat. Got lucky, I guess. Guys up front didn't make it."

He stood up straight. "No armor in our flooring, Dan, thanks to Congress. Penny-pinching bastards."

"Is that why you got into politics?"

"It wasn't about the Humvees, Dan. We never should have been in Iraq in the first place. But Bush and Cheney wanted a victory somewhere, so they could thump their chests to the world. Thousands of our guys paid for that. I paid for that. And I don't want to see anything like that ever happen again. *That's* why I got into politics. And sure as shit Rebecca Pierce will have us fighting in some worthless desert the second she's inaugurated. Probably give herself a fifth star."

"But Becker can't win."

"Of course he can't."

"So why not tell them to close up shop and get behind Sheffield."

"I made that point."

"Barely. Why?"

Powell considered his response as he slipped his hands inside his pockets. "Because if I was Megan's age, I'd ignore me, too."

Dan leaned up against the same truck. "How're they going to do?"

"You don't want to know."

"What's their best-case scenario?"

"Best case? They win Nevada."

Dan frowned. "*Realistic* best case."

"He gives Sheffield a hell of a scare. He could strike a nerve, Dan, and in this business, timing is everything. A thousand things would have to go right for him, but sometimes these things take on a life of their own. See Donald Trump."

"Have you told this to Megan?"

"That girl doesn't need anyone planting those kinds of fantasies in her head."

"Tell me about it. She thinks Walter can win."

Powell gave him a dismissive wave. "That's her heart talking, not her head. Trust me, deep down, she knows better. And a little secret about your daughter. Seven chances out of ten, I'm working for her someday."

Dan let out a long breath. "I know the feeling."

CHAPTER 15

Hello America. I'm Rebecca Pierce, and I'm running to be your next President and Commander in Chief.

It's been a few weeks since we last spoke, and I wanted to share with you some of my recent experiences. I've been traveling all across this great land, and I've had the privilege of visiting with so many extraordinary Americans, just like you. Americans who the corrupt and incompetent Washington insiders forgot about long ago. I met steelworkers in Pennsylvania, textile workers in the Carolinas, dairy farmers in Wisconsin, coal miners in West Virginia, and auto workers in Michigan. These men and women are the backbone of America.

Like you, they are fed up with our so-called leaders in the current Administration. Disgusted with their failed economic policies, and appalled by their shameful, global retreat in the face of foreign adversaries. I want you to know I've also had it with these swindlers, and I'm ready to fight on your behalf. It's time to put these people where they belong – a stockade – and get our country back on track.

I am also so humbled by the support for our campaign continuing to pour in from coast to coast. Make no mistake, panic is gripping Washington right now. Change is coming, and the corrupt and incompetent politicians who have diminished and denigrated this great country know it.

I promise you, as your President, I will never forget you. I will fight for you, each and every day.

But wait, there's more.

We are an incredibly diverse nation, and that diversity is, without question, one of our greatest qualities. But we are also one nation, and we must recognize and celebrate those aspects of our culture that unite us and define us as Americans.

Everyone in this country, no matter their ethnicity, heritage, religion, or creed, wants to be an American. We share common values, common ideals, and a common vision for a strong and prosperous nation. We unite behind our flag and our national anthem. And we should unite behind the common language we share. That is why I want to make English the official language of the United States.

We cannot thrive as a multi-language country. We live in a world where communication is the driver of economic prosperity and cultural harmony. The many immigrants I have spoken to all want to speak English. They want their children and grandchildren to speak English. It is a wish that has been true for generations.

Establishing English as the official language will give us a national identity, ensuring our commerce, our schools, our elections – every meaningful activity sponsored by the government – is conducted in our common language. I have asked one of my former company commanders, West Point graduate and retired Army Captain Roberto Herrera, a native Nicaraguan and a Medal of Honor winner, to spearhead this initiative, should I be elected as your next President.

Finally, I want to report the incredible success of our effort to fund this campaign entirely from small donations. Last month, 826,000 of you contributed $20 or more, sending more than $26 million to our campaign. What an army you've become. And what an incredible message you are sending to Washington and the country. In order to spread our message further, I'm asking each of you to send an additional $20 to jointhefight.com. And this time, I'm also asking you to convince just one family member, friend, or co-worker to match your donation. Together, our army can take back our country, and free us from *the unconscionable corruption and incompetence of the Vance-Sheffield Administration.*

Yes, we can do this, America. We can do this, for America.

Join the fight.

CHAPTER 16

January 25
Twenty-Eight Days to Primary Day

The sprint was on. Four weeks remained to persuade Nevada Democrats to shift their allegiance from a well-entrenched frontrunner to a virtual unknown. One lacking a single day in political office or government service. It would be a Herculean task even for the most battle-hardened campaign veterans, but in Las Vegas, it was left in the hands of two mostly untested youngsters, with little experience and even less margin for error.

They heeded Marc Powell's counsel about connecting with key constituencies, and their early outreach efforts scored several successes. The largest Latino student organization on campus agreed to sponsor a social event with the professor. Two colleagues from the school's Hispanic Studies program joined Walter in a panel discussion at the campus library. Even a cold call to the city's Latin Chamber of Commerce bore a future speaking opportunity one week before Primary Day.

They targeted older voters as well, with an assist from a student's father who was active in the local chapter of Jewish War Veterans. He invited Walter to address their quarterly meeting and provided additional contacts in fraternal organizations to further widen their reach.

Dan cautioned about traveling down that road, arguing veterans were far more likely to gravitate to Sheffield or Pierce, both retired military. But Walter was resolute, convinced the Cure Initiative and its rallying cry to every American would reverberate among former servicemen and women. That was their message today at a VA center in North Las Vegas, where they began an unusually brisk morning by greeting arriving staff and visitors outside the main entrance, handing out graphics-laden flyers detailing Becker's grand vision. Most scurried by, eager to reach their heated offices inside.

The small number of workers and patients who did engage were of mixed views. Some were fervent backers of Pierce, sniffing at the offense of someone who hadn't ever worn the uniform casting aspersions on such an American patriot. Others were more indulgent, graciously accepting the flyers and hearing Walter out. The team eventually moved indoors for the scheduled event Evan had coordinated, expecting a mostly friendly audience for what had been billed as a public forum to discuss the health of the nation's veteran community. It began with a short talk from Walter, mirroring his remarks at the dairy and drawing a connection between the declining health of older veterans and his vision for stamping out the diseases afflicting so many. He then fielded a number of questions; much to even Dan's dismay, not one referenced the Cure Initiative.

Instead, the attendees stood, one after another, to talk politics, and vent about the implications of Walter entering the contest. Many were self-described Democrats and union members, more than bothered by the prospect of Walter drawing even small numbers of votes the Vice President desperately needed. A few didn't mince words, casting Walter as a spoiler, and suggesting his campaign was nothing more than an exercise in vanity. Recognizing the common threads in their remarks, Dan suspected the long arm of the Sheffield campaign at work.

When the event finally ended, Megan and Evan were nearly despondent. As they lumbered to the parking garage, Walter tried to shake the two from their doldrums with a reminder they had long anticipated some degree of pushback from the party faithful. His words were little comfort to Don and Darla Quixote.

Walter quietly pulled Dan aside, insisting the younger duo needed a break. It was hard to disagree. The campaign managers had exhausted themselves for ten straight days, juggling schoolwork, part-time jobs, and the remnants of their social lives. When they reached the Explorer, Walter declared a rare afternoon off the campaign trail, mandating a team lunch at his favorite eatery. Even Dan brightened at the welcome respite, until he learned the destination, confounded for years by the West Coast fascination with *In-N-Out Burger*.

As they finished up their repast, he stared bitterly at the remains of his, knowing the modest two pounds he had recently shaved from his frame would soon re-appear, thanks to the Double-Double roiling in his belly.

He didn't have to be there, of course. As had been the case from the outset, no one was holding him at gunpoint, and he could have easily dropped them all at the restaurant and found an acai bowl somewhere. And yet here he was, by his own choice, food coma and all. No longer a bystander to their plotting, but a witting contributor.

Dan knew in his heart what began as a simple ploy to bond with Megan had evolved now into something else. The campaign had been more alluring that he expected, and from the periphery, it was as if he was watching Megan and the others on a lifeboat, battling the gales and high seas as they tried to stay afloat. The urge to join with them was growing, the intoxication alive again in his bones, a long dormant zeal revived.

Equally affecting was Walter Becker. Even in their limited time together, Dan could see why so many were drawn to the man and the lifeforce he exuded. In every one of their conversations, Dan was struck by the professor's prose, and his ability to verbalize every thought so effortlessly. There was depth there too, his insights perceptive and penetrating, with hidden messages and droplets of wisdom lurking everywhere. He made Dan think, and articulate his own thoughts. And for all his oratory gifts, the professor was also an avid listener, gleaning some life lesson from every anecdote or recollection Dan shared.

Beyond his growing regard for Walter, the campaign itself had progressed further than Dan thought possible, a credit to the abilities and resourcefulness of Evan and Megan. In a matter of days, it was beginning to resemble...a campaign. Evan, in the role of field director, pieced together a daily schedule of events, capped every evening with a review and planning session at the library. Megan and Hope managed the online side of the operation, shaping their messaging, pushing it out digitally, and amplifying it across the social media domain. With the students shouldering so much behind the scenes, it was Dan and Walter who spent the better part of their days together, crisscrossing the Valley from event to event, tacking on an occasional medical appointment or UNLV home game.

It all consumed most of Dan's waking hours, leaving little room for exploring job opportunities, or pursuing anything he once thought might occupy his retirement years. And while he would sooner thrust a fork into his heart than admit it out loud, he knew how much he was enjoying himself. Far more so than in December, when he was eating cereal for dinner and tuning into Rocky marathons like they were the 1969 lunar landing.

He watched Walter push away his tray of half-eaten food and study the two campaign managers, both still wallowing in misery. The resuscitation powers of a milkshake were clearly less potent than the man thought.

"Megan, Evan, if I may, please don't lose heart over this morning. You both did a wonderful job organizing the event. I know some of the waters were a bit rough, but that was to be expected."

"That crowd," groused Megan, "and not a single reporter there. A blessing, maybe, considering all the flak you took."

"They'll come, we just need to stay persistent. I promise you, there will be better coverage."

Evan was equally downcast. "Better? I'll take any."

"We've made it into some stories."

"Not enough. And barely a word about the Cure Initiative. I don't get it. How is that not the lead story in the R-J, let alone on CNN? Don't they care?"

Dan snickered and they all turned to him.

"What?" Megan asked.

"Nothing," he insisted, composing himself again. "Really."

"Come, Mr. Cahill. Share."

Dan wavered for a moment before giving in. "I don't mean to sound harsh, but it's not the lead story because no, the media doesn't care. And no, they aren't taking you seriously."

"They're not, or you're not?" teased Walter. "Let's assume the former. How do we get them to take us seriously?"

"Drop out," he grinned.

Megan looked away, and judging from the silence around the table, he had chosen an inopportune moment for humor.

"Look, you had a nice week. No, you didn't exactly make CNN, but that was a decent showing on campus with the Hispanic students. And even today, you had the chance to shake all kinds of hands and make your case to hundreds of people. You're getting support out there. Maybe not as much as you hoped, but you're winning some votes. And you heard Powell. Sheffield needs every vote he can get. So, use whatever support you've gained, get him to back the Cure Initiative and add it to his own platform."

"Come on, Dad—"

Walter held up a hand. "In exchange for endorsing him?"

"Why not?" Dan saw the protests forming across the table. "This campaign will be over in a month. But it's the Cure Initiative you care about, right? If you had an opportunity to elevate it, and keep it in the national conversation, wouldn't you consider that a win?"

"Suppose we did as you suggest," Walter said. "Suppose Sheffield endorsed it, even adopted the idea as his own. Suppose, even, he was our next President. What are the chances, you believe, he would actually follow through, and bring our plan to fruition?"

Dan was quiet, realizing his misstep.

"Zero," Walter answered for him. Dan nodded in grudging agreement.

Evan was struggling to follow. "Why? He's not my favorite guy, but if he campaigned on it, why wouldn't he see it through? Like you told Powell, it's good policy *and* good politics."

"That's not how Sheffield thinks," Dan explained. "He would see the Initiative as high-risk, high-reward. If it succeeds, he's the hero of the century. If it fails, he's in Herbert Hoover and Donald Trump territory."

"So, it's a gamble for him."

"Right. And Sheffield never gambles. On anything."

Walter turned to Megan, having noticed a change in her demeanor, suddenly brightening as she scrolled through her phone.

"We can't get your father to stop talking, and yet you've been uncharacteristically quiet."

Megan waved her phone. "Has anyone seen what Hope did with those photos the banner crew is taking?"

She flipped the device around.

"She's created an Instagram account for them. BannerDaze. Looks like she started it yesterday, and she's already got 14,000 followers."

Megan clicked on the latest post and they all leaned in. The photograph showed two of their student volunteers, standing on one corner of an intersection and waving at cars as they gripped the ends of a ten-foot banner. The words *A NEW VOICE* were painted in midnight blue against a gold background with *Vote Walter Becker* in smaller letters. The post had more than 8,000 likes in an hour.

Evan shook his head in awe. "How does she do it? I've got 2,500 followers, and that took me six years."

Walter rapped his knuckles on the table. "I have an idea that might make the splash we've been looking for. It's a bit of a Hail Mary. What's this campaign missing so far?"

"A sex scandal!"

They all smiled, though Dan knew Megan's observation was actually quite astute. As a young agent in the Boston Field Office, he was frequently seconded to

John Kerry's local detail for his presidential campaign and had soaked up quite a bit of lore from a few of the veteran campaign operatives. One universal truth: national campaigns, filled with energetic youths and withering emotional stress, were often ground zero for dating escapades.

"I was thinking more along the lines of a debate. Our Republican friends staged one here two months ago. They have another scheduled in Reno two days before the primary. The Democrats haven't had a single one, and I was thinking perhaps we should issue a challenge."

"They haven't had one," Dan pointed out, "because until you jumped in, no one other than that loony Socialist was running against Sheffield."

"Actually," Megan countered, "there's also a Green Party candidate who qualified, and I heard Marc Powell say there's a debate in the works. I think one of the education groups is the sponsor. He says Sheffield will have to be in it."

Evan snapped his fingers. "That's our play, then."

"Actually, I was thinking we should issue the challenge to Rebecca Pierce."

They all regarded Walter.

"We're still in the primary."

Walter turned to Megan. "So?"

"So, why would she debate us? I heard Marc say with her lead here, Pierce may even bail on the Reno debate with Anna Morales, just so she can focus on South Carolina."

Morales was the youthful, plucky governor of New Mexico, and a late entrant in the GOP presidential primary. She had chosen to bypass Iowa and New Hampshire, doubting a Latina could fare well with those demographics, and was instead devoting her time and resources to Nevada and South Carolina and their far more diverse electorates. Her campaign was middling though, attracting nominal support thus far as Rebecca Pierce continued to dominate the national conversation.

"Oh, I have no expectation she'll actually accept. But there may be value even in just issuing the challenge and showing a little moxie. I think there are scores of Democrats growing quite tired of the media, Sheffield, and everyone else tiptoeing around that woman, terrified to contradict a single one of her mindless edicts. I think it's time to show everyone which candidate is willing to stand up to her. So, we stage a debate, whether she shows or not."

Dan opened his mouth, then changed his mind, burned once already in this conversation.

Walter noticed. "Please, Mr. Cahill, you have something to add?"

"I see what you're trying to do. It's just – everyone will know it's a sham. I know what you want people to see, but I think you're just going to reinforce an image of a fringe candidate. If you want to be taken seriously, you can't be pulling stunts like that."

"Dad—"

Walter held up a hand. "No, Megan, it's a fair point. Many will perceive it just as you suggest, Mr. Cahill. But this is an unconventional campaign, lacking the stature or resources necessary to remain competitive if we rely solely on traditional means. This morning was a case in point. So, let me ask you this. Do we have anything to lose?"

Dan held up his hands, painted into a corner once again.

"Mr. Worley, Miss Cahill, your thoughts about challenging Pierce to a debate?"

"Bring it on."

"Let's do it."

"Splendid. We'll need an appropriate setting to issue our challenge, and I think I have an ideal backdrop. It'll require a short trip to Reno."

"Reno?" asked Megan, her head spinning.

"Do you think your friends up there with our banner can meet me? I'll need as large a group of supporters as they can muster."

"I think so," answered Megan. "This is the Hail Mary you were talking about?"

Walter smiled, leaning back in his chair. "No, that would be Syd Milburn."

Syd Milburn? Dan shook off the whiplash. The man could change course in a nanosecond.

"The casino guy?" Evan asked.

Walter unfolded a newspaper clipping from his pocket and placed it on the center of the table.

"Did anyone see the R-J this morning?"

"I did," Megan said, her eyes scanning the headline. "But I didn't see this."

"It was buried in the Entertainment section. The London Towers is having its five-year anniversary celebration this weekend."

"And?"

"And, I think we should be there."

"Why?" asked Megan. "You a fan of the Kardashians?"

There was a response to Megan's glib remark from someone, but Dan hadn't heard it. He picked up the clipping, a feature story filled with effusive words about Milburn's entrepreneurial success and gaudy profits. What did this have to do—

"Jesus," he blurted out, slapping the table. "Did your wife teach you this too?"

Walter smiled. "I came up with this one on my own, Mr. Cahill. I've always been drawn to the lifestyles of the rich and famous."

Dan turned to the others, tapping his index finger on the last paragraph of the article. "The labor unions are picketing the Towers on Saturday."

Megan shrugged. "They've been doing that for years. Milburn won't let his workers unionize."

Evan turned to Walter. "You want to join the picket line?"

"It's more than a picket line this time. The Culinary Workers have a permit to demonstrate, from eight in the morning to four in the afternoon. The County is even marking off space for them on the public sidewalk and the access road leading up to the hotel. The union is hoping to put a damper on Milburn's celebration."

Megan and Evan exchanged pensive looks. Unusual, considering the pair had a habit of reacting to the professor's ideas like he just invented the Internet.

"Why Milburn?"

"Why not Milburn?" Walter responded to Evan. "The vast majority of those workers on the picket line are almost certainly Democrats."

"So is he," Megan pointed out, working her phone screen with both thumbs.

"He's also not just a Democrat," Dan noted. "He's the rock star of Nevada Democrats."

"Who's given a hell of a lot to the community," Megan added. "The rec centers. The hiking trails in Red Rock Canyon. And he's been a huge supporter of the party. He was on Obama's finance committee. I'm pretty sure he's on Sheffield's finance committee."

Evan snapped his fingers again. "He is, and that's the point, isn't it? Sheffield is holding hands with the most anti-labor businessman in Nevada."

"But it's not just Sheffield," Megan argued, studying the dollar figures listed on her screen. "Milburn has been a huge donor to the State Party. Federal races too. Supported just about every Democratic nominee for the House and the Senate. Marc will flip out if we attack his cash cow."

"So, Milburn's political and charitable donations inoculate him from any criticism?" Walter asked. "His workers don't deserve the same labor protections, the same wages and benefits, as other workers on the Strip?"

"I didn't say that. I'm just asking if it makes sense to attack a guy who has done so much for the party. And Nevada."

Walter turned to Dan. "Do you have an opinion of Syd Milburn?"

"Everyone in Vegas has an opinion of Syd Milburn." Dan thought for a moment. "His place was a frequent stop for our protectees. I worked pretty closely with his people; we were familiar with how he operated."

"And?"

Dan exhaled. "I know you don't want to hear this, but everything there was on the up and up. I could care less about the man's politics or political donations, but Megan's right. He's given a boatload of his money to this community, and to the Democratic Party. You take him on, you're pissing off a lot of heavyweights in your own party. And losing a lot of potential voters."

"And gaining plenty of others," crowed Evan. "The union will love it. And if the union gets behind the professor—"

"Who said we're siding with the union?"

The room was quiet again. Even Dan, often a beat faster than the students in deciphering the man's intentions, was lost.

"Blessed are the peacemakers, says the bible verse." Walter smiled as he rubbed his hands. "I'll tell you what. Today is Tuesday. The protest is in four days. Do your homework on the man. And their dispute. Above all else, keep an open mind. *Embrace the unconventional.* Let's meet again tomorrow evening and see where we all stand."

"Uh, one question," said Evan, raising his hand. "Can we go back to the Reno thing?"

CHAPTER 17

January 29
Twenty-Four Days to Primary Day

It was a sun-drenched Saturday morning, and the warm air pouring down from the canopy of blue above was a welcome change from the overcast skies bedeviling the city of late. The architectural lines of the London Towers Resort and Casino painted a spectacular image across the cloudless sky, with the trio of iconic structures rising up from the earth, as if reaching for the heavens. Commemorating the resort's milestone birthday, the upper tiers of each structure had been wrapped with perforated vinyl imprinted with larger-than-life images of celebratory cakes and candles, bursts of fireworks, and even a glamorous young couple strolling through a shower of hundred-dollar bills.

Syd Milburn wasn't relishing any of it from his vantage point, a personal suite on the 44th floor of his signature tower. The 42-year-old folded his arms across his Burberry blazer as he stared hundreds of feet below, at a scene far from festive. The mass of protesters at least had been herded onto a parcel far from the resort's grand entrance.

Not far enough, Syd grumbled to himself.

Through the thick glass, he could hear their faint chants rising from a sea of angry fists punching into the air. He shook his head in grudging due. The labor bosses, led by the venerated Culinary Workers, had called for an all-hands turnout, and their union brothers and sisters had answered in droves.

Syd's attorneys had fought to prevent it in a permit hearing weeks ago, framing the planned demonstration as nothing more than an attempt to embarrass a respected local businessman on his own property. Not only had every objection been soundly rebuffed, the county granted the petitioners a bonanza of allotted space. The designated site encompassed the public sidewalk fronting the sprawling resort as well as one of the access road lanes leading from Las Vegas Boulevard to the valet and taxi drop-off. Police were diverting traffic around the protesters, but it was still morning and arriving cars and taxis were few. That would soon change, creating a bottleneck for visitors, and a migraine for Syd.

He had fought back as best he could, taking his case public and granting rare media interviews to refute the union's usual hyperbole about third-world working conditions and depressed wages. His public relations team distributed quotes and fact sheets, countering every misleading claim with statistics and testimonials, and his workers were openly encouraged to speak to the press about London Towers management and working conditions.

While Syd played the happy warrior in public, cheerfully defending his practices to anyone within hearing range, privately he seethed, incensed at hearing his name sullied by those he had never met, their political agendas championed by the same elected officials Syd bankrolled into office. He punched a fist into his open hand, still livid with the county for its feckless caving at the permit hearing and the unprecedented access granted to his property. A property generating millions for local municipal coffers.

The timing of the protest below was skillfully planned. They were targeting his greatest vulnerabilities: his wallet and ego. Hundreds of thousands of dollars had been invested in the day's festivities, including exorbitant appearance fees and travel expenses of celebrities due to arrive from New York and Los Angeles in just hours. He would have to smuggle them into the resort through less visible access points to avoid confrontations, undercutting the entire purpose of their pricey services. His wallet would survive, but the damage to Syd's reputation, and the portrait of a maniacal tyrant his critics were selling to the public, could not be easily remedied.

An audible sigh escaped Syd's lips. In his 125,000 square foot casino below, games of chance and skill were decided in favor of either the house or the players, making Milburn a winner in either case. But that unyielding mob, with their phony claims and groundless petitions, gnawed away at a man who believed in his own magnanimity. Syd would never shy away from a brawl with anyone who dared to malign his virtue and integrity, but as he looked down on the gathered masses, he faced two competing truths. He would not, *could* not, give in to those people. Yet his appetite for prolonging this food fight without end was rapidly waning.

Unlike his casino, no one was holding a winning hand.

. . .

Two miles away, Dan eased the Explorer into Walter's driveway. A brief downpour had soaked him earlier that morning as he finished the second mile of a pre-dawn run. An immaculate sunrise soon followed, finally giving way to clearing skies. A symbol, perhaps, of the first dividends finally emerging from his determined struggle of late to defy the laws of aging.

He was running daily now – three miles along Charleston Avenue as it rose up to meet the western edge of the valley – while still braving twice-weekly torture sessions at Lifetime Fitness. There were at first the expected protests from muscles and joints pathetically out of shape, but the aches were beginning to subside. Another month, and he might be able to overtake some of the Social Security recipients hobbling around his neighborhood.

With Walter's weekends free from teaching, Evan had pieced together yet another whipsaw Saturday. From the morning demonstration at the London Towers, Dan would ferry the professor to a neighboring MGM property where he could greet arriving casino workers. Then a lunchtime speaking engagement at a local American Legion post, followed by a side trip to campus for some brief filming with Hope. It would have been a grueling slog for anyone, let alone a 76-year-old unused to such a pace.

And now there was an added wrinkle. Walter's personal safety had to be accounted for after the campaign had received its first threats. The caustic emails flowed into the professor's university account two days ago, shortly after he let slip to a Reno-area podcast host that if elected, he would make "mincemeat" of the 2nd Amendment.

Dan parked next to an unfamiliar, pint-sized Chevy Spark and climbed out of his SUV, offering a friendly wave to the Metro cop parked on the curb.

"Bang!"

Startled, Dan whirled around at the sound of the voice. During his peak days on the Detail, his hand would have been a blur as it moved toward his hip, his palm instantly slapping around the butt of a holstered Sig Sauer. But that was an eternity ago, and with his only sidearm locked up in a bedroom closet, and his feet frozen to the cement, the former agent could only stare in disbelief at the source of the voice.

"Jumpin' Junipers, Dan, my three-year-old grandson could get the drop on you."

The twang was familiar. As was the tone of disapproval. Her face, however, was as inscrutable as ever.

The ageless Barb Patterson was as arresting as when Dan last saw her so many years ago. Still trim in figure, her back was ramrod straight and anchored a pair of perfectly squared shoulders. A thin, belted black leather coat was wrapped around her waist, and designer jeans and heeled shoes completed the outfit. Her hair was still jet black, pulled back in a braid, without a single strand either graying or out of formation. Cosmetics continued to remain mostly foreign to her complexion.

He mumbled something unintelligible.

"Speak English, bucko. And don't get all misty-eyed on me. Tony Jarrett said some sawed-off loonies were coming after your principal. Said you might need a hand."

"I don't," Dan managed, finding his voice. "The locals are on it."

Barb grunted. "You mean the kid in the front seat of that cruiser chugging his Frappuccino with his eyes glued to his phone? Don't snap my garters, Danny Boy."

He felt the burn on the back of his neck, her words stinging him now as much as they did so many years ago. She may as well have been wagging a finger in his face.

"That kid had half a dozen deployments with Army special forces before they found a heart murmur. He's a ringer and a dead shot, and I asked for him every time we had a foreign dignitary in town."

"Think he could outdraw a 62-year-old grandmother who once KO'd a 250-pound Russian goon?"

This time, Dan couldn't hold back the smile. That was a true story.

"I didn't think so." Her face softened for an instant. "How are you, Dan?"

"I'm okay. What about you? All sorts of rumors about what you've been doing the last ten years."

"Oh? Like what?"

"Best one was you were running a detail for Christian Bale."

"Fiction. You know the rule, Dan. You can't protect someone you've slept with."

He couldn't help the laugh. Her face remained stoic, but there was light in her eyes now.

"So, to answer my question—"

"To answer your question, Metro PD is—"

And just like that, the light flickered away.

"What about this car, Dan? Do you even have a V6 in there? Looks like it has the acceleration of a school bus. And you left it overnight in your unsecured garage. Did you happen to notice the small box I slipped into your back seat last night? Since you're now sweating like a whore in church, I know you didn't."

Shit. Dan quietly fumed. Her presence had awakened a swirl of memories and emotions. Somehow, inexplicably, it warmed him to see her again, but he could also feel resentment bubbling to the surface. He wasn't some impertinent young agent anymore, obliged to listen to her incessant barking. Still, his insides were churning and he knew why. She was right.

The professor, of course, would have been indifferent about it all. He'd been dismissive about the threats, refusing to consider any precautionary measures other than having a marked cruiser parked outside his home. Dan hadn't pushed back, a clear mistake. He could have been more assertive, reminding Walter of the special breed of gun-toting extremists dwelling in Southern Nevada, and what they were capable of.

There was judgment on Barb's face, and the spite within Dan surged forward again. This was the woman who aided and abetted the spoiling of his career.

"Are you just here to bust my balls? Tossing me off the Detail wasn't enough?"

If he expected a denial, or even an ounce of contrition, it would not come from the likes of Barb Patterson. Instead, she grinned, an act Dan once thought might cause her face to crack.

"Consider it a job application. Am I hired?"

"Hired for what?"

"The professor's security. Come on, I can be the driver."

"I'm the driver," Dan shot back, mortified to hear his own voice staking out the least coveted turf in the history of executive protection.

"Then I'll take the house. I can sack out on the man's sofa at night. I hate hotels."

Dan chewed his lip.

"Why are you pretending to mull this over, Dan? You know he needs me."

"What do you get out of this?"

Barb snickered. "Besides the mountain of cash and public adulation? Not much. Maybe I'm just a bored divorcee, looking for a little post-menopause adventure."

He glanced at her hip. "You carrying?"

"You seriously asking that? Buddy boy, I'm from West Texas. If you're not carrying, you're not breathing."

Dan sighed. "Come on. I'll introduce you. He's a little cranky in the morning."

"Oh, I like him already."

The professor was not only awake and dressed, he had been preparing for the day, watching clips of Syd Milburn on YouTube and browsing old press accounts of the casino owner's feud with local labor leaders.

Walter greeted Barb with his usual affability, his charm all but lost on the crusty former agent. She gave the professor a handshake that nearly wrenched his arm off as her eyes explored the house, taking inventory of entry points and other potential vulnerabilities.

She eventually returned her scrutiny to the professor, leveling her trademark glare at him.

"Three rules, Professor. First, you don't step outside this house without Dan or I in tow. For the next twenty-four days, the only privacy you'll have is under this roof. You want to go for one of your morning constitutionals, that black and white outside will be right behind you."

"Even in my own neigh—"

"Second, dial down the rhetoric on the 2nd Amendment. You're not going to win any more votes by tweaking noses, and all you're doing is squattin' on your spurs while making our jobs ten times dicier."

Walter turned to Dan. "I'm getting the sense I'm not in charge anymore."

"You should hear her do all this in German."

Barb, as usual, had icicles in her eyes, but Dan was sure he saw a trace of a smile.

"Don't listen to this man, Walt, he'd argue with a wooden Indian."

Walter nodded his concurrence. "Third?"

"Third, I want a new coffeemaker."

"A cof—"

"I see what's on the counter over there. What is that, a 1984 edition of Mr. Coffee? Not going to cut it, Professor. I'm going to need some quality Joe here, and don't expect Dan to splurge. He'll squeeze a nickel 'till the buffalo screams. Capiche?"

"Capiche."

"Now why don't you boys shoo out and scrounge up some votes? I'm going to check these Ikea windows and make sure—"

"I did that already," Dan injected.

"And *make sure* it was done correctly."

Barb moved to the stairs and the two men fled the house, with Dan conspicuously checking the back seat and rear compartment of the Explorer. They began the short drive to the Strip, quickly becoming ensnared in construction-slowed traffic on East Tropicana.

Walter fiddled with the radio, finding a familiar station. "Ah," he said, sitting back as his finger flew through the air like a conductor's baton.

"My old man liked jazz too."

"There's jazz, Mr. Cahill, and then there's Coltrane. Your father was in the Secret Service as well, right?"

"Yep. He was on Jimmy Carter's detail, then Reagan. Ran the Washington Field Office after that. He died when Megs was in grade school. Lung cancer."

"Are you a chip off the old block?"

Dan chuckled. "Not quite. Barb would say the apple fell off the tree and rolled a few miles away."

"And your mother?"

"Passed away about ten years before Dad. What about you? Any kids?"

"No, children were never in the cards for Hannah and me. But young people were always part of our lives and careers."

Dan switched lanes as the traffic began to thin.

"Your friend, Ms. Patterson—"

"She's not my friend."

"You're not friends?"

"I don't have friends."

"Well, whoever she is, Ms. Patterson seems quite...efficient."

"That's one word." After a moment, Dan nodded in concession. "You have no idea."

"Did you work with her?"

"I worked *for* her."

"Really, on the President's security team?"

"The Detail, we call it. And before that. We were at the Winter Olympics together."

"You two were Olympians?"

That made Dan laugh again. "Not exactly. We were working the Salt Lake City games in 2002. The Service was in charge of security out there. Sporting events weren't normally our responsibility, but the Olympics were a completely different beast. And it was just a few months after 9/11, so everyone was prepping for the next attack from al-Qaeda."

"Trying times for us all."

Dan's eyes were on the freeway, but his thoughts drifted back more than two decades.

"You must have been quite young."

Another nod from Dan. "I was a shiny new agent, barely a year on the job. Working out of the Boston Field Office, but anyone with a pulse was sent to Utah. Hell, we were drafting border patrol agents and forest rangers to help us out. We had something like nine hundred square miles to cover, from Salt Lake to Provo."

He tapped the brakes as some maniac rocketed past on a motorcycle. Dan was consciously aware of the traffic. He could sense the weight of his foot on the pedals, and his gentle grip on the wheel. Yet the memories from two decades ago were coming alive in his mind. The white-capped mountain range and glacial temperatures. The falling snow on the back of his neck. The black, moonless evenings when visibility measured in mere inches.

"I was posted up in Park City, where they had most of the ski and snowboarding events. They had me working midnights, standing post on the back side of a mountain. It felt like the other side of civilization, but someone had to watch the back door. As the FNG, I had—"

"FNG?"

"Fucking new guy. Sorry."

It was Walter's turn to laugh. "As the FNG..."

"I drew one of the short straws. Had to cover a patch more than a mile wide on my own, all night long. They had built little huts for us, hot boxes we called them, about the size of a phone booth. I had a radio, a flashlight, my weapon, and a shovel to dig myself out in the morning. It snowed every night, and I practically froze solid my first night out. Sometimes, at some crazy hour, we had to wander out, by ourselves, into the wilderness. You could barely see your hand in front of your face. All because some furry beast was tripping our sensors."

He paused, feeling a stab of hurt he had not felt in so long. It had been years since he had spoken of it.

"My third straight night in the box, around four in the morning, I had a visitor, too early to be my relief. It was Barb. She was one of the chiefs in our protective ops division back then. Pretty much running the entire show out in Utah. She was a big wheel in the Service, kind of a legend, and here she was, at the door of my crappy little hut in the Arctic Circle, miles away from her command post. She handed me a thermos of coffee and gave me the news."

"What news?"

"We lost a baby. Michelle had a miscarriage. She wasn't due for another two months."

He could still see Barb standing before him, as taciturn as ever, as she delivered the blow.

"Michelle had sent word to headquarters, which sent word to the command post, and voila, here's the lady in charge of just about everything, tramping through a blizzard to tell me in person."

"Sounds like a pretty good boss," Walter said quietly.

Dan turned onto Las Vegas Boulevard and immediately moved into the exit lane for W. London Way.

"Wait for the kicker. Barb, she orders me to hoof it back to base camp and call my wife. I told her I couldn't abandon my post, and she tells me she'll cover for the next two hours until my relief comes. I was floored. This woman was responsible for the entire fucking Olympics. She should have been in a Holiday Inn somewhere sipping hot chocolate, making sure 8,000 Olympians live another night. But there she was, at four in the morning, relieving a rookie agent, so he could call his wife."

"And she was your supervisor when you were protecting the President?"

"Yep, a few years later."

"You must have enjoyed serving under her."

"I did. Until she had me exiled out here."

Walter turned to him in surprise, and Dan fell silent for several moments, his eyes on the traffic signal they had stopped at.

"Long story. Not her fault. I did enjoy serving under her. She was the best. What she did for me in Utah, she would have done that for any of her people. And she wasn't alone. I always took it for granted, but now that I'm on the outside...Don't get me wrong, we had our share of blockheads. But all in all, man, it was a hell of an organization."

"So why did you leave? Megan tells me you were close to retirement."

Dan finished the turn from the Strip and gunned the Explorer up the access road.

"Saved by the bell. We can hold that story for another time."

Walter pointed to the digital clock above the radio. "Speaking of time, how do you do that?"

It was two minutes before ten, and Dan gave a proud grin as he slowed the Explorer, passing what seemed like hundreds of sign-waving protesters along the access road. There were several parked buses as well, disembarking passengers and adding to the growing flocks. Dan edged past it all and entered the self-park garage, where Megan stood near the gate.

He smiled. Progress.

It would be just the three of them today, with Evan back on campus canvassing for more volunteers. They left the Explorer and followed Megan through a labyrinth of trimmed hedges, lush gardens, and sparkling fountains, eventually emerging near the grand entrance. The chants grew louder as they neared the protest site, and Dan caught sight of a podium and microphone. Megan pointed to a silver-haired lady scribbling on a clipboard.

"Is that the gal in charge?"

Megan turned to him in horror. "Did you just call her a *gal?*"

Dan's smile evaporated as he saw how mortified his daughter was.

"What?"

"Dad, you can't call women *gals.*"

"Come on, Megs, I didn't mean—"

Megan cut him off. "Please don't do it again, especially in front of her. She has a name."

Dan bit his tongue, wondering exactly how many women were going to chew him out today.

Her name was Claire Levin, and she offered Walter a warm greeting. The longtime Secretary-Treasurer of Culinary Workers Union, Local 226, was in her early sixties, a rotund woman with a face full of vitality and intelligence. Walter made the introductions to the two Cahills, but his words could barely be heard above those of the speaker at the podium, the man's voice amplified by a pair of 4,000-watt speakers. As Walter and Claire shouted in each other's ears, Dan scanned the crowd. It was impressive, both in numbers and energy, but he had seen such rallies before, and knew what was missing.

Claire followed his eyes. "Quite a showing, eh?"

"Yeah," Dan admitted, matching her raised voice. "But why no media? You've got a huge turnout."

The labor leader stepped on her tip toes to reach Dan's ear. "We've been here on Milburn's doorstep, in one form or another, for years. The media doesn't exactly consider our protests breaking news. But fear not. Miley Cyrus is arriving for a pool party at 1:30. The cameras will be here for that, I assure you."

"Can I ask you a question?" Megan asked.

"Sure."

"Years? No offense, but you don't seem to be hurting his business very much. So, what's the point?"

Claire and Walter shared a smile. She signaled them to follow her several feet away, behind one of the amplifiers, where it was blessedly quieter.

"These things just take time, that's all. I was a cashier at the old Frontier when we first tried to unionize there. Took us six years to get our bargaining rights. A quarter century later, we took on the foreign bankers who owned the Cosmopolitan, and when they sold, the new owners came straight to the negotiating table. We got family health insurance with no premiums, retirement contributions, and higher wages for every worker. Not everyone is so enlightened, and there's always holdouts. It just takes vigilance, and patience. But I promise you, this dam will eventually break."

Claire shifted her attention to Walter, and there was sudden strain in her voice. "Walt, I didn't want to get into this over email, but you know we're backing Sheffield. I don't like he has ties to Milburn, but so did Obama. And in the Senate, he voted with us every time. From a right to work state, to boot. If we don't support him, we'll lose all kinds of credibility on the Hill and with the party."

"I understand, Claire. I know what kind of position you're in."

"I'm not sure you do. I appreciate why you're here, but I hope you're not planning on using our cause as an opportunity to take a swing at the Vice President. This demonstration isn't about presidential politics, and if it becomes tethered to the election, we lose all kinds of leverage. If you're goal here is to pull votes from Sheffield, I can't let you up there. We've formally endorsed him, and we'll be working hard to elect him President in November."

"Claire, I promise you, I'm not here to promote my candidacy, or fire any volleys at the Vice President. I'm here to speak for 2,500 disadvantaged workers who have no bargaining power. I promise, no attacks."

"Okay then," Claire smiled, signaling to the young man managing the podium. "You're next. I've asked everyone to limit their remarks to five minutes."

They waited while the current speaker finished, pounding the lectern to accentuate each point as he whipped the crowd into a near frenzy. When he stepped down from the makeshift stage, Claire took to the microphone and gave a welcoming introduction to the man she described as an old friend and fellow warrior for working families. She and Walter shared a peck on the cheek, and once the ovation waned, Walter leaned into the microphone.

"Thank you, Claire, for that hearty welcome. I am so pleased to be here with you this morning. I have so much admiration for all of you, and those who came before you, who fought for basic fairness and to make sure your members had adequate compensation and benefits so vital to the well-being of working families. And I want to thank every one of you for your devotion to this crucial fight for the common good."

More applause rose from the crowd, but Walter did not wait.

"Like most Las Vegans, I have been aware of the quarrel between Syd Milburn and the unions for years now. There is, sadly, no end in sight. Your side and his side seem intractable. I've heard Mr. Milburn claim his wages and benefits are competitive with other properties on the Strip, including those with unionized workers."

A smattering of boos could be heard but Walter continued on, his voice rising above the din.

"I have also heard his claim that allowing his workers to organize would cause him irreparable financial harm and hinder his ability to invest and expand his operations. An expansion that would create new jobs and enhance the pay and benefits for his current workers. I confess. I have never owned my own business, nor have I ever had to manage a workforce. So, I'm certainly not one to judge whether Mr. Milburn's claims are credible or not. But given his indisputable success in the hotel industry and knowing the extent of his philanthropy in our community, perhaps Mr. Milburn has earned the benefit of the doubt."

The crowd fell silent. There were a few nervous laughs, some thinking Walter might have resorted to sarcasm and humor. Dan regarded Claire, and there was no misunderstanding there. Her face was like stone, with rage in her eyes as Walter pressed ahead. Megan stood on her tiptoes, holding her phone high as she recorded every syllable.

"On the other side, I have known Claire Levin for more than thirty years, and I can say with absolute certainty her claims *are* credible. The workers at this property receive less compensation and fewer benefits than workers at comparable properties. That is an irrefutable fact. And without the ability to collectively bargain, they will fall behind in the future. If we have an economic downturn, their standard of living will further erode. That is the risk these workers must live with every day.

"So, where does that leave us? With two opposing sides, unbendable in their convictions, both drawing lines in the sand. Caught in the middle is all of you, and the workers and families you are fighting for. Thousands of people in this community. My fear is the inability of the two sides to communicate and compromise will leave these issues unresolved forever. And that is unacceptable.

"We need to find common ground. And right now. So, I say to Claire and Mr. Milburn, you are each mired in paralysis, unable to bridge the issues dividing you and impacting those you serve. I would like to show the warring political factions in Washington that we in Nevada can do better. That you can show them the way. So, Mr. Milburn, we've tried your approach of denial and avoidance. Claire, we've tried your approach of protest and picketing. All to no avail. So, what do you say we try something different? I am inviting these two to join with me, just the three of us, on neutral ground, for some conversation. No cameras, and no lawyers or staff. I'll be there to moderate, to guide the discussion, and help identify common ground. And maybe keep the two of you from strangling each other. And if the two principals want me to leave, I'll leave. But let us see, after more than five years of intransigence, if we can solve this problem in one afternoon."

"Claire, what do you say?"

CHAPTER 18

February 3

Nineteen Days to Primary Day

"I've said it over and over again. I'm willing to sit down and talk in good faith. I'm not willing to be lectured by someone who has never created a single job or had to meet a payroll, let alone—"

"And we're not willing to turn a blind eye to you treating your workers like second-class citizens, just so you can see your name on the Forbes billionaires list."

Dan rubbed his eyes with his fingertips, tempted to gouge them out. The bickering was chipping away at his sanity, as the pair hurled contempt-filled daggers across the table with little regard for decorum, or even complete sentences. With neither side conceding an inch, the trench warfare was sure to continue without end.

Five days had passed since Walter floated the idea of a parley. Both sides accepted, but only after the local press – namely, an obscure metro reporter named Stu Valentine – badgered Syd and Claire for official responses to Walter's public challenge. Neither could refuse, each unwilling to chance a public backlash for rejecting a civil discussion. But neither also considered it a serious venture.

When Dan and Walter pulled into the library parking lot earlier that morning, they were surprised to find Syd already there. The casino owner was patiently leaning against his SUV, clutching a gas station coffee while reading a folded edition of the *Review-Journal*. So much for Dan's preconceptions. The man was punctual, had sourced the best coffee in town, and judging from the lack of any staff or entourage in sight, was unpretentious. His vintage Land Rover, coated in desert dust, appeared even more ancient than Dan's early model Explorer.

Syd and Walter introduced themselves, with the casino operator giving Dan a wary once-over. He held the newspaper up.

"You see these results from last night, Professor? Looks like you might have an opening."

"I've been arguing for more citizen participation in the civic process my entire career, Mr. Milburn. It's difficult to delight in such dismal numbers."

And dismal they were. Less than 140,000 Iowans had shown up to vote in that state's Democratic caucuses, where the Vice President was the only Democrat on the ballot. More than a quarter million Republicans caucused for the GOP, and with Anna Morales conceding the state, Rebecca Pierce too was essentially unopposed. The disparity in enthusiasm between the Pierce and Sheffield camps was glaring, and yet another troubling omen for the Democratic frontrunner.

Milburn tucked the paper under his arm. "No argument there. Sure hope someone lights a fire under our guy, or it could be a long four years."

Dan was surprised by the man's affability. His mussed hair, weathered face, and sapphire eyes evoked a middle-aged Robert Redford. As tall as Dan, his skin had an earthy shade and when the two shook hands, his callused grip was strong and confident. He wore jeans, rawhide boots and a flannel shirt; a proper rig, he explained, for tending to his acreage in Southern Utah, where he planned to escape for a few days of serenity following the cage match he was anticipating ahead.

It started with surprising civility. They were seated in the familiar conference room when Claire pushed open the door with her hip, balancing a tray of coffees in one hand and a box of donuts in the other.

"I can see you haven't been to many of these," she remarked to Syd, who quickly stood to reach for the tray. "It's tradition for the future winners to bring the future losers breakfast."

The multi-millionaire examined the box of donuts. "Arsenic or anthrax?"

Even Claire smiled appreciatively.

"My husband wanted to invite you over to Lasagna Night. I went with the donuts." She gestured to Dan with a frown. "I thought it was just the three of us. Our counsel is livid I'm doing this without her."

"Mr. Cahill has to drive me to a senior center in Henderson when we're finished here. I didn't want him to have to wait in the car."

"I promise I won't say a word."

"He won't," assured Walter, "but I have found him to be a keen observer."

The two sides grudgingly consented, but that was fifteen excruciating minutes ago, and the last point of agreement in the room. It took seconds for the first jabs to be thrown, followed by occasional uppercuts, including the last one against a now-heated Syd, the blow clearly hitting home.

"Second-class?" He gave his foe a hard glare. "You don't know a damn thing about the relationship between me and my people."

"We've spoken to plenty of your people, Syd. And trust me, they're not as infatuated with you as you think."

Syd crossed his arms. His biceps pushed against his shirt sleeves as he sucked in a deep breath and exhaled, willing his temper to remain even.

"Look, Claire," he started, more calmly than he felt, "I know the history of the labor movement in this country, and I'm grateful for it. Child labor laws, safe working conditions, worker benefits. I know how much of it we take for granted. Do I think there's a place for unions today? You bet I do, where they're needed. But not at the Towers. We have a good thing going."

"A good thing? A housekeeper at the Towers earns $2.10 less per hour than a housekeeper at the Bellagio. That's $80 a week, Syd, and more than $300 a month. Real money for these people. It's not the difference between a Toyota and a Lexus. It's food on the table, bills, childcare. The Towers had net operating income of more than $700 million last year. Are you going to tell me you can't afford to offer another two bucks an hour, so your people can be on a level field with workers at MGM and Caesars?"

Syd bristled at the mention of the two corporate beasts. Other than the London Towers, the Venetian, and a few other holdouts, nearly every resort on the Strip flew under those two banners. They were ruthless competitors who didn't take kindly to upstarts, as Syd knew from their past efforts to smother the Towers in its infancy.

"You think I'm putting that money in my pocket? I need that revenue to expand, Claire. I've spent months trying to acquire decent land in North Las Vegas to build a sister property. That's potentially 3,000 new jobs, in a marginal part of the Valley. Jobs with good pay and generous benefits. And more revenue for the state, which goes toward education, social services—"

"Oh, yes," Claire interrupted, her voice laced with mockery. "You're doing it for the children."

"I won't be doing anything for anyone if my labor costs preclude any capital investments. Employment at my place is voluntary, Claire, and if there are better paying jobs on the Strip, my people are free to leave any time they wish. But no one leaves. No one. We've been named one of the *100 Best Companies in America* for three straight years. I've got twenty applications for every service position opening up. We take care of our workers, every one of them."

Claire scoffed. "Except when it comes to wages and health care. Other than that, how was the play, Mrs. Lincoln?"

"Our wages and benefits are competitive. And I need every nickel I can scrape together to expand. I'm trying to create thousands of good new jobs—"

"Enough with the self-adulation, Syd. It's hard to take such altruistic claims seriously from a man who would low-ball wage employees while paying a Food & Beverage Director half a million dollars. She's quite the looker, by the way."

Syd balled his fists. A local gossip columnist had somehow acquired the confidential salary information months ago and spiced up the story even more by hinting of a relationship between the executive and the famously unattached owner.

"Unbelievable," sputtered Syd. "Even for you, Claire. I pay Annette that much because her side of the house is a third of my revenues, and she's the best in the city."

Syd turned to Walter. "You understand I'm not exactly dealing with Mother Teresa here, right? We had a concert we booked last fall with Tina Tiggs and the Chase Brothers headlining. A fundraiser for the Boys & Girls Clubs. We sold out the venue – 22,000 tickets – and raised more than $3 million from pre-sales and sponsorships. But Claire's union friends in Washington did a smear campaign against us, told everyone it was tainted money. Leaned on their allies in the music industry, and every act backed out a week before the concert."

"Some people have principles, Syd. Maybe they didn't want to be a part of your phony PR campaign to make it look like you give a damn about those kids. Or maybe—"

Her words were cut short as Syd abruptly rose from his chair, back kicking the folding metal chair. It crashed noisily against the wall, and the sudden violence of the act caused Dan to spring from his own seat. Syd turned from them and faced the wall, shielding the fury in his eyes. Eyes that were distant now, in another place and time.

Alton Sydney Milburn was born into an affluent real estate family, his only aspiration to follow his father's path to the high-wire world of finance. Jack Milburn was a self-made man who spent a lifetime acquiring a wide collection of apartment buildings, parking garages, and high-rise condominiums across the greater Phoenix area. As a child, young Sydney worshipped his father, awestruck by the power he wielded and respect he commanded from others. Syd desperately wanted to become what his father was. A force, with a fortune built from his own initiative and ingenuity.

It would not come easy. Syd struggled with his studies, hampered by the dyslexia he begged his parents to keep secret. At the time, Syd told himself it was to avoid perceptions of weakness, knowing how much his father had prospered by projecting strength, real or illusionary, in every negotiation. Looking back, Syd could now admit that was only partly true. Like any adolescent, it was the teasing and ridicule he dreaded more than anything.

He left college after a single semester but still managed to obtain a commercial real estate license, using it to claw his way up the ladder of one of the largest brokerages in Phoenix. Taken under the wing of a senior associate and working assiduously six days a week, Syd became a skilled market analyst with a nose for hidden commercial gems floundering under stifling regulations and liens. He took out a loan to open his own brokerage, and within months, he was signing multi-million-dollar deals for industrial centers and retail spaces. His meteoric rise landed him on the glossy cover of the industry's leading trade publication, and he was flying high. Too high. When financial institutions began collapsing without warning, and the local market tanked, the world came crashing down around Syd, who found himself overextended, overleveraged, and forced into bankruptcy.

He was hardly cowed, and with less than a thousand dollars to his name, Syd moved to Las Vegas, taking refuge in a dilapidated motel charging by the week. He swallowed his pride and borrowed money from his parents, shifting trades to buy a struggling brew pub half a mile off the Strip. He was a tireless promoter with a burning determination to amass another fortune, and Syd squirreled every nickel away, a grander vision in sight. He paid off the note from his parents and opened a second pub off Fremont Street, a former pawn shop he filled with go-go dancers and – courtesy of his newly minted gaming license – slot machines. Syd was soon swimming in cash again, with enough capital to invest in a startup providing off-road Jeep rides in the desert to cash-laden tourists and thrill-seekers. His revenues soared after cutting a deal with a major airline to distribute coupons to inbound passengers, and on his 35th birthday, he sold the business for some $4 million. He then unloaded the two pubs, thickening his bankroll even more.

Backed by a trio of venture capitalists, Syd acquired the long vacant Emerald Casino, gutting the main gaming floor of the aging downtown property and adding hundreds of refurbished rooms and luxury suites. The renamed Cowboy

Inn Resort and Casino opened with much fanfare, partnering with Lyft to shuttle in local seniors and fete them with the usual freebies and red-carpet enticements. Less than three years later, the Cowboy Inn was generating annual revenue in excess of $100 million. He brought in more investors, and plowed every available cent from the property into his next venture, the purchase of an empty lot on prized Strip real estate where a onetime Vegas landmark, a relic of the Rat Pack era, once stood. The ink on the contracts was barely dry when Syd broke ground on what would become his crowning achievement, the $1.7 billion London Towers.

Besides the 5,500 rooms luxury rooms, the resort was home to the largest casino in the Valley, a sprawling events center hosting the most prolific musical acts on tour, and an array of fine dining establishments fronted by the world's most renowned chefs. It soon became a magnet for those with money to burn, drawing film and television stars, recording artists, and the occasional Saudi prince.

Syd had reached the pinnacle of his entrepreneurial ambitions. With his lofty success came the necessary evil intertwined with gambling since the first slot machine opened in Vegas a century ago. Politics. To the dismay of his competitors, Syd was a quick study with natural instincts. He mastered the art of political patronage while cultivating an image of a titan with a conscience, donating generously to local charities and forging a well-publicized partnership with the Boys and Girls Clubs of Southern Nevada.

It may have started as image building, but Syd took his community activism to heart. He presided over the construction of a network of recreation centers across the city for at-risk youths and established a foundation for preservation efforts at state parks across the Silver State. He contributed millions for a dazzling new facility to house UNLV's esteemed hospitality college. In a short time, Syd became a man of considerable prestige, and there were whispers of a possible mayoral campaign if the Goodman family ever decided to step aside.

Syd's passion, however, extended far beyond municipal government. He busied himself directing political dollars to left-leaning organizations and Democratic candidates, more of the Milburn lineage at work. This time it came from Syd's mother, Francine, who was a finance chair for Bill Clinton and a fiery activist for women's causes. Syd followed suit, becoming a patron and sought-after invite to big-dollar fundraising events, where he hobnobbed with Senators, Governors, former Presidents, and sometimes the big man himself.

There was, however, just one glaring incongruity between his progressive political views and his business practices. Since the day the Towers opened, Syd firmly refused to allow his workers to unionize. It was a stance that was anathema to his party, and it put him in the company of rogues like the operators of the non-unionized Venetian Resort, universally loathed by Nevada Democrats.

Syd's obstinacy on that single issue drew the expected ire of the most aggressive political force in the state. Though their national influence had diminished over the decades, organized labor was still a kingmaker and king slayer in Nevada. The resorts were filled with thousands of housekeepers, casino workers, bar and restaurant staff, and other low and mid-wage employees. Led by the Culinary Workers Union, labor in Nevada had long proven a mighty voting bloc, even fighting to allow caucus events on resort grounds and organizing fleets of buses to transport workers to polling places.

Many bent to their will. But not Syd Milburn, peeved by the notion of outsiders dictating to him the terms of everything he had built on his own. He considered himself a generous and conscientious employer, providing benefits and wages that were more than fair. His people were family, and Claire's stinging accusation was a blow to both his heart and pride.

His chest still pounding, Syd willed himself to control his voice, but the words still came out through a clenched jaw.

"Maybe you should ask the Boys & Girls Clubs what they believe. And what they hoped to do with that money. That kind of BS is why I won't cave to you people. And why organized labor is dying. You had something once, Claire, but your membership rolls are dwindling every year. Why? Because business and industry has changed. This isn't the 1920s anymore. It's all far from perfect, I know, but picking fights with the good guys isn't going to help your cause."

"Business and industry changed because of us. You think it was their humanity? Better angels at work? Demean organized labor all you want, Syd, but we've got 60,000 members here, in a right to work state. Our health plan – which you won't let your employees join – covers 130,000 men, women, and children in Nevada. Comprehensive coverage our members don't pay a single penny for in premiums. Do you see your competitors suffering? Putting their expansion and investment plans on hold? And I've got news for you, Syd. Those picket lines aren't going anywhere. For six years, five hundred of us picketed the Frontier. We kept that picket line going twenty-four hours a day, seven days a week, and not a single striker ever crossed it. When it was over, all five hundred went back to their jobs. With better wages, and better benefits."

"And where is the Frontier today, Claire? Gone, in a pile of dust and rubble, with those five hundred jobs. You want my workers to join a union, so they can receive a higher wage? How much are you going to charge them for that privilege? How much are your monthly dues?"

Claire shifted in her seat. "Our dues are voluntary."

"$40? $50? Let's say forty bucks a month. I've got 400 housekeepers on my staff. That's more than $16,000 a month they alone would be paying in dues. Every single month. Nearly $200,000 of their money each year, right into your coffers. That's real money, Claire, out of their pockets. Money that could be used to put food on the table, pay bills—"

Claire's face tightened. "Your workers would consider that a bargain in return for free health care and real retirement—"

"Then why don't you ask our workers—"

"Because you won't let us—"

"Enough!" roared Dan, slapping the table with his palm, the sharp noise ringing across the small room. Heads turned outside the glass wall, and inside, the room fell silent. Even as the two blood enemies glowered at each other, they both seemed grateful for the break, perhaps secretly tiring of the circular arguments splitting labor and management since the beginning of time.

It was Walter who spoke next. "Thank you, Mr. Cahill, on behalf of all mankind. That exchange was curling my toes. Mr. Milburn, will you re-join us?"

The professor waited for Syd to take his seat again. "Speaking as a neutral party, it seems to me the central issue here, the one each of you refuses to budge on, is whether workers at the Towers will have the right to form a union and bargain collectively. Let us for a moment take that issue off the table."

"Off the table?" Claire cried. "Are you serious? You're going to side with—"

"One minute, Claire." Walter turned to Syd. "Would you consider doing more for your workers if Claire promised to end the picket lines?"

"I'm not promi—"

"Claire, please!" The words were pointed, surprising Dan.

"Mr. Milburn?"

Syd looked wary. "Like what?"

"Let's start with a wage increase. Something meaningful, and closer to what your competitors offer. But won't jeopardize your acquisition efforts, or move you closer to the red."

"Every nickel Claire bleeds out of us will move me closer to the red."

"Oh, come now, Mr. Milburn. You can absorb some losses in the short-term. If you can write a personal check for millions of dollars to the Boys & Girls Club to cover the losses from a single canceled concert, you can find enough spare change between your sofa cushions to give each of your workers a two dollar raise."

"How did you—"

"You did that?" Dan asked, surprised. "A personal check?"

Syd eyed the professor. "We're going to have a little talk later about how you get your information. That's not for public consumption." He rubbed the back of his neck as he considered what Walter proposed. "A one-time, one dollar raise, and the picket lines go away?"

"I think $2.10 would be more appropriate."

"I'm not making that deal," Claire exclaimed. "This is Fantasy Land."

"And health care," Walter declared. "100%."

Syd laughed.

"What do you offer now, Mr. Milburn?"

"We pay 80%. That's better than the civil service for Christ's sake."

Claire wagged a finger. "Leaving your workers with a significant sum to pay out of pocket every month. For a high-deductible policy geared toward the young and healthy, and with far less coverage than what our plan offers."

Walter turned to the union chief.

"How so?"

"Huh?"

Walter sat back in his chair. "What coverage does Mr. Milburn fail to offer that the union does?"

"I...I'm not sure. I'd have to check. Orthodontic care is one example, but there's far more that—"

The professor looked at Syd crossly. "Orthodontics can be a significant cost for workers with young children."

"I put $2,000 in an HSA for every worker every year. That money—"

"Braces cost $5,000 a year, Syd," derided Claire. "If you have two kids in them at the same time, those monthly payouts are devastating. And if you've blown through your HSA on orthodontic care alone, what about all your other out-of-pocket expenses?" She turned back to Walter. "That's just one example. Orthodontic care is the tip of a very large iceberg."

"Can you find out specifically how the union plan differs from what Mr. Milburn offers? Beyond orthodontic care."

"I guess I can email you—"

"No. Right now. Can you call someone?"

Claire exchanged a look with an equally mystified Syd. "Call someone?"

"Yes. It's very relevant to this discussion, wouldn't you say?"

Claire sat still, her face blank.

"Please," Walter implored.

Claire threw her hands up in exasperation. She pulled her phone from her purse and left the room.

Syd pitched his paper cup in a nearby wastebasket and reached for one of the coffees Claire had supplied. "Well, this is new. Didn't think I'd be talking about braces today."

Walter smiled. "I didn't think we'd be talking about anything today. You surprised me, Mr. Milburn, agreeing to participate."

"I don't like to be pushed around, Professor. And I don't like anyone suggesting I'm just a profiteer with no values or principles. I would be happy to cut a fair deal and end this today. But they've never wanted to seriously negotiate. They want their picket lines."

"Do you really believe that?"

"I've lived it. Trust me, I've seen this movie before. Let's see how far you get today. Prove me wrong."

The door opened and Claire returned. "Walt, can we speak in private for a minute?

"No objection from me," Syd said, tipping his chair back as he eyed his watch, estimating he'd be at the ranch in under four hours.

Walter exited, pulling the door closed behind him as Syd studied Dan.

"So, what's your story? Don, right?"

"Dan."

"Dan, sorry." Syd grinned. "No offense, but I've been around plenty of campaigns, and you seem to be a little long in the tooth for this kind of work. Average age seems to be about nineteen, and they're usually wearing flip flops and UNLV t-shirts."

"My daughter, who wears flip flops and UNLV t-shirts, is running this campaign."

Syd squinted at him. "I know you."

"Probably."

"How? Have we met?"

"Not really." He was going to end it there, still unused to speaking openly about his past profession, but shrugged it off once more. "I was with the local Secret Service office. We had a few protectees that were regulars at your place. You always greeted each one personally when they arrived."

Syd clapped the table. "That's it. Photographic memory. Blessing and a curse." He stared at the ceiling for several moments before snapping his fingers. "Singapore?"

"Singapore," Dan confirmed with surprise. "That was last summer. We had another two years ago—"

"Costa Rica."

"That one I'll have to look up. Even I don't remember."

Syd smiled in triumph. Then his expression changed. "Walter Becker is getting Secret Service protection?"

Dan laughed. "No, not quite. I'm retired. Recently. A bit involuntarily. I'm here on my own time."

"Involuntarily?" It came to him. "You're the Platinum guy. The two bodyguards from Greece."

"Cyprus."

"Right, Cyprus. You got fired for that?"

A pause. "So, you think the Knights will make the playoffs?"

Syd smiled, nodding his understanding. "Got it. But Dan, hey, no shit. Thank you. What you did took real guts, letting the public know what happened in there, risking your career. I like to think something like that could never happen at my place. But this is Vegas, and stuff goes on I can't always control. A $100 bill moves mountains in this town. For what it's worth, we talked to all our guys after that incident, laid down the law. Told them we won't tolerate anything like that. But I'm not naive."

Anything like that. Anything started with the world's oldest profession, and one of Vegas' oldest traditions. Though the practice had been outlawed in Clark County since 1971, prostitution in Las Vegas was far from a struggling trade. On any given evening, Strip properties like the London Towers, the most target-rich environments in the Western Hemisphere, were teeming with hookers.

Syd shifted gears. "So, you've known Becker a long time?"

"Just a few weeks. He's my kid's professor."

"A few weeks," Syd repeated, amused. "And now you're sitting in the middle of a presidential campaign, brokering world peace between the Hatfields and McCoys."

"It's a dream come true."

"Can I ask you a question about Becker?"

"Depends on the question."

"Does he really think he can win?"

Dan considered his response. "No. But the kids working for him, including my daughter, think he walks on water."

"The man must be pretty inspiring."

"He knows how to make a speech. Put him in a debate with either Sheffield or Pierce, and he'd clean the floor with them."

"He's that good?"

Dan craned his neck so he could see past Milburn and through the glass. A short distance away, Walter and Claire were engaged in an animated discussion, with dueling hand gestures.

"We'll soon find out."

.   .   .

Outside the meeting room, Claire led Walter to an exterior corridor near the restrooms, and the two barely managed to keep their heated words from echoing across the facility.

"What the hell's happening in there, Walt?"

"Progress, I think."

"Progress? In what direction? You're asking me to give up our most fundamental tenet. How can you expect me to betray the principle of collective bargaining when—"

"That principle is getting those workers nothing, Claire. Nothing. And you know it. It's not your fault. You could picket that man for twenty-five years and you wouldn't get him to budge an inch. So, where does that leave the workers you purport to be fighting for?"

"If we back down, they'll be left with no one to fight for their futures. Whatever nominal concessions you might get out of Milburn today, the gap between his workers and those we represent will only widen down the road. And if we're taken out of the equation, they'll all be left twisting in the wind."

"Which is exactly what will happen if you stay the course. You will get nothing for these workers and their families. For God's sake, Claire, *nominal*? You have an opportunity to put real money in their pockets. Expand their health coverage. The union can declare victory for that!"

"Victory?" Claire flared. "Think about what kind of precedent we'd be setting here. For every losing standoff we have with the Milburns and Adelsons of the world, we have a success story like the Cosmopolitan and Platinum. We drop our demand for collective bargaining and no one will take our picket lines seriously. They'd expect us to fold in a heartbeat, for the price of a few breadcrumbs."

"I'm not trying to decide the future of the labor movement, Claire. I asked you both to come here because I wanted to bring the two sides together, see if cooler heads could prevail. If we could improve the lives of thousands of families who live in our shared community. And if we couldn't end a war, at least end a battle."

"You don't get it, Walt. If my side surrenders this battle, we've lost the war."

Walter leaned one shoulder against the wall, his frustration visible now.

"A cautionary note, Claire. You walk away from this, think about what will happen. Word will surely get out he was willing to deal, and you weren't. His workers will know they could have received raises and benefit increases, and the union said no. He'll probably call your bluff to have a secret ballot, to see whether his workers really want the union, and you'll lose. So not only will you deny those workers their raises, you'll give yourself a very public black eye."

The silence lasted nearly ten seconds, Claire's gaze turning ice cold. "Word will get out. A threat?"

"A caution."

Claire gave him a mirthless smile. "You know, Walt, I thought you wanted to be different. A new voice, you're calling it. Sounds like the same old voice to me."

"Let's be fair here, Claire. One of us sees this as a fight for what's in the best interests of organized labor in this country. The other, for what's in the best interests of thousands of local families. That doesn't make either one of us, or Syd Milburn for that matter, a villain. It means we have different visions for reaching an end. Your approach hasn't worked."

"Really? Tell that to our 60,000 members, Walt. And one good...caution...deserves another. In the last election, those members knocked on over 200,000 doors, and spoke directly to more than 50,000 voters across Nevada. We made this state blue and can be very helpful to those who support our cause.

But we'll work equally hard against those who stand in the way of basic fairness and equitable treatment."

"Come on, Claire, you've already endorsed Sheffield. Which is ironic, considering Syd has done the same. So, as you can see, I have nothing to lose or gain here politically. I'm the only honest broker in that room."

Walter softened his voice. "You've been my friend for years, Claire. And whatever happens today, I hope that will continue. But this is a moment. And you have a chance to do some real good for thousands of people. Think about that. Thousands. You were one of those workers once. A cashier barely scraping together her rent money from minimum wage. Put yourself in her shoes again. What would you want to happen here?"

The two fell silent, but the professor could see the uncertainty washing over his old friend. A muted Claire returned to the conference room with Walter following close behind. Sixty minutes later, she was studying the words on the hastily scrawled proposal the professor had penned. She gave a sad nod. They had a pact, pending formal approval by the union and matching armies of attorneys.

"No one touched the donuts," Syd noted.

"Tradition," Claire sighed.

CHAPTER 19

The Levin abode was sited along the very eastern edge of Henderson. The upscale suburb had a rich history, rooted in World War II, when it sprang up next to a magnesium plant producing the "miracle metal" of Franklin Roosevelt's Arsenal of Democracy. The single facility in the Nevada desert, with more than 14,000 workers at peak production, was vital to the manufacturing of bombers, munitions, and other war material fueling the Allied victory. Several years after the war ended, an aspiring young politician visited the expanding community, deeming it a "city of destiny." By the 1990s, Jack Kennedy had proven prophetic, with Henderson surpassing Reno as the second largest municipality in the state, more than 300,000 residents within its boundaries.

The split-level home, just three years old, was the handiwork of Sam Levin, who logged three decades as an electrician before starting his own contracting company. He considered his dozen employees and well-honed crew of subcontractors – all union members of course – the finest craftsmen in the valley, and their fingerprints were on nearly every fixture, fitting, and accent in the house.

Both Levins were industrious workers, clocking in from dawn to dusk, but even after thirty-five years of marriage, their evening meal together remained a ritual seldom missed. They were halfway thru their supper when the doorbell chimed. Sam, nearing his sixty-fifth birthday, pushed back from the table but Claire beat him to it. Her sneakers squeaked across the Spanish tiles as she whisked toward the foyer, their beagle padding to the door at his owner's feet.

Claire was smiling, the dinner hour interruptions like clockwork this time of year. With Spring fast approaching, and the street brimming with young athletes tied to pricey club teams, the Levin home was a popular bullseye for neighborhood kids with a fundraising quota. Sam was the easier touch, but even Claire couldn't resist a pitch from a 12-year-old hawking frozen pizzas or holiday wrapping paper.

She swung the door open, her smile dissolving in an instant. The figure standing on her porch was no neighborhood kid. And despite the man's cheery smile, she felt her temper spiking before a single word had been voiced.

"You."

"Me," answered Syd. "Am I intruding?"

"Intruding? Was Genghis Khan intruding on Asia?" She wrinkled her nose. "What are you doing here? I thought you were heading to your estate in Utah."

"My *estate* is barely fifty acres with a firetrap of a farmhouse probably built by Lewis and Clark. And I was headed there, but I had a craving for lasagna."

She still hadn't invited him in. "There's a dozen restaurants in your resort, Syd. No one makes lasagna?"

"Eighteen restaurants, actually. They're all overpriced."

"You said you were in a rush to get out of town," she persisted.

"I was halfway to Bryce Canyon. Then I turned around."

"Why?"

"I was hungry. And I wanted to talk to you. So, two birds."

A voice called out from an adjoining room. "Let him in, Claire. You can't refuse a man your mother's lasagna."

Claire clucked her tongue, gesturing Syd in and leading him into the dining room. She made the introductions before retreating to the kitchen to retrieve an extra place setting. Syd sat next to Sam, the two exchanging small talk as the dog competed for attention. Claire returned, scowling at the dog who now had his head in Syd's lap as he received a healthy rub behind the ear.

"And who's this?"

"His name is Hoffa," replied Sam.

Syd looked at him. "You're kidding."

"No, I'm not kidding. He's always disappearing."

They both laughed, as Syd endeared himself to one host while the other simply groaned, having suffered through more than three decades of Sam's amateur stand-up routine.

"His name is Teddy," Claire said, dishing up a serving of pasta and handing the plate to Syd. "Now talk."

Syd offered Teddy one last pat on the belly before forking a corner of lasagna and popping it into his mouth.

"I had an idea." He swallowed another bite and poked at the food. "That's fantastic."

"You're going to start treating your workers humanely?"

Syd lowered his fork to the table, staring at his plate.

"Claire," her husband said quietly. "The man is an invited guest in our home."

"He invited himself!" Claire took a deep breath, placing her hands flat on the table. "Damn it. I need more wine," she declared, looking at Syd. "Merlot or Cabernet?"

"Merlot. Bring the bottle."

Sam waived Claire off this time, fetching the Merlot from the kitchen and another stemmed glass from the nearby buffet. He offered Syd a full pour before topping off his wife's glass.

"That's good stuff," Syd said approvingly, licking his lips. "But I'm not kidding. This lasagna is outstanding. I'd put it in one of my restaurants."

Sam patted his forearm. "Her mother's secret ingredient. Ground filet mignon."

"I'll send you the recipe on Pinterest, Syd. Now, please, the suspense is killing me," she added dryly.

Syd pointed his fork. "I want to have a press conference, Claire. Together, just you and me."

Claire and Sam shared a look. Her husband gave a barely perceptible shake of his head, sensing an eruption of monumental proportion. Claire narrowed her eyes at their caller.

"Are you joking?"

"No."

"Do you have any idea of the phone calls and emails I've already received since our deal was announced? I'm being treated like a Nazi collaborator. And you want me to take a victory lap with you?"

"Who's treating you like a Nazi collaborator?"

"My colleagues. The mother ship in Washington. Friends in Congress."

"How about the workers at my hotel? The ones you were fighting for. Are they part of it?"

"I think you know the answer to that."

"Tell me."

Claire took a long sip from her glass. "They are quite grateful. I know that's what you want to hear, but spare me the self-congratulations. You put short-term cash in their pockets. Hurrah. Guaranteed popularity points for you. But you and

159

I know what that means for their health and retirement benefits, now and in the future. So, I'll pass on the victory lap. I lost the war."

"You didn't lose the war. You just haven't won it."

"Semantics. And I'm not going to try to walk between the raindrops in front of the press. I'm happy your workers are getting some increases they very much deserve. I just don't want to be part of any effort to trumpet—"

"That's not what this press conference would be about."

Confusion crossed Claire's face.

"It wouldn't have anything to do with that piece of paper we signed," Syd continued.

Sam rubbed his hands. "You're going to finally lower your table limits?"

"I can't wait to hear this," muttered Claire, downing the rest of her wine.

Syd sucked in a breath. "I'd like for us to join together, mutually pull our support from Sheffield, and endorse Becker for president."

Sam chortled and Claire couldn't help but smile. But Syd remained quiet, watching her intently.

"Come on."

"Claire, think about—"

"You're asking me to turn my back on the nominee, and support a novelty candidate polling at zero percent? You can't be serious."

"Sheffield isn't the nominee yet. And Becker isn't at zero percent. Just hear me out."

"Have you made it your life mission to destroy my reputation? To make me an eternal pariah in the labor movement? You are absolutely certifiable. Why would I abandon Paul Sheffield?"

"Paul Sheffield is going to lose, and you know it."

"We don't know that. The party will eventually rally around—"

"What are we doing here, Claire?"

"Letting a good lasagna get cold," Sam wisecracked.

Syd kept his eyes fixed on Claire.

"I gave ten million dollars to support his campaign last year. His people are asking me to double that this year. They're also leaning on me for the convention in August. I'm helping to bankroll this man, yet for the life of me, I can't tell you what he stands for. He's not Rebecca Pierce, they say. Terrific. I get that. But is that the best we can do? Is that the best thing I can say about a man running for President of the United States? That he's not someone else?"

"Becker can't win, Syd. You know that. At best, he'll get a few thousand votes in the city, all of them under the age of twenty-five. Whatever you think of Sheffield's chances, you'd be throwing your vote away."

"I agree. Becker can't win. But what if we weren't throwing away our votes, and we were actually making our voices matter? What if by endorsing Becker, we made Sheffield a better candidate?"

The Levins were both quiet.

Syd leaned back. "You're looking at me like I have a third eye."

"You've lost me."

"Me too," admitted Sam, apologetically.

Syd pushed back from the table and stood. He was all energy now, and began pacing back and forth, with Teddy at his heels.

"Sorry, I need to stand. Look, the Paul Sheffield you're supporting, that I'm supporting, that guy is not going to beat Pierce. That's your wasted vote. We have to change Sheffield, and we can't steal second base with one foot on first."

"By endorsing Becker? That would be perceived as nothing less than a public rebuke of Sheffield. I can't do that to the man, especially after what just happened in Iowa. And how in the world would that help him?"

"If he does nothing in response, then yes, he's weakened. But Claire, he's weak right now. His campaign is completely rudderless. That was the lowest turnout in Iowa in eighty years. He has to run a better campaign, and he has to become a better candidate. It's his only hope for November."

Claire stared at the casino operator. Hours ago, she wanted to run him over with a tractor. Now she found herself agreeing with nearly every point he was making.

"So, you think he *could* win?"

"Not that cardboard cutout we're currently seeing out there, propped up by the DNC."

"Suppose I agree. You haven't explained how endorsing Becker changes Sheffield."

"We box Sheffield in on Becker's National Cure Initiative. Get him to endorse it. Embrace it. It's exactly the game-changer his campaign needs. But he won't do it on his own. He knows Pierce would attack him for it, say he's showing his true liberal colors. He'd worry about losing the center. But I think that's dead wrong. I think the Cure Initiative *wins* him the center. I'm open to other ideas, but my money and your voters carry a lot of heft here, Claire. Let's use that to fundamentally change this race. Maybe force Sheffield's people to understand they need to start campaigning like Becker. Start acting like they want to win votes, instead of not losing them."

Claire took another swallow of her Merlot as Syd returned to his seat, cleaning half his plate in seconds.

He wiped his mouth with a napkin. "It won't happen, Claire, unless people like you and me start taking a stand. You and I matter here. Nevada matters. And we've still got nine months until Election Day. We could change the entire trajectory of this election, right here, you and me."

Her voice was quiet. "We're not negotiating over orthodontic benefits anymore, are we?"

"We agreed this morning to come together for the benefit of thousands of families in this community. Maybe it's time we set our sights a little higher."

Claire gave him a long look, taking the measure of a man who for years she thought of only as an intractable obstacle to everything she hoped to attain for Nevada workers.

"Syd, I'm starting to suspect you're not the worst human being in this city."

"Does that mean I can have seconds on the lasagna?"

There was a long silence as Sam spooned another serving onto Syd's plate and Claire fell deep into thought. It was her husband who finally spoke.

"Tell him," Sam urged, his eyes twinkling at his bride of so many years.

"We vowed not to tell anyone."

"It wasn't a divine promise. Tell him."

She stared at the table for several seconds before turning to Syd. "We're voting for Walter."

The casino owner blinked. "What?"

"We had a daughter, Syd. Long ago, when we were still living in Michigan. Sophia. She was three years old when she was diagnosed with neuroblastoma. It's one of the rarest forms of childhood cancer. We lost her a year later."

Syd's face fell. "Christ, I'm so sorry. I didn't know."

"We haven't shared that with many people. It's why we moved here. We needed the fresh start. The loss was devastating to us both."

Claire was glassy-eyed, the heartrending memories tugging at her. She closed her eyes as her husband reached across the table and stroked her forearm. She wiped away a tear and spoke again, her voice halting now.

"Walt's National Cure Initiative spoke to us, as you can imagine. If I thought for an instant it was nothing more than a political ploy, and he was harboring anything but absolute sincerity, I would have called him out for it. I wanted to strangle him this morning, but I've known him too long. Hannah was one of my dearest friends. I believe in Walter. And however cynical we've all become about Washington, his Initiative could work. We both believe that. We have to believe that. And whether wasted or not, he has our votes. In Sophia's memory."

Syd sat back, dumbfounded by the revelation. He hadn't known Claire Levin before today, they had never met in person. He only knew *of* her, and her reputation among those in his circles as soulless and uncompromising. Now, there were those in her own circles labeling her a Nazi collaborator for bargaining with someone like him. How little they all knew about her. How little they all knew about him.

"When are you announcing this?"

"I'm not." The mettle was back in her voice. "Publicly, I'm still supporting Sheffield. I have to, Syd. My endorsement means something here locally, and I have to think about the best interests of the workers I represent. The organizer in me has to support the candidate who has the strongest record of fighting for worker rights. And doing whatever it takes to ensure the candidate who would like to see our movement eviscerated isn't elected. But who I actually pull the lever for, well, that's just for me."

She turned to her husband with a disapproving glare. "What's with the potted plant routine? Stop pretending you don't have an opinion."

Sam rubbed his jaw. "You know he's right about Sheffield. You've said it yourself a hundred times at this very table."

"I've also said I have a responsibility to separate how I feel personally about issues and candidates. My job is to advocate for the best interests of the workers I represent."

Sam leaned toward her, wrapping both hands around hers. "Isn't it possible, dear, what Syd is proposing, would do exactly that?"

•   •   •

The ad began airing a few days later. The concept was simple and unorthodox, avoiding the use of actors, graphics, or other technical wizardry so routine now in modern political advertisements. The script was penciled out over a bottle of wine; a compelling declaration literally in Syd and Claire's own words.

Having shared their intentions with no one, the sixty-second spot rocked the Nevada political establishment. With Syd's personal checkbook, they managed to inundate the network airwaves, bookending prime-time programming for three straight evenings. The digital buy was even more robust, the ad popping up in the news and social media feeds of journalists, political figures, and local celebrities across Southern Nevada. The odd pairing, coming on the heels of their brokered labor agreement, was news in itself, but it was their message that resonated so deeply. The video soon spread like wildfire.

Dan and his daughter saw it minutes after it was first released. They were enjoying a Sunday dinner together when the text and link came in from Evan. Their Persian kabobs were quickly forgotten as they watched in stunned silence.

"I'm Claire Levin, Secretary-Treasurer of the Culinary Workers Union, Local 226. I've been fighting for Nevada workers since my days as a cashier at the Frontier, decades ago."

"And I'm Syd Milburn, Chairman and CEO of London Towers Resort and Casino, and a proud employer of those same Nevada workers."

"Syd and I have had our share of battles."

"Like the Hatfields and McCoys."

"But as we've recently learned, sometimes we have to come together for the common good."

"Today, Claire and I are joining together for a new battle. As Democrats. As Nevadans. As Americans."

"We are announcing our mutual support for a truly inspiring initiative put forward by our fellow Las Vegan, Professor Walter Becker.

"We know Walter as a man of intelligence, of integrity—"

"And ideas. Claire and I believe in the history of presidential elections, there has never been a more inspiring idea than Walter's National Cure Initiative."

"We have both lost close family members to cancer. Syd's mother was forty-seven. My precious daughter, just four. More than fifty children will learn today they have cancer. Fifty more will hear that tomorrow, and another fifty the day after that."

"Today, we're stepping forward to say, enough is enough. Despite our past differences, we know nothing is more important than the health of our families and communities, and the workers we represent and employ."

"*Cancer knows no political parties and no ideologies. No boundaries of geography, ethnicity, or wealth. It will never be defeated until we – Syd, myself, and all of you – join together and fight this war together.*"

"*It's time for change and unity. It's time for us to get behind a new idea.*"

"*To learn more about the National Cure Initiative, and how you can sign a petition calling on each presidential candidate to support it, please visit Cure4America.com.*"

"*Join us. Join the real fight for America. Support Walter Becker's vision. Support the National Cure Initiative.*

"*If we can come together, so can you.*"

"*Enough is enough.*"

CHAPTER 20

February 7
Fifteen Days to Primary Day

The following day, Dan found himself with Walter again, this time at the professor's cramped office on campus. In contrast to his uncluttered home, the office resembled a debris field following a tornado strike, with enough paper and file folders strewn about his desk and bookshelves to fill an Office Depot. The professor sat behind an L-shaped desk, holding a mug of herbal tea and surrounded by mounds of graded exams and term papers. Dan sat across from him, shifting his frame in a dented metal chair likely fabricated during the Reagan Administration.

"Remind me why I'm here."

"One, because Evan and your daughter are helping with the banners today. And two, they don't trust me unsupervised. Besides, I've told you how much I value your perspective."

"Are we going to have time to make your appointment?"

Walter waved a hand, unconcerned. "Our visitor assures me he won't require more than thirty minutes. I may have neglected to mention we'll be going to a different medical office today. This one is off of Lake Mead Boulevard."

"Why not? Seems like we've hit every other medical office in the city."

"One of the great benefits of the golden years. A daily regimen of poking and prodding."

Dan glanced over. "Everything okay?"

Walter gave him a resigned shrug. "Standard operating procedure, Mr. Cahill. Not everything works as it should when you reach my age, and there never seems to be any shortage of young doctors wanting an opportunity to check under the hood and find some new ailment."

There was a short knock on the doorframe and they rose to greet their visitor. He was close to Walter's age, balding and with a trim beard flecked with gray. More sprightly and stylish than Dan would have expected for an egghead type, his twill pants, russet-colored shirt, and herringbone blazer could have landed him on the cover of GQ. After the introductions, they seated themselves around the desk, peering at each over the piles.

"Thank you for taking time to meet with me," their guest started, his tone guarded but not unfriendly. "I know how busy you must be."

"Jerald Coates speaks very highly of you, Dr. Atwell. You worked together?"

"Please, it's Stephen. Jerry and I were the UNR representatives on the Governor's education panel before he transferred down here last year."

"And you teach in the UNR medical school?"

"No longer. I'm still an adjunct there, but for the last few years I've been serving as the Director of our Clinical Research Center for Molecular Medicine."

"That's a mouthful," remarked Dan.

Atwell winked. "You should hear the Chinese translation."

Walter set his tea down. "Dr. Coates mentioned you wished to discuss our Cure Initiative? I confess, even though we were pressed for time, we should have consulted someone with actual expertise before we settled on the particulars."

"Then you would have been the first political candidate in American history to have done so."

Dan smiled. He was warming to this man.

"Let me begin, Professor, by saying I've followed your recent advocacy on behalf of the student population here. Kudos to you for that. And I applaud your efforts to draw attention to the acute needs of the medical research community. Self-serving, I know. But raising awareness among the public so they fully understand the challenges we face is vitally important to our existence."

Walter spread his hands. "Very kind of you to say. But I have a feeling you're not here to offer an endorsement."

Their visitor bowed his head in regret. "That would be inappropriate, of course, given my position. Politics is an arena we strive mightily to stay out of."

"I know the feeling," murmured Dan.

Walter leaned forward. "Certainly. But I suspect whatever compelled you to take a flight down here from Reno is something we may not like hearing."

"Indeed," Atwell said quietly. "Let me caveat this by saying I represent no one other than myself. This is just one man's opinion, and I'm not speaking for my profession or my center. And I'll be direct, which I know you will appreciate. The grand effort you are envisioning, even if it were a rousing success and exceeded all expectations, raising billions of dollars and significantly expanding available resources, would, I fear, do little to bring us any closer to the cures for these horrific diseases we are all so desperate for. The needle, in all likelihood, would barely move."

Dan scoffed. "Come on."

"Again, I'm not here representing the entire medical field. I'm sure there are other researchers, clinicians, academics, and others who would disagree with what I have to say. I can only speak to you based on my experience in this field. And my views are this. For too long, the public has been led to believe curing cancer is a simple equation of time and money. That the two correlate, and the more money we funnel to NIH and the research community, the more breakthroughs we will experience, and the faster we can discover those cures. Many look at it almost as an engineering challenge, like building a bridge from San Diego to Honolulu, or flying a manned spacecraft to Mars. A misguided belief that with enough money alone, we can simply reach any end point."

"And you're saying that isn't the case here?"

"I'm saying, Professor, that fighting cancer is about scientific discovery, and there is nothing predictive about how or when that will occur, no matter the scarcity or riches of resources."

"So, the fundraising drives, the 5k races for breast cancer research, the billions of dollars we appropriate every year, those are all just useless endeavors?"

"I certainly don't mean to suggest that. Money is good, and necessary to continue the research and experimentation that are the bedrock of discovery. But any sort of promise that a massive influx of new money will accelerate those discoveries, or vaccines, or groundbreaking therapeutics, is where you get into far more uncertain territory." He paused. "Forgive me, I'm a cardiologist by training, and managing expectations is a creed in our line of work."

"Then if money *is* necessary, why are you here?"

"I'm here to present an alternative suggestion for you. A cause where I believe there is far more certainty an infusion of resources and greater public awareness could significantly improve public health. It lacks the notoriety of cancer, but it's a condition imperiling millions, and warrants its own national call to action."

Dan shook his head in disbelief. "The primary is in two weeks. Early voting starts next Tuesday. And you want him to unring a bell and completely change the platform he's been running on?"

Walter leaned forward. "It's a reasonable question, Doctor. You don't seem to be denying additional resources would accelerate your efforts, it's just a question of degree. So, we're not misleading anyone, right? The money is still greatly needed, no? And if that's the case, I'm not sure how I can walk away from the Cure Initiative at this point."

"You can't," Dan said firmly.

"Gentlemen," Atwell soothed, "I'm not a politician, but I am a realist. And I know what I'm asking you to consider is extraordinary. But I still feel duty-bound to steer you to the other course I alluded to."

"Which is?"

"Obesity."

Atwell saw their shared reaction and raised his palms.

"Hear me out. It has become a true epidemic in this country. Let me quote you some statistics before you dismiss it." The doctor fished a folded slip of paper from his inside pocket. "Heart disease is the number one killer in America, even more so than cancer. One in four deaths in this country is attributable to heart disease, and obesity is a proven and significant contributing factor. As it is with Type 2 diabetes, strokes, I could go on. Roughly forty percent of Americans – 100 million of our fellow citizens – are obese. Not overweight. Obese. By definition, that means you are carrying enough body fat to induce significant health issues, as those I've just described. It has also been tied to various cancers – breast, colon, pancreatic, liver, prostate. All increased likelihood if the subject has obesity."

"You said contributing factor," Dan queried. "Not the direct cause."

"Correct. But please understand, there is wide consensus within my profession that obesity is a public health crisis right now. If we don't reverse the trends, or at least slow the rising numbers, we will see the physical health of our country continue to plummet. And while I could rattle off statistics all day long, here is the one that always stops me in my tracks. One in five children today – one in five! – is already considered obese."

Dan wasn't sure he heard right. "One in *five?*"

"Yes. We have an entire generation of ten-year-olds out there who you can almost guarantee a diagnosis of diabetes or the like in their future. And yet parents are still spoon feeding them fast food and sugary drinks like there's no tomorrow.

There are plenty of studies out there to support what I am telling you. The American Journal of Public Health would be an excellent start. Or talk to the AMA."

"I'm not certain that's necessary," Walter said. "I think you know your trade quite well, Doctor. And you've certainly given us some things to think about."

Atwell smiled. "I didn't make a dent, did I?"

"Not for lack of trying. You made a forceful case, and I doubt nothing you stated. Rationally, you are almost certainly right. But this is deeply personal to me, Doctor. Cancer took both my parents, and Mr. Cahill's father. I know this shouldn't be personal, and that in running for president I need to weigh the public good and make the soundest choice for the greatest number of Americans. But there's something else, Doctor."

Walter leaned forward, putting more force behind his words.

"Beyond the public health benefits, the country desperately needs this. Everyone, from the left and right, needs to get behind something. Something that can unite us and bring us together as Americans. The polarization in this country is so deep these days, we demonize everyone who disagrees with us, whether the issues are great or small. I fear we've forgotten who we are, and what we're capable of. We saved the world from the Nazis. We split the atom and put a man on the moon. It wasn't just Democrats who pulled on those oars, or Republicans. It was every American. And don't mistake what I'm saying for the jingoistic rubbish coming out of Rebecca Pierce's mouth. She's using cheap devices to drive a wedge through this country. Them versus us. I want a clarion call, not a dog whistle. I want every man, woman, and child to set aside their partisan differences and self-interest, and work together for a goal so grand it would take an unprecedented, national-level effort to reach it."

Atwell sighed. "And that's not obesity, is it?"

"Cancer is a great evil, Doctor, and it has incurred the wrath of so many of us. I'm not sure I can say the same of a Snickers bar. Please don't misunderstand me. I don't mean to belittle your cause, and logically, you may be right. But it is cancer I believe everyone can most relate to. And, in all candor, I can't compete in this contest, as improbable as it all is, unless I'm fighting for the cause closest to my heart. I hope you can understand that."

"I can, and I do." Atwell rose to his feet. "I admire your passion and conviction, Professor. And please don't misunderstand *me*. What you are advocating would be of tremendous value to my community, and our country at large. Once your Cure Initiative is on the road to success, I hope obesity is something we can tackle in your second term. Together."

Walter stood as well and the two men clasped hands. "A forward-thinking man."

Atwell gave a rueful smile. "A realist."

CHAPTER 21

February 11
Eleven Days to Primary Day

Unlike the stately sophistication of its namesake, Parliament Hall was a mostly forgettable space, particularly by Las Vegas standards. The lower-level, monochromatic room, wallpapered in more shades of beige than Dan knew existed, was spacious enough to accommodate a small wedding. Impressive, if they had been standing in a Marriott. But this was the London Towers Resort & Casino, which showcased enough conference space to host a small country. The Parliament was a relative broom closet compared to other available venues within the resort's Special Events Center.

It was dwarfed, ironically enough, by Buckingham Hall, one level up. Syd Milburn liked to boast the Buckingham was as cavernous as the Louisiana Superdome, and the arena-like feel was no exaggeration. It was a room Dan was intimately familiar with. Just two years ago, he stood on its stylishly carpeted floor, managing security and logistics for a fundraising gala hosted by the Democratic National Committee. The majestic room had been filled to capacity that evening with an ocean of humanity. Thousands clad in black tie and designer gowns, sharing Kobe beef medallions and lobster bisque as they feted President Vance, congressional leaders, and multiple cabinet secretaries.

The scale of the event wasn't unprecedented for the Secret Service, but the timing left even the most tested agents on edge. It had been just ten days since a car bomb detonated near a security checkpoint across from the U.S. Capitol, maiming a dozen pedestrians and two Capitol Police officers. In the heightened threat environment that followed, and with numerous protective details operating under one roof, public scrutiny of the Towers event mushroomed. A parade of media commentators and former law enforcement officials took to the airwaves, decrying the event as ill-timed while second-guessing every reported security measure and precaution.

It was a watershed moment for Dan, fourteen years after he left the White House. The weight of responsibility for safeguarding not only the nation's highest elected leader, but more than 2,000 guests, resuscitated something within, a long dormant hunger for front line duty he hadn't felt since his expulsion to the field. He and Anthony Jarrett, both veterans of the Presidential Detail, sat in long planning sessions with the advance team and coordinated with the many police, fire, and other emergency response teams that would be roving nearby during zero hour. For nearly a month, Dan had been dialed in with the preparations, his function a vital component of a choreography that could have matched a Bob Fosse production. Volumes of sensitive secrets, contingency plans, and other operational minutia filled his head as he worked exhausting 18-hour days to prevent the worst national security disaster in American history.

Oh, how the mighty have fallen, Dan muttered to himself, taking in the current backdrop.

He scanned the relatively diminutive Parliament from end to end, concluding the only viable threat would be if some madman attempted to separate Evan's hand from the Styrofoam cup of coffee he was gripping like the last canteen in a desert. The over-caffeinated campaign manager was swaying in place, his eyes darting about like a petrified rabbit.

Though Dan had misgivings about the entire charade, the students had at least well-executed the visuals. There were two lecterns on the podium, angled inward, at the front of the room, each topped by a placard bearing the name of the expected occupant. It was all theater of course, but the media seemed willing to play their part. Scattered among the first two rows of chairs were several local scribes with phones and notepads in hand, mingling with each other.

Their presence was a head scratcher for Dan. Surely they knew Rebecca Pierce couldn't possibly walk through those doors. The Republican frontrunner had spent the previous day in Manchester, attending get-out-the-vote rallies from morning to midnight. Though bleary-eyed New Hampshirites had just started casting ballots, press accounts had Pierce already en route to South Carolina, confident of the day's outcome. And unless her aides had secretly commandeered a supersonic jet and strapped her in, there was zero chance she would be surfacing in a state she had been snubbing for weeks.

Walter, of course, not only predicted the general's absence when he first conceived the debate ruse, he was counting on it. He shared that with Dan as they traveled together to Reno earlier in the week. Goaded by Barb Patterson, Dan shelled out his own money to accompany Walter up north, then watched as the professor issued his debate challenge to Pierce while standing within view of a fleet of aging military aircraft. Dan kept his glum doubts to himself, certain the entire ploy would flop. Nor did he share his concern it may backfire, the local press sure to be insulted by the gimmickry.

Or not, judging from the attendees filling in the chairs.

With a signal from Megan, the professor stepped in front of the twin lecterns, not a single note or talking point in hand.

"Thank you all for joining us this morning. As you know, we invited Rebecca Pierce as well, hoping to have a hardy public debate on the issues so important to the people of our great state. She is, we've been informed, quite busy. Indeed, by our count, since we issued that invitation, she has hosted seven fundraisers, attended a college basketball game, and even flown out to California to appear on *The Tonight Show*. She has also held campaign events in South Carolina, Ohio, and Florida. And while Nevada is next on the primary calendar, with our election less than two weeks away, she refuses to visit our state.

"Like all of you, we have puzzled over this. Maybe she doesn't want to defend her call for severe reductions in legal immigration that has more than alarmed our expanding Hispanic population, many of whom voted for the Republican nominee in the last election. Or explain her opposition to modernizing the twelve C-130 aircraft comprising the Air National Guard's 152nd Airlift Wing in Reno. I'm sure you recall the debate in Des Moines last month, when Pierce called for shifting already-approved funding for upgrading our ancient C-130s to a fleet of new Tempest helicopters for the Iowa Army National Guard. And now she can't be pried loose from South Carolina. I think we can see where Nevada stands on her list of priorities.

"So, my apologies we were unable to persuade the general to visit us here in Nevada and discuss these issues in public. In the absence of a debate, I'm happy to field any questions you might have. Mr. Byers?"

A thickset man in the front row dropped his hand, his face registering surprise. He had heavy jowls, a wispy silver beard, and wire-rimmed eyeglasses perched on the end of his nose.

"You know me?"

"I feel like I know you. I'm an avid reader of your column."

"That makes three of you," joked the newspaperman with false modesty. Tom Byers was the dean of print journalists in the state, and during his nearly three decades as a political reporter, had nurtured relationships with every elected official from Las Vegas to Carson City. He wasn't just widely read in Nevada. Party officials in Washington dissected every column and tweet from the veteran correspondent, knowing his fingers were clamped to the pulse of the local political scene.

"I'd love to sit down and chat one-on-one at some point, see if maybe I can pull together a piece on your campaign."

"I would enjoy that. The tall gentleman in the back is our press secretary. I'll have him reach out to you."

"Let me ask, what were you hoping to accomplish here today?"

Walter started to respond before breaking out a sheepish smile. "I feel somewhat imperious standing up here. Do you mind if join you, maybe pull up a seat?" He stepped down from the riser, turning one of the chairs around and sitting among the bemused journalists.

"Much better. I'm sorry, your question again, Mr. Byers?"

"Since we know Pierce won't be here today, what are you hoping to accomplish?"

"You know, I'm not certain. I really hoped she would surprise us."

Byers tilted his head down, peering at Walter from over the rims of his eyeglasses.

Walter smiled. "You believe this is all just a show, designed to kindle media interest in my campaign. Well, no doubt I am very happy to see all of you here today. But for the record, I honestly did hope, with ample notice, the general might have made some effort to be here."

Dan, standing in the rear, elbowed his daughter.

"The guy isn't even taking notes. Or recording this."

"So? He just offered to interview Becker later. That's a win, Dad."

"So why is he here now?"

Megan shrugged. "In case Pierce actually showed?"

Dan started to respond, but another reporter jumped in with a question.

"Our polling shows Pierce with a sizable lead here over Governor Morales. Why *wouldn't* she skip Nevada and focus on other states?"

"States like South Carolina, where she has an even greater lead? And the UNR poll released yesterday shows her with just a seven-point advantage here in the general election."

"Against Sheffield. Any concern your candidacy is hindering the Vice President's ability to close that margin?"

"I suspect if my name were added to the poll, we'd see the Vice President hindering *my* ability to close that margin."

Byers snorted as a harried, late-arriving young woman approached Walter, clutching a microphone as she waved her trailing cameraman into position.

"Hi Professor, Samantha Nagumo, KLVT Channel 4. We're going to set up right here if that's okay, maybe ask you a few questions?"

"Sure, that sounds lovely," Walter said, rising from his chair.

The cameraman finished securing his equipment to a tripod and signaled Nagumo, who raised the microphone to her chin.

"Professor Becker, you've been in the race for almost a month now, but most observers believe Vice President Sheffield is still comfortably ahead here. Have you considered dropping out and endorsing him?"

"No, I haven't. The election is still eleven days away, and we believe we're gaining ground every hour."

"The Pierce campaign claims long-scheduled commitments are keeping her in South Carolina today. Are you disappointed she didn't accept your debate challenge?"

"Disappointed, yes. Surprised, I guess not. The general has shown little interest in answering tough questions about the issues most voters care about, ringing herself instead with that braying mass of sycophants. She's become a bottomless reservoir of undemocratic thought, and I think it's high time someone challenges her on all these absurdities she keeps waxing on about."

Byers jerked up in his seat with sudden interest, while Nagumo tightened her grip on the microphone. She and her media colleagues had been craving this for months; a public figure with the temerity to take on Pierce. The other reporters also stirred, as Byers, wielding his phone now as an audio recorder, held it toward Walter.

"Professor, you don't seem interested in Vice President Sheffield, the frontrunner in the Democratic primary. Why not issue a debate challenge to him?"

Walter gave a tired smile. "You sound like my team. But the Vice President has had plenty of opportunities to speak to Nevadans about these issues, and to call out Rebecca Pierce each time she has tendered one of her thoughtless proclamations. He has chosen to remain disturbingly quiet. We need strong voices, not more shrinking violets."

Byers leaned in. "Are you saying Sheffield lacks the character to stand up to Rebecca Pierce in November?"

Dan coughed loudly, and Walter cast a glance to the back of the room, acknowledging the not-so-subtle warning with a droll smile.

"I'll let the Vice President answer that question but consider this. The history books are filled with the names of demagogues who blackened the world's doorstep and stood for little more than social injustice, empty rhetoric, and unchecked power. Every one of them was empowered and emboldened by those too meek and intimidated to dissent."

"So, the Vice President is meek, and intimidated by Pierce?"

"Judging by her absence today, one might conclude Pierce is the one who is meek and intimidated."

A hand went up from one of the back rows. "Chad Kinney, *Scarlet and Gray Free Press.*"

"Ah, Mr. Kinney, I'm familiar with your editorials."

"UNLV student paper," Megan whispered to her father. "The guy is a Pierce fanatic."

"Vice President Sheffield has refused to take a position on General Pierce's call for a Constitutional amendment to make English the official language of the United States. Does that prove she's right on the issue?"

"No, it proves you don't have to be a Washington politician to come up with an asinine idea."

The gathered journalists grinned in delight, while the unamused Kinney plowed forward, a sharper edge in his voice now.

"Are you saying sixty percent of the American people, who also support the idea, are asinine as well?"

"Let's talk about that sixty percent. What we've seen from Rebecca Pierce is nothing more than a devout eagerness to champion causes that tap into the disappointments and resentments of our fellow citizens. She's also quite adept at fanning flames among those who assign blame to others for their misfortune. The likes of Rebecca Pierce have been preying on the aggrieved since the beginning of time, using them for their own political ends. My own parents spoke no English when they arrived here, and yet you and Pierce would have them afoul today of the Constitution they cherished so much. Mark me as part of the forty percent, Mr. Kinney, who are disappointed to see Pierce so joyfully stoking and inflaming such animosity towards others, especially those who look and sound different than her supporters. For my money, it's the most unpatriotic proposal we've seen in a generation."

"Unpatriotic?" Kinney protested, as the others were no longer smiling, losing patience with the young grandstander. "General Pierce has three decades of service to this country leading our nation's soldiers. Maybe it's hard to see from your ivory tower the anger Pierce is responding to, and how—"

"Oh, I can see what she's responding to. And what she's not. Set aside the nonsense she's trying to sell and think about the issues she's intentionally avoiding. We are the wealthiest, most technologically advanced country on Earth, and yet we rank near the bottom in terms of poverty and income inequality. Our investments in renewable energy and infrastructure are anemic. We pour untold resources into education, with ho-hum results. Those are the issues haunting this country, Mr. Kinney. If Rebecca Pierce would instead like to center her campaign around what our official language should be, then she should pitch that drivel to Yosemite Sam and other likeminded, intellectual equals. I believe, however, that America deserves a more serious candidate, willing to confront issues and challenges that may or may not be popular, but touch on the essence of who we are, and what we want to aspire to. That's leadership, my friends."

"I could not agree more."

They all turned as one at the new voice. It came from just behind Dan, where a tall, slender figure stood just inside the double doors leading into the room. Dan recognized her on sight, having seen her occasionally on cable news. Judging from the reaction in the room, he wasn't alone.

Perhaps a decade younger than Dan, she stood nearly six feet in her patent leather heels. Her eyes were the color of caramel, and framed by a dark, oval face and a small, upturned nose. A mass of thick dark tresses was swept into a bun, held in place by a trio of hairpins. She was smartly dressed in a black pantsuit and square-neck, lilac-colored blouse, accented by a loop of ivory pearls. She strode into the room, flanked by an even younger woman with strawberry curls clutching multiple devices.

Megan and Evan stood open-mouthed, and the reporters in the room were suddenly alert and erect in their chairs. Even Walter, nearly impossible to fluster, smiled uneasily as the newcomer approached.

"Governor," he said amiably. "You are a pleasant surprise. Welcome."

Anna Morales offered her hand and a wide smile, revealing rows of even, snow-white teeth. "Thank you, Professor. I understand you hoped to have a debate with Rebecca Pierce."

Walter shrugged. "We tried. She wouldn't agree."

"Welcome to my life for the last two months."

The reporters followed the conversation like a tennis match. It was Byers, of course, who spoke first, holding up his phone again.

"Governor, you took a shellacking in Iowa, and polls suggest you won't fare well in New Hampshire today. A number of prominent Republicans, including former President Trump, the Senate Minority Leader, and the Speaker of the House, have called on you to drop out of the race and throw your support behind General Pierce. What's your response?"

Morales turned to Byers and his colleagues, their devices held high, as Nagumo's cameraman continued to record it all.

"As you know, we chose not to compete in those two states, and are focusing our efforts instead in Nevada and South Carolina, where we're doing quite well. But before I take further questions, could I have just brief minute or two alone with Professor Becker?"

Morales whispered to her aide before leading Walter to the far side of the room.

"Well, Governor, I thought I was the clever one here, but you have one-upped me."

"How so?"

"Well, we put on something of a show here, to draw in some of the local press. But I suspect they'll be far more interested in printing whatever you have to say."

"I hope you don't mind my dropping in."

"Mind, no, surprised, yes. Why are you here, Governor?"

"We just arrived in town. I have an event in an hour with a business roundtable, and then a private fundraiser in Henderson. I heard what you were doing here, and in the absence of Pierce, I thought maybe you and I could have our own debate, or maybe even just a discussion, about issues we both care deeply about. That's what you were hoping for, right?"

Walter cast a skeptical eye. "What would we be discussing?"

"Whatever you like. We'll let Byers moderate. His ego won't let him say no, and then he'll write a puff piece, touting us as underdogs and insurgents. We'll both get good local ink out of it. I just wish I had more time."

Walter hesitated. "Would you mind if I consulted with my team?"

"Sure. And hey, no pressure here. If you're not comfortable with it, I'll just pretend I was stopping by to meet you. If you need to chat privately, I can—"

"That's not necessary," Walter said, waving his campaign stewards over. The professor quickly recapped the governor's proposal.

Evan chewed his lip. "You've never been in a real political debate. She's a pro, probably been in, like, a hundred."

Morales offered her hand. "You must be Evan Worley."

The young man flushed. "How did you—"

"Leila, my campaign manager back there, knows all. I suspect you two come from the same bloodline. I appreciate your caution Evan, but I promise, I'm not looking to pull a fast one here. I've been urging more public debates since I entered this race. I may not see eye to eye with Professor Becker on every issue, but I think voters would benefit from hearing us out."

Walter turned to his other campaign manager. "Megan?"

"I say we do it. For a Republican, she doesn't seem that horrible."

"Thanks," the governor said, her smile genuine. Megan returned it.

Walter looked at Dan. "What do you think?"

"Me?"

"You. Speak out, man. The apathy routine really no longer suits you."

Megan crossed her arms. "Yeah, no one's buying it anymore."

Dan sensed Morales appraising him, a thought he found unnerving, and felt a surprise pang inside. He raised his eyes to hers – a mistake – before quickly looking away, his train of thought entirely derailed. *What the hell?*

Walter coughed, and Dan realized the others were waiting on him. He forced himself to concentrate on a response, having become unmoored by a single momentary look from a woman he didn't even know.

"Evan has a point," he said weakly.

Morales eyed him with curiosity. "Leila didn't say anything about you. Mr..."

"Dan," he stammered. "Dan Cahill. You can call me Dan."

Walter saw it was time for a rescue, the man struggling now with simple English. "Mr. Cahill is our acting press secretary."

"Not by choice," Dan retorted. He faced Morales again. "I'm really not involved."

Morales pressed her hand into his, offering a gentle squeeze.

"Well, Mr. Not Involved, I swear to you, to all of you, I don't bite. I'm still relatively new to this game as well. But I've always stood for more open debates and honest discussions and letting the chips fall where they may. I'm also down to about ten minutes before I have to jet. All I'm suggesting is a little one-on-one in front of this crowd, show them all we both have something to contribute to this contest. But again, if you're not comfortable with it, no hurt feelings. Promise."

Walter looked again to Dan. He gave the professor a quick nod, as did the two students.

"Okay, Governor," Walter said, then added lightly, "*en garde.*"

Moments later, the two candidates had taken station behind their respective podiums. Morales' aide zipped in to snatch the placard bearing Pierce's name, making a show of tossing it in a nearby trash can.

Morales checked her wristwatch. "Okay, Mr. Byers, you're on. Start the clock, eight minutes."

The newsman cleared his throat. "Just to be clear, you want to debate real issues, nothing personal or tawdry, and no mention of absent third parties, right?"

"Right," the candidates answered in unison.

"Pity," said Byers, tugging on his beard as he considered his options. "Well, Governor, you're the visiting team, we'll start with you. I gave Professor Becker's website a quick look, and he's proposing a national-level program to encourage young people to enter public or community service. Would you be willing to support such an idea?"

"I'm not familiar with the elements of his proposal, but there is no question many of our communities are in desperate need of more first responders, nurses, schoolteachers, and the like. What I fear is the host of practical problems associated with the federal government managing such responsibility. Top-down approaches have doomed similar, well-intended efforts in the past, rendering them difficult to implement and largely ineffective."

"Professor?"

"Well, Governor, as my father used to say, those sure are a lot of ten-dollar words. But I welcome others with differing experiences and perspectives. If you agree this is a praiseworthy objective, why not join with me to find a way to make it implementable and effective?"

"With all due respect, it's more than just implementation, Professor. I find considerable fault with the underlying principle. There is something unseemly about the notion of bribing young people to serve their communities and country. And do we really need yet another federal program to address local needs? As Winston Churchill said, those who fail to learn from the past are condemned to repeat it."

"Actually, Churchill was paraphrasing a philosophy professor at Harvard, who was hardly denouncing the notion of selfless service to others. And contrary to popular myth, the federal government can be a very efficient administrator."

"The people of New Mexico would disagree. We find Uncle Sam to be quite heavy-handed most of the time."

"Nothing is more certain than the indispensable necessity of government," retorted Walter, "and it is equally undeniable, that whenever and however it is instituted—"

"The people must cede to it some of their natural rights in order to vest it with requisite powers."

Walter smiled in delight. "Well done, Governor. I normally don't enjoy others finishing my sentences, but it appears I must make an exception."

"Federalist Number Two," Morales said, returning his smile. "James Madison, I believe. My father was an enthusiast."

"It was John Jay, and consider me an enthusiast of your father. But the point stands."

"So it does. I'm a governor, Professor, so I've been on the receiving end of these kinds of programs. And I simply have little faith in anything administered and managed by Washington bureaucrats. For those of us in state government, flexibility is paramount. Maybe Colorado needs more forest rangers, but New Mexico needs firefighters and Pennsylvania needs educators. So instead of a one-size-fits-all framework, may I suggest you consider providing the states with block grants, and allow each the discretion to establish and manage a community service program tailored to their unique needs?"

Walter darkened the moment she referenced Washington bureaucrats. "Block granting good programs is a proven recipe for failure."

"Not in our st—"

"And I assure you, Governor, Washington does not have a monopoly on ineptitude. Left to their own devices in the past, plenty of states have utterly destroyed well-intended programs, either through mismanagement, inefficiency, or outright corruption."

Megan and her father shared a look of concern. Walter's mood had abruptly shifted. He seemed suddenly cross and his patience frayed, his earlier joviality abandoning him as he continued to fume.

"I know charlatans like Rebecca Pierce have tried to drum a notion into the American people that every corner of Washington is corrupt, but truth matters. State houses in Carson City, Santa Fe, and Sacramento are as susceptible as anyone in Washington to scandal and malfeasance. So, let's dispense with the fairy tale that state governments are models of purity."

Morales hesitated, carefully choosing her words as she too heard the clear change in tenor.

"Respectfully, Professor, national-level solutions rarely allow —"

"And what about my proposal to mobilize our country for a war on cancer? Would you like to mock and ridicule that idea as well? Argue the NIH is as dysfunctional and useless as the rest of Washington?"

Dan watched Walter in surprise, the professor's white-knuckled hands clutching the edges of the podium. It was the first time he had heard the man snap at anyone. Evan was attempting to signal Walter, but the candidate's eyes, full of fervor and frustration now, were focused on Morales, awaiting the governor's response.

Morales remained silent at the lectern as she composed her thoughts. After several moments, she turned again to her opponent, and when she spoke, her voice was deliberate and even.

"No, Professor, I wouldn't like to argue that point. I would venture we share more than either of us knows. I have read about your Cure Initiative, and I think it is a fine idea. Should you become our next President, I hope to be one of its fiercest advocates. Should I become President, well, please take no offense, but I hope you would consider coming to work for me. I believe you could provide the leadership and vision needed to make it a success. There are some issues that transcend not only partisanship, but traditional views within my party about the role of the Federal government, and of the states."

Walter was quiet as he absorbed her response before slowly shaking his head. His sudden fatigue was visible now, and when he spoke, his tone was far more subdued and devoid of the curt delivery from seconds ago.

"No offense taken, Governor. I welcome every American to that fight, no matter their political faiths. And you'll forgive me for my boorishness. I seem to have momentarily forgotten to practice what I preach."

Morales gave him an easy smile. "There's nothing to forgive. The public deserves a robust discussion, no matter the issue. Unfortunately, I promised I would take questions, so I'm going to have to end our...discussion. I have a full day here and fly out in the morning to Charleston. Pierce may actually show up for that debate."

"You'll probably enjoy it more than this one," Walter said apologetically.

"I highly doubt that." She moved closer to Walter for one last handshake, lowering her voice as the reporters rose up to envelop them. "Before the piranhas attack, I wanted to see if you might join me for dinner this evening."

"Dinner? Why?"

Morales shrugged. "You're an interesting one, Walter Becker. And I could use a new dinner companion. So, it's either find some fresh blood, or listen to Leila catalog historical voting patterns in Bucks County, Pennsylvania."

"Well, I'm flattered, Governor, And I could never turn down a request from such a worthy adversary. Your event is in Henderson? We have a few soccer moms and dads to canvas this afternoon, but what do you say we rendezvous at the Green Valley Resort? They have a lovely Italian restaurant inside, just off the casino floor."

"I'll find it," Morales said. "Let's make it seven, if that suits you."

She eyed the pack of reporters moving to surround them and offered a sigh.

"Feeding time."

CHAPTER 22

Just steps from the casino floor, DePippa's Italian Bistro provided a refuge for players hemorrhaging cash at the slots and table games or pining for the restaurant's signature carbonara. The cuisine and décor matched the Mediterranean inspiration of Green Valley Ranch, the luxury, off-Strip property catering to far more locals than out-of-towners. It was a resort the Cahills knew well, once Sunday brunch regulars after first arriving from Washington and moving into the attached neighborhood.

As always during prime dining hours, the restaurant was bustling, mirroring the jammed gaming tables outside. Dan passed through the open entryway, grateful to trade the clamor and stench of tobacco for the far more inviting aromas of Northern Italy. The governor was easy to spot, seated on a bench near the hostess stand and towering over her companion, the same redheaded aide who was at her side earlier that morning.

It was the moment Dan had been dreading. He considered a sharp U-turn, his arrival still unnoticed as the two women stared intently at the aide's phone. Judging by their deep consternation, a no-show from another campaign might be the least of their worries. But his hopes for slipping away evaporated the moment Morales glanced up, a welcoming smile glinting in his direction. She craned her neck to peer past his shoulder, undoubtedly searching for his constant companion.

"You made it," she said, rising to offer her hand. "Where's our esteemed professor?"

"Resting at home. He's a little under the weather."

"Is he alright?"

"Yeah, but it was a pretty strenuous day. We had no contact number for you, and he asked me to fill in tonight. I know the second team isn't what you had in mind, so if—"

"I'm sorry to hear that. About Walter. I was really hoping to chat with him about a few things. I could use some words of wisdom."

Dan almost laughed. With her stunningly successful rise to power, the 34-year-old certainly didn't need any pointers from a college professor likely polling in decimal points.

"He just needs a little breather. He'll rebound in the morning."

"I've heard about the pace he's keeping. I'm surprised he hasn't collapsed yet."

So was Dan, who had somewhat understated the professor's condition. They hadn't returned to the house until late in the afternoon, having spent hours in balmy sunshine at a youth soccer complex glad-handing a flood of waiting parents. It was wilting work, and Walter had barely been able to keep his eyes open by the time they pulled into his driveway. Barb Patterson greeted them at the door, startled by Walter's appearance as she and Dan all but carried the man to his living room sofa. Barb argued for a visit to Urgent Care, but Walter insisted rest was all he needed.

His color returned an hour later, but Barb dismissed any notion of the professor leaving the house again. Walter conceded, on the condition Dan take his place at dinner with the governor, whom they could not reach to cancel. Dan balked at first. There were far worse imaginable tasks than sitting across from Anna Morales for an hour, but he knew it would not end well, as he was sure to drop some contemptuous remark about politicians before their water glasses were filled. Walter stood his ground, aghast at the idea of standing the Governor up, and Dan eventually relented. It wouldn't matter, he reasoned aloud, as Morales was certain to back out once she learned her invited guest had sent his driver in his place.

When Dan departed, Walter was sitting up on the sofa, cradling a mug of steaming tea in both hands, his legs covered by a handmade quilt.

"Mr. Cahill?"

Halfway through the front door, Dan turned back to the professor. "Someday you're going to call me by my first name."

"Someday you're going to admit you're more than just a driver."

"Tell that to the field marshal," Dan said, gesturing toward the kitchen, where the sound of a knife blade could be heard beating out a tattoo on a bamboo cutting board. "She keeps sending me out for groceries."

"A question for you, Mr. Cahill. All those issue discussions we've had in the car. Taxes, health care, immigration, international affairs. I'm not sure we've shared a single position on anything."

"Just like my ex-wife. And for the record, you were doing most of the talking." He paused, grinning. "Just like my ex-wife."

"And yet here you are."

"Here I am."

"You told me in your past profession, you had responsibilities existing irrespective of political views or even personal differences. But I imagine from time to time back then, there came a point when the performance of your duties intersected with some degree of personal loyalty to the person under your charge. Perhaps even, dare I say, with friendship."

"You're asking if I was friends with Bush?"

Walter smiled. "No. And I know how much you valued your professionalism. You would have afforded every person you were protecting with the same level of fidelity, regardless of personal or political sentiments. But I imagine if you did respect someone you were protecting, and had any sort of attachment to them, it would have given you a great deal of pride in your work. Hypothetical, of course."

"That I can't argue with."

"Then I also imagine the inverse is likely true. Those who you were protecting, if *they* respected and had an attachment to *you*, would have been immensely proud to have someone of your caliber, and character, by their side."

"I like to think so," Dan said quietly. A small smile. "Hypothetical, of course." Walter nodded. "Of course."

That exchange stayed with Dan the entire drive to Henderson. He returned his attention to Morales. The aide had broken away to arrange their seating, and the governor's eyes were searching his while jubilant cheers erupted from a craps table in the distance.

She gave her footwear an embarrassed glance. "My apologies for dressing like its karaoke night. I can't eat when I'm not comfortable. Hopefully you didn't notice."

He noticed. Her Santa Fe garb – close-fitting jeans, cowboy boots, and a snug, white cotton blouse – was more than alluring, and Dan felt self-conscious now about his own attire, more suitable for pledging a fraternity than greeting a governor and presidential contender.

"Speaking of apologies, the professor asked me to offer you one for any inconvenience. If you need a lift anywhere I—"

"Do you have somewhere you need to be?"

"Excuse me?"

"I have to eat and you keep trying to bail. Aren't you going to join me?"

Dan looked at her skeptically. "You don't even know my name."

"Sure, I do. You're Dan Cahill, Mr. Not Involved. Former Secret Service agent. The guy who got canned after the Cyprus incident."

"I didn't get canned, I resigned. And how do you know that?"

"I told you. Leila knows everything. I can barely function without her, but we tired of each other's company about a month ago. So, you're stuck with me for dinner. I promise not to ask for your vote or money."

Dan laughed. "You call yourself a politician?"

"One caveat though. Leila is trying to make sure we have a table with some privacy, but I'll be recognized out there. You know the drill. Assume every person in view has a phone camera pointed at us. I hope you'll stay, but I can't promise you there won't be a headline in the *New York Post* tomorrow declaring you my new sex toy."

"I can work with sex toy," he grinned, unable to keep his cheeks from coloring. It was madness to stay, with his foot destined to be soon planted in his mouth, but her charm and confidence were magnetic, and he was filled with curiosity about this woman. He vowed to stick to club soda.

Leila returned, handing a laminated index card to Morales.

"Tomorrow's schedule," the governor explained to Dan, pocketing the card.

"And some reading materials," Leila said, handing her a thick binder, which went into a large handbag. "In case Ethan Hunt gets a bat signal and has to bail. I'll be back at the hotel editing the new direct mail piece, and Zach promised he'll shoot us the speech for the Chamber of Commerce in Charleston sometime tonight. Text me when you're finished here, and I'll send Vic with the car. Nice to meet you, Mr. Hunt."

The manic aide was gone in a trail of vapor. Dan had known carbon copies of Leila in years past. Like Megan and Evan, they were the lifeblood of every campaign.

All at once, the governor seemed to breathe easier, as if every weight and burden of a presidential election had been lifted from her shoulders the moment Leila was out of range. A hostess led them across the dining room, with Dan a step behind Morales and fighting to keep his eyes from wandering anywhere ungentlemanly. As advertised, heads began turning and several diners whispered among themselves, reaching for their phones. They took their seats on opposite sides of a corner booth, tastefully set with a white tablecloth and array of small candles.

"I have two questions," Dan started as they opened their menus, and a server filled their water glasses.

"I'll give you one answer and one dodge."

"Don't take this as insulting, but aren't you a little young to be President?"

"Pro tip, Dan. You can't insult a woman my age by telling her she looks young. And the answer is no, according to the Founding Fathers. That Constitution thingy says a president has to be thirty-five, and I'll hit that the week before Inauguration Day. Though I'm not sure the powdered wig crowd had someone like me in mind. What's your second question?"

"No security?"

"Aren't you the professional?" Anna smiled, studying a wine list. "I have a State Police detail at home, but on the campaign trail, Vic and a couple of his guys travel with us. Depending where we are, he coordinates with the locals if we need more support."

"Vic is your driver?"

"He's a bit more than a driver."

Dan laughed.

"What?"

"Nothing. Sorry. Is he somewhere nearby?"

"He's in the resort somewhere, enjoying a thick steak. It may be the only upside to being so down in the polls. I can still go out for a relatively quiet dinner."

"Can I ask – are you enjoying it?"

"That's a third question. Campaigning?" She set her menu down. "You know, I think you're the first person who's asked me that since I announced. The truth is, yeah, I'm enjoying it. I love it. I mean, there's plenty of wackos out there, and people who want to bend your ear all day because they're convinced black helicopters have smuggled the next E.T. into Roswell. But for the most part, talking to people, engaging them – I get off on that."

Her eyes moved away, and Dan at first thought she might have regretted her choice of words. But there was a wistful smile, and Dan could see now she was lost in some past remembrance. After a few moments, she returned to him.

"Sorry. I was just thinking back to my first campaign. It was such an eye opener. I can't describe what it's like when people pour their hearts out to you, share with you their aspirations, their fears, their anger. There's nothing like it."

She paused, the passion in her voice palpable. "It's like a drug, Dan. Or a tonic. Maybe both. Some of their stories are so inspiring, others...heartbreaking. My first time out, it was overwhelming at first. But after a week on the campaign trail, I knew I made the right decision. I wanted to hear it all and fix it all. And since then, there's nothing else I've wanted to do."

"I always had the impression politicians hated campaigning. Especially the fundraising."

"Most do. And with good reason. The money chase is self-debasing. The public is beyond fickle; every time you're finally able to satisfy one constituency, another starts throwing poison darts at you. And your life is under a 24/7 microscope. But the payoffs rock. For me, at least. I'm guess I'm old school on this, but serving in office, serving the people, improving their lives – screw the poison darts. And I'll take the pitchforks of disenfranchised constituents on the campaign trail over the venomous infighting in Santa Fe or Washington every day of the week."

"Do you think you have a chance against Pierce?"

"Well, you're definitely not the first person who's asked me *that*." She propped her chin on her hand. "What do you think?"

"No way," he laughed. "Not going there. But you do seem to have quite a climb ahead of you."

"It's fucking Mount Kilimanjaro, Dan."

"So, no chance?"

"Are we speaking on the record or off the record?"

"Come on. Do I look like a reporter?"

"Another pro tip, Dan. In politics, there's no such thing as off the record. Make sure Walter knows that. And assumes everything coming out of his mouth will be on the *Drudge Report* the next day. Like the 2nd Amendment remark he made. But no, you don't look like a reporter, so I'll say this."

She softened her voice and leaned toward him. Dan caught a whiff of her perfume. Ralph Lauren perhaps.

"Any objective observer would tell you I have no chance. Pierce has got the core constituencies in the party locked down, and the RNC has leaned on every major donor and delegate to rally around her. It's Hillary all over again, but on the right now. I don't think it's healthy for the party or the country, so the more they circle the wagons around Pierce, the more I want a shootout. Look who she's speaking to, every single event. Evangelicals, pro-life groups, the gun-toting militia crowd, country club Republicans. Who doesn't she speak to? Young people, minorities, true small government conservatives who still believe in environmental protection and civil rights. Those are the voters who put me in office. But Pierce doesn't want them. And her demonizing of Democrats means we'll go back to four more years of Trump-style paralysis in Washington, regardless of who wins."

A server materialized and they ordered their entrees, agreeing to share a bottle of Pinot Grigio. So much for the club soda.

"So, you're running for the moderates?"

"That's how the media portrays it, but it's not that simplistic. Pro-choicers don't exactly think of me as a moderate. Nor do the doves in either party."

"So why are you running?"

"Do you know who my father is?"

As of an hour ago he did, thanks to Google. Most search results that came up under Anna Morales led with the same two bullets. She was the youngest governor in the history of New Mexico, and she was only the second most famous member of her family. Her father Frank was one of America's most admired military figures, a retired three-star Army general and former head of the United States Special Operations Command. As an Army Ranger during the Gulf War, he was awarded a Silver Star for carrying three wounded squad mates to safety under fire. A surgeon later pulled five pieces of shrapnel from his neck and shoulders, ending his combat career. He rose steadily through the ranks until the prestigious appointment to USSOCOM, where he oversaw the hunting down of the most wanted terrorists in the world. After retiring, he taught leadership courses at the Army War College and Harvard, while serving on multiple graybeard panels and advising two presidents. Lieutenant General Morales, Dan learned, was an accomplished, formidable man.

With an accomplished, formidable daughter.

He breathed in deeply. Definitely Ralph Lauren.

Anna audibly cleared her throat as she drummed her manicured nails on the table. He quickly searched his memory for the question she had posed.

"Sure," he recovered. "Everyone knows who he is."

Their wine arrived and after a generous pour from the server, they clinked their glasses in an unspoken toast.

"When I was in college, I flew up to New York for his retirement ceremony at West Point. We met in Manhattan, where he'd been invited to speak at a National Guard armory. We're taking a taxi from LaGuardia, and the driver, straight out of central casting, Queens accent and all, sees my father's uniform and starts going off on him, the Army, and the government. The cabbie's got three kids, who live with his ex in Jersey City, where his kids' schools are falling apart. The garbage collectors are on strike, and they can't get the city to take care of the stray dogs in the neighborhood. Forty-five minutes this goes on, and the whole time, my father is practically egging the man on, asking him questions, stirring him up. When we got out of the cab, I asked my father, why waste time talking to some nut you'll never see again? I'll never forget his response. Anna, he said, his eyes blazing, what did you hear that man tell us? I told him I heard a lot of griping about garbage men and barking dogs. No, he said, what you heard was everything you need to know about tax policy in the United States."

"Tax policy? How so?"

"My question too. He first reminded me his father drove a taxi in the worst *barrio* in Guadalajara. He then told me if I ever wanted to go into politics, I damn well better listen to what people like that have to say. That taxi driver needs the government's help. He's a hard-working Joe, the kind who doesn't like handouts. He's willing to pay, and he does, through taxes. But he wants – expects – something in return."

"More garbage men and fewer barking dogs."

"Exactly. But Anna, my father told me, if I ever teach you anything in life, remember this one thing. That taxi driver has value. Everyone has value."

She paused again, remembering. "Then he said the day he stopped caring about his soldiers in the foxholes would be the day he abdicated any notion of being a leader."

She picked up her glass and sat back in her seat, savoring the memory of a life lesson more than a decade ago.

"Sounds like quite a man."

Anna ignored the buzzing of her phone. It stopped, then rang again, and she picked it up without a single glimpse at the incoming caller, powering the device down and slipping it into her purse.

"Do you need to check on the professor? I get a call from Leila every twenty minutes in case I've fallen and can't get up."

"He's got company."

"He a widower, right? Does he live alone? I heard he had some trouble with those gun rights people."

"They'd be walking into a hornet nest. His sofa is currently occupied by a trigger-happy grandmother who sleeps with an arsenal under her pillow. And when he's out, he's either with me and my daughter or a police cruiser."

"Your daughter?" Her eyes immediately moved to his left hand, and a ring finger that had been bare for years.

"Yeah, she's one of Walter's students. And now she's one of his campaign managers. That's how I got lassoed into this. Twenty years old. Gets her politics from my ex."

A brazenly obvious word-drop at the end, and Anna's reaction told Dan it hadn't gone unnoticed.

"Ah, I remember her from the debate this morning. Beautiful girl. Is she anything like you?"

"Surly and sarcastic?"

She laughed. "I was going to go with funny and intelligent."

"You forgot devilishly good-looking."

"Well, if I said it out loud, we'd lose some mystery here, wouldn't we?"

He rolled his eyes – partly out of modesty, partly to avoid hers – and sipped his wine.

"What about you? Family? Significant other?"

She looked at him playfully. "What did Google tell you?"

"Divorced, nothing much beyond that."

"So, you did check me out."

A grin. "Pro tip, Governor. You have a Wikipedia page."

"It's Anna, please." She poured herself another glass and topped off his. "Seth and I met in college. We were both athletes, moved in together after graduation, then pushed each other into a marriage neither of us was ready for. Some indiscretions ended things, not even a year in."

"He cheated on you?"

"I cheated on him. Nothing I'm proud of, Dan, he didn't deserve it. But we married for all the wrong reasons. It's no justification for what I did, but I think we both knew the marriage was over before it really started."

"I'm sorry."

She waved it off before a surprising realization swept over her.

"You know what? Leila has been at my side forever, since she was my PA at the news station. We've been through three elections together, now four. And I've never told her how Seth and I fell apart. I've known you for thirty minutes, and

I'm already telling you a life secret the National Enquirer would pay half a million dollars for. Why is that?"

Dan held up his glass. "Worthy of trust and confidence. It's the Secret Service motto. Or, maybe it's because you know you'll never see me again."

"I won't?"

"You seem to be a little occupied at the moment."

"True. I wouldn't take it you ever find yourself in New Mexico from time to time? We have some big universities, lots of elderly professors you could drive around."

Dan felt her foot brush against his knee as she re-crossed her legs under the table. He had to remind himself this wasn't a date. His dinner companion was mesmerizing and captivating, but still, by definition, the opposition. Yet something was amiss. Starting with the pair of salads, untouched by two people so absorbed in conversation they hadn't noticed the server dropping them off minutes ago.

Following her lead, Dan started in on his plate, thinking back to what she had said, and what he had learned of her extraordinary rise in New Mexico and national politics.

Then he had his own realization.

"What?" she asked, seeing the look on his face.

He finished chewing a mouthful of kale and pointed his fork at her. "It doesn't add up."

"What doesn't add up?"

"I told you I checked you out. You ran for governor because you wanted to break the partisan gridlock in the state capital and actually get things done. I believe that. I mean, it's kind of cliché, but I believe it's what you wanted to do."

"Gee, thanks."

"That's why you're running for President too, right? Restore bipartisanship, move the country forward, blah blah blah."

"I like to think I'm somewhat more articulate than blah blah blah."

"Everywhere you've gone, you've achieved results. Your news program. The State Senate. Governor."

"Maybe you should be *my* press secretary."

"It doesn't add up."

"I'm having déjà vu. What doesn't add up?"

"The notion you'd rather be in Washington than New Mexico. A place where absolutely nothing gets done. Don't get me wrong. There are plenty of narcissistic, self-aggrandizing politicians out there, always looking to move up a notch in the food chain, just for the sake of moving up a notch in the food chain. But that's not you, is it?"

A waiter removed the unfinished salads and set down their main courses. Tilapia for him, penne pasta in arrabbiata sauce for her. Neither reached for a fork, and Anna sat expressionless, her eyes burning into him. Finally, she moved her plate aside and rested her chin again on her folded hands.

"Forty minutes now, we've known each other. Every political instinct in my body is telling me to laugh off your question. Tell you you're misreading things and assure you I'm going to Washington because I believe I can do more good there, and better serve the people of my state."

It was like he hit a nerve. "I didn't mean to suggest you don't care about people. You have—"

"I'm far from perfect, Dan, and I have my share of shortcomings. But dishonesty isn't one of them. I'm going to Washington because I believe I can do far more good there, and for far more people."

She paused, taking a long sip from her wine as she contemplated her next words.

"And yes, you're right, there's more to the story. But sharing that with a stranger would be more than reckless. Just like it's unwise, if not self-destructive, to continue this conversation."

"And yet we're still talking."

"And yet we're still talking."

"Vic is a phone call away."

Anna leaned forward again, her eyes exploring his. "What is this between you and me? Or do you not have any idea what I'm talking about?"

He knew exactly what she was talking about. "I – I don't know."

"How can I possibly trust you with my future? How can I want you to know more about me? How can I be thinking of slipping you my room key?"

They stared at each other wordlessly until Dan speared a piece of fish and lamely attempted to change course.

"You stole some of our limelight today."

Anna smiled at his redirect. "Did I?"

"Crashing a pretty well-staged media event, completely uninvited."

"Our state capitol is a roundhouse, Dan, and we had a saying about keeping confidential conversations 'in the round.' So now that we're talking shop again, let's keep this chat in the round, okay? The fake debate with one candidate facing an empty podium has been played out."

"I know. I tried to tell them."

"Journalists stopped covering those twenty years ago. They're not interested in props and Kabuki theater anymore."

"Then how do you explain—" Dan stopped himself.

Of course.

She smiled at his comprehension.

"They were there for you," he sighed. "You told them you'd be there."

"I hope you're not cross with me."

Dan laughed, shaking his head. "Just another reminder none of us knows what we're doing. Is that why you were hoping to see Walter tonight? To confess to your crime?"

"And offer some help. He's been trying to shoot quite a few arrows at Rebecca Pierce."

"And you can help."

"I need to help."

Her voice had abruptly changed, with a note of urgency now. As he watched her from across the table, he was struck by the sternness suddenly washing over her face, and the depth of emotion in her eyes. He saw a glimpse of something else, something so familiar. What he saw in the mirror every day. A show of strength, projected outward, intended to obscure any visible signs of softness or vulnerability. There was also conflict in her eyes, an internal one, and one he also knew all too well. Feeling bound by some mystery obligation to share nothing, but secretly yearning to find that trusted soul to share everything.

He lowered his fork, no longer hungry. It would never be found in anything as overt as her actions or words, but it was there, and only he could see it. She was reaching out.

"Life is short, my old man always said. And since we both know slipping me your room key would likely be the lead story on Drudge tomorrow, let me ask you just one last question. Not for the press, or the campaign, or the people. Just me."

Her eyes glowed like two small lamps. Encouraging him. Already knowing the question.

"Anna Morales, why are you running for President?"

She quickly scanned the dining area before pulling her phone from her purse. "What do you know about OPSEC, Dan?"

Not what he was expecting.

"Operational security? Lots."

She gave a grim smile as she swiped through screens. "So does my father. Let's hope he doesn't learn what I'm about to show you."

CHAPTER 23

The decisive moment came as their plates were cleared and the server spotted Anna swallowing her last drops of the Bordeaux they had moved onto. *Another round?* Such a harmless question, but as Anna regarded her intriguing new friend across the table, she was well-acquainted with what another round could mean. Caving to her impulses was a non-starter, the consequences nearly inconceivable should the evening turn an unexpected corner. Yet she was certain the hunger and isolation so clearly etched on his face was matched by her own. As the server waited for a response, a flurry of unspoken thoughts passed between the two, each tempted to throw caution to the wind even as they both knew they never would.

It was a moment she would not soon forget.

"Well, Dan, thank you for staying. I confess, I've never had dinner with someone from a rival campaign."

They were outside now by the valet pickup. Others were within earshot, so they kept their voices low.

"Speak for yourself. I'm meeting Rebecca Pierce for drinks in an hour."

She laughed. "Well then, I better let you go. Maybe our paths will cross again on the campaign trail."

"Walter's path won't be crossing the state lines. I'd suggest some path-crossing when the campaign ends, but Washington is a little far for me."

"Aren't you the optimistic one? You know there's a slight chance I just might end up back in Santa Fe."

"Then I just might have to visit Santa Fe. I'd like to see this roundhouse. And maybe one can find a decent Bordeaux in New Mexico."

"Maybe one can."

They were suddenly doused in headlight beams as a foreboding black Lincoln Navigator eased to the curb, prompting an awkward and reluctant parting. Aware of a watchful eye from behind the tinted glass, Anna could only offer her dinner partner a hasty farewell peck on the cheek, but her hands still found his as she backed away. And in those fleeting seconds, as she felt the warmth of his touch and the strength of his grip, she knew intuitively she had not seen the last of Mr. Not Involved.

Pulling open the passenger door – she refused to ride in the back – she greeted the driver and climbed in, powering her phone back on. Anna's uncanny gift for compartmentalization immediately kicked in, walling off every emotion and extraneous thought as she pulled herself back into campaign mode. She had little choice. The clock was ticking.

She patted the forearm of the stoic, muscled figure behind the wheel. He wasn't her father, but the next closest thing. Anna was seven months old when Frank Morales deployed to the Kuwaiti desert to fight Iraqis, the first of many prolonged separations during her adolescence. By the time he returned from his final tour in Afghanistan, her mother had fallen gravely ill, and the diagnosis was later verified by the finest oncologists on the East Coast. Anna's mother succumbed two years later, an agonizing bout that shattered their small family.

Frank barely had time to mourn before returning to his post, keeping the sacred promise he pledged to his wife in her waning days. He continued his advance through the Army's upper echelon, with high-level postings in Germany and at the Pentagon, capping off his career with the appointment to the much-heralded special forces command in South Florida. Anna became a standout at her Tampa high school, captaining both the volleyball and debate teams while serving as assistant editor of the campus newspaper. She enrolled at New Mexico State University – her mother's alma mater – on an athletic scholarship and became quickly taken with the climate and character of the Southwest.

Four years later, with a communications degree and several internships under her belt, Anna was hired as a local reporter at the NBC affiliate in Albuquerque. Within months, her workhorse approach won over the station GM, who green-lighted Anna's request to produce her own stories showcasing the plights of local businesses and non-profit organizations struggling against intransigent government regulators. She became a sensation among the local populace, and a force on social media where she plugged her efforts to expose bureaucratic mismanagement and abuse.

With growing popularity, and an effortless, on-camera poise, Anna was awarded her own Sunday morning current affairs program. The hour-long show drew a sizable audience across all demographics, elevating Anna from news reporter to news maker. She was a natural in front of the camera, amiable and quick-witted, and her sparring with local politicians and community leaders catapulted her ratings. She shied away from no topic, elevating the public discourse on everything from education reform and social services to local land disputes. She was twenty-four years old.

After two years on the air, Anna, a budding celebrity in New Mexico, left her colleagues and viewers in dismay when she announced her resignation from the station and a departure from the news industry altogether. She revealed nothing further until the closing seconds of her final Sunday broadcast, brandishing the papers she intended to file as a candidate for the New Mexico State Senate.

Few took her gambit seriously. The political establishment was particularly dismissive, seeing it as a hopeless fantasy for the young and recently declared Republican. Timing the announcement in the midst of a very public and acrimonious divorce was further viewed as a telling sign of her political naiveté.

Anna ignored the sniping, following instead the counsel of her most trusted adviser. Frank Morales had long known journalism quarters were too confining for his indomitable daughter. He sensed a greater calling and was the first to encourage Anna to explore a political run, particularly considering her home district, long held by Democrats, was expected to be far more competitive with newly re-drawn boundaries. Anna needed little convincing. In addition to her own ambitions, she was her father's daughter, born to fight.

The election proved to be a cakewalk no one saw coming. Anna had countless admirers, and for the masses who had connected with her on the airwaves, she was like family. The other contenders followed a political playbook from years past, espousing 20th century solutions to 21st century challenges. Anna articulated an inspiring vision for New Mexico's future, one that included an economic rebirth and a reimagined social fabric designed to offer more opportunities to New Mexico's impoverished communities. After besting an open field of other Republicans, she routed the five-term Democratic incumbent by ten percentage points.

Catcalls soon came pouring down from those in the party's most conservative wing, casting their doubts on Anna's core beliefs. Republican power brokers in Santa Fe ignored the noise, knowing they had an ascending star on their hands. As a freshman senator, she notched several legislative wins, earning wide praise from editorial boards and fellow lawmakers across the state, and later coasted to re-election. When the sitting governor accepted a Cabinet post in the Vance Administration, a special gubernatorial election was called, and Anna wasted no time throwing her hat in the ring. It was a whirlwind campaign, but one the untiring Anna relished, crisscrossing New Mexico and packing her schedule day and night with community events and speaking engagements. Endorsements and donations rolled in, and a few short months later, Anna was swept into office, winning sixty-three percent of the vote in a state that had voted blue in the past three presidential elections. She had just celebrated her thirtieth birthday, the third youngest governor in American history.

She made an immediate mark, becoming the most unconventional of chief state executives. It began with her Inaugural Address, where she pledged to embrace a nonpartisan approach to policy development and appoint qualified candidates to key posts regardless of political affiliation. Party loyalists were outraged, but she charged ahead anyway, determined to solve the thorniest issues that had vexed both political parties for years.

Her first test came a month into her Administration, when she formed a bipartisan panel to examine the state of education in New Mexico. An uproar ensued when her appointees prescribed a series of emergency measures to fix a public-school system deemed in crisis. Anna, already familiar with the institutional failures plaguing local and tribal school districts, embraced the wide-ranging recommendations without reservation, dismissing the political risks flagged by her advisers. She vowed to back any legislator from either party who supported the panel's slate of reforms, including raising teacher salaries, investing in school construction, expanding choice options, and declaring an education emergency in tribal districts.

In her path were two great obstacles, the teachers' unions and school choice advocates, each irate the other stood to gain in the legislation. Shunning the ideological purists in both camps who refused to cede ground, Anna barnstormed the state, rallying the public and local elected officials to her side and overcoming the opposition more easily than anyone thought possible. Her Students First initiative, a mix of new resources and inventive reforms, sailed through the State Legislature in a matter of months. It was an eye-popping triumph, and with soaring popularity and a campaign committee raking in cash, Anna was a lock for a second term.

But Anna wasn't finished with her surprises. The capstone came three months ago, when she set much of New Mexico and the nation's capital afire by declining to run for re-election. Instead, she pushed her chips to the center of the grandest of poker tables, declaring her candidacy for President of the United States.

The shock waves rippled through Republican National Committee headquarters. While pleased with her early political success, most in the party hierarchy still considered Anna little more than a neophyte. Her timing was baffling as well, announcing her candidacy so late in the year, and forsaking the conventional norm of declaring many months earlier to endlessly court voters in Iowa and New Hampshire.

And then there was Rebecca Pierce. National Republicans had been bullish throughout the autumn, as their not-yet-declared but unofficially anointed candidate surged in polling against Paul Sheffield, the likely Democratic nominee. A Pierce candidacy held the promise of uniting the party and drawing support from independents, suburbanites, and other swing voters who had drifted leftward in recent elections. Having already goaded several other potential GOP candidates out of the race to clear a path for the recently retired general, party emissaries were dispatched to Santa Fe to convince Anna to reverse course. She rejected every appeal.

By the new year, with both women officially in the race and Anna struggling to close the gap, those who had played hardball – counseling against her candidacy and then working to sink it – continued to send signals all would be forgiven if Anna quietly folded her tent. They even dangled a future cabinet position.

Anna tuned out the pleas, except one. She could not ignore Leila, and her empirical, data-centric reasoning. The Morales campaign continued to barely register with Republican voters nationwide. The donor base was mostly tapped out. And after the drubbing in Iowa, little new money or support was coming in.

To Leila's frustration, there was never any rebuttal from Anna. Just a simple refusal to change course, and a single-minded focus in forging ahead no matter the storm winds. Anna would even make light of their struggles, often quoting the former Chinese communist premier and his famous reflection that it was always darkest before it was completely black. Leila, loyal to her core, stayed on.

For Anna, the polls did not matter. Nor did the ire of the national party. Iowa, New Hampshire, her political career – none of it mattered. She had reason to gamble it all.

. . .

Anna settled into the leather upholstery. As usual, the car was at a morgue-like temperature.

"How bad is it?"

"Twenty-four points. About two-thirds of the precincts reporting."

Anna closed her eyes. "Could have been worse."

Vic grunted. "Could have been better."

She turned to him. "New Hampshire was never part of our strategy."

The driver grunted again.

"What?"

"It's politics. Perception is everything. Reality don't mean shit."

"Dad says the most important decision in any battle is choosing the ground you fight on."

"So, what ground you gonna fight on?"

"Charleston."

"Charleston?" Vic calculated that in his mind. "This soon? You clear that with Foxtrot Mike?"

Anna smiled at the nickname. Vic branded everyone using their initials and the Army's call sign alphabet. Leila was Lima Tango.

"He's already en route."

"Well then, fuck New Hampshire."

She laughed, toggling to her email inbox. "Where are we tonight?"

"A Hilton Garden Inn on the other side of town," replied Vic in his raspy voice, the product of a lifetime tobacco habit. The man had a future playing mob bosses in audio books.

"Why does it always seem like we're staying at a Hilton Garden Inn on the other side of town?"

"I've told your girl you need to start staying at places more...presidential."

"My girl is a woman, and her name is Leila. And I like Garden Inns. They always leave those little candy bars."

"They leave Goodbars, which rank up there with chocolate Blow-Pops and watermelon Jolly Ranchers."

Anna gave up trying to catch up with her email and put her head back, closing her eyes. "If only your Goodbar hate was our biggest problem."

"We have problems?"

"That's what they all seem to think."

"Who's they? Your date?"

"Anyone in politics. Or with cognitive skills. Or who can read a poll. And he wasn't a date."

"Russ Feingold."

"Who's Russ Feingold?"

"He was a young guy once, back about when you were born. A state legislator in Wisconsin. No one outside his district has ever heard of him, he's got nothing but the change in his pocket, and he decides he wants to be a U.S. Senator. A month before the primary election, he's at ten percent, way behind a sitting congressman and some millionaire. No one gave him a chance. A few weeks later, he wins the primary with seventy percent of the vote. Two months after that, he wins the general."

Anna was unsurprised by the recitation of random Wisconsin political history. Like most senior enlisted, Vic was a walking encyclopedia.

"Russ who?"

"Feingold."

"And you think I could be the next Russ Feingold?"

"Hope not. Ever hear of President Feingold?"

She smiled, closing her eyes again after another wearisome day in the books. They quickly snapped open.

"Why do you think it was a date?"

Vic didn't miss a beat. "Those jeans. That handshake."

"I thought I was having dinner with an old man when I put these on."

"Good thing he didn't show. Would've had a heart attack."

The man was part warrior, part Jewish mother. The credentials in his suit coat pocket identified Victor Parish as a Special Officer with the New Mexico Department of Public Safety, but the 9mm Beretta strapped to his hip wasn't standard police-issue. It was left over from his days as a career soldier, retiring as Command Sergeant Major, 75th Ranger Regiment. And in the decade since becoming a civilian again, the most trusted friend and confidante of his one-time commander, Lieutenant General Frank Morales.

Having enlisted after high school, Vic was still in his prime when he finished his thirty years in the Army, just weeks after his goddaughter became governor of her state. Too young to retire to a rocking chair, Vic was summoned to Santa Fe, and sworn-in as a member of Anna's security detail after the necessary hiring waivers were approved.

When campaigning, he and Leila were always at Anna's side, but in vastly different roles. Obsessed with politics, Leila was the most intuitive strategic thinker Anna had ever known. She was also a master coordinator, managing their traveling team of field organizers, press flacks, and advance staff with unmatched energy and efficiency. She wasn't much of a conversationalist though, and when the campaign was over, Anna had resolved to introduce the 29-year-old recluse to online dating.

While Leila held the campaign together, Vic was Anna's personal anchor. A man who always knew more than he seemed to, and never shied away from privately voicing views far more insightful than those of the pricey consultants they splurged on after first entering the race. She owed much of her sanity on the campaign trail to his biting humor, and though he rarely smiled, the occasional press photo of the two together made him glow like the proudest of papas. They were quite the mismatch. She, the long-legged, radiant Latina, always striding one step ahead of the stout, stern-faced soldier, with the ebony skin, shaved head, and ever-alert eyes.

The Navigator pulled up to the hotel and Anna climbed out, leaving Vic to his nightly indulgence, the Baccarat Luchadore cigars he discovered while stationed in Central America. Passing through the lobby, she waved to Pete Wickham, another plainclothes NMDPS officer, pretending to read a newspaper from one of the sofas. Arriving at her third-floor room, she swiped her key and heard the lock clicking open. Leila was in her usual perch, sitting cross-legged on the floor with an iPad in hand. She was encircled by her usual-colored folders, each adorned with an array of Post-It notes. It was her never ending struggle to mesh a daily schedule with their campaign strategy, without causing their logistics guru in Santa Fe to hurl herself from a cliff.

"Back from your date so soon," Leila murmured, her eyes zipping between her iPad screen and the purple folder at her knee.

"It wasn't a date. That speech come in yet?"

Leila threw a handful of Skittles in her mouth with a Diet Coke chaser as she waved toward a stack of papers on the nightstand, topped with a miniature, yellow-wrapped candy bar.

"Up there. I told Zach we need to lay off the education stuff. You can't come off as a one-trick pony. And honestly, Anna, we don't have time."

Anna reached for the speech and settled herself on the edge of the bed, skimming the opening lines. "Time for what?"

"Dating. We're getting creamed in New Hampshire, and we need you to focus on—"

"We aren't even competing in New Hampshire, and for Christ's sake, you and Vic need a hobby. It wasn't a date."

"Right." Leila looked up from her papers. "He's cute."

Anna grinned at her. "Think so?"

Her aide brightened. "Would you go out with him? If he asked?"

Anna chewed her lip. "Good question. Not exactly the best timing, and I—"

"It was a trick question," Leila moaned. "You're not dating anyone right now, Anna. We're not exactly getting quality ink out there and dating a Democratic campaign operative isn't how most candidates in a Republican primary would try to bring their numbers up."

"He's a retired Secret Service agent, not a campaign operative. All he's doing is driving a college professor around."

"A college professor with a guardian angel."

"What do you mean?"

"The casino guy, Syd Milburn. Politico has a story he's told the DNC if Sheffield doesn't endorse the professor's Cure Initiative, he's not giving another dime to Sheffield or the Democratic Party. Not to mention the buy he made here for that ad with the union lady."

"Big?"

"It's been running on the local affiliates and all over digital media for almost a week now. That's serious money."

"Is it helping Becker? Have we seen any numbers?"

"Nope. No one has bothered to poll their race here, because it wasn't a race. Sheffield may have some internal numbers, and if they show Becker drawing any real support, they'll come down on that old man like a ton of bricks. They can't have another embarrassment like Iowa. But whatever happens, the nomination is Sheffield's. They got no one else."

Anna kicked off her heels and laid back on the bed, leaning against the headboard.

"Good," she said, slitting her eyes. "I can take Sheffield."

"Yes, you can," Leila allowed. "But first we need the nomination, and you can't be making unforced errors in these early states. Including the ones we're competing in."

Anna roused herself. She knew her campaign manager too well. "Meaning?"

"South Carolina."

"Ah. This again."

"This again. It's not too late to pull out."

"I thought we already discussed this."

"I lost the argument, so I don't consider that a discussion."

Anna sat up, bracing herself for the tropical storm her campaign manager could mutate into on a dime.

"You can't be serious. The debate is in less than forty-eight hours."

"I know it's not the best optic, and the press—"

"The press will roast me alive and have a field day with the hypocrisy of ripping Pierce for limiting our debates and then pulling out of the one we've both agreed to. Our donors will flip out and wonder why they're still writing checks to us. What do we say to them?"

"We say you're standing up to the party bosses who rigged everything in that state. Who pushed every county chair not declared for Pierce out of their posts. Who gave Pierce the keynote at their state party convention last month. Who staged the one debate on a military campus, where her supporters will outnumber ours twenty to one."

"We're not pulling out."

Leila threw her hands up. "Look at the polling, Anna. That state worships Pierce. They resent you. Did you see the *ABC/Washington Post* numbers from the Super Tuesday states? We're in single digits in every one them. Every one of them, Anna. I'm fighting like hell to get you and Pierce on a stage together next week in Pennsylvania. But a slaughter in South Carolina and the networks will bag the whole idea if they believe re-runs of *Shark Tank* will get higher ratings."

Anna was quiet, and Leila persisted, urgency in her voice now. "We're down to our last $12 million, and you won't let me spend it. That's barely enough for a single ad buy for Super Tuesday. Or we can keep the lights on in Santa Fe for maybe another month. Not both." She paused. "I'm starting to feel like we're at the beginning of the end. You go to South Carolina, and it's a no-win situation for you. What did your father say once about walking into a minefield with snowshoes on?"

The governor moved to the window, folding her arms as she surveyed the lighted parking lot three floors below. She could see the glow from Vic's cigar, the bulky retired soldier leaning heavily against the SUV. Anna would not waver, but she also wasn't unmoved by the despair in Leila's voice. Her campaign manager was almost always unflustered, but for the first time Anna sensed defeat in her tone. Anna couldn't blame her. The nomination belonged to Pierce, and they both knew Anna had long ago forsaken any hope of joining the ticket or serving in a future Republican Administration.

Neither, of course, had ever been Anna's wish.

There was much even Leila wasn't privy to. Two others were. One was in his Kia Sorrento, clawing up the Florida panhandle on his way to Charleston. The other was outside, subsumed by a cloud of noxious Honduran tobacco fumes.

Anna flinched. *Make that three,* as she mentally added a retired Secret Service agent to the list. A man drummed out of his agency and now working for an enemy camp. A man whom she knew virtually nothing about. And yet as thoughts of their dinner filled her head, she could see herself smiling in the reflection of the window.

She faced Leila. It was time to add a fourth.

"You know who Mike Tyson is?"

As the words left her, Anna felt more at ease than she had in weeks. Leila was the most faithful friend she ever had, and for Anna, coming clean after so long to someone so close and sisterly felt almost like absolution.

Leila didn't look up, her head buried again in a layers of scheduling notes, having abandoned the previous argument.

"Of course, I know who Mike Tyson is," she said absently. "Creepy face tattoo guy."

"He was a great boxer. My father's favorite. He quotes him all the time."

"And?"

"Everyone has a plan," Anna parroted, "until they get punched in the mouth."

Leila lowered the sheath of papers in her hands, turning now to her boss.

"You're planning on punching Pierce in the mouth?"

"I need to make a call to Ira Painter. Tonight."

"Who?"

She swiveled to Leila. "You heard me."

"Why the hell do you need to talk to the editor of the *New York Times*?"

"Lei, it's time to fill you in on some things."

. . .

Across town, other strategists were plotting as well. By the time Dan arrived at the library from his dinner with Governor Morales, it was nearing closing time and the two campaign managers were powering down their laptops. Their candidate, of course, was still resting at home.

Megan and Evan took turns updating Dan on the ongoing fallout from the surprise push by Syd Milburn and Claire Levin. Milburn's digital marketing team was particularly effective, with new traffic swamping the campaign website and thousands of visitors downloading their one-page infographic on the Cure Initiative. Syd's hired guns were also hitting the streets, with more than 30,000 Nevadans already signing petitions for the Initiative, circulated across the Valley by an army of clipboard carriers. Levin, too, was knocking on doors with a handful of other union employees who had joined their cause. The *Review-Journal* had reported her formal offer to resign from the union, and the ensuing outcry from the rank and file for their national leadership to reject it.

Evan pulled his coat on. "You didn't have to come out here, Mr. Cahill."

"Yeah, Dad," Megan chimed in with a teasing smile. "We heard about your big dinner. How'd it go?"

"Lousy. Best carbs in Vegas and I had to order fish. How's the old guy?"

"I called him and he said Calamity Jane was taking good care of him, whoever that is. I was going to swing by if you want to come with me."

The heavy glass door was pushed open and a breathless Marques Newsome filled the doorway. He was one of the original student ringleaders that fateful evening weeks ago at Greenspun Hall, but a broken arm in an intramural flag football game sidelined him until recently.

"You guys hear the news? About New Hampshire?"

"What's happening?" Evan asked, reaching for his iPad.

"Polls closed two hours ago," Marques said, caressing the soft cast wrapped around his forearm. "Ninety percent of the precincts reporting."

"And?" Megan asked. "Blowouts on both sides, right?"

"Pierce and Sheffield are both winning," Evan confirmed, scanning headlines on his small screen. "Looks like a rout for Pierce. They called it as soon as the polls closed."

"Sheffield too?" Dan asked.

"No," Marques answered. "That's why I'm here. My moms and pops have been phone banking in Manchester all week, drove there from Philly. News people ain't reporting it yet, but Sheffield's only ahead by three points."

"Three points?" Megan shrieked, turning a number of heads from the tables outside their room. "There's no one else on the ballot!"

Evan scrunched his forehead. "Wait, why aren't they reporting it if ninety percent of the precincts are in?"

Marques grinned. "Because it's taking so long to validate all the write-in ballots."

Megan furrowed her brow. "Write-in bal – NO!"

"Yep. He's up three points on a write-in candidate." Marques used air quotes at the end.

"Oh my God," Evan gasped, his expression a mix of shock and delight. Only Dan remained expressionless, puzzling over who the write-in candidate could be. Certainly not Walter. There was no chance that many voters in New Hampshire had heard of their campaign. Megan quickly filled him in.

It had started a month ago with a single, disillusioned voter. A retired climate scientist and steadfast Democrat, whose forbearance for Beltway creatures like Sheffield had reached a breaking point. Irate over the lack of any viable alternatives, she erected a billboard on her apple orchard flanking Highway 3, just outside Nashua, exhorting New Hampshire Democrats to write in a "None of the Above" vote, permissible under State ballot laws.

Students at Dartmouth heard about the sign and took up the cause. They produced a quirky music video featuring a purposely awful "Check the None" rap song that became wildly popular and shared across the Granite State. National media outlets picked up the story, sparking doubts that ricocheted across New Hampshire as more and more Democrats began openly questioning the Vice President's ability to inspire even the most loyal party members. State Democratic leaders remained unalarmed, certain no one would take seriously the preposterous idea of a mock write-in-candidate at this late stage. What now appeared to be a grave miscalculation.

The campaign team departed the library as the lights flickered off behind them, and a short drive later, Dan and his daughter found the professor still ensconced in his living room, watching election returns on CNN with Barb Patterson. The race was down to two points between the Vice President of the United States and a glib slogan, and a gallery of pundits was offering bleak assessments of Sheffield's prospects in the general election.

"Well, this may help us draw a few more votes," Walter said, watching Dan stare at the television. "Penny for your thoughts, Mr. Cahill."

Dan shook his head in wonder. "Just imagining all the panic buttons being pressed in DC. This is looking like a bloodbath in November."

Walter smiled, holding up his iPhone. "Panic buttons indeed. I've received six phone calls in the last two hours. All from the 202-area code."

"Washington," Dan said, unsurprised.

"I haven't listened to the messages, but I can imagine who they're from."

"Sheffield's campaign?" Megan ventured.

"More likely the DNC. And there was one very interesting number. It started with 456."

Dan's eyes widened, and he shared a look with Barb. "You're kidding."

"What, Dad?"

"That's a White House number," Barb offered.

Megan put a hand to her mouth. "Holy shit. Sheffield has been in New Hampshire, so maybe its Vance, calling to ask you to drop out."

"I don't think they want to invite me over for bundt cake. But I doubt it's the President. More likely the Chief of Staff or another aide, looking ahead to our race. I agree with your father. Sheffield's people must be quite on edge right now."

"What are you going to tell them?"

"What do you think I should tell them, Megan?"

"That maybe it's time to ask themselves if they picked the right candidate."

"Yes, Mr. Cahill? I saw that face."

Dan let out a long breath. "Since they're not going to abandon Sheffield, and the usual grab bag of Democratic hits like health care reform and saving the spotted owls aren't working for him, you could suggest his people find a new issue to rally around."

Megan pouted her lips. "Back to this?"

Dan stayed focused on Walter. "You wouldn't want Sheffield to endorse the Cure Initiative?"

"Of course, I would. But not out of political expediency."

"Dad, Sheffield just got plastered in New Hampshire, and before that, the debacle in Iowa. Two of the biggest Democratic players in this state just endorsed our campaign. Why would we—"

"They didn't endorse the campaign. They endorsed the Cure Initiative."

"Same thing."

"Not the same thing. And let's talk about that. Milburn and Levin smoke a peace pipe, pour ungodly amounts of money into this race to elevate the one issue you're running on, but purposely stop short of backing you. Why?"

"Because they believe in ending cancer? Or is that too naïve, Mr. Cahill?"

"Way too naïve. And they're not trying to help your campaign, otherwise they would have said so. They're up to something else."

"What?"

"I'm not sure. Maybe—"

His words froze in mid-air as he caught Megan staring into the distance. Her eyes were indecipherable, but he could see the wheels turning. Then a quick scowl, and he knew she had found the answer still eluding him. He shook his head in wonder. The girl had more than a knack for this game; she had next-level instincts Dan could only have dreamed of when he was her age.

"Maybe *what*, Mr. Cahill?"

"Maybe my daughter can tell us."

CHAPTER 24

Hello America. I'm Rebecca Pierce, and I'm running to be your next President and Commander in Chief.

Let me begin by thanking the great people of New Hampshire for our overwhelming win in the primary yesterday. I am so grateful for your incredible support and enthusiasm. The Granite State knows how to fight.

And you aren't alone. Americans across the country are sending an emphatic message for change in Washington. They want to see an end to the corruption and incompetence. They want to see strong, moral leadership restored to the White House. They want to fight for what this country once stood for. And I am so proud to carry that banner on your behalf.

But wait, there's more.

To win back our country, it's long past time to take on the influence peddlers in Washington and remove power from the hands of those who have long abused it.

Our sacred Constitution is full of so much foresight and wisdom. But it was written in different times, by public servants of a far different caliber and character than those we find in Washington today. Those same Founding Fathers wisely provided a mechanism by which the Constitution could be modified to adapt to a changing world, and address failings in our governance framework.

That's why I want us to take a good, long look at Article I. Our Founders conceived the powers of Congress in an era where elected leaders were most loyal to their country, and the people they represented. But with the Capitol awash today in corruption and incompetence, what was once a hallowed institution is now a hollowed institution. Can we really trust the security of our nation and the prosperity of our economy, with a Congress bought and paid for by special interests? As John Adams once said, one useless man is a disgrace, two are a law firm, and three or more a Congress.

I propose we start by slashing their exorbitant salaries. Like many of you, I consider $175,000 a year for a three-day work week a brazen misuse of taxpayer dollars. I also want to amend the Constitution to return Congress to the citizen-legislature our Founders intended. We'll not only cut their pay, we'll cut their office budgets, and their overseas travel. We'll make it harder for them to raise your taxes, and harder to pass job-killing laws.

That's what I'm going to fight for. That's what we'll fight for together.

So, continue to make your voices heard. Continue to send us your small donations.

Join the fight, and take back your country.

CHAPTER 25

February 13
Nine Days to Primary Day

Along the banks of the Ashley River, in the heart of Charleston, lies the Military College of South Carolina, widely known as The Citadel. Throughout a rich heritage stretching across three different centuries, the institution had weathered the turbulent history of the American South, often from the center of the storm. Most famously, it was young cadets from The Citadel who fired the first cannon shots at Fort Sumter – the lightly-manned Federal installation guarding the mouth of Charleston Harbor – marking the commencement of the Civil War.

Like South Carolina itself, the school evolved from generation to generation, and had made a concerted effort in recent years to diversify its student body and promote greater tolerance on campus. But with rebellion in its blood, change had been a long, winding road for The Citadel, and came neither swiftly nor easily. The first black cadet wasn't admitted until 1966, and thirty more years passed before the first women were welcomed on school grounds.

While today's Corps of Cadets, 2,300 strong, certainly had a different cultural profile than past eras, The Citadel remained a deeply conservative institution. As a public university, the school was barred from political advocacy, but there was no shying from presidential politics among the cadets. Indeed, there was little doubt the evening's debate among the two Republican presidential candidates was being held on the home field of the retired Army general who at every turn crowed about her Southern roots and traditional values.

The bond was evident earlier in the day as senior cadets accompanied Rebecca Pierce on a campus walking tour with local news cameras in tow. What began as a small escort swelled into an impromptu rally, drawing hundreds of young admirers traversing the grounds between classes. Their embrace was almost rabid, the cadets electrified by a candidate finally willing to shake a long overdue fist at America's foreign enemies and weak-kneed allies. It was as if George Patton had reincarnated before their worshipping eyes.

Just as Leila had predicted, South Carolina had proven to be challenging terrain for those praising the virtues of a wider tent, and the Morales campaign had made few inroads among primary voters here. It was once thought Anna's lineage might be an asset. The Palmetto State revered its military icons, and though the name Frank Morales still carried considerable sway here, not a single coattail had emerged for his daughter.

As the candidates entered the closing segment of their nationally televised debate, the seated audience had shown little hostility toward Anna thus far. Like the Pierce campaign, those in attendance likely considered the governor a mere nuisance given her anemic poll numbers in their state. Anna becoming a threat to Pierce seemed as likely as Cadet Colonel Broxton Hale – the burly regimental commander – taking up yoga. It was evident again now, as Anna wrapped up her response to the last question. Each time she spoke, few seemed to notice or care how ably she shredded Pierce's positions, or eloquently articulated her own. Most in the audience simply tapped their feet in irritation, anxious for the limelight to return to the star attraction.

"And that, General, is why I reject the premise of the question. The Viper isn't a fighter plane, it's a financial sinkhole, paid for with blank checks and IOUs. I would prefer we invest those resources in our servicemen and women instead. Double the child tax credit for military families. Provide greater accessibility to counseling and other mental health services for combat veterans. Create subsidies for continuing education so there are better opportunities when they retire from active duty. Our people should be our priority. We don't need another Pentagon boondoggle plagued by cost overruns and test failures."

The lead moderator from CNN held up a hand just as the red light came on. "Thank you, Governor. Sixty seconds to respond, General."

In this phase, the candidates were required to pose questions to each other. The format was intended to liven the debate and add an element of unpredictability, but both Pierce and Anna were well-prepared, nimbly evading one another's pointed questions and using their allotted time to recite rehearsed talking points before pivoting to friendlier territory.

Pierce, basking in her ample leads in just about every state and national poll, wore a satisfied smile. With a confident and well-honed delivery, she held a command presence on the stage. Of average height and solidly built, she had shoulder-length, tawny hair, and behind a set of dark, emerald eyes, one sensed both steel and shrewdness. Her attire – a Merino wool jacket fitting neatly over matching slacks and a button-down, ivory blouse – was likely pleasing to both campaigns. She could not have presented a greater contrast to Anna, who wore a sleeveless, Mulberry-colored sheath dress and matching heels.

The former general began her next response with a dramatic head shake, as if slighted by the notion of a civilian daring to challenge her, of all people, on the worth of such a program. Pierce began her Army career in a helicopter cockpit, eventually commanding an air wing, and later, the Aviation Center Logistics Command. She went on to hold leadership positions in the infantry, serving as a division and corps commander before her appointment as head of U.S. Army Forces Command. From there, she was named Army Chief of Staff, earning her fourth star and becoming the highest-ranking soldier in the entire service.

Three years later, she was steamrolling to the GOP nomination. Tossing back her hair, she spoke to the camera again, having readied a kill shot in response to the young governor's claims.

"Let's be clear," she started, in her most forceful voice. "The F-44 Viper is the future of American military power. A strike fighter that ensures we continue to dominate the skies for the foreseeable future and remain well ahead of the Chinese and Russians. Oh yes, Governor, this is indeed about our servicemen and women. As someone who knows what it's like to strap into the pilot's seat to safeguard this country, I believe we owe these brave men and women the very best technology and weapons systems, no matter the costs. Unlike you, I will not put a price on their lives. It's that simple. That's why this program has the support of our Republican majorities in the House and Senate. Your opposition, Governor, puts you in the same corner as the Democratic President and Vice President, while the Russians and Chinese..."

Anna lowered her head as she scribbled gibberish on a notecard. It was pretense, of course, her attention no longer on Pierce's rambling response. The critical moment had arrived, and Anna was mentally preparing her next broadside. She pried her eyes back up, sensing the audience hanging on Pierce's every word, their adoration reaching a pitched level. For the briefest of seconds, Anna wavered, twinges of doubt coursing through her. A vital detail they may have overlooked. Potential retreat among her accomplices. The vengeful, scorched Earth assault on her character that would soon follow.

She quickly pushed it all aside. Every element was accounted for. The two dozen men and women in her fold were fully committed, and none were the type that would ever falter in the face of opposing fire. Like her, they were driven by noble ideals and the sanctity of public trust, all far outweighing whatever personal risk was in the balance. Most significantly, the man at the center of it all would never fail her.

As Pierce wrapped up her rant, Anna's eyes swept across the hundreds seated before her. Fellow Republicans all, but a different breed than those she knew out West. In the blaze of nearly blinding light from above, she could not see her faithful sidekicks, Leila and Vic, camped somewhere in the front row. But she knew they were there, alongside the trio of youngsters managing her ground game here. What devotion, she mused. Three young people, barely out of college, willing to operate in a state with swarms of belligerent, flag-waving conservatives holding little affection for the opposite wing of the party, most particularly anyone who stood against Rebecca Pierce.

There were more than a few military uniforms visible in the rows closest to the stage. The cadets had been heard from every time Pierce spoke, roaring their support as she railed against the futility of multilateral initiatives while demanding sweeping new investments in American air, ground, and sea power. It was no accident Pierce's spending plans would send a river of cash into South Carolina, Pennsylvania, Ohio, and select other states, all linchpins of her electoral strategy.

Anna's eyes drifted to the rear of the auditorium as she searched for a courtly figure likely seated in the very last row. He would not be in a uniform, but his hardened features, wooden posture, and perfectly knotted necktie would mark him as an old soldier. The distance would make difficult any mutual acknowledgment, but just the twinkle in his eyes would be enough. A familiar, momentary flicker of light and love that always took her back to the very first time he held her tiny hand in his and told his little girl how much she resembled her mother.

And then, she found him. Somehow, his silhouette took form, and she felt his eyes meetings hers. There was an unspoken question, one nagging at her all evening as she fretted about the repercussions to him, and the peril she knew she was putting his reputation and legacy in. And then, as if reading her thoughts, she saw a firm nod and a hand moving to his chest, tapping what she knew would have been the ever-present pin on his lapel. The red, blue, and gold of the elite 75th Ranger Regiment. His first major command. His beloved soldiers.

Anna stiffened, self-discipline filling her again as the moment approached. She was risking a presidential campaign and her political career. He and the others were risking so much more.

"Governor Morales, your question."

Anna turned to her adversary, greeted by an almost taunting glare that did little to cloak the general's sense of superiority. Anna sensed impatience as well from someone surely accustomed to deference from others, if not submission, and likely pondering why she was sharing a stage with a second-tier challenger drowning in every poll.

"My last question for General Pierce is a simple one. You have been running on a platform of strength and leadership, citing your military experience as your greatest qualification to serve as president. So, my question is, how do you square that with the dishonor and disgrace you have brought to the uniform you once wore?"

A pall settled over the audience, the charge instantly shocking the boisterous cadets into silence, other than a few murmurs of stunned disbelief. The explosive words had been lobbed at the most celebrated military figure in the country with the subtlety of a hand grenade. Quickly recovering, the cadets began to stir, gripped by the horror of hearing such slander delivered on their own soil. For these young men and women in uniform, a word like dishonor was more than insulting, it was incendiary. In a different era, such an accusation would have been met with dueling pistols.

At home, millions of viewers froze as well, startled by the break in etiquette and precipitous shift away from the banal platitudes and policy esoterics that had thus far marked the debate. The split screen captured the heightened drama onstage. A defiant Anna, standing tall, across from a clearly shaken Pierce, who stared into the camera with a mix of uncertainty and outrage.

The moderator cleared his throat. "Is that your question, Governor?"

Those few seconds were all Pierce needed to collect herself. She slowly turned to Anna, marshaling every ounce of indignation, practically spitting her response through clenched teeth.

"How dare you, Governor," a scornful Pierce began. "And how desperate you must be. Coming from someone who has never worn a uniform, let alone served her country in any—"

"Many Americans, General, serve their country without donning a uniform. Nurses, teachers, public servants. Americans you keep vilifying on the campaign trail. And please know I was born in a military hospital, and raised by the most honorable of Army officers, a man decorated three times for valor. Like you, the Army is the only family I've ever known. Unlike you, I have never betrayed that family."

Pierce's jaw dropped an inch, and this time a collective, audible gasp rose from the audience. The young cadets, appalled by language usually associated with the likes of Benedict Arnold, cried out, their boos and hisses filling the air.

Pierce inhaled deeply, understanding the gravity of the moment. It was a test she hadn't foreseen, but one she welcomed, nonetheless. How she countered this salvo would soon be dissected and analyzed by every armchair pundit in America. It would have little impact on the primary, already essentially over, but they would see Pierce's response as indicative of how she might later fare against a polished campaigner like Paul Sheffield. Knowing flag officers of Pierce's stature were rarely challenged or criticized in person, her team had her well-prepared, and when the general faced the camera again, the words came easily.

"Governor, I don't know what your ploy here is, but it is truly offensive and beyond the pale. You dare to question my personal honor? I understand your frustration. Your campaign has not fared well, and you're finding little support in the Republican Party. But I thought we were here to debate the issues and challenges facing our nation. Not engage in petty insults and unfounded character assassination. I didn't expect that from a fellow Republican. Assuming you are still a Republican."

The cadet corps reacted as expected, whooping with approval. As if Pierce had parried Anna's thrust and delivered a fatal strike of her own. There was a different take among the veteran political pros in the audience, as they anxiously awaited the next barb. Unless this was some pointless bluff, whatever cards the young governor was holding had not yet been played.

"Sixty seconds, Governor," the moderator intoned.

Anna turned away from Pierce and ignored the jeering from the front rows. It was time to speak to a wider audience.

"I do not choose my words lightly. Nor does it bring me any joy to expose wrongdoing within an institution I have loved my entire life."

The tension in the room was oppressive, as was the anticipation among millions of television viewers, the assembled media, and perhaps even Mike Tyson.

"Minutes ago, my campaign loaded several documents onto our website, Morales4America.com. Documents that you, General Pierce, took many steps over the years to bury. The first document relates to your brief tenure as head of the Aviation Center Logistics Command back in 2009. You were a recently promoted colonel then. The document is a memorandum to you, signed by your deputy, warning of repeated mechanical failures in the avionics of the S-88 Tempest, at that time the Army's newest helicopter and still in its testing phase. The second document we've shared is the report you filed to the Secretary of the Army two months later, finding pilot error for a training accident involving a Tempest at Fort Rucker, Alabama, where you were in command. That crash killed the crew and four other soldiers onboard, and yet for some curious reason, you overruled your own investigative board, suppressing its findings. Six weeks after filing this report, and just six months after your promotion to colonel, you were made a brigadier general, and deputy commander of the 2nd Infantry Division."

"Governor Morales," the moderator injected, "your time has expired." But his voice was lost among the blare in the audience. Not that he cared. The man had been a broadcast journalist for thirty years and was well aware of what he was presiding over.

"If you are insinuating I—"

Anna cut Pierce off. "But wait, General, there's more."

There were few neutral observers in the audience, but every one of them guffawed at Anna's appropriation of the line. A rotund figure sprang from the front row and dashed to an outer hallway leading to the event control room. Anna could not see his face, but knew it was Pierce's acerbic, high-octane campaign manager.

He knows, Anna thought to herself, the man's muffled outburst reverberating inside the hall.

Pierce shot the moderator a look. Her signature bravado had vanished, and her eyes were imploring the man to enforce the mutually agreed upon rules. Before he could intercede, Anna barreled on.

"Four months after you departed the Aviation Center Logistics Command, there was another accident involving a Tempest, this one at Fort Benning. The pilot, his crew, and six Army Rangers perished in that crash. Your successor at Fort Rucker, with the support of the Army Chief of Staff, grounded the entire fleet pending a full investigation. On our web site, the public can find an account of the Fort Benning crash, and the results from the subsequent investigation. Including a finding of the same faulty avionics you covered up at Fort Rucker. It should be mentioned that the Tempest, built by Quantica Aviation, was an $18 billion acquisition program."

At the mention of the name Quantica, Pierce visibly blanched, and Anna could discern frantic movement among the media members in the very front row.

"Anyone care to guess what company, years later, put General Pierce on their Board of Directors with a seven-figure salary, the day she retired? Joining the retired three-star who secured her promotion to flag rank. A company that has funneled millions of dollars into a Super PAC supporting the general and provided the private aircraft that flew her here from New Hampshire two nights ago."

Anna turned to Pierce once more, the general speechless again.

"Fifteen soldiers, needlessly killed, General, so you could shield your patrons from financial loss. Duplicity for which you were richly rewarded. A higher rank and prominent command, at first, and now blood money. That doesn't sound like leadership to me. So, let me ask you this final question, General. Is it corruption, incompetence, or both?"

. . .

Two days later, the tremors from the Charleston debate were still reaching far beyond the South Carolina coastline. As Anna's father had anticipated months ago, the national media sank their teeth into the story, as budding young sleuths from the *Washington Post* to the student newspaper at the University of Pennsylvania meticulously scrutinized every facet of the design, testing, and deployment of the S-88 Tempest.

Once the dam was broken, other serving and retired officers began talking to the press, adding fuel to the spreading fire. Among the lowlights, bewildering personnel decisions among those under Pierce's command, interference with acquisition and procurement matters outside her responsibilities, and even an inappropriate relationship with an allegedly coerced subordinate. Searing headline after headline rocked the Pierce campaign, and her public support began to wane as her numbers on character and truthfulness tumbled. Meanwhile, Morales was gaining ground, more than doubling her previous share in South Carolina, Nevada, and a host of Super Tuesday states.

Still, it was far from a knockout blow. Pierce assembled a tenacious defense, denying every allegation involving the Tempest, and citing a long history of bipartisan support for the program, from the Obama and Trump Administrations to both Republicans and Democrats on Capitol Hill. She accepted responsibility for her marital affair, even as her surrogates were blanketing the airwaves, defending the episode as consensual and commonplace in military circles. They raised the specter of a double standard, noting male officers were rarely demoted or reprimanded for the same offenses. An argument that had much resonance among women voters.

The expected counterpunches came as well, as Pierce and her allies attacked Anna relentlessly. Super PACs supporting Pierce launched full barrages, painting Anna as a career politician willing to say anything to get elected, and an underground liberal who identified as a Republican only to boost her electoral chances. Right-wing bloggers chimed in, repeating lurid gossip swirling in remote corners of the Santa Fe statehouse for years that Anna's relationship with a female Democratic state lawmaker went beyond the traditional boundaries of friendship.

A week after the debate, it appeared Pierce might have withstood the worst. Her numbers stabilized, and though large swaths of supporters had defected to Anna or the undecided column, Pierce preserved her leads in the early voting states.

The one exception was Nevada. Once up by a dozen points, Pierce was now neck and neck with Anna in the Silver State. The Pierce campaign poured more resources into the Las Vegas and Reno media markets, confident a win in Anna's Southwestern backyard, followed by a triumph in South Carolina, would snuff out the last of the resistance to her nomination.

Anna knew differently. This was all just the beginning, not the end. No matter the vast resources at Pierce's disposal, and no matter how low Pierce was willing to stoop, Anna was her father's daughter, and retreat was nowhere to be found in her lexicon. She could hear her father's voice, the words he spoke to her the day she announced her candidacy for the New Mexico State Senate.

As long as we persevere and endure, we can get anything we want.
Another Mike Tyson gem.

CHAPTER 26

February 16
Six Days to Primary Day

Even the façade of a building reminded Dan how strangely foreign the current political cosmos was from that which he recalled of his youth. The Nevada State Democratic Party was housed in a contemporary, glass-encased structure just off of Russell Road. A far cry from the drab, threadbare campaign offices Dan and other Massachusetts Republicans once toiled in. Housed in unleased strip malls, those makeshift spaces were often windowless and sparse, with the exception of the battered metal desks and other secondhand furniture liberated from corporate scrap heaps. They were prison wards compared to the confines these Nevada Democrats were working from, the contemporary design resembling an off-shoot of the renowned Google campus.

The invitation from Marc Powell wasn't entirely unforeseen. They had long expected causing enough of a local stir would likely prompt some sort of call to the principal's office. That call came yesterday, and with Megan and Evan spearheading the leafleting of neighborhoods with their dwindling supply of flyers, it was left to Dan to accompany the professor to the State Party's woodshed.

They negotiated a late morning meeting. As the campaign entered its final week, Walter would not ease up on his stakeouts at grocery stores and shopping centers, determined to engage every last voter in Southern Nevada. Nor would he pare back his teaching schedule, despite the clear toll the endless stumping was taking on his physical condition. He was no longer able to rouse himself at dawn, and, lacking the energy for his mile-long walks to campus, he became a fixture in Dan's passenger seat. By mid-afternoons of late, he could barely keep his eyes open, and Dan knew he and Barb were in unspoken agreement: the end of the campaign couldn't come soon enough.

On the ride to Powell's office, Walter seemed mostly alert, relieving Cahill. It wasn't likely to be a pleasant discussion, particularly given the names of other attendees Powell had shared, so the professor would have to be on his game. As Dan accelerated down Tropicana Avenue, Walter queried him on what he thought they might hear.

Dan proffered his best guess, suggesting it would be cordial at first, with ample flattery to soften the professor up. They would then prevail on Walter to bow out and throw his support to the Vice President, warning unless Sheffield emerged from Nevada with a far stronger showing than Iowa and New Hampshire, there would be little hope of stopping Rebecca Pierce in November.

Walter was firm; there would be no dropping out, and Dan expected no less. The man's loyalty was to his students, not the Democratic Party, and he would never walk away from them, let alone abandon a cause he was clearly so wedded to.

After arriving at the office building, they were led to a sun-filled corner office decorated with vintage Marine Corps recruiting posters from the two world wars and souvenirs from Powell's postings in Okinawa and Iraq. The Political Director waved in greeting from behind his desk as two other guests stood in welcome.

"Good to see you again, Mr. Powell. Hope we haven't been causing you too much heartburn."

Powell shrugged, clasping the older man's outstretched hand. "Heartburn is all we got around here, Professor. But like Truman said, if you can't stand the heat, go sell table saws at Home Depot."

Four chairs had been arranged in front of the desk and they all took their seats. Handshakes and names were exchanged before Powell turned to Dan.

"Where's my favorite data entry girl who never does any data entry?"

"In Southern Highlands, going door to door. Probably won't run into anyone from the Vice President's campaign out there."

The younger of the two strangers loudly cleared his throat. The strategist ignored it and faced Walter.

"I have some good news for you."

"Oh?"

"And our visitors have the not-so-good news."

Walter crossed his legs, appearing far more relaxed than Dan felt. "I suppose they're not here to volunteer on our campaign."

The other two men remained unsmiling as they shifted anxiously in their seats. The tension in the room was thick as sludge. The younger of the two was practically sneering at Walter in disapproval, his stooped posture and narrowed eyelids reminding Dan of a Doberman straining at his leash.

Powell gestured toward the older man first. "Cole here is a vice chair of the DNC. Alan is their Western Regional Director. They flew out just to meet with you."

"Why don't you tell us the good news first, before these two gentlemen rough us up."

"You have to promise me it doesn't leave this room." Powell waited for confirmation from both Walter and Dan before continuing. "According to our internal polling, your numbers are ticking up. I can't give you the data, we keep that all in-house. And you're not leading, or even close to the Vice President. But you've come a long way in just a few weeks."

It was indeed good news. They had no polling until now, as the only public numbers released in recent weeks had focused on the expected general election matchup between Sheffield and Pierce.

Walter winked at Dan. "Not bad for a bunch of wide-eyed idealists and an old bag of bones."

"You forgot the driver."

"You're the old bag of bones."

Dan laughed and even Powell seemed to crack a smile before the younger visitor coughed into his fist.

"Unfortunately," Powell continued, making no effort to conceal his irritation with the party man, "people are taking notice."

Dan held out a hand. "People like these two."

"Perhaps, Mr. Powell, people have noticed our Cure Initiative is resonating across Nevada."

"Perhaps. But sometimes if the mice play a little too loud, they wake up the cat."

Walter offered a faint smile. "The *mice* are *playing*, are they?"

"I didn't mean—"

"Let me guess," Walter stopped him, facing their visitors. "The Vice President is asking me to withdraw from the race, for the sake of party unity and our common goal of vanquishing Rebecca Pierce in November."

"We don't work for Sheffield's campaign."

It was the first time Coleman Baldinger had spoken. With his silver mane, formal manner, and pressed, three-piece suit, the heavy-set Baldinger reminded Dan more of a bank manager than a political mastermind. He spoke with a deliberate tone, and his bearing was self-assured, suggesting a man who commanded attention. There was keenness too in his eyes, as well as something darker.

"Like Marc, we have remained neutral in the contested states, making sure any qualified candidate has equal opportunities throughout the primary process."

Dan couldn't help an eye roll that would have made Megan proud. "Would that include convincing Sheffield to debate us? Our campaign manager has tried to reach you people for three days now. Not one returned call."

Walter smiled at him. "*Us*, is it? Why, Mr. Cahill, you're starting to sound *involved*."

Alan Perlman's face coiled into a scowl. Reed-thin and decades younger, he was Baldinger's opposite in nearly every way. More stylish to begin, with a tailored Hugo Boss sport coat molded perfectly over a lavender Oxford shirt. And much more sullen.

"No one has asked us about a debate," he sneered, with all of the charm of a prison guard. "Your *campaign manager* seems to be stretching the truth a bit."

Dan felt the professor's hand on his forearm. Beyond the swipe at Megan, it had taken considerable prodding to finally persuade Walter to challenge the Vice President. Even Barb Patterson added her voice to the chorus. Walter was reluctant at first, mindful of how fruitless and transparent his debate ploy with Pierce had proven. The others wore him down though, convinced they were running out of time and a shake-up was desperately needed in the closing days. He eventually relented, but it proved a moot point. Every overture to party officials had been completely ignored.

"That campaign manager is my daughter, and she hasn't worked in politics long enough to know how to stretch the truth. And these kids aren't as stupid as you think. They had a Plan B. The debate sponsored by the Nevada State Education Association. It was supposed to be tonight. Sheffield was on board, as was the Green Party candidate. We contacted the SEA, and they agreed to put

Walter on the stage. The next day, they told us they had to scrap the entire event. Why? Because you guys threatened to pull out unless every declared candidate was invited to participate."

"We believe in an inclusive—"

"Inclusive? Are you fucking—"

"Mr. Cahill," Walter warned.

Dan stopped himself. He spoke again, his voice calmer but still curt.

"They *had* an inclusive debate. Sheffield, Walter, and the Green Party. But your edict would have included a bunch of nutjobs and bomb throwers who made it on the ballot, turning the debate into a complete circus. So the SEA cut their losses and killed it."

"We had nothing to do with their decision," Baldinger explained. "And I assure you, I don't approve of such tactics. You can believe that or not, I do not care. But check my reputation, if you must."

Dan already had, the moment Powell told them who called the meeting. Baldinger was a longtime congressman from Orange County, and former chairman of the House Energy and Commerce Committee. The ink was barely dry on his retirement a decade ago when every high-powered lobbying firm in Washington began jockeying to put his name on their letterhead. With his Rolodex alone a gold mine, he landed one of the most sought-after perches in Washington, heading the government liaison shop for the Motion Picture Association of America. As Hollywood's top man in the capital, Baldinger split his time between cornering former colleagues on electronic piracy and copyright infringement issues and hosting lavish events and movie premieres at the MPAA's opulent office, just blocks from the White House.

He left after just two years; a lifetime partisan tired of playing nice with the same Republicans he had clashed with his entire career. Chummy with Obama, loaded with political connections, and still a prodigious fundraiser, he was awarded a top post with the national party. Considered the backbone of the leadership apparatus, Baldinger was regarded by many as singularly responsible for the party's post-Trump resurgence.

Dan cast an eye toward Powell, perplexed by the man's uncharacteristic silence. He hadn't expected the former Marine to be so cowed by party henchmen parachuting into his state.

"Mr. Baldinger," Walter said, "I may be new enough to presidential politics, but your name and reputation are well known to anyone who reads a newspaper. Whatever brings a man of your stature all the way out here cannot be trivial. So please, what can we do for you?"

Baldinger leaned forward. "We were contacted by a woman named Elise Haynes, who lives in the San Francisco Bay Area. Does that name mean anything to you?"

Walter squinted, searching his memory. "No. Should it?"

"She met with one of our attorneys and made several astonishing claims. And, well, I'll get to the point. The party has an investigative firm on retainer. They are very capable, and very discreet. It didn't take them long to verify the allegation from Ms. Haynes."

"And what does this woman I have never heard of allege?"

"She is the sister of Julia Stillman."

The reaction from Walter was instantaneous, his face suddenly darkening as his eyes dropped to the floor. The room went still, and only the deadened voices of phone bankers on the other side of the wall chatting up potential donors could be heard.

To Dan's surprise, Baldinger was plainly uncomfortable. Whatever message the party dean was here to deliver, he was not relishing the task. His younger cohort seemed to have no such aversion, the man's demeanor resembling a circling vulture.

When Walter finally spoke, his words were almost a whisper. "Oh, the lengths you people will go to."

Baldinger shook his head. "We did not instigate this, Professor. We merely validated it."

The younger visitor was contemptuous. "Did you really think this wasn't going to come out? Maybe you can get away with that crap in Vegas, but not—"

"Alan," Baldinger said quietly, with enough menace to silence his colleague. His voice toward Walter remained gentle. "We're not here to re-open old wounds, Professor."

Dan continued to eye Walter closely. The name clearly had a jarring effect on a man so famously composed and unruffled. His skin seemed a shade paler, and he appeared almost unable to speak, as if a crushing weight had fallen on his chest. Something was seriously awry, but Dan was his only ally in the room, and felt compelled to fill the void.

"Then what the hell are you here for?"

Baldinger sighed. "It isn't in the interest of anyone in the party for what we've learned to become public. Our national chairman has contacted the woman and convinced her not to share her story any further. But given the assortment of people she has already revealed it to, we have to assume it will likely get out."

"Convinced?" asked Dan, dubious.

"Convinced. A phone call, sir. We're not the mob."

Dan turned to the professor. "You want me to step out so you can continue this in private?"

Walter's face was ghost white now. "Go ahead, Mr. Baldinger. Let Mr. Cahill and Mr. Powell hear what you've learned."

Baldinger nodded, his tone reluctant but not lacking assurance. "It was 1993, and you were in your eighth year at the university. You had an affair with Ms. Stillman, who was just twenty-one years old and one of your undergraduate students. She got pregnant, and when she learned you had no intention of leaving your wife, she tried to take her own life. They pumped the pills out of her stomach, and she lost the baby. Her parents threatened to sue, and there was a settlement. The dollar amount was never disclosed, but it was contingent on Ms. Stillman leaving the university. This is what Ms. Haynes is claiming. Do you deny any of it?"

Dan was holding his breath, dazed by the charges. He waited for Walter's denial and umbrage, any display of emotion. Rage surely, that members of his own party would manufacture such an absurd charge, or deliberately misconstrue some unfortunate past episode to cast a troublesome foe in the worst possible light. But the professor simply sat still, his face inexpressive, unwilling to repudiate a single word.

The party official leaned back in his chair. "I see. I'm sorry, Professor, but I hope you can understand our position. For the moment, the DNC will continue to remain neutral, both here in Nevada and nationwide. This is Marc's backyard, but I'm sure he considers this a precarious time to have such controversy flare up and risk damaging our Election Day prospects as a whole. So, I'm here to ask you to consider whether moving forward with your candidacy is in the interest of the shared outcomes we are united behind. There is so much riding on this election, Professor, far beyond the White House. Congress, state houses, the courts, they're all in play. The brand of our party must be strong. It has to be inspiring, and unassailable. The ideals you have expressed in your campaign, they are aligned with our every endeavor on the national level. So, I'm asking you to think beyond your own candidacy, and consider instead the broader interests of the country."

There it was, just as they had anticipated, but there was no grand, defiant response from Walter. He stood slowly, his shoulders sagging, and Dan knew he was watching a beaten man, unable to make eye contact with any of them now.

"Finish this meeting for me, will you, Mr. Cahill?"

"Me? Where are you going?"

"Home. I have some things to think about."

"I don't need to be here. I can drive—"

"Call me an Uber, please."

"An Uber?"

"Yes. And stay here, please. I suspect these gentlemen are not finished." He tilted his head toward the others. "I thank you for making the trip out here. And you, Mr. Powell, I – I'm sorry."

They watched the old man walk out, closing the door quietly behind him.

"I should have worked at Home Depot," muttered Powell.

Dan finished ordering the car service from his phone and glowered at Baldinger.

"You have your scalp now. Happy?"

The older man looked at him unkindly and his voice had a harder edge now. "Don't be naive, son. Marc has told me about your background, so I know you've seen the rough and tumble of presidential politics before. It's never pretty, and Walter is lucky."

"Lucky," sneered Dan.

"Yes, lucky. He can still get out before any of this hits the press. That will at least dull the pain somewhat. Not everyone gets that chance."

"Not everyone *deserves* that chance," chimed in Perlman.

"Fuck both of you."

Baldinger started to respond but stopped himself, sharing a look with his colleague. "I think that's our cue."

The two men left without goodbyes, leaving Dan and Powell alone. The strategist hadn't moved the entire time, the back of his chair still tipped against the wall, his hands tented on his belly.

"I guess you got what you wanted."

Powell scowled at him. "You don't know what the fuck I wanted."

"A clear path for Sheffield. Just like them."

Powell laughed, but there was no humor in it.

"Wide right, rookie, wide right. I've known Cole Baldinger for more than a decade. I know how he operates, and I know who he works for. We're both dyed in the wool Democrats, and we believe in the same issues and vision for the party. Beyond that, we don't have a goddamn thing in common. I'm not like them."

"You want Walter out of the race, don't you?"

Powell tilted his chair forward until it rested on all four legs. He flexed his artificial limbs, rubbing the back of his thighs.

"I know how much this stings, Dan. But he had an affair with a student, and then got her booted from campus to keep his secrets and save the university the embarrassment. It's not unforgivable, but there are political realities here. You get that?"

"I get it. He stays in, the story gets out while the election is still front-page news."

Powell shook his head. "Forget whatever kind of 'dull the pain' bullshit those assholes were slinging. The story is coming out, very soon, whether or not Walter gets out of the race. It's six days before the primary, Dan. Six days. Even if he dropped out, his name would still be out there, and he'd still draw votes away from Sheffield. The party can't have that. They need his reputation to take a hit. Right now."

"Why do they care how many votes he draws? Sheffield will still win. And Baldinger said he didn't want the party damaged right before Election Day,"

"People like Baldinger don't consider Walter the party. They're focused on the big picture, racking up wins in the primary, state-by-state until every Democrat is lined up behind Sheffield. If that means a day or two of bad headlines, just to make sure Democratic voters aren't tempted to pull a lever for Walter and run up his numbers here, that's a trade-off they're willing to make."

Dan felt nauseated. "What should he do?"

"For most people, I'd tell them to quietly drop out and stay out of sight. Ignore the crappy headlines and let the storm pass in a few days. Everyone can rehab in time."

Powell paused, thinking it all through. "He won't do that, though. The man is a fighter, and he cares too damn much about his students to pull up stakes now. So, his only other option is to confront it head-on, explain things, and give a mea culpa. The people he cares about – his students, his colleagues, his friends – they'll forgive him. He'll get thumped in the election, but the life he knew before? He can still have it back. Most of it, at least."

"Only one problem with that."

"What's that?"

"I don't think he wants to go back to that life."

"Then what does he want?"

"He wants to cure cancer."

"I know," Powell said, a wry smile on his face. "Why do you think I'm voting for him?"

CHAPTER 27

The dining room table was worn and chipped, an apt description of the man seated at its head. Walter had spoken fondly of the table, hand carved from California walnut by his father, who labored as a carpenter's apprentice in his German youth. Walter and Hannah breakfasted here every day of their marriage, and the table had witnessed more than a few heated discussions over the years. There were no such spirited exchanges at the moment, the mood far more somber now. The voices around the table were muted, filling the room with awkward silence and frayed trust.

They were still absorbing all that Walter had painstakingly shared. His voice had been uneven throughout as he struggled to get through the unsavory details, his embarrassment more than evident. There was genuine remorse, but Dan also sensed bitterness behind the words. He sympathized, well-experienced with having his own reputation marred by a single lapse.

There was much emotion from the two student leaders. The pedestal they had hoisted their mentor upon for so long was crumbling before their eyes, and neither was taking it well. Megan had many talents, but masking disappointment wasn't one of them, and her face was lined with desolation. Evan also hid nothing, though for him that was routine. Dan pitied them both. While the day had been long coming for dashed hopes, even a rout in ballot returns would have been far less cruel than what they were now sitting through. Barb Patterson was a quiet observer from the breakfast bar, but Dan suspected his former colleague was unmoved by the disclosures, having witnessed far worse from her years in the West Wing.

Walter finally broke the long silence.

"As I've said, I'm so sorry to have disappointed each of you. I won't defend or obfuscate what I did. My actions and deceit, to my wife and this community, were completely wrong. I know that now. I knew it then. Megan, Evan, if either of you believe what I did is inexcusable – a more than reasonable view – we can end this campaign this very minute. Whatever your decision, I will be forever grateful for your incredibly hard work on my behalf these last many weeks."

"What about the woman?" Megan's voice was barely a whisper.

"What about her?"

"You apologized for disappointing us. You said what you did to your wife and this community was wrong. What about what you did to *her*?"

Walter nodded solemnly. "Of course. It was completely wrong and inappropriate, and I will reach out to her with an apology as well."

Megan couldn't look at him. "Would've been nice if you had mentioned that first."

It was Evan's turn. "Why did you keep this from us? That first night, Megan's dad asked you if there was anything in your past. You joked about it."

"I never believed any of this would come out. I thought the matter was closed decades ago. And I never imagined we would have presented enough of a threat to invite this level of scrutiny. To his credit, Mr. Cahill warned me explicitly about people digging into the past. I wish I could explain why I wasn't more forthcoming with all of you. Undoubtedly, shame had much to do with it. As did the thought my students, in particular the two of you, who I have so much affection and regard for, might forever look at me differently. I acted inappropriately, and wronged an innocent, undeserving young person. I deceived each of you, and so many others. And for that, again, all I can offer you is my most sincere apology."

"I'm not exactly thrilled you kept this from us," Evan said. "But Megan, if he told us, what would we have done? Walked away from this campaign? Made him go public with it?"

"Maybe."

"Maybe, maybe not. I'm as pissed as you we weren't told, but let's think about what happened thirty years ago, and what it should mean today."

Megan looked at him thoughtfully. "You mean, should something like this be disqualifying?"

"Yeah."

Dan grunted. "If it was, we wouldn't have a Congress. Or half our past presidents."

"That's my point," Evan said, turning to Megan again. "I'm not trying to trivialize what he did. But it was thirty years ago. And as long as he acknowledges it and apologizes, I think most people would be willing to continue supporting him."

All eyes were on Megan. She started to speak but was interrupted by another voice.

"Whoa there, you got a big hole in your fence there, son."

They all turned in surprise toward Barb. She moved to the table, taking the only remaining seat.

"Let's talk about what there is to *acknowledge*. I had a track coach in high school. He was young, maybe a few years out of college. The man was as full of wind as a corn-fed horse, but he was handsome and funny, and always touching me. Innocent, you know, a hand on my shoulder, or a half-embrace after a win. Until his hand would brush down to other areas. By accident, of course. And that wasn't all he did. It was wrong, and in my later years, I'd have plugged him full of lead. But I was sixteen then, and as confused as a goat on AstroTurf. I didn't breathe a word."

Barb paused, meeting Walter's eyes.

"Your relationship with this young woman, was it consensual?"

"Yes."

Barb swiveled her head to Megan, who looked sickened.

"No, it wasn't, Professor."

"Not even close," seconded Barb. "She was your student, Walt, and you put her in a terrible position, whether you think you had consent or not. You need to understand that."

The professor leaned back in his chair, his eyes glassy. "You're both right, of course."

"That's the point I need you to understand," Megan said. "It's not just about betraying your wife and deceiving everyone else. And it's not what you did *with* Julia Stillman. It's what you did *to* her. That's what you need to acknowledge and apologize for. And I think you need to do it publicly, right now."

"Yes, I agree," Walter said.

Evan's voice rose in alarm. "Wait. I get where you're coming from Megan, but if he says that in public, we're dead in the water. Can't he do it after the election? We're talking about one week."

"No," Walter declared, his voice firm. "These ladies are both absolutely right. I cannot hide from this, and it's time I was held accountable for my actions. If I'm asking people for their vote, they have a right to know. As does everyone who has worked on my behalf. I want to see this campaign through, but if any of you have lost faith in me, and cannot see us going forward, I will, of course, completely understand."

The quiet lasted nearly a full minute, each of them weighing the choices. Evan spoke first.

"Megan, I'm not blowing this off. What he did was wrong, way wrong. But I'm not going to walk away from him or this campaign because of it. We dragged him into this, and we need to finish it."

"No one dragged me—"

"I can't leave now either," Barb added, slapping the table as she rose from her chair and moved toward the kitchen. "I've got more soup to make, and I'm still hoping one of those militia types tries to crawl through one of these windows so we can have some target practice."

Megan turned to her father. "Dad?"

"You need to figure this one out on your own, Megs."

"I think I have, but I need you to tell me if I'm right."

Dan let out a long breath.

"Someday you'll look back at this day, and realize it was the moment you discovered someone close to you, someone you admired so much, was actually far more human and imperfect than you once thought. He made a God-awful, boneheaded mistake decades ago, no question. But maybe you need to ask yourself what kind of standard you're holding him to, and how fair that is. Clinton fooled around with an intern in the Oval Office. When I was your age, I thought that was the crime of the century. Then Trump sold his soul to the Russians, and now Pierce wants to re-write the Constitution."

"You're saying I'm making too much of this?"

"No, not at all. I'm just saying sometimes we need to give some thought to how we move forward. I promise you this, by the time we all get to Walter's age, we'll make our own God-awful, boneheaded mistakes. Some of us already have. Here's what I would ask. Is he a good man? Did he learn from his mistake? Does he deserve forgiveness, trust, maybe even a second chance? Or are you going to go with a one strike and you're out policy?"

Megan nodded, knowing where this was all coming from. She wasn't the only one. The clamor of dishes and pots in the kitchen had fallen suddenly silent.

He turned to Walter. "I think you can guess where I stand. So, whatever you decide to do, and wherever you decide to go, I promise you, day and night, I'll be there to make sure you know how to order an Uber on your own."

They all smiled at that, even Megan.

Evan turned to her. "Well? We need you."

She closed her eyes, deep in thought. When they opened again, she gave a firm, encouraging nod to Walter, but her words were soft, lacking their usual verve.

"I'm still in."

Walter nodded in return, but he heard it in her voice. They all had, and Dan could read it on the man's face. The loss of something precious he knew would be difficult to regain.

"You kids are truly extraordinary, and far kinder to me than I deserve." Walter paused. "I promised myself, long ago, that I would be a better husband, and a better person. I'm not sure if I succeeded, but I can say one thing with certainty. I hope I'm judged someday by the character of those at this table today."

He stood slowly – wincing as he straightened his back – and politely excused himself before retreating to his bedroom for needed rest. Undoubtably, it had been a draining day, and Barb quickly shooed everyone out of the house, promising to text them all when the professor was ready to resume whatever Evan had on the calendar. Dan agreed to give Megan a lift to the spa; she still had a six-hour shift ahead of her. As he piloted the Explorer through the winding residential streets, only the car radio could be heard, his daughter staring forlornly out her window.

"You okay?"

She sighed. "Not the day I thought it was going to be."

"He's still a good man, Megs."

"Is he? Maybe it's not fair to him, but I really thought he was different. You know, above it all."

"You're hurting, I can understand. But he is different. All of us stumble from time to time, and all of us have regrets. That's life right there." He paused. "You feel like you can still do this?"

"I feel like I have to. I mean, I believe him when he says he's truly sorry about it all. And I know everyone deserves forgiveness and a second chance. But to be honest, I care more about the Cure Initiative now than I do him winning. Does that make sense?"

"Absolutely. And Walter has been saying it from the beginning. This wasn't about him. It was always about the Cure Initiative and bringing the country together. Let's just not get too caught up in these last days and forget there's a human being back there. A 76-year-old man, all alone in his life."

"I know. And I'm still going to fight for this. We started something pretty cool, and I think we've achieved something, no matter how bad we lose next week."

"Are you kidding? Megs, you've achieved what most people would consider the impossible. You had a month and Walter's piggy bank to work with. You and Evan, taking on the Vice President of the United States, and an army of professionals bankrolled with millions of dollars. You two managed to make a mark – a real mark – on this election. What happened this morning is proof of that. You've also put an important issue on everyone's radar absolutely no one was talking about a month ago. And you're the engine for it all, Megs. You never let up, and you work your tail off. I don't know how you do it; I'm not even part of the campaign and I'm wiped out."

"Ha! You're part of it, Dad, and you know it. You've been a huge help. Really. I wish you'd been with us for the tuition fight."

"No thanks, I think I've had all I can handle. And keep me off the invite list for future crusades, please. Once has been enough."

"Deal," Megan said, turning again to her window and gazing out at the passing homes and businesses. They were only a few blocks from their destination away when she abruptly spun in her seat, the light burning in her eyes once again.

"Remember last month, when we were talking about school? And I told you about maybe taking some time off?"

"Yeah."

"I changed my mind. I want to finish and get my degree."

Dan raised an eyebrow. "Your mom will do cartwheels. Change in plans?"

She turned again, her eyes drawn to her window, fixing on some distant object. Her voice was so low only she could hear the words.

"Exactly. A change in plans."

. . .

Hope Sullivan tapped the screen on her phone, the device clamped to a tripod she had expertly rigged. They were in the professor's campus office, with Walter seated behind his now spotless desk, the mountains of paper temporarily relocated to the floor. He sat up straight, his hands clasped before him and resting on the surface of the desk as he ran through the salient points he intended to make. His mind was focused, knowing it all had to be pitch perfect.

Despite his exhaustion, he'd been unable to sleep a wink at the house. His mind was racing, the angst and turmoil that had shaken him since leaving Marc Powell's office turning into something very different now. This was his opportunity. Not to right a wrong – it was too late for that – but to own up to his failings and give relief to a conscience that hadn't felt clean in decades. Let others know precisely who he really was. His faults, his imperfections, and his penance. Then let them judge.

As the task ahead crystalized, he reached out for Hope, their resident goddess of Instagram, the one person he would need an assist from. He left the house before Barb could lodge any objection, making the short trek to campus on foot as the LVMPD cruiser trailed from a block away. His gait was slow, the mild ache in his lower back more persistent now, but the extra minutes gave him needed clarity, allowing him to organize his thoughts and sort through the precise words he would employ. Hope met him at the office, lugging the simple equipment of her trade.

"You're on, Professor."

"I can start?"

"Yep."

Walter looked at his hands. "Where do I begin?" The question was to himself, but it was heard by those in the live audience who had tuned in to the largest social media stage on the globe. He inhaled deeply, lifting his head as he forced his eyes to look into the tiny lens, Hope's long curls a blur of copper in the background.

"Well, first, thank you all for joining me and providing this opportunity to address what I understand will be in the news very soon. What you will likely hear is mostly true. In an act of true irresponsibility and terrible judgment, I had an affair with an undergraduate many years ago. I will waste no one's time denying this, or equivocating, or shirking any responsibility for my actions. I abused my position then and betrayed the trust of so many people. A young, impressionable student, first and foremost. But also, my wife, and my larger UNLV family. The wrong person was forced to leave the campus then, and that is a shame I will forever carry. I cannot apologize enough to her. I am truly, truly sorry.

"I wasn't a perfect person then, and I'm far from a perfect person now. So, for those who are questioning whether to cast a ballot for me next week, all I can do is ask for your forgiveness. I have strived to improve myself these last many years, and it is my great hope my personal shortcomings do not detract from the vitally important proposal we have put forward during this campaign. The National Cure Initiative stands for great and lasting change to our public health and this country. It's an opportunity for all of us, irrespective of our political persuasions, to unify behind the most imperative objective for humanity – keeping our loved ones alive and healthy. It's a message far outweighing its messenger, and however you vote on February 22nd, I hope you will continue our fight to make the Cure Initiative a reality. Thank you."

Hope tapped the screen again, giving a nod of approval. She removed the phone from the clamp and began collapsing the tripod.

"I have to run to class but looks like a few thousand people were on. People were already posting and sharing. I can give you a total head count later today, and the number of hits."

"No need for that. I trust this will be seen. I've seen your magic."

"Roger-o, Professor," the young woman said, gliding to the front door, cracking her gum as she shouldered the tripod like a baseball bat.

"Hope?"

She turned, her jaw practically on spin cycle. "Yeah?"

He settled into the supple leather of the ancient chair, its springs squeaking in response.

"What did you think?"

Hope shrugged, tucking a loose curl behind her ear with her free hand. She had a petite frame, but Walter knew she was an energetic whirlwind, running her social media platforms while on pace to graduate this spring with honors from the school's mechanical engineering program.

"Doesn't matter what I think. Only matters what *they* think."

"Fair enough. But I'm asking about you."

She considered a response as her fingers caressed a charm dangling from a silver chain around her neck.

"I like politics, but I'm not obsessed like Megan and Evan." She moved the gum to a back corner of her mouth. "I won't follow dolts like Sheffield and Pierce because all they do is post what they think people want to hear and see. The ads they run, they're like a veneer. Shiny on the outside, just to get your attention. Sand it away, though, and all you've got it plywood. But in my world, you get a hot, Hollywood actress to post a selfie with no makeup and no filters, she'll get a million likes an hour after it's up. People want real, Professor, not plywood. That's what you always want to shoot for. Get it?"

"I think so. I should be the hot Hollywood actress without makeup."

Hope grinned, the gum cracking again. "Exactly." She turned serious. "Don't take this the wrong way, but maybe those people out there don't really care about you. Maybe they just want to cure cancer."

"To be honest, Hope, that's why I'm staying in this race. It's why I got into this race."

Hope chewed her lower lip. "I got something, Professor."

"You got something?"

"Yeah, on the Vice President. Something he wouldn't want to come out."

Walter gave her a quizzical look.

"It's a report from the Senate Ethics Committee. Someone sent it to me anonymously, hoping I'd post it. Said it was buried a long time ago, when Sheffield was a new Senator, and was only seen by a few people."

"What report?"

"Apparently Sheffield was tapping his Senate office funds. Getting reimbursed for an apartment he wasn't paying rent for. And there was a woman."

"Hope—"

"That's serious fraud, Professor. I checked. We get that report out there, what you did a hundred years ago is a snoozer by comparison. I can make it viral in sixty seconds."

"No." His voice was hard.

"Why not? Don't you think voters have a right to know?"

"I do. And if that really happened, it will come out. But I don't want a hand in it."

"It took thirty years for your secret to come out. And his people were happy to screw you with it. Maybe they need a taste of their own medicine."

"An eye for an eye?"

"My grandmother would have said do unto others."

Walter chuckled as Hope lowered the tripod to the floor. She sat in the chair opposite the professor, her expression quite different now as they regarded each other. Behind the Instagram maven cracking her gum, he sensed there was something more to this young woman. Much more.

"I have a little brother. Eight years old, fighting leukemia."

Walter sagged. "Oh Hope, I'm so sorry. I can't imagine what he and your family are going through."

"It's awful, what he's had to put up with." She paused, lost in thought, and Walter could see the pools in her eyes. "I hate watching it. I want to scream and cry every second I'm with him at the hospital, and yet there's nowhere else I want to be."

Walter nodded in understanding. "He's experiencing one form of hurt, and you another. It must be excruciating and maddening for your family. It's such a blight on us all and there's nothing crueler about cancer than its indiscriminate preying on young children. It's why I wanted our voices to be heard, Hope. We must do better."

Her eyes were pleading. "You have to win next week. Let me help you."

"You are helping me, Hope. And I appreciate your good intentions. Your passion to fix what ails your brother, desperate for any solution, I've been there. I know what that pain in your heart feels like. But I didn't get into this race to destroy others. I never wanted to be in a competition among rivals and enemies. I wanted to be in a competition of ideas. Ours are better, that I am certain of. And if this election proves I'm the wrong messenger, I want to see an army of others, like you, who will carry our movement forward. And make the Cure Initiative a reality."

Hope stood, unenthusiastic, but at least offering a grudging nod as she lifted her tripod again.

Walter smiled at her. "Your integrity, my dear, and my conscience, will remain intact. But fear not, the Vice President will one day learn the same inescapable lesson I am now experiencing."

"What's that?"

"As the Buddhists say, there are three things that cannot long stay hidden. The sun, the moon, and the truth."

CHAPTER 28

February 20

Two Days to Primary Day

The results from the final statewide poll before Primary Day came as no surprise when they were finally published. In a final return favor, Stu Valentine from the *Review-Journal* had given Dan a late-night preview, sharing numbers the newspaper's readers wouldn't see until morning. His chat with Valentine reminded Dan ten weeks had passed since the episode at the Platinum. It felt more like ten years.

Lacking resources to commission their own poll, the campaign team had been eagerly awaiting the R-J's results, unsure how harshly voters would judge Walter for the recent revelations. As Marc Powell had warned that first day, online stories began surfacing before nightfall. Local media outlets joined the fray, and by the next day, there were few registered Democrats left in the state who hadn't heard the name Julia Stillman.

Most had also viewed Walter's on-camera confessional. That was not only courtesy of Hope's social media talents, but whatever deep-pocketed mystery figure was underwriting an effort to flood the digital landscape with the public apology. A certain renegade casino owner was the primary suspect, but whoever the culprit, they all crossed their fingers Walter's heartfelt contrition would serve as an effective counterweight to the sensational headlines.

An effective counterweight, indeed. Dan blinked when he read the poll numbers Valentine had texted. Walter was closing the gap, with the survey now finding twenty-one percent of likely Democratic primary voters supporting the professor. Considering the countless headwinds they had faced since Day One, it was a stunning number.

But there were no illusions of victory in the poll, either. Sheffield was maintaining an insurmountable lead, his support holding strong at sixty-three percent.

Megan had spoken to Powell, who somehow acquired the critical drilldown data, known to professional survey takers as the crosstabs. As expected, the Vice President's supporters weren't prioritizing policy principles or leadership qualities; they were simply rallying around the only candidate they believed capable of defeating Rebecca Pierce in the fall. It was bitterly frustrating to Megan and Evan, and even Powell conceded a candidate like Sheffield was the Republicans' dream opponent. But Nevada Democrats, unable to see Walter as a viable nominee, saw no alternative to charging down such a path, no matter how doomed it was.

As for the Republican side, national polling showed far more upheaval. What had been a fairly under-the-radar process to clear an uncontested path for Pierce to the convention had devolved into a street fight since the South Carolina debate. As more of the general's former colleagues and subordinates stepped forward with accounts and accusations, the media continued to mine Pierce's record for buried treasure, splashing new exposés across their printed pages and digital sites.

Not that Anna was coming through it all unscathed. Pierce's monied supporters hammered her without mercy, releasing a series of scorching ads framing her as a wolf in sheep's clothing and secretly embracing leftist sympathies. They started a whisper campaign within GOP circles, with the wildest, most unsubstantiated claims of Anna's personal life they could fabricate. They even coaxed her ex-husband into stepping before the cameras and sharing with the world Anna's infidelity that ended their marriage and left him heartbroken.

Anna was hardly deterred, and if Pierce's backers believed the fusillade in Charleston was a last gasp, they were grossly mistaken. Following the debate, Anna unleashed a multi-million-dollar ad buy in a handful of pivotal states slated to vote on March 1. She went all in, using the last of her war chest to target nearly half of the total number of Republican delegates needed to win the nomination. If it worked, the small, early voting states of Iowa, New Hampshire, Nevada, and South Carolina – where Pierce had already triumphed or was leading in the polls – would become numerically insignificant. If it failed, the Morales campaign would be penniless and essentially finished, with Pierce holding nearly every advantage heading into the most consequential phase of the primary.

Pierce, meanwhile, was like a wounded animal, lashing out and fearsomely dangerous. She was swimming in cash, with reportedly over $200 million on-hand,

and still wielded a sprawling campaign organization. Almost every national party luminary remained in her corner, brushing off the damaging headlines continuing to materialize, and betting they would have little influence with Republican voters. Time would tell.

Dan maneuvered the Explorer into Walter's driveway. It was just after seven in the morning and there was a light haze over the city, lingering evidence of the spate of forest fires engulfing parts of Southern California. As the headlight beams danced across the stucco façade, Walter emerged from the front door, clad in his familiar khakis but otherwise out of uniform. His ever-present Rockports and powder blue Oxford had been traded for hiking boots, his lucky UNLV sweatshirt, and a nearly blinding dayglow squall coat that could likely be seen from Reno. Walter slid into the passenger seat, grunting as he folded his legs, but still armed with his cheeriest smile.

"Good morning, Mr. Cahill."

"What's with the Eddie Bauer ensemble? And the pre-dawn pickup? Sergeant Slaughter chewed me out when I cut our session short."

"I was hoping we could go somewhere different this morning. Play a little hooky from the campaign."

"I gathered that. You want me to drop you at a construction site? Or are you flagging traffic today on I-15?"

"Funny stuff." Walter's eyes moved to the two paper cups in the center console as he sniffed the air. "That doesn't look like your usual."

"Hot tea for both of us. Made a deal with Sergeant Slaughter. I go three days without coffee, I get pizza."

"You're going to drink hot tea?"

"He says it has cleansing properties. Care to fill me in on our plans? We'll get there faster if you tell me the destination."

"Red Rock."

"The resort?"

"The canyon."

Dan instantly soured. He loved the park, but he wasn't dressed for trekking through winding trails and expansive rock formations, and the rugged terrain would wreak havoc on his Bostonian loafers. At least they would not be venturing far, considering Walter's physical limitations. The closing days of the campaign had become truly grinding, and it was having a noticeable effect on the man, far less spry than when Dan first met him six weeks ago. Not that Dan was in any condition for vigorous exercise either. His legs were like rubber at the moment, thanks to the hundreds of lunges and squats he had finished barely an hour ago with a supplement-chugging fanatic screaming in his ear.

Walter sipped his tea. "Fear not, Mr. Cahill, no marathons today. I just want to show you something. Some scenery I think you'll enjoy."

With early voting underway and polls opening in less than forty-eight hours, Dan couldn't see how they had time to spare for scenic drives. Any further prodding was pointless though, as Dan was familiar enough now with Walter's fondness for mystery. He backed the Explorer out of the driveway and steered towards I-215, the local Autobahn looping around the bulk of the city and skirting the ranges of mountains framing the valley.

"I have a small grievance."

Dan raised an eyebrow. "Really. Can two play? I'd like to start with all the gas money you owe me."

"I understand Anna Morales is now under the protection of the Secret Service."

"True. And you want the same? You've got Doc Holiday back at the homestead. Trust me, she's all you need."

"Doc Holiday was a dentist and a drunkard and died at a young age. I'm not sure Ms. Patterson would appreciate the comparison."

Dan turned serious. "The Service wouldn't be there unless there were credible threats. It's not about poll numbers, it's about the threat. You shouldn't feel slighted."

"Yes, of course. A poor attempt at humor on my part." Walter watched him. "You look...concerned."

"The threats, the ugliness. I'm just so sick of what's happening in this country. And Pierce just eggs it all on. Did you see the ad they're running claiming Anna wasn't born in this country? She was born in an Army hospital in Germany for Christ's sake."

"*Anna?*"

Dan gave an embarrassed smile. "Governor Morales."

"I can't say I agree with her on most issues, but she seems like quite a gal."

"Woman," corrected Dan, "not gal. Trust me on that one. And yes, she's quite a gal."

A gal he had been trading messages with since their dinner together at DePippa's. How she found his email address he had no idea, but once they began exchanging notes, he found himself refreshing his inbox incessantly, eager for her latest missive. He marveled at her ability to find time for him, considering the post-Charleston slugfest she was mired in. Her messages came in at the oddest hours, each one a mix of humor and commentary, and an occasional deep-dive into some aspect of society she wanted to right. Her writing was raw and emotive, like a journal entry, and he knew his return notes were much the same.

Their exchanges became increasingly personal, bantering about past relationships and the mistakes they had made. They migrated to WhatsApp for more confidentiality, and Dan cautioned about the chance she was taking should their liaisons ever became public. But it all continued unabated, including one series of notes where Anna helped Dan sort through competing feelings about Megan's recent epiphany. That chat pushed into the early morning hours, wrapping up just two hours before Anna was due to address the Rotary Club of Charlotte.

"Do you think she hurt Pierce in Charleston?"

Walter's question and the blaring of a car horn brought Dan back to the present, and he stepped on the accelerator to catch up to the procession of cars passing the Explorer.

"Hard to tell. Pierce seems to have the same cultish following Trump had. Independents, suburban women, others – they may be a different story. Pierce has been selling herself as some paragon of military virtue. Her entire campaign is about her being the next George Washington or Dwight Eisenhower. But if the middle begins to see her as a fraud, it could all backfire on her."

"I have to say, Mr. Cahill, you've proven to be quite the political analyst."

"Those weren't really original thoughts. I was paraphrasing someone much smarter than me."

Walter smiled knowingly. "Your daughter?"

"Exactly."

"I had a text from her this morning that some letter is coming out?"

"It's an op-ed, in today's *New York Times*. I haven't seen it yet, only heard of it."

"The author?"

"The last five chairmen of the Joint Chiefs of Staff. Three of them served under Bush or Trump. They're coming out against Pierce and endorsing Anna – Governor Morales."

"You don't sound as beguiled by this as Megan."

"I'm not sure how many working-class people in Nevada and South Carolina read the *New York Times*. But they can work it into ads, and the timing is interesting. Pierce has a big press event today in Virginia with some former generals and admirals who have signed onto her campaign. And hours before she steps in front of the cameras, this op-ed comes out."

"Is that unusual? Hannah used to talk about campaigns having a rapid response team."

"This was no rapid response. It had to be weeks in the making. Their coordination has been really something. Hitting Pierce at the debate. Rolling out this list of military endorsements. Some bill signing ceremony she's got on tap for veteran's health care in New Mexico. Another major ad buy in Texas and California. The lady is executing a plan."

They drove the remaining way in silence, nursing their tea, as twinkling lights from homes and streetlamps winked at them in passing. The sun was just beginning to inch above the horizon as they passed through the main park gate.

A dozen miles from the Strip, the Red Rock Canyon National Conservation Area was a precious gem few visitors to Vegas were even aware existed. Established in 1967 as a 10,000-acre set-aside by the Bureau of Land Management, it was one of the first surprises the Cahills discovered when they arrived from Washington. It had long been a favorite of Megan and her childhood friends, all avid rock climbers, and they were hardly alone. The ancient formations and sandstone walls attracted nearly two million visitors every year, including the climbers who scaled La Madre Mountain and it's 8,000-foot peak.

They parked the car and each took a turn in the public restroom before Walter led them to the Moenkopi Look, one of the gentler trails just past the Visitors Center. Still early, there were few others on the path, and after a quarter mile or so, Walter stopped at a large boulder, topped with a smooth, level surface. Already winded, he gingerly made the six-foot climb, using the smaller adjacent rocks as steps while gripping Dan's arm for balance. Dan climbed up to join him as Walter shed his squall coat, using it as a cushion as he lowered himself to the hard surface. The older man stretched his legs out, absorbing the breathtaking expanse before him, and the radiant sun rising into the blue umbrella sky.

"I take it you've been here before," Dan remarked, sitting next to the professor.

A young couple power walked past, snickering as they glimpsed up at Dan's footwear, his loafers coated now in trail dust.

Walter nodded distractedly before turning to Dan.

"Megan tells me your family came here quite often when you first moved here."

"Yep. Michelle and I both grew up on the East Coast. We didn't expect this kind of real estate here. And Megan loved it, climbed all over every one of these rocks."

"What was she like?" Walter probed. "As a kid."

Dan rested his forearms on his bent knees. "If I'm being honest, I wish I knew. She was two when I went to the Detail, so I missed a lot of those younger years. I thought the one advantage to coming out here would be more family time. But with all the protective visits here, plus my caseload, there were far more working weekends and late nights than I expected. Things went south with Michelle and I moved out. Megan wasn't even twelve. We still talked, and she stayed with me twice a month, but it was all so...forced. I just felt disconnected from her. I thought retirement would finally be the chance to repair all that. Better late than never, right? Figured she would resist, probably still pissed I ignored her all those years. But she surprised me, said she was willing to give it a go. And now, we've had more conversations in the last six weeks than we had in the last six years."

"You make it sound like you wronged her. I highly doubt that's the case. She certainly doesn't seem to think so."

Had he wronged her? He had missed so much of her life. The little he hadn't had always stayed with him, those few memories he held so close and were still so vivid in his mind. The day Megan was in the net for the state high school championship game stood out more than anything. It was four years ago, and he had managed to take a leave day then, a rare occasion. The sights and sounds of that day slowly came alive again in his mind, as if he was witnessing it all over again.

She was just seventeen, under so much pressure at the moment, not only as team captain, but facing a blue-chip rival in the opposing net who was headed to Arizona State in the fall. Megan had already overcome so much in her young life, including a ghastly leg injury the year prior. Seconds before kickoff, she stood in front of her net, waving wildly to her mom, seated with the other clusters of parents in the midfield stands. Her eyes swept through the other sections, hurriedly, as the referee placed the ball at center field, raising one hand in the air. And then, just before the opening whistle, she found her father, off by himself, and jubilantly waved both arms over her head as if she had discovered one last present under the Christmas tree. It was, he knew, a silent thank you being there, and for taking a leave day. A thank you she thought he deserved. He knew better.

"Do you regret your absences?"

"Of course, I do." Dan caught the professor's eye. "You're asking if I would do things differently."

"Would you?"

"I like to think so. The last few weeks have made me see that." He paused, looking down. "Easy for me to say that now."

"What do you mean?"

"When we were in Washington, and Megs was a toddler, I was gone so much because I *had* to be. That's life on the Detail, and I knew what I was signing up for. Everyone goes through it; the Service should have divorce lawyers on retainers. But here, I had choices. I could have worked less, pushed cases off, delegated more to others under me. Spent more time at home. But I didn't."

"Why not?"

"I'm not sure. Maybe because I loved the job, more than I realized. Didn't really see it at the time, but looking back, man, I couldn't wait to clock in every day. See my guys, hit the casework, manage our protective details. Maybe that's why I never thought of it as a choice. But it all seems so meaningless now."

"I wouldn't wring your hands too much, Mr. Cahill. You may have loved the work. I'll buy that. But don't fool yourself into thinking you loved your job more than your daughter. And, by the way, she managed to turn out okay, didn't she?"

"That she did." Dan squinted at the faint contours of the Strip far off in the distance. "I don't know where she gets it from."

"Gets what from?"

"That spirit she has. Her optimism."

"A born leader," offered Walter.

"Yeah, that too."

"Remind me, Mr. Cahill, did you not lead people here, in what you constantly refer to as the most elite law enforcement organization in the world?"

"I did, but my people followed my orders because they had to. We had a chain of command. It's different with Megs. Those kids follow her because they want to."

"You said you were politically active when you were her age."

"I was, but man, what a different ballgame back then. Yeah, character was an issue, and I know politics has always had a dark side, but the viciousness is just out of control now. I remember during the Clinton years, there was a congressman who shot a watermelon in his backyard, all to prove some zany conspiracy theory that Hillary had a White House lawyer murdered. I wanted Bill and Hillary out because they wanted to nationalize health care and he was hitting on interns in the Oval Office. But murderers? That congressman was a nutjob, an outlier, and every Republican I knew rolled their eyes when his name was mentioned. Today, that guy would have millions of Twitter followers. The flakes with the zany conspiracy theories are all mainstream now, left and right. And the labeling. Every Democrat is a socialist and every Republican is a fascist. Them versus us, on every single issue."

"That doesn't sound like your daughter."

"It's not. And she thinks she can make it better. Credit Michelle, my ex-wife, for that. Made her a true believer, one who could save the whales, and democracy."

Walter sighed. "I can see I won't be able to convince you of your own influence at work with that one."

"Nope. But I do need to thank you. Spending all this time with her, seeing this fantastic young woman she's become. It's like having a new lease on life. I mean that."

"Well, we may not carry Nevada," Walter said lightly, "but if we can bring a father and daughter closer together, at least we've accomplished one deed."

Dan loosened his arms. "Okay, the suspense is killing me. I don't think you brought me out here to talk about Megan. Or show me any scenery."

Walter smiled, taking a moment to absorb the grandeur of the rust-colored canyon before turning to his companion.

"Our conversations of late, Mr. Cahill, I sensed you experiencing some regret. Looking back on your life, questioning the path you chose, like what we just discussed. I wanted to explore that with you a bit."

"Why?"

"It's a common phenomenon, I imagine. You reach a certain age, realizing time is slipping away. I'm sure the questions come to us all. Have I done enough? How will I be judged? But once the matter is no longer in doubt, the questions become more pressing, and the answers more consequential."

"What are you talking about?"

Walter hesitated. "I guess you could say my future here is no longer in doubt, Mr. Cahill."

The words were delivered with an even tone, and as was often the case with the professor, shrouded in ambiguity. Dan might have spent a few moments distilling their meaning, but it wasn't needed. There was an off note in Walter's tenor, one that stood out, and unmasked each word for what it was. And as the realization took hold, it hit him like a hammer.

Dan hadn't ever spent much time among anyone Walter's age – both his parents had passed away before the age of sixty – so perhaps he could be forgiven for not piecing it all together. What he simply regarded as everyday limitations for a man with advancing years, others might have recognized as the onset of something far more dire. But for someone who once prided himself as a crack investigator, it pained Dan to think how oblivious he had been. The clues had been there, lurking in the open since he first heard the man speak at Greenspun Hall, but blindly chalked up by Dan to the demands of the campaign trail and the fragility of old age.

The most obvious sign, however, had somehow been the most elusive. Walter's willingness to throw himself into an unwinnable contest, and his impassioned efforts in the weeks that followed, were rooted in something far deeper than political disaffection. The last several days were like the long-distance races the man once competed in. He was staggering, but determined to push through the stumbles and obstacles, and cross the finish line. Dan could see now what should have been plainly obvious. This entire endeavor was the mark of a man writing his final chapter, and coloring in the last details of his own life story.

He finally breathed. "How long?"

"Months, perhaps. More likely weeks."

Dan felt an ache deep within. "Weeks? Walter, I'm so sorry."

His companion tittered. "There is little we can do to guide the hands of fate, Mr. Cahill. I'm at peace with it. My lifetime has been a gift; shorter than some, longer than others. It's simply my time. And though I don't relish the many forthcoming goodbyes, there is one consolation. One so meaningful I cannot think of it as a consolation, but as a gift. I get to see my Hannah again."

"Do the kids know?'

"No one knows. Until now."

"Isn't there anything the doctors can do?"

"Stage four pancreatic cancer? Not likely. It's in my lungs and liver now. I fear this might be my last physical excursion for some time."

"But you go to that clinic two, three times a week. They're treating it, right? Can't—"

"Palliative care, Mr. Cahill. They're doing what they can to ease the symptoms and make me more comfortable. Nothing more."

Dan leaned back, his palms resting on the cool stone behind him, deep torment pressing down on his chest as a thousand thoughts raced through his head.

"You're going to tell Megan and Evan at some point, right?"

"On Sunday, when it's all over." He gave Dan a wink. "We wouldn't want to dampen their eagerness, would we? I need every vote I can get."

Dan could have objected. It was difficult to imagine the emotional wallop coming Megan's way. Not from the election returns. For all her outspoken insistence that a miracle was still within reach, Marc Powell was right, she was too levelheaded not to see the inevitable outcome. Losing Walter though – her mentor, her friend, and, despite the recent admission, probably closer to a father figure than Dan ever was – would be utterly devastating.

"I also don't want this getting out, lest someone accuse me of playing the cancer card to win this campaign."

"Is that why you chose this platform? The Initiative?"

"I know it must look that way. Damned cancer is gunning for me, I should take my revenge, no? But I think you know me well enough to know I would never have proposed such a thing for personal reasons. I've said the Cure Initiative is vital to our very existence, and I believe that. Not only what it means to so many of us who have suffered, either ourselves or through our loved ones, but the importance of uniting the country behind such a common cause. You've heard me say this, Mr. Cahill, but it's not some talking point I mindlessly regurgitate. I truly believe an effort such as this may be our final chance to pull this country back together again, before this rancorous hatred between the two parties is irreversible and consumes us all."

"Well, whatever happens on Saturday, I hope you appreciate how far you've come these last six weeks. It would hardly be a failure if the Initiative didn't happen."

"Ah, Mr. Cahill, always the doubtful one."

"I think of myself as the clear-eyed one."

"Do you. I want to show you something."

Walter took a small envelope from his coat and removed a 4x6 color photograph, handing it to Dan. It was on Kodak paper, yellowing at the edges, and judging from the colorful wardrobe of the subjects, dated to sometime in the 1960s or 1970s. The young couple was sitting side by side on a large rock, their legs splayed out in front of them, both leaning back with their palms on the ground, just as Dan had been sitting moments ago. The dark-haired girl was unfamiliar, but even the poor technology and grainy imagery could not obscure her bright eyes, shimmering with life and good humor. The young man, with his roguish smile and eternally tousled hair, was instantly recognizable.

"We're sitting in this spot."

"Yes."

"That's Hannah?"

"That's my girl. 1972, a few years after this park opened. We asked a ranger to take that. Ten minutes later, I proposed to her. Right here. The ring was in my pocket."

Dan returned the photo, and the professor scanned it again as he must have a thousand times before, a longing expression on his face.

"So much has changed since then. The university, the city, our society, all so different now."

He turned to Dan, a sudden intensity in his voice. "And *we've* changed, Mr. Cahill. I'm not the same man who sat here fifty years ago, the son of a milk truck driver. Who could have taken a place in Vietnam next to the poor and underprivileged, but instead chose to use his college deferment instead. Who proposed to his sweetheart, a true angel, only to betray her some years later. And you're not the same man who walked into a campus lecture hall not long ago, full of disillusionment, with a broken spirit and resentful outlook toward everything and everyone in his life. I've discovered recently there is little utility in dwelling over our regrets. But we can learn from them. What did you call it? A new lease on life?"

Dan nodded. "I owe you for that."

"Do you? You've said I inspire those kids. But I look at a young woman like Megan, and I see everything this country should be. Virtuous, compassionate, selfless. No, Mr. Cahill, it is those young people who have inspired *me*. And for that, for her, I owe *you*."

Neither man spoke for several minutes, allowing the sun to warm their faces as they each reflected on what the future might hold. It was Dan who spoke first.

"What are your plans? After Saturday."

"Since we started all this, it's been difficult to think past Election Day, and perhaps that's been a blessing. First order of business is to find a way to express my gratitude to all those who made this past month the most invigorating and rejuvenating experience of my lifetime. After that, teach as long as I can. And then take whatever time I need to make my peace."

"You sound like you've already found your peace."

"I've had a good life, Mr. Cahill. Far from perfect, as Julia Stillman would tell you. But I've had it better than most. A wife who deserved better. A rewarding career. Mostly good health. And what I'll always prize the most, outside my marriage: the opportunity to engage with so many magnificent souls, young and old, who I've learned so much from. Starting in a Mississippi classroom all those years ago."

"I think they probably learned quite a bit from you as well. I have."

"Well, I guess that's what friends are for, eh?"

"I've told you before, I don't have friends."

"And I'm telling you now, Dan. That's no longer true."

EPILOGUE

One Year Later

"Exactly how much does this pay if you win?"

Megan washed down the last of her Italian sausage with a long slurp of Diet Coke. "Between the salary and the per diem, about $25,000 a year."

"You're kidding."

"You're surprised?"

"Yeah, I am. I know it's not the British House of Lords, but you're not exactly flipping burgers at *Five Guys*."

Megan shrugged. "It's a part-time job. Most of them are doctors and lawyers, so money isn't an issue."

"You're not a doctor or lawyer, so money *is* an issue."

"Dad, they're old people with kids. I'll be twenty-two. I'll get by."

Dan chewed a mouthful of romaine. "You have any polling yet?"

"Nope. Media won't poll state assembly races, even a special election. I think the State Party might have some numbers, but Marc's not sharing, other than reminding me not to underestimate the opposition. Thanks, Captain Obvious. Every time I ping him, he tells me to go knock on another five hundred doors."

"You still keeping count?"

A nod. "Evan says we hit the five thousand mark on Tuesday. You should see the neighborhood maps he carries around with voting histories and registrations. That binder has to be worth a fortune."

"Impressive." He meant it. That was a hell of a lot of doors, especially with a full semester of coursework and two shifts a week at the spa.

"Marc was right, it really does matter to people. You should see their reactions when I'm on their doorstep and explaining why I'm there. Super annoyed at first, like I'm a human telemarketing call just showing up uninvited. But then I ask them for their opinion, or advice, or what issues they care about, and most of them just open up. It's amazing."

Dan smiled to himself, his daughter's zeal for retail politicking familiar. He heard much the same from an ardent young governor months ago, as she described the charge she felt from connecting with people and serving as an elected representative. He also had little doubt Megan was making headway. A few minutes with her though a screen door might reveal little to a potential voter, but her earnestness shined each time she spoke, and that would be remembered.

He sat back, watching her finish her meal as he thought about the sea change in their relationship from a year ago. He took measure of the bond between them now, and how much he had learned about his daughter since their odyssey with Walter Becker began. It was truly astounding what they had pulled off. A handful of dogged college students and their senior citizen draftee, armed with nothing more than ideals and vision, up against a competitor with every advantage and desperate for a convincing win in Nevada.

And he got it. Paul Sheffield bested Walter Becker in the Nevada primary by thirty points. But Walter won the support of a third of voting Democrats in the state, an extraordinary feat, leading to the team's one small triumph that day. It came during Sheffield's victory speech, when the Vice President offered a gracious nod to his opponent, followed by a full-throated endorsement of the National Cure Initiative.

There was much rejoicing over the surprise declaration. Among Megan and Evan, of course, but also elsewhere in the city, where a casino magnate and a retired labor leader held their breath with cautious optimism, hoping it marked a turning point for the Vice President's campaign. It wasn't to be. The attacks from Rebecca Pierce rained down almost immediately, berating the Cure Initiative as a socialist and liberal spending fantasy. Sheffield, conditioned by an entire career of sacrificing principle for consensus, hastily backpedaled, re-casting the Initiative as some downrange goal the country should one day aspire to. His election night calls for a massive infusion of resources were never heard again.

The primary loss and Sheffield's folding did nothing to quell the fire within Megan. Dan recalled the day Walter's past surfaced; the same day Megan divulged her future aspirations. She raised the prospect again after the election, this time revealing the details and immediacy of her plans. She walked her father through her scrupulous research, including the arcane recall procedures and state campaign finance laws she had sifted through.

She was also now racing to complete her degree by May, freeing herself from her studies so she could commit herself entirely to the budding campaign. A campaign that if successful, would make her the youngest elected representative in the history of the Nevada Legislature.

Dan suspected his daughter was not alone in her scheming. If Marc Powell didn't have a hand in it, he at least had taught Megan how to play the long game. It began with a recall engineered by Megan and Evan in the weeks following the Nevada primary. In their crosshairs was Eleanor Jeschke, the fossilized eighteen-term assemblywoman and chair of the Committee on Taxation who championed the tuition increase that roiled the UNLV community a year earlier. After collecting the necessary signatures, the pair rallied the State Democratic Party to their side as Megan began renting a rundown apartment in North Las Vegas, a roach palace sitting squarely in the middle of Jeschke's district.

Six months later, the recall was a trouncing success, compelling a special election the following November to fill the seat. An election now nine months away.

"Are you still working for Syd Milburn?"

Dan pushed his half-finished salad aside, unable to stomach the wilted lettuce amid the cruelly tempting scents drifting through *State Street Dogs*.

"I'm not working for Syd Milburn," he said. "I'm helping him spend his money."

"Claire said he wants to open some new Boys and Girls Clubs next year."

"Three. And the scholarships we're – he's – establishing at UNLV in Walter's name."

"She also said she signed up the first volunteer for our campaign."

"Let me get this straight. Claire Levin is your Field Director?"

"Yep."

"And she reports to Evan?"

She grinned. "On paper, yes. In reality, it's the other way around. Don't tell Evan that."

"I take it she has some free time in her retirement."

"Speaking of free time, her first volunteer..."

Dan shrugged. "Well, I heard the screening process might be pretty discerning, so thought I would get a head start."

"Maybe I can put in a good word for you."

They shared a smile.

"Don't even ask me to start driving you—"

He stopped, seeing his daughter's attention drift past his shoulder.

Dan twisted in his seat, following Megan's eyes to the imposing figure pushing through the glass door. The man swept the dining area with a practiced eye, his dour expression and Brooks Brothers suit woefully out of place and drawing attention from every corner of the restaurant. His searching eyes finally settled on Dan, and he marched in their direction, ignoring the stares and whispers of those who filled the nearby booths. He slapped Dan on the back and held out a fist the size of a ham to Megan, a broad, disarming smile spreading across his face.

"Assemblyman Cahill."

Megan grinned, bumping his fist back. "I'll settle for future-Assemblyperson Cahill."

Dan stared open-mouthed. "What in God's name are you doing here?"

Anthony Jarrett slipped off his sunglasses and slid into the booth next to Megan, using his hip to shove the youngster aside while wrinkling his nose at the remains of her dinner.

"Not eating this crap. Are those cheese fries? Girl, how do you stay so thin eating that garbage?"

"I run five miles every morning. Plus, lots of sex with my boyfriend."

Jarrett knitted his brow. "I didn't hear that."

"Neither did I," Dan said, flashing a scowl at his daughter before turning to his old boss. "What the hell are you doing here, Tony?"

Jarrett folded his hands as he scrutinized his old friend.

"Who're you working for now, Jenny Craig?"

Megan laughed but her father was still waiting on an answer, question marks filling his eyes.

Jarrett softened his voice. "I didn't get a chance to speak to you after the old man died. It was my second week on the campaign, but no excuse."

"I got your email."

"I should have called. I know what he meant to the two of you. I'm sorry."

"Appreciate that Tony, but really, I know your head has been spinning since last summer."

It was an understatement. Jarrett's long-anticipated posting to a senior position on the Presidential Detail had come in August, just after the two political conventions. With the general election campaign in full swing, he was detoured from the White House to the Republican nominee, who was already setting a torrid travel pace barnstorming the country. Following her inauguration last month, Jarrett finally rotated to the White House, settling into the Deputy SAIC slot he had long coveted.

Jarrett turned to Megan. "And look at you now. I've heard about your campaign. Sounds like the professor made quite an impression on at least one voter."

Megan looked meaningfully at her father. "Two."

Jarrett scoffed. "Don't tell me Ebenezer Scrooge here believes in Christmas now."

Dan smiled as Jarrett slipped a hand into his inside pocket, removing a phone and giving the screen a quick read. Dan knew enough not to ask, though he could imagine the messages flashing in. His old friend had reached a stature that once, long ago, Dan had wished for. There was no resentment, though, and no regrets. Whatever cards fate had dealt Dan, they had led him here, sitting across from his daughter, a part of her life once again.

His thoughts shifted to other memories, and the agonizing journey she had been through the past year, including those despairing final days with Walter in the hospice center. Consoling Megan through her grief, and his own, hadn't been easy, but Dan had lost both parents long ago, and death was not unfamiliar. Still, the deep sorrow he felt for the loss said something about the man he knew for barely three months.

Walter had no family, but dear friends aplenty, and those who had been at his side during those frantic February days were all there in the final moments at his hospice bed. It was, as Syd Milburn quietly remarked to Dan, not a terrible way to go.

Jarrett turned back to Megan. "I heard you gave quite the talk at the funeral. Lit up the room."

Megan was coy. "Says who?"

"I saw Barb Patterson at the Director's holiday reception. Said she'd never been to a memorial service like that."

Neither had Dan. The funeral itself had been a small affair, just the campaign team and a handful of university colleagues, as the professor's casket was lowered into the ground beside his beloved wife. The memorial service, held at the Clark County Library, was a different story. Hundreds attended a standing room-only event filled with peers, former and current students, and so many others whose lives had been touched and inspired by a lifetime of teaching and an improbable, 36-day run for the highest office in the land. There were profoundly touching eulogies from Megan and Charlie Drummond, each blending levity, tears, and fire. They were all there, grieving, but also celebrating the man's life, and his quest to restore a sense of decency and purpose to the country he loved so dearly.

"Dan?"

His friend's prompt brought Dan back. "Sorry. So, how're things in DC?"

Jarrett's expression changed. It was almost...impish. "Yeah, I wanted to talk to you about that."

"Deputy SAIC, right? PPD?"

"Right on both counts."

"Meaning you have no life and the twins don't recognize you anymore. So, what the hell are you doing here? Since when does anyone on the shift get to jump on a plane to Vegas without POTUS."

"They don't. I'm here with POTUS."

That stopped him. "She's in Vegas?"

Jarrett didn't answer, a mischievous smirk slowly spreading across his face.

"Wait, how did you get away—"

And then it hit him.

He was chagrined at first, as he mentally cataloged the telltales he had inexplicably missed. The distinctive, color-coded pin on Jarrett's lapel. The barely visible earpiece, clamped firmly in place and cued to the thumb-operated mic, peeking out of the agent's sleeve and tucked into his left palm. And over his friend's shoulder, the pack of dark-suited agents, quietly ushering nearby diners to other tables, clearing out their back corner of the restaurant. Jarrett, reading his thoughts, grinned at him as another agent passed through the glass door, holding it ajar with one hand, the other hovering near the service weapon on her hip.

Patrons and servers gawked in fascination at the bizarre choreography unfolding. Dan understood it all, of course, leaping to his feet as a communal gasp rose from the other side of the room, and the most famous figure on the planet marched through the door. She halted for a moment, taking in the surroundings, then followed the lead agent's arm extending toward the back of the dining area. She shared a nod with Jarrett, also standing now, before the large man backed away, the slightest of curls on his lips.

"Hi, Dan."

His mouth was bone dry. He could see Megan in his periphery, still seated, but speechless as well. A rarity.

"Madam President. What are—"

She held up a finger, turning to Megan as she offered her hand. "I believe we bumped into each other during the primary. Anna Morales."

Megan shook her hand, the initial shockwave quickly giving way to opportunism. "Hi. Can I...You gotta let me take a selfie."

Dan nearly groaned. "Megs."

But Anna was smiling, enjoying the moment.

"Sure, no charge. But won't that hurt your chances? I'm technically on the other side."

"Who cares? It's a State Assembly seat, and you're the fucking – sorry, you're the President of the United States."

She bounced out of her seat, standing next to the President and holding her phone high as Anna broke out her marque smile. Megan pointed at her, dropping her jaw in an exaggerated gape as she recorded a photo that would soon rocket across the Southern Nevada social media sphere.

"Anything I can do to help your campaign?"

Megan couldn't hold back the grin. "Help...my campaign?"

"I know we're in different parties, but from what I hear, the Republicans aren't even bothering to run someone, so you just have to make it through the primary, right? Seems like we've all been down that road before. Besides, I want to support good candidates, not good partisans."

"I appreciate that. I really do. And I know it's probably kind of nuts for me to say this, but I kinda want to do this on my own."

Anna smiled. "Believe it or not, Megan, I know exactly what you mean. Mind if I have a few moments with your father?"

"Sure. He's single. Hasn't dated anyone since Nicole."

"Megan!"

Anna beamed. "Who's Nicole?"

"Long story. Good night, daughter."

Megan said her farewells and was a few steps toward the door when she stopped, turning around as she chewed her lip.

"Madam President, can I just ask you one thing?

"Of course."

"That Viper plane you and Pierce argued about during the campaign."

"Ah. You heard about the *Wall Street Journal* piece."

"You promised to end the program and spend the money on military families and veterans. But now they're saying you're going to keep it. Is that true?

Anna grimaced. "Officially, I haven't released my budget request yet. Unofficially, yes, I'm going to keep the damned airplane."

Megan's face was blank, but it wasn't difficult to read.

"Barely on the job a month, and I'm already breaking a campaign promise, right? All I can tell you Megan, is that as President of the United States, I'm privy to some things now I wasn't privy to as Governor of New Mexico. I can't get too into it, but let's just say I want to do what's best for our national security, and what's best for the men and women in those cockpits."

"Isn't that just what Pierce said? If you—"

She stopped herself, shaking her head. "You know what, never mind, I've bugged you enough. It was very nice meeting you. I mean that."

"You too," Anna said, watching the young woman walk away again.

"Megan," the President called after her. Megan stopped, turning again in surprise.

"I want to earn it."

"Earn what?"

"When the President has to do something that might be unpopular, or something she doesn't *want* to do, because she believes it's necessary for the greater good, I want people to believe her. I want them to accept her word on face value, and stand with her, because they have faith in their President, and believe she's doing what's best for the American people. I know that sort of faith and trust doesn't come easy and has to be earned. I promise you, Megan, I will earn it."

Megan nodded in understanding. "I want to earn it, too."

"I know you do. That's why we have more in common than you might think. Like I said, if you ever need my help, you can count on me. I'll be there for you."

They shared a final smile, and then Megan lifted her chin, showing the familiar resolve her father knew so well, before departing again. The glass door swung closed, and other than the onlookers from across the dining area, each under the vigilant eye of nearly a dozen armed agents, Dan was alone with the leader of the free world.

"Tony says she's quite a young woman."

"She's definitely cut from the same cloth as you. What are you doing here?"

Anna grinned. "You said you liked surprises."

"Surprises, as in birthday cakes, or winning a free car wash at the gas station. Not the President of the United States crashing my dinner with my daughter."

Anna leaned forward, planting her elbows as she rested her chin on her hands. "Well, I couldn't exactly call and ask you to meet me at Starbucks. And since Tony has created enough standoff distance so these people can't eavesdrop on us, maybe you can call me Anna."

"I kind of like Madam President."

Her eyes sparkled. "So do I. But I'm willing to make an exception."

Madam President. A year ago, they were in an Italian bistro a mile from this very spot. Two strangers then, alone in their cocoons, unexpectedly baring their souls over a few glasses of wine and sharing their innermost feelings with a mutual trust neither could explain.

And now, here she was, the single most powerful individual on the globe.

Like Walter, Anna had not fared well in the Nevada primary. Even with her bounce coming out of the Charleston debate, and Pierce all but ignoring three million Nevadans, Anna fell a few thousand votes short of an upset.

Elsewhere in the country, the Republican race became a riveting spectacle. A steady march of Pentagon officials and senior Army officers, some retired and some still on active duty, continued to step forward, week after week, unburdening themselves with accounts of Pierce's duplicity reaching back nearly two decades. With the national media converging on the frontrunner, Anna put her campaign into overdrive.

On the ground, she campaigned almost exclusively in California and Texas, significantly raising her profile in the two grand prizes of the Super Tuesday primaries. New money poured in, providing the needed resources for Anna to introduce herself on the airwaves in the other battleground states.

She broke even with Pierce on the delegate tally that day. Considering from how far behind she had come, it was perceived by voters and commentators alike as a victory, and Anna's momentum began to snowball. With crippling headline after headline, Pierce's trademark buzzwords of corruption and incompetence morphed into a national punch line, and her congressional allies, most locked into their own grueling reelection bids, began quietly withdrawing their endorsements. High-dollar donors and other prominent backers followed, and Pierce's support soon cratered across the country. By mid-May, Anna claimed the necessary delegates, clinching the GOP nomination.

From the outset, the general election between Anna and the Vice President was a stark contrast of styles and imagery. There were vast policy differences, but voters thirsting for change saw it as a race between a youthful, charismatic governor of color, and an aging, lackluster caretaker of the status quo. Anna outdueled Sheffield in all four of their nationally televised debates, even stealing his home state of Virginia from under his feet as she rolled to a landslide victory in November.

Shortly after her historic swearing-in, Anna made good on the two "Day One" pledges she unveiled in her Inaugural Address, where she declared America's struggle with incurable diseases the single highest priority of her Administration. She framed the coming year as a bucket brigade moment, where every American could step forward and be counted, and join a movement that would reshape the nation's health, now and for generations to come.

Her pledges were truly groundbreaking. She signed her first executive order, elevating the Director of the National Institutes of Health to a cabinet-level position and detailing new, far-reaching responsibilities and authorities. And she sent her first legislation to Capitol Hill, immediately introduced by the Speaker of the House as H.R. 1, *The National Cure Act of 2025*.

The legislation was hailed as landmark, drawing favorable comparisons to past efforts that spawned Social Security and historic civil rights protections. The bill established the trust fund Walter Becker first conceived, plus the necessary mechanics for the collection and disbursement of funds. It authorized billions of federal dollars to bolster the ranks of America's cancer-fighting corps, also aligning with Walter's plan. But Anna went a step further, not content with adding medical researchers and health specialists alone, and called on the brightest and most imaginative minds in America to lend their talents to this historic enterprise. Her principal lure, beyond the cash bonuses Walter had devised, was the challenge she issued to her fellow Americans, to join the most ambitious scientific undertaking since the age of atomic discovery, and unravel the greatest puzzle in human history.

Just weeks after the Cure Act was introduced, tens of thousands of Americans stepped forward and applied for federal service. They answered her call for talent from disciplines far and wide, including computer scientists, physicists, mathematicians, engineers, logistical wizards; anyone, in their President's words, with a pioneering spirit and a passion for serving their country.

"I haven't heard from you since early November," Dan noted. "So, what's new? And don't feed me the old 'the NSA took my cell phone' excuse."

She laughed with him. "I miss my phone. The one they gave me is great for checking the weather and firing off our nukes, but that's about it. What's new? Let's see, the Chinese and Russians are still taking turns trying to kneecap us. Outside that door, there's an armored car, with a lieutenant colonel wearing too much aftershave and clutching a briefcase full of launch codes that could incinerate the entire world. And I've set a record with the Secret Service for death threats received in my first month in office."

"You beat Obama?"

"I lapped Obama. He was black. I'm Hispanic and a woman."

"How's your father doing?"

There was a touch of sadness in her eyes. "He's fine. It wasn't easy for him. He has close friends who won't speak to him anymore."

"They were part of it? Covering up the accident, getting her promoted?"

"They knew about it and said nothing. Which my father considered equally abhorrent. Went against everything they're taught at West Point. But, like I said, they were his friends. One was his classmate."

"How did he find out about it? You wouldn't tell me last year."

"His classmate confided in him when Pierce joined the Joint Chiefs. The man was liquored up and gave something of a confessional about the crash at Fort Rucker. My father back-channeled it to the White House, and their solution was to keep it under wraps but find some excuse to pass her over for Joint Chiefs Chair. They thought the damage was done and exposing it publicly would hurt too many good officers. My father thought the dead soldiers and their families might argue otherwise. He'd also heard the White House was shielding some of their own appointees in the Pentagon who were also culpable. He put Vic on the case, who dug up those initial documents. Never underestimate the eyes, ears, and reach of a command master sergeant, my father always says."

"He must be quite proud of you. You pulled off a miracle."

Anna's smile faded, uneasy now as she leaned toward him. But her eyes were like embers.

"I need you to know something, Dan. I didn't get into the race as an instrument of my father, or for the sole purpose of taking down Rebecca Pierce. And I didn't expose who she really was just to win an election. I wanted to be President, Dan, for the same reason I wanted to be a governor and a state senator. To represent other people, to work on their behalf, and to serve my country. I need you to believe that."

"Last time I checked," he said, "you became President because you won a general election. Where you were outspent, I believe, by a three to one margin. You won that election because fifty-seven percent of the country saw exactly the same thing I see now. When I said your father must be proud, I wasn't talking about the takedown of Pierce. That's not what the first line in the history books will say about you."

"Oh? What will they say about me?"

"They'll say on November 4th, 2024, America stood up and said Anna Morales, we want you to be our President. Not because you're a woman, or Hispanic, but because we know who you are at your core. A leader, who wants the best for every American, and has the heart, brains, and passion to pull it off."

She sat back, smiling at him appreciatively. "Well, Mr. Not Involved, you sure know how to charm a President. And yes, my father is proud. He knows about the death threats, by the way, and he's a little pissed your former agency thinks Vic is too old to have at my side."

"Tony and his people are pretty good."

"Considering they're in my lap all day long, I'd agree."

"So, you hate being President?"

"I love it. And I'm going to have the 22nd Amendment repealed so I can do this forever."

"Very Trumpian. Any drawbacks?"

"Sure. Washington. And dinners in the personal residence by myself are getting a little old, though I bring my father to town whenever I can. So, I'm coping."

"Is that why you're here? You miss the Southwest?"

Anna hesitated. "I'm here to attend to a personnel matter."

"Personnel?"

"Tony tells me they still haven't backfilled his position yet. The Las Vegas office needs a manager."

"We call it a SAIC and—"

"We?"

"—they have an acting one."

"Tony said his name is Chief Wagon?"

Dan laughed. "Chief Wiggum. From *The Simpsons.*"

"I don't follow."

"Greg Childers isn't one of the Service's brightest stars. They brought him down from Reno until they could fill the billet."

"You're a bright star. Or you were. You should be running the office. And you look like you've been training for the Olympics."

"I was a bright star two decades ago. Now, I'm more of an old asteroid."

"How much weight have you lost?"

"You should never ask a girl that. Fourteen pounds. And my cholesterol is down to 138."

Anna swept her hand across the restaurant. "This place must be a torture chamber."

"Why are you here, Anna?"

"I told you. A personnel matter."

He paused, attempting to read her teasing eyes. He shook his head.

"It's not that simple. I'm retired."

"I can un-retire you."

"And there's a whole process for selecting a new SAIC. They have to put it on a bid list and then—"

"Bid list? I'm the President, Dan. I get to decide who works for me. Do you want it or not?"

"Why not just make me Director?"

"I thought about it. Then maybe I wouldn't be dining alone so often. But you'd have to be confirmed, and Tony says you and Senate hearing rooms don't mix so well."

"True."

"He also says you need two more years to get your full pension."

"Tony seems to tell you a lot. So?"

"So, you could be here for a couple of years, and watch your daughter make history."

"I could do that without coming back."

"But there's nothing you want more than to come back. Finish the career you started."

"You say that like we're lifelong friends. Like you know me so well."

"Tell me I'm wrong."

He waited a few seconds. "There would be talk. About you. About us. By jumping the line, I'd be the most resented guy in the Service."

"You don't give a damn. You stopped caring what people thought of you some time ago."

"There you go again. My lifelong friend."

"Tell me I'm wrong. Tell me you don't want to come back."

Dan remained quiet, unable to pull his eyes from the table.

"I have to admit, Dan, this wasn't originally my idea."

"Oh?"

"Tony introduced me to a friend of yours. She came all the way to Washington to see me. Turns out she grew up seventy miles from the New Mexico border."

It took Dan a second or two to put it together. "Barb Patterson? You met with Barb Patterson?"

"I did."

"And this was her idea? She asked you to offer me the Vegas office?"

"I feel like I was told more than asked."

Dan laughed. "That's Barb."

"Tony seconded it. What do you say, Dan? I can make it happen with one call to the Director."

She was staring at him intently, and he had to avert her eyes. She was right. It had been fourteen months since he walked away, and the pull still lingered. Partly because he missed the work and the mission. Partly because he walked away. He let out a long breath before he was able to meet her eyes again.

"I can't. I'm incredibly grateful for the offer, but it wouldn't be right. Wouldn't be fair to the others bidding for that slot. They've done everything the Service asked of them. I didn't. I'm sorry, Anna, I can't do it."

"I know," she said, her lips curling into the slightest of smirks.

Dan straightened. "You know?"

"Of course, I know. You've told me more than once you never wanted your father's help. He offered to make a call once, right? Keep you on the White House detail? And you refused. You never said why, but I know. You're just not the string-pulling type, Dan. And a small confession; you're not alone. That was a phone call I didn't really want to make."

Dan shook his head, unable to comprehend it all. "If you knew I was going to turn you down, why are you here?"

"Vic taught me the value of having contingency plans. Which leads us to door number two."

"And what's behind door number two?"

"The District of Nevada needs a United States Marshal."

Dan gazed at her, incredulous. The U.S. Marshal's Service was the oldest federal law enforcement agency in America, the first marshals appointed by George Washington. The organization was best known for its celebrated past on the frontier, when grizzled federal lawmen policed the Old West from Tombstone to Dodge City. Today, a few thousand deputy marshals and investigators were responsible for safeguarding the enormity of the federal judiciary, from prisoner escort and witness security to the protection of some three thousand judges. They also hunted down wayward fugitives, as famously sensationalized by an Oscar-nominated film thirty years ago.

"What do I know about being a U.S. Marshal?"

"Probably more than the last guy, who came out of the local police department. No jumping the line with this one, Dan. Marshals are presidential appointments, and from what I'm told, most come from outside the Marshals Service. I'm also told they have a full plate here in Nevada. You won't be just punching a timecard; you'll have protection duties and casework. And you'll get to close out your twenty-five years, retire with a full pension whenever you please."

Dan was speechless, knowing the validity of every word she just spoke.

Anna tapped a finger on the table. "There's a price though."

"This should be good."

"You have to ask me out."

"I have to what?"

"You heard me."

"You want me to ask out the President of the United States?"

"No, I want you to ask out Anna Morales."

"And she would say yes?"

"She might. She's fifty-fifty right now."

"So, I ask you out, and in exchange, I become a United States Marshal. You realize you're a terrible negotiator? The country should be worried."

"The country doesn't eat alone in the White House residence."

"This sounds like a quid pro quo."

"It absolutely is. Impeach me. But I want an answer. And make it quick, I have an Air Force One to catch. I'm free this Friday."

"Friday is Valentine's Day."

"So it is. Haven't celebrated one of those in a while. I'm waiting, Dan."

A fifty-fifty shot. Maybe even sixty-forty. Dan reached across the table, covering her hand with his. There was a tender squeeze as a dozen phone cameras captured the moment from across the room for the rest of the country. She wasn't waiting for an answer, but a question. One so laughable Dan wasn't sure how to form the words. But they came, spoken with a conviction and confidence he hadn't expected, driven by the emotion of the moment and one inescapable truth.

The worst she could say was no.

ACKNOWLEDGMENTS

A few notes about people and events in the story. All of the characters are fictional, and are not intended to represent actual individuals in the U.S. Secret Service, the Nevada State Democratic Party, or any elected office. The events are fictional as well, although the necessity of closing off private aircraft to Ronald Reagan National Airport was very much an issue in the years following the 9/11 attacks. A Congressional hearing similar to the one I described in the Prologue actually occurred, though I took license with the date to align with the storyline. Finally, at the time of publication, Nevada was still using a caucus system in the presidential primaries. A number of conversations with well-connected friends in the Silver State convinced me that would likely change by 2024, with the state likely shifting to a traditional primary system.

As always, my greatest gratitude is reserved for my special clan at home – Stephanie, Maddie, and Ben – the threesome who inspire me every day with their indomitable spirit, humor, and support. A special note of thanks to my wife for gifting me a space heater; no longer must I battle the frigid elements in my basement office at home.

As always, my early readers provide such an invaluable service in shaping and perfecting my story and writing, and I'd be lost without them. Elizabeth Harvey, who has weighed in on all three of my books, performing lifesaving microsurgery on each; Eben Carle, whose critiques of my writing are not only always spot-on, but full of such witticisms and humor they should be published as their own work; and Dean Strang, the legal legend from my hometown of Madison with an eagle-eye for detail and nuance. Each was a goldmine of edits, perspective, and course corrections, and I cannot thank them enough.

I want to also thank a number of individuals who provided their expert advice and guidance on this project. First and foremost, to my former colleagues on H Street: John Gill, Paul Irving, Brian Dunlop, and Tim Koerner, to whom I owe so much authenticity in this story, on everything from the career experiences of my protagonist to agency procedures and jargon.

I relied on the professional acumen of so many others for this story, including Rachel Hirschberg, political campaign consultant extraordinaire; Professors Michael Green and Ruben Garcia at the University of Nevada-Las Vegas, the former for his rich knowledge of Las Vegas history and politics, and the latter for his experience with labor relations in the state; and Dr. Howard Bailey and Dr. Edward Prendergast, highly regarded oncologists who provided their expertise and insight for all story pieces relating to medical conditions, care, and research.

Finally, a special thank you to my one-time employer, former Senator Richard H. Bryan. The truest public servant I have ever known, Bryan is the inspiration for much of this story. He dedicated the entirety of his long and storied career in Nevada politics and elected office to the constituents he served, never caring an iota about personal enrichment or his own political fortunes, and treated those he employed, from his Chief of Staff to the unpaid interns, as sons and daughters. An eminently earnest, selfless, and compassionate man, he represents the core of everything *Honorable Profession* is intended to stand for.

Andy Kutler
December 2021

ABOUT THE AUTHOR

Andy Kutler is a writer and author of two award-winning novels, *The Batter's Box* and *The Other Side of Life*. Andy has also written extensively for The Huffington Post and The Milwaukee Journal Sentinel. Over a 28-year professional career, he has worked in the United States Senate, the U.S. Secret Service, and the national security community. A Wisconsin native, Andy lives with his wife and two children in Arlington, Virginia.

NOTE FROM THE AUTHOR

Word-of-mouth is crucial for any author to succeed. If you enjoyed *Honorable Profession*, please leave a review online—anywhere you are able. Even if it's just a sentence or two. It would make all the difference and would be very much appreciated.

Thanks!

Andy Kutler

We hope you enjoyed reading this title from:

BLACK ROSE
writing™

www.blackrosewriting.com

Subscribe to our mailing list – *The Rosevine* – and receive **FREE** books, daily deals, and stay current with news about upcoming releases and our hottest authors.
Scan the QR code below to sign up.

Already a subscriber? Please accept a sincere thank you for being a fan of Black Rose Writing authors.

View other Black Rose Writing titles at
www.blackrosewriting.com/books and use promo code
PRINT to receive a **20% discount** when purchasing.